Advance Praise for Hal Sisson's
Modus Operandi 9/11

"This informative novel relegates the fictional *9/11 Commission Report* to the dust bin of history, where it belongs."

— *Joyce Lynn,* Journalist

"Hal Sisson is at it again. With humorous synonymic names like Rick O'Shea, Eileen Dover, Pat Hand, Mosey Long and Sarah Bellum, you know you're in for a wild ride. But add in some very serious information regarding the attacks of September 11, 2001, and you've really got a book to contend with. It's a bit like having 9/11 explained to you by Benny Hill. But don't laugh it off. Sisson has done his homework and presents a novel that may get you thinking in between the laughs."

— *Jim Marrs,* best selling Author/Journalist,
Crossfire; Rule by Secrecy; and The Terror Conspiracy

"Puts into perspective what could have happened regarding 9/11, and not only that, but plausibly what likely did happen."

— *W. Leon Smith,* Publisher & Editor-in-Chief,
The Lone Star Iconoclast

MEMO TO READERS

The main story line of this novel relates to various events that the author visualized as having happened between the attacks on the World Trade Center on September 11, 2001, and the date of publication of this book in February 2007. Many of the minor characters you will encounter herein, will be met only once or twice, but never pursued further. Except, that is, for the main plot line, whose characters include: Slippery Jack Danielson, Zack Zapata and Bill Bailey, who appear at regular intervals throughout, and whom you may regard as the guys wearing the white hats – as opposed to Nick 'the Nostril' D'Amous, Bob Loblaw and Mosey Long, wearing the black hats.

This is an historical novel. Technical material describing the events before, during and after 9/11 is all on record as being quite possible. However, most of the names, characters, places and incidents are either products of the author's imagination or used fictitiously – except for the names of the patsies: Osama bin Laden, Mohamed Atta, et al. Any other resemblance to actual events, locales or persons, living or dead, is entirely coincidental.

Hal Sisson, Q.C.

All truth passes through three stages:

First, it is ridiculed,
Second, it is violently opposed,
Third, it is accepted as self-evident.

— Arthur Schopenhauer (1788-1860)

Modus Operandi
9/11

Hal Sisson

Published by Global Outlook™
www.GlobalOutlook.ca

Modus Operandi 9/11

First Edition

Cataloging in Publication Data:

A catalog record for this publication is available from the National Library of Canada.

Book Jacket Design by Modernia.net Copyright © 2007
Back Cover Photo of Protesters by Jan Hoyer (3/28/04) DigitalStyleDesigns.com Copyright © Jan Hoyer 2007

Printed and bound in Canada. First Printing: February 2007

ANCIENT FOREST **FRIENDLY** This book is printed on acid-free paper that is 100% Ancient Forest Friendly (100% post-consumer recycled), processed chlorine free and printed with vegetable-based, low VOC (Volatile Organic Compound) ink.

Paperback ISBN: 0-9731109-2-9

Requests for permission to make copies of any part of this work should be mailed to the address below:

To order this book directly from the publisher please call toll-free (North America) 1-888-713-8500 or 1-705-720-6500 (from overseas) or you can order it on-line at www.GlobalOutlook.ca.

Any other inquiries can be directed by mail to:

Global Outlook
P.O. Box 222, Oro
Ontario, Canada   L0L 2X0

info@GlobalOutlook.ca
www.GlobalOutlook.ca

Contents

> "We are on the verge of a global transformation.
> All we need is the right major crisis
> And the nations will accept the
> New World Order."

> — *David Rockefeller, Chairman of Chase Manhattan Bank,*
> *at the United Nations, September 14, 1994*

I – Cui Bono?

Washington, D.C., September 11, 2001, 7:00 a.m.

Nicolaus D'Amous was part of the world where money was no object – it was a mere detail, no more significant than a date on a check. By money, he meant other people's money, taxpayers' money, drug money, laundered money, any money that greased the wheels of the New World Order.

The meeting he had arranged was to take place in a private dining room in an exclusive hotel on Capitol Hill. On his way into the room, Nick caught his reflection in the glass of a smoked wall mirror. His Windsor knot was just so, his shirt crisp, his Savile Row suit a perfect fit. The touch of gray in the black at his temples added an air of distinction. An immaculate perception, he thought as he straightened his shoulders and admired the fit body beneath the expensive clothing. Nick signaled to the butler who entered the room accompanied by a waiter bearing condiments for the breakfast table.

"A glass of Ambrosia, please."

"Certainly, sir." The butler popped the cork on a bottle of Moët & Chandon, added the orange juice and brought the drink over to Nick's table by the tall windows at one end of the elegantly appointed room.

As he sipped the drink and gazed out over Washington, Nick's encyclopedic mind recalled – verbatim – the words of

Sir Josiah Stamp, a former Governor of the Bank of England, on the subject of money:

> *The modern banking system manufactures money out of nothing. The process is perhaps the most astonishing piece of sleight of hand ever invented. Banking was conceived in iniquity, and born in sin. Bankers own the earth. Take it away from them, but leave them the power to create money, and with the flick of a pen, they will create enough money to buy it back again. Take this great power away from them, and all great fortunes like mine will disappear. And, they ought to disappear, for then this would be a better and happier world to live in. But if you want to continue to be slaves of the bankers, and pay the cost of your own slavery, then let bankers continue to create money, and control credit.*

Stamp had it right, which was precisely why Nick's ultimate employers were bankers. Private banking was a slick operation indeed. For example, despite its name, the U.S. Federal Reserve Bank was not a federal department or agency, and there were no reserves. The Fed was owned by American, Japanese and European member banks that were themselves owned by the power elite of those nations. Nick was the *de facto* CEO of this cult of super-rich bankers, profiting from the interest on trillions of dollars of debt incurred by countries that were borrowing money created by the banks with a stroke of a pen. The greater the debt, the more the interest, and the greater the profits enjoyed by the bank owners. In Nick's view, that kind of systemic deception constituted an investment scam on a colossal scale. Yet he was happy to be part of it.

As he took another sip, he thought about what David Rockefeller had to say at the Bilderberg meeting in Baden-Baden Germany exactly ten years ago to the day:

> *The supranational sovereignty of an intellectual elite and world bankers is surely preferable to the national*

auto-determination practiced in past centuries.

Rockefeller had it right too. There was an excessive amount of democracy then, as now, and it was time for a change.

D'Amous' musings were interrupted by a swarthy heavy-set man sporting a mustache and a wide grin under his bald pate, who strode confidently into the room. Nick advanced, shook hands with his guest and waved him to a seat.

Lt. General Abdul Dabulbulah, Pakistan's Chief of Inter-Service Intelligence (ISI), had been a central figure in the military coup that ousted the government of Nawaz Sharif and installed a new president, who, at least in theory, was more sympathetic to the United States. By force of habit Abdul settled himself with his back to the wall.

"The others will be here shortly," said Nick, signaling for a libation for the other man. "We have a moment to talk."

"By all means," the ISI Chief replied.

"The money was successfully transferred to Mr. Atta. Thank you for seeing to that."

"I am always happy to be of service."

"And you've met with your counterpart at the CIA?"

"I have indeed. You may recall that he made a quiet visit to Pakistan last May to see the General. I think we can continue to provide great logistical support for your country's geo-strategic imperatives in Central Asia; just as we did during our clandestine little war with the Soviets in the 1980s."

Nick lowered his voice a notch. "I'm told General Massood, the leader of the Northern Alliance in Afghanistan, is dead."

"He met with an unfortunate accident; however, some are suggesting he was assassinated by members of the ISI-Osama bin Laden-Taliban axis."

"I'm sure nothing could be further from the truth," said Nick sarcastically.

"There's an old saying back home: *Truth is the safest lie.*"

"Speaking of Osama, which is mainly why I wanted a private word with you, Abdul, what gives with our skinny rug rider? Where's he holed up now?"

"I am not certain, as he has a habit of being rather elusive. However, we have passed on the CIA's message to him: 'We created you, we armed you, then made you an enemy. It is time for you to start acting like one, in sufficient degree to make the world believe it must do whatever it takes to deal harshly with you and your al-Qaeda organization.'"

"Is he cooperating?" asked Nick.

"I am surprised you ask – because no doubt you know, or perhaps the CIA could inform you that, like it or not, Osama will be fulfilling his role in the charade later this morning."

"Things seem to be in place, then. There's one thing I want you to keep in mind. No matter what some military type may tell you, or ask you to do at some future time, we never want to see Osama's ass on the witness stand; mind you, if he ever did get caught, he'd likely get killed trying to escape rather than let himself be questioned, if you know what I mean."

"I completely understand," Abdul said, nodding slowly. "He has been a valued asset of both U.S. and British intelligence for many years. That lengthy acquaintance makes him a dangerous fellow, does it not?"

Nick looked around, signaling an end to this part of their conversation. "The others should be here for breakfast soon."

"Who is attending this meeting?" asked Abdul.

"Senator Graham Roberts, the chairman of the House and Senate Intelligence Committee, Representative Patrick Gross, Senator Kyle Johnson and your ambassador to the U.S."

"Will Dick Underwood be coming?"

"If he can make it. This is a very busy time for him. As you're aware, he's a member of the Council on Foreign

Relations in New York, the International Institute for Strategic Studies in London, the Fulbright Association and the Council of American Ambassadors.

"Didn't he serve on the staff of the National Security Council and the U.S. Senate Intelligence and Foreign Relations Committee?

"Yes, as I said, a busy guy," said Nick.

"If we are to be discussing the nations surrounding Afghanistan, then his presence would be invaluable, especially if you are seeking an expert in crisis management."

As opposed to the damage control I do every day, Nick said to himself.

Dabulbulah continued: "In any event I assure you, Nicolaus, we desire very close collaboration between our great countries."

"As do we," Nick replied smoothly. "And in both our cases, *ducit amor patriae*. Love of country guides me." Nick spoke flawless Latin, and wasn't above demonstrating the fact at every opportunity. "I'll arrange further meetings for you with the Secretary of State. Oh, and one last thing, we'd appreciate a heads up on any oil-producing nations that might be thinking of screwing around with the petrodollar. If you hear anything about any more of them seriously considering the creation of a stock exchange that would trade oil and gas in euros instead of American petrodollars, or mess up our deal with OPEC, we want to know about it right away."

"Certainly, Nicolaus."

"Here they are now." Nick and the General stood to greet the other guests.

The false-flag *War on Terror* against Muslim and Arab States – the next step in creating a global Pax Americana – would begin in a little over an hour at the World Trade Center. Only God, Allah and the shadow government of the U.S., of which D'Amous was an integral part, knew how long that war would last.

> "I don't know if there are men on the moon, but if there are, they must be using the earth as their lunatic asylum."
>
> — *George Bernard Shaw*

II – Slippery Jack Danielson

New York City, September 11, 2001, 8:40 a.m.

Through half-closed eyes he watched the blonde with the big breasts hovering over his open mouth with a sharp metal instrument in her hand. Rather than being frightened, Jack was thankful to be in a dentist's office for a relatively painless cleaning. *This was a piece of cake*, he thought, *compared to being attended to by a sadistic root canal specialist, or worse still, finding himself in the office of a belligerent proctologist.*

Jack's mind wandered as the hygienist probed and scraped between his teeth. *What was the name of that little bird that goes into the mouths of large mammals, like crocodiles, and cleans their teeth?* Jack knew there was a name for that kind of mutually beneficial activity. *Was it 'symbiosis'? But what was the bird called? If he could recall the name, he'd mention it to the blonde dental assistant. Their union could maybe use it as a logo.*

Soon afterwards, the hygienist relieved him of his bib. Jack's mouth felt clean and his teeth gleamed brightly as he got out of the chair and walked out to reception to pay the bill.

The receptionist appeared to be in shock, gasping as she asked him, "Did you hear? Some kind of a plane hit one of the Trade Towers! We can't see it from this side of the building, but it's all over the news!"

"Didn't hear a thing about it," Jack replied. He came out onto Sixth Avenue and began walking quickly toward the Twin Towers of the World Trade Center. Long before he got close, he could see a tall column of smoke billowing out of the North

Tower, near the top of the skyscraper. *How'd the military let a plane get down here, right into friggin' Lower Manhattan?!* Jack wondered. He eased his way through the crowds of gawkers packing the streets of Manhattan.

His watch said 9:03 a.m. *Jesus Christ, here comes another one. It's going to hit too!* Just before it did, Jack thought he heard an explosion at ground level. Then he heard a massive explosion overhead, accompanied by a fire-ball which shot out from the side of the building as the plane angled into the South Tower. The craft's starboard engine sliced through the building, came out the other side and flew all the way to Barclay Street, landing sixty feet from where Jack was standing. He stared at the smoking hulk of metal. His gut was urging him to take off in the opposite direction, but the scene literally drew him forward. He joined the few people still drifting toward the towers, like zombies out of a Hollywood film. The rest of the crowd was fleeing, trampling anything in its path. By this time Jack was close enough to help the stunned men and women streaming out of the towers.

Fire trucks were running their hoses into the North Tower. Then a great cry went up from the crowd. Jack looked up and saw people leaping from the windows above to escape the terrible smoke, flames and killer toxins. Desperate jumpers struck the pavement and in moments the ground was littered with mangled flesh. Jack stepped over one bloody mess, realizing it had once been someone's head. Chaos, the oldest of the Greek gods, reigned everywhere.

Just before 10:00 a.m., there came a series of unbelievable explosions, and people dove for cover or pelted up the street. Jack, no neophyte when it came to building collapses, watched the scene in amazement. He felt the ground shake just before he heard another unmistakable sound – *chi, chi, chi, chi, chi, chi, chi.* It was the noise of cutter explosions ringing around the South Tower. He felt and heard these things before the start of the terrible reverberations that heralded the collapse of the tower. The twisting and ripping of steel as explosives cut beams into sections. The steel hitting the ground, the ground shaking, everything moving, human voices screaming in terror.

"They've pulled the friggin' building," Jack yelled in disbelief. "Why on earth would they do that?!"

A massive toxic cloud of pulverized concrete roared at him as he tried to escape. It was almost on top of him as he dove behind a fire truck and tried to pull the stacked hose over his body to protect himself from the falling debris. Too late. Something struck his head and knocked him out.

* * *

10:28 a.m. Bruised, shaken and dazed, Jack crawled out from amongst a tangle of fire-hose, coincidentally just in time to see the collapse of the North Tower. Struggling to his feet, he hoped nothing major would fall on top of him. A powerful wind from the collapse suddenly picked him up and flung him across the street. Jack started crawling, trying to get out of the scary hot darkness that suddenly enveloped the streets of New York. Paper and powdered glass flew through the air. Debris was everywhere. A layer of gray concrete dust was up to four inches thick in some places. The acrid stench of burning chemicals irritated his lungs.

From what he could tell, the Twin Towers were no more. In their place was a 110-degree hell, with smoke hovering over everything. Ashes fell like snow. Scared shitless, Jack continued to crawl his way out of 'Ground Zero', as it became known – named after the two nuclear explosions which took place during the bombings of Japan in WWII. It was like someone had poured sand in his mouth. He began to realize how many computers had been in those two towers, and pondered the health hazards of inhaling the remains of ink, fax machines, cadmium, the liquid metals inside millions of batteries, watches, cellphones and pagers, along with keyboards and monitors, freon, mercury, asbestos, benzene, lead, manganese, vanadium, PCBs and dioxins. There had to be thousands of gallons of ammonia, bleach and cleaning fluid, glass and gyprock – all reduced to a fine dust that not even protective gear would be able to withstand.

The air was so thick you could chew it. Jack was coughing, his nose bleeding. No more time to think or cry. He crawled along a fire-hose and came to a fire truck's pumper, which provided some water. Jack splashed water on his face and hands and cleared his throat, but the contamination was so horrific he couldn't breathe anything that resembled air. One half of someone's head stared at him from the foot-thick debris on the pavement. He saw a shoe with a foot in it, a pair of sneakers with legs and feet attached to them. Gazing skyward, he saw that some of the bodies that had fallen from the towers had been skewered on steel beams. He reached a line of hospital workers and paramedics who were standing by with empty stretchers. They gave him some oxygen and cleaned the blood and dirt from his face.

Jack leaned on the hood of a police car, feeling guilty to be alive. *I'll remember this for the rest of my life. And just to think I helped the bastards who pulled these buildings!*

Jack Danielson, a good-looking Irish-American citizen, in his early thirties, a demolition expert, member of Alcoholics Anonymous, divorced with no kids, was dry-eyed on the outside but crying on the inside.

He hitched a ride home, where he removed more encrusted debris from his body. His eyes felt extremely irritated. He studied the bruise at the hairline over his left eye. A small cut but a large lump. He made an ice pack from cubes of ice in the freezer and applied it to his aching forehead. Was he heading for the last round-up, he wondered? Something awful seemed to have seized his lungs in a vice grip. Swallowing several Tylenol in hopes of easing the pain in his chest, Jack crashed into his dark bedroom to sleep off the effects of his horrendous experience.

He awoke the next day still feeling like he should call in dead. His left eye was bloodshot and hurting terribly, forcing him to go to emergency, where an ophthalmologist removed several ultra-fine particles of glass.

Three days later he felt able to return to the downtown scene, now one of surreal chaos. Hundreds of people were working on site cleanup, gathering up parts of dead bodies in buckets. Jack began to help. A few burly firefighters told him the steel beams that reached down to bedrock in the seventh level tower basement remained too hot to approach. They wondered how that was possible with fires of short duration on the top floors. Jack knew, but decided a closed mouth gathers no feet. When Jack got home he studied all the news on television and in the papers. This was the greatest atrocity ever committed, an iconic event of biblical proportions to mark the first years of the new millennium.

* * *

Less than two days after the attacks, the administration began leaking their conspiracy theory to the press, who quickly ran with the story: a gang of nineteen Arab terrorists had perpetrated this heinous act, led by a hate-filled Muslim fanatic named Osama bin Laden, who operated a sinister, massively powerful organization called al-Qaeda with headquarters in a cave in Afghanistan. These terrorists hated all Americans and all Christians, the story went, and they must be brought to justice quickly and made to pay for their crimes against humanity. The reports went on to say there had been no useful advance warnings of the attacks. No one in the military or the administration had ever imagined that terrorists would use commercial airliners as bombs to demolish American landmarks.

Now that is the mother of all conspiracy theories, thought Jack. *They want us to believe that nineteen evil Middle Eastern Muslim terrorists, using pocket knives and box cutters, hijacked four commercial airliners, all at the same time, in broad daylight, catching the U.S. authorities completely off guard. Then they somehow flew these huge planes, with only minimal flight training, into three out of four targets – the Twin Towers and the Pentagon – without interception by NORAD and the U.S. Air Force, circumventing the most sophisticated radar system on Earth, killing themselves because of their love of Allah and their hatred for our freedoms. The whole operation was directed by a rich Saudi with a laptop computer hiding in a cave somewhere in Afghanistan, of all places. Further, that these aluminum aircraft, after they had crashed into the Twin Towers, caused such super hot fires that they, in turn, caused these steel structures to collapse at free fall speed. Unbelievable!*

Jack, who'd heard plenty of scuttlebutt during his obsessive returns to the scene, was amazed that no mention was made in the media of Building 7 which had collapsed at 5:20 p.m. on '9/11', as it became known. Nor of the pools of what appeared to be molten steel that had congealed in the foundations of the buildings, many levels underground. Also, there was no mention that *never before in history* had a steel-framed skyscraper collapsed due to being gutted by fires. Yet, the media implied that it was natural, even though the debris at Ground Zero was uncharacteristic of a gravitational collapse due to fires. Instead of chunks of concrete, it was pulverized to a fine powder. Instead of long, twisted steel beams, they found short pieces of steel, no more than twenty feet long.

The authorities maintained that no flight recorders, or black boxes, from the aircraft had been found. No further details were released by the FBI or the military, who cited national security concerns for their refusal to do so.

Watching this coverage and hearing its tone, Jack got the impression that anyone, including himself, who offered a different explanation for what had happened would immediately be branded as an unpatriotic son of a bitch and would run the risk of internment in some secret black hole of a prison, his ass stuffed with broken glass and his body immersed in a bathtub full of Tabasco sauce.

The government's 'official story' depended on alleged evidence that couldn't be tested or proven. The Pentagon and the various intelligence agencies supplied the media with their in-house news releases and reconstruction of the hijacking, but refused to release the many surveillance images in their possession, using the standard excuse of 'national security'.

Whoever these alleged terrorists really were, they had to have had one helluva lot of help to pull off this horrendous false-flag caper, Jack said to himself. *I'd better have a talk with my buddy Sean.* Sean Hennessey had paid Jack to help him wire the basement of the Twin Towers – for some obscure reason – a few weeks prior to 9/11, on behalf of Guided Destruction Engineering Inc. who'd been hired by the landlord.

And it was only then that the name of the bird he'd been trying to think of in the dentist's office popped into Jack's mind – the Egyptian Plover, who flew into the open mouths of crocodiles on the Nile, picking away at debris and scar tissue.

I may be doing the same thing, thought Jack. *Crocs eat birds, but they don't eat the Plovers that provide them with a service. Can you say the same thing about the American government?*

But another bird immediately jumped into his head, one whose etymological name Jack could not immediately remember either – one which was nicknamed, the bare-bummed Blackbird. This bird, which was only found in desert areas and whenever there was a sand storm, had learned to fly ass backwards.

"My only regret was I had but one life to give for my country. If I'd had two, I would have had felt a lot better."

— Anonymous Soldier

"All wars are popular for the first thirty days."

— Arthur Schlesinger

III – Zack Zapata

Parris Island, May 6, 2003, 4:30 a.m.

The sun failed to break through a colorless sky above the parade square of the marine base.

"Drop your cocks and grab your socks, and start to shovel shit!" shouted the corporal as he marched down the length of the barracks, his hobnail boots clanging on the cement.

What a God-forsaken time to get out of bed. Zack Zapata was tired; he hadn't slept well. The recruit in the next fart-sack suffered from bad dreams, and at odd times during the night had yelled out, "Aye, aye, sir! Do I have to kiss your ass, sir?"

Roll call was at 5 a.m. and you'd better be on your feet and in shape to run five miles in combat boots before breakfast.

As he stood awaiting inspection, Zack wondered if he had forgotten to do anything. He usually had; there was so much to remember. Drill Instructor Manny Grudges felt Zack's chin and found stubble under it. That was usually enough to get you assigned to the goon squad, but the sergeant merely ordered him to do fifty push-ups on the spot. In good shape, Zack managed it easily and rose to his feet.

"Ten-HOWN," bellowed the DI, and Zack snapped to with alacrity. But the head games weren't over yet. "Is that a grin on your face, recruit?" Grudges snarled at him.

"No, sir! Not at all, sir!" Zack replied, trying to suppress the grin that formed on his permanently tanned Hispanic face whenever he was nervous. And Grudges made him nervous, all right.

"You've got nothing to smile about, soldier. Do you call that a shine on your boots?"

"Yes sir! I worked hard on them, sir!"

"Let's see the insteps."

Zack complied.

"Just as I thought," said the drill sergeant, "Nada. A total disgrace to the corps."

"Give me fifty more push-ups."

His new good buddy Terry Dunbar, standing in the line behind, could see the sweat trickling from Zack's close-cropped haircut. Zack was single, while Terry was married with no kids. Both were a little older than average for marine recruits, but they were determined to become changed men.

They were training to join the ranks of the U.S. marines – the proud few, the best in the West and the East didn't count. Basic training was the ultimate male bonding experience, where young men and women who wouldn't ordinarily meet in normal life exercised, ate, slept, learned the ropes, got dirty and fired weapons together for thirteen weeks. It was a test of character and a test of what they could endure together: calisthenics, runs, rope climbs and obstacle courses, plus the dreaded gas chamber. You had to do a hundred sit-ups in two minutes with a drill sergeant bellowing, "Did I say stop? Keep crunching!" Punishing physical training that shed pounds of fat and created sculpted muscle.

The recruits learned close-quarter combat moves like the horizontal hammer blow, the vertical elbow strike and the eye gouge – a thrust of the hand with fingers spread. One guy had lost an eye on that one, and was back on civvie street. "Probably selling pencils," one recruit had quipped when they got the news.

Zack's platoon became proficient with the rifle and could fire the M-16 accurately from a standing, lying or kneeling position.

But the toughest test came toward the end of training: the Crucible, a 54-hour endurance drill of challenging tests accompanied by sleep and food deprivation. The recruits donned camouflage uniforms and applied green paint to their faces to make the exercises seem real. Gun shots rang out at random every few minutes as recruits traversed the 16-mile course of barbed wire, logs, empty pipes, mud and a bridge. At each burst of gunfire the soldiers threw themselves down on their bellies and crawled forward a few yards before standing, running and yelling, "I'm up!" then "They see me! I'm down!" before hitting the dirt again.

"I used to think I'd die someplace else," Zack commented at the lunch break.

"Don't abandon ship, buddy," Terry Dunbar replied. "We'll make it, and then forever be known as marines."

"Easy for you to say," Zack snapped. "That bastard Grudges likes to mess with me all the time."

"I gotta be thankful it's not me. But don't let him get to you, that's what Manny's waiting for."

They all survived the Crucible. During the countdown to graduation, no two days were the same except for the physical effort involved. But each day started on the parade square.

"Okay Zapata, let's have a look at those insteps this morning." Zack lifted his feet alternately to show the sergeant, having made damn sure the insteps were highly polished.

"Just as I thought," growled the instructor, "Brown-nosing! Trying to suck up to me, eh? Okay, give me fifty push-ups, you sorry excuse for a soldier."

Rumors flew about the platoon regarding what rituals were to be performed as a rite of graduation. What was required was something that proved your fearless animalism. One grunt staunchly maintained that before graduation you had to either bite the head off a chicken or bite a snake in half. "Bullshit," stated another. "That's only for Special Forces Branch."

A week later, graduation arrived with final uniforms issued and tailored, the CO's general inspection, and no snakes or chickens. What better way to be shaped as a person than the military? *Let me count the ways*, thought Zack. They'd just found out they were being shipped out to Iraq right after graduation, to fight al-Qaeda. Zack wasn't afraid to go. Iraq looked good after Parris Island; it'd be a respite from that goddamned drill instructor Grudges. Zack figured bringing democracy to a country that had threatened the security of America on 9/11 wasn't such a bad idea. And if they encountered terrorists, the marines had now been trained to shoot on sight and without question as to age or gender.

They were allowed to talk to family members for five minutes, but with a marine corps officer present. The plane was taking off that afternoon. Zack walked by as Terry greeted his mother, who had bused in for his graduation ceremony. She urged him to be careful as she kissed him goodbye.

Zack discovered that DI Grudges had gone on leave by the time the newly minted marines had begun heading for the plane. Opportunity often knocks but once, and Zack took it. He hung back so as to be the last to leave the barrack block. The drill sergeant's cubicle was walled off at one end, his footlocker at one end of his bed. Zack picked the lock and opened the box. He unzipped his fly, whipped out his johnson and took a long piss before closing the lid. *Grudges had better not show up in Iraq or I'll shoot the bastard*, Zack vowed. He slipped out the door and was on his way to war.

* * *

They got in just before a storm warning diverted all planes from Baghdad airport. An eerie yellow glow enveloped everything as a blinding sandstorm hit the city. Visibility dropped to less than 3-feet and they had great difficulty reaching their barracks. Howling winds whipped up the desert sands, coating the Green Zone with a gritty opaque haze.

"You're lucky you didn't get caught out on patrol," an old hand told Zack as he stowed his gear. "It's brutal out there in the city. You can't breathe, and anything that moves is reduced to a crawl. And still those shitheels will take advantage and attack you. Fighting these people is like trying to chase goats off a garbage dump. The Iraqis have electricity maybe a couple of hours a day and what they call drinking water would kill you or me. The daytime temperature is around 120-degrees. I got trapped inside the city once. Most awful night of my life. Welcome to Iraq, soldier."

> "Only two things are infinite,
> the universe and human stupidity,
> and I'm not sure about the former."
>
> — *Albert Einstein*

IV – Bill Bailey

February 12, 2004, 11:00 a.m.

Bill Bailey was awestruck at the sheer number of people jammed into the civic auditorium that was the site of Tallahassee's largest-ever politico-religious rally. The Dominionist Congregation event was being hosted by a Moral Majority televangelist, a Congressman and a bigshot mover and shaker in the Republican Party. Bill was one of just six young Congregation members selected to partake of coffee and conversation with the VIPs at the conclusion of the convention.

As God-fearing as Bill's rural Florida upbringing required, he could certainly talk the talk; but rather than seeking a spiritual booster shot, he was hoping that cruising the rally would yield him a better job, or at least some solid leads. He was a lowly laborer in the carpentry trade, barely surviving on the minimum wage and determined to move up in the material world.

Fifty state flags festooned the rafters. Two video screens flashed religious slogans reclaiming America for Christ. Several thousand staunch Presbyterian and Baptist Christian fundamentalists were in attendance. Banners and posters exhorted these evangelical members of the nation's most effective political machine to continue their holy war against the Godless forces of secularism and infidel religions.

Eager and faithful hacks dashed around the hall snapping public relations photos. The crowd around the main stage punctuated the speaker's words with excited roars of "Amen, Amen!" Prayers flew heavenward like the souls of dying sinners, while minions bearing collection plates worked the room for cash like bird dogs flushing quail. There were indeed some ultra-rich, generously inclined individual and corporate representatives in this assemblage of the Dominionists – biblical literalists who believed God had called them to take over the U.S. government. No fly-by-night, flash-in-the-pan religion this. No siree, this was a modern, civilized, neoconservative religious movement looking for a lot of modern civilized cash in exchange for spiritual satisfaction, salvation music and hellfire and brimstone speeches.

Bill looked up into the balcony and picked out the political pundit Nicolaus D'Amous, known to choose his public appearances with particularity. Maybe Bill could get his ear over coffee, an opportunity not to be missed. He figured the slender, gray-haired guy sharing the box with D'Amous was Frank Porter, one of the most influential evangelists in the States. Controller of a TV-and-radio audience of three million Jesus-loving, Bible-thumping listeners who weren't going to save America soul by soul, but election by election; and a man who was now a five-star general in the Christian Army that selected Presidents and advised them on matters of federal policy.

Checking his program, Bill noted that another luminary gracing the convention was the Rev. R. Albert Mohler Jr., president of the Southern Baptist Theological Seminary in Louisville, Kentucky, who preached 'full quiver' theology, as in Psalm 127: "Children are a gift of the Lord, the fruit of the womb is a reward. Like arrows in the hand of a warrior, so are the children of one's youth. How blessed is the man whose quiver is full of them." To Mohler and the Baptist press, raising children was both a God-given duty and one of the most critical opportunities for the making of saints. Marriage, sex and children were part of the same package. To deny any part of this wholeness was to reject God's intention in creation, and his mandate as revealed in the Bible. Bill recalled the quote attributed to Mohler in an article he'd read recently: "To breed or not to breed, that is the question. Animals breed, but human beings procreate and raise children to the glory of God."

Bill saw that the chanting and hollering were loudest in the center of the floor, but the wildly gyrating crowd was blocking his view of the speaker. He threaded his way through until he was ten unruly rows back. His shouted question into his neighbor's ear elicited the excited response that the speaker was the Reverend Dixie Lund, a top lobbyist for the sixteen-million-strong Southern Baptist Convention, and a ranking Republican.

Red-faced, his arms waving, Dixie shouted, "We've got the Holy Spirit's wind at our backs!" He urged the crowd to recite with him the oath the Dominionists dreamed of hearing in every classroom: "I pledge allegiance to the Christian flag, and to the Savior for whose kingdom it stands. One Savior, crucified, risen and coming again, with life and liberty for all who believe."

Dixie's speech was all over the place like a blind man in a nudist colony. It was a touching sight, reflecting his ongoing efforts to turn public schools into forums for evangelism, and to stamp the neocon insignia on every major institution the Christian Right did not yet control.

"The most humble Christian is more qualified for office than the best-educated pagan," he declared, stabbing his index finger at the audience. "We have already built a grass roots anti-abortionist group who has taken over many school boards.

Now it is my burden, and your duty, to multiply that success all across America.

"Today I want every one of you at this Reclaiming America Convention to get behind Davie Jones and his Houses of Worship Free Speech Restoration Act, which will permit ministers to endorse political candidates from their pulpits, effectively converting our tax-exempt churches into Republican campaign headquarters. Now I'm going to ask our Congressman Davie Jones to say a few words." Lund moved aside, leading the applause as Jones stepped briskly to the podium.

"America is under assault," thundered the Congressman from the podium, shifting immediately into religious warp drive. "You cannot have a strong nation that does not follow God. Our job is to reclaim America for Christ, whatever the cost. As the vice-regents of God, we are to exercise dominion and influence over our neighborhoods, our schools, our government, our literature and arts, our sports arenas, our entertainment media and our scientific endeavors; in short, over every aspect and institution of human society.

"But in the meantime, we need a little help from our friends! So take this great opportunity to bring God back into the public institutions and judiciary of our country. Donate generously to the cause, I beseech you. Please God – God, please – save America!"

To a chorus of wild applause, stamping of feet and whistling, the next neocon fundamentalist speaker graced the stage. He was the Reverend Mosey Long, pastor of the Wonderful World Tomorrow Church, although detractors were more apt to call it the Holier Than Thou Church of the First Thrown Rock. Long was the owner of his own television network and a multi-million-dollar personal fortune, a man on intimate terms with the most powerful Republicans in Washington, and the most popular evangelical preacher in the South. He was about to hit the audience over the head with God and brimstone. 'Take out some Insurance against Hell' was the theme of his sermon from the mount.

"Listen to the words of hope now being brought to you by Jesus visionaries like unto myself," Mosey exhorted his audience. "The Second Coming is upon us. There are undeniable signs of Jesus Christ's return. The Bible warns us to remain watchful for the Day of the Lord, and that is exactly what I have done. I have seen the Lord with my own eyes – a miraculous encounter with Our Savior as he prepares to announce his divinely appointed return, when he will be unveiled before the world.

"I saw a blazing light, a white light, but not like a fire. My eyes got used to the light and I could see a man wearing bright, blinding white robes. He looked at me and smiled, and said, 'This is not your time. This is my time. I am returning to bring peace to the world. Watch for my return when you march to Jerusalem.'

"And where will he return, dearly beloved friends? Over a battlefield to the north of Jerusalem where American troops are already clashing with the guerilla army of the Devil. The final battle will be not far from the Mount of Megiddo on the Plains of Armageddon. So support our God-guided patriotic troops in Iraq who daily decimate the infidel terrorists.

"In Matthew 24, Christ tells his disciples that the generation that witnesses the return of the nation of Israel will also witness his return. Also, the proof of Christ's return comes from the Book of David, the Book of Revelations and the Book of Daniel which foretells the collapse of an eastern kingdom – perhaps Iran – from which springs the 'false king' or anti-Christ, just as the al-Qaeda terrorist network sprang from Soviet-occupied Afghanistan and the breakaway Republic of Chechnya.

"Current events are predicted in Revelations, such as global warming, which is the burning of Earth and all living things, and the outbreak of the Four Horsemen of the Apocalypse – war in Iraq, famine in Africa, plague in Asia and death by natural disasters as seen in the tsunamis in the Pacific and the hurricanes in the Americas. Each of these signs indicates Christ's return.

"And what is Christ's message to you, dearly beloved? 'Blessings upon you, my faithful children. Though darkness surrounds you, never forget the shining light of love for your neighbors and for your guiding pastor, which is the same as your love for me.'

"Hold no money or worldly treasure tightly in your hands, for soon will come a time when such things will pass away. Prepare now for my reign; purify your hearts and act always in a way pleasing to the Lord who reigns in Heaven. Take out some insurance against Hell! Don't let the Beelzebugs get you, for they are Satan's devils in the form of mosquitoes that get into your bedroom at three in the morning and cannot be cast out.

"Collection plates will be passed amongst you and Jesus wants you to give generously to his cause here on Earth. The days grow darker, and to all you who have ears to hear, abandon everything that stands between you and a guaranteed entry into the Kingdom of Heaven, which is the reward for your generosity here on Earth. Again, blessings upon you, my faithful children. Praise the Lord and Hallelujah!"

* * *

Leaving the chorus of wild applause, stamping of feet and whistling, Bill Bailey wandered around the hall, pondering how to make his pitch at the power coffee meeting. He spotted a lone figure in the back row, writing furiously in a notebook.

In the spirit of camaraderie Bill grabbed a chair, dragged it over and sat down next to the writer.

A shadow of annoyance on his face, the stranger looked up from his work as Bill introduced himself. Seeing such a friendly smile accompanying the proffered handshake, the writer shoved his pen into his breast pocket, stuck out his hand and said, "Manuel Controles. Glad to meet you, Bill."

"You a reporter?" Bill asked.

"That's right. I'm a stringer for the Southwest Secularist News Service."

"What are you doing here?"

"On assignment, that's all."

"So what do you think of the 'big show' then?"

"How tough a Bible puncher are you? My poison-pen opinions may hit you like hot pellets of fire raining from a volcano."

"T'ain't like I didn't ast ya, pardner," Bill replied. "Which bein' the case, I could hardly complain."

"Okay, then." An intense expression on his face, Controles leaned closer to Bill. "Religion is a universal conspiracy for idiots. You'd think the notion of a Christian would be a good, moral thing, but these Dominionist types are no more following the teachings of Christ than the Clean Water Act is about clean water. These fundamentalist holy rollers figure the Founding Fathers never intended to erect a barrier between politics and religion. They argue that the constitutional guarantee against a state-sponsored religion is actually designed to shield the church from federal interference, so Christians can take their rightful place at the head of the government. Their Alliance Defense Fund is made up of some 750 lawyers trained to fight abortion and gay marriage in the courts. Like chimpanzees, you can train lawyers to do anything, then persuade the government to appoint right-wing judges to the Supreme Court to agree with them. Like Roy Moore, former Alabama Chief Justice, who installed a 5,300-pound granite memorial to the Ten Commandments on top of the State judicial building, and once called for the state to execute practicing homosexuals."

Bill interjected, playing up his cowboy impression, "Whoa, boy, them pellets is hittin' me right in the gut. But I'm prepared for your next ones, so fire away, pardner."

Controles barely missed a beat. "Like Opus Dei and the Jesuits, the Dominionists operate the business of religion like self-styled saints running a whorehouse. They think they can control the actual psychos running the government they helped to elect, but they haven't got a clue who's really in charge. Their ultimate goal is to plant the seeds of a faith-based government that will last far longer than the current presidency, until the Second Coming of Jesus Christ."

Bailey stared at the reporter. "Holy H. Smoke! Smile when ya say that, stranger. You've about filled me with lead. And this kinda talk could get ya ridden outta here on a rail, and I'm only half kiddin'. Personally, though, I 'preciate yer straight shootin' and I hear what you're sayin'."

Needing no encouragement at all, Manuel Controles went on. "The fact is, these Judas priests wouldn't even recognize Jesus if he miraculously showed up again. If he didn't vote the Republican ticket, they'd kick the living shit out of him. It'd make Mel Gibson's *The Passion of the Christ* look like a Sunday school picnic. Picture this: a bearded Christ, looking suspiciously like Osama bin Laden, walks into a Worst Eastern Motor Hotel, hands the clerk a handful of nails and says, 'Can you put me up for the night?'"

Not used to this type of humor, Bill forced a smile.

"The next scene is Christ's extraordinary rendition to Guantánamo Bay, where he's tortured: electric shocks to the genitals, fingernails pulled out, waterboarding, objects inserted into his rectum. Then the Palestinian hanging, where they tie his hands behind his back and suspend him from the ceiling. This causes his shoulders to pop out of their sockets and makes it tough for him to breathe. His interrogation by CIA agents can't extract any information from him except 'Forgive them Father, for they know not what they do.' All they can do is ask him, 'Where'd you pick up that left-wing, liberal communist bullshit, Jesus? We'll teach you to get sarcastic with us and attack American family values, you bearded son of a bitch.' Finally, Jesus dies while lying face down on the cold prison floor, his manacled hands tightly bound and twisted behind his back while attack dogs – Dobermans and German Shepherds – lunge and snarl inches from his face."

As Controles finally ran out of wind, Bill got to his feet and tugged on the brim of his imaginary Stetson. He pretended to draw a six-shooter and empty it into the reporter. Manuel clutched at his chest, as if staunching the blood flow from the imaginary wound, as Bill sauntered away.

"I counted, and you've still got one shot left, Bill," said Controles as he slumped to the floor.

"I'm savin' that," said Bill, spitting into an imaginary frying pan to see if it was ready to bake biscuits, "in case I run into a drunken preacher who tries to stop me from ravishing a beautiful half-breed dancehall girl."

The convention ended with cheering, hosannas and amens. Bill made his way to the lounge set aside for the coffee klatch. He was 22, stood a wiry five-foot-ten, and wore his hair a tad longer than most of the conventioneers would consider manly. His brown eyes spilled nervous energy despite his attempts to control his anxiety.

Introductions were made and he found himself seated next to, of all people, Nicolaus D'Amous, who smiled at him, revealing a set of white teeth that would have made Count Dracula envious.

"What do you do, young man?" D'Amous asked, trying to set Bill at ease.

Bill told him about being a carpenter, then added, "Not that I'm very happy with my job. Seems like a dead end."

D'Amous smiled at the wording, because what he was about to recommend to this young specimen of American manhood gave a much more literal meaning to 'dead end.'

"Have you ever thought of joining the military, Bill? They can teach you a trade, further your education. When you get out you'll most likely find yourself a much better job. And you'll have served your God and your country in the meantime."

"I'll give that a lot of thought, sir. Thank you for the suggestion." Small talk ensued, during which D'Amous learned that Bill was unmarried, had a steady girlfriend, and that he'd enjoyed the rally immensely. In keeping with protocol for the meeting, Bill got up to move to another table.

"One last thought," Nick said to him. "The root of all evil is to run out of money, and you can make a good living in the army." Bill smiled a farewell and turned away.

* * *

Bill told his girlfriend Helen Weills about the convention later the same evening. She thought D'Amous' suggestion for Bill to join the army was brilliant, so Bill took himself off to the recruiting office the next day.

"Can I pick my trade after I finish basic training?" he asked the sergeant behind the desk.

"Of course. What are you interested in?"

"Something that involves engineering, maybe, like bridge building. I've also always been interested in computers."

"Those trades are possible. I'll make a note of it, and I'm sure we can get you into one of those."

"How about deployment? Tell you the truth, I'm not keen on serving overseas, especially in the desert."

"Is that right? Well, I'll put a note about that in your file as well," said the sergeant, as he played x's and o's on the margin of the intake form.

* * *

Bill soon learned that you couldn't believe anything the military told you. They didn't lie, they just failed to tell you the truth. The second you signed on the dotted line, they owned your ass – lock, stock and two smoking gun barrels. You were government property to do with as they saw fit.

And how they saw fit in Bill's case, after he completed basic training, was to send him post-haste to Iraq, where they were badly in need of fresh boots on the ground. Instead of engineering or computer tech training, the army taught him about explosives, demolition and land mines. He complained to his superior officer without getting permission to speak, so they docked him half a month's pay for insolence.

In Iraq his job as part of a foot patrol was to place explosive charges against an Iraqi citizen's front door and blow it off, while five or six of his young buddies rushed into the household looking for teenage terrorists, hauling off all the males to Abu Ghraib. After a hundred such occasions of house breaking and entering, the only terrorists Bill had seen for sure were himself and his buddies.

"Nothing is more dangerous to man's private morality than the habit of command. The best man, the most intelligent, disinterested, generous, pure, will infallibly and always be spoiled at this trade. Two sentiments inherent in power never fail to produce this demoralization; they are: contempt for the masses and the overestimation of one's own merits."

— *Mikhail Bakunin,* Power Corrupts the Best, *1867*

V – Nicolaus D'Amous
a.k.a. Nick 'the Nostril'

April 2001, FEMA Office Building, Washington, D.C.

The President of the United States had a nickname for everyone he knew, and Nicolaus D'Amous, the czar of his shadow government, was no exception. He was known to the President as Nick 'the Nostril', because Nostril D'Amous sounded like Nostradamus, who was one of the President's heroes, a man who had foreseen Armageddon, the end of the civilization over which God had intended an American President to preside. None dared call Nicolaus, *the Nostril,* to his face, but they often did so behind his back.

A cynic could hardly be blamed for thinking 'the Nostril' was conducting choir practice when he spoke in front of a conglomeration of party hacks, political attack dogs, smooth-talking lobbyists, bagmen and money launderers, shameless propagandists, naïve, willingly-deceived liberals, right wing ideologues, ex wet-ops agents and old Iran-Contra drug smugglers. These were the usual suspects of the neoconservative GOPUSA, whose goal was the continual consolidation of power and money into ever higher, tighter and righter hands.

The administration's economic plan was to use the national debt to pay for the endless disproportionate tax cuts to the rich and the horrendous expense of militarization. When the Bush-Quayle team left office, one percent of the nation owned 57 percent of the private wealth of the United States. In the current era, the public was seeing that trend continue toward the goal of one percent owning 70 percent of all the nation's wealth.

The meeting of the shadow government took place behind a curtain of secrecy, in the FEMA building in D.C.

FEMA, the Federal Emergency Management Agency, was the forerunner of the Office of Homeland Security, the largest and least understood spy organization in the United States, created by Presidential Executive Order #13228. Although critics of Homeland Security depicted them as previously unemployable authoritarian hacks, the job of these men was to build up the American Empire – to create situations where as much of the planet's resources as possible flowed into the possession of American corporations which increased their control over the American government. Over the previous fifty years, this plan, this economic policy, had built the largest military empire in the history of the world, concomitant with the largest debt ever owed to international bankers – 3.4 trillion dollars, thus ensuring America's subservient compliance to their dictates. And the New World Order corporate-military oligarchic government was currently contemplating another holy crusade against the Middle East. America was addicted to war; in fact, without it, the economy would fold like a circus tent.

Although not mentioned in the Constitution, executive orders issued by the President had the same legal effect as laws passed by Congress, allowing the President to legislate independently of that elected body.

Only long-standing employees of the Federal Executive Department, possessing the highest possible security clearances, were being allowed through the newly installed metal security doors of this powerful agency. The entrance was not only staffed by fundamental Christian and neoconservative Republican types, but was heavily laden with, and led by, political cronies of the administration.

"Gentlemen," said Nick D'Amous, exuding a sober, practiced and well-tailored confidence, "as you know, this meeting is sponsored by the World Bank, the International Monetary Fund, the World Trade Organization, and supported by sundry private mega-corporations such as Halliburton and Bechtel. You have all expressed your interest in becoming part of PNAC – the Project for a New American Century – and your willingness to work by whatever means possible for the long-term greater good of the United States of America."

Nicolaus was a member of the Bilderbergers, the Council on Foreign Relations, the Trilateral Commission, the Royal Institute of International Affairs and the Canadian Institute of International Affairs. In fact, he was the czar of the Global Union and nothing of significance happened within these secret elite organizations that he did not directly or indirectly control.

"There are some God-forsaken liberals who say we are immoral, that criticize our methodology," Nick continued, "and who would have you believe that we use economic manipulation, through alleged cheating and fraud, to seduce people into our way of life, luring poor countries into debt and then forcing them to open their markets and natural resources to U.S. investors and corporations. People who tell you that are wrong thinkers. If you are a wrong thinker, please leave now. Only patriots of the highest order are welcome to stay."

No one left the room.

"May I propose a toast to our founders," continued D'Amous as he raised his wineglass. "To Harry Truman, Dickie Nixon and Henry Kissinger. It is to such truly great men, and many others, like Edward Lansdale, Alan and John Foster Dulles, Frank Wismer, William Colby, John Poindexter, Oliver North and Richard Secord that we should be thankful; for their past efforts helped create the most powerful organization in the United States, and therefore the world. For the protection and good of the public, FEMA has the power in times of real crisis or civil unrest to take over when the President declares a state of emergency, and provide continuity of government. Remember, *Americae est imperare orabi universo.* It is America's destiny to rule the world."

The whole group raised their glasses and chorused "To FEMA and PNAC."

"Now, if you will all repair to your previously assigned target-designated policy groups," said D'Amous, who was chairing the meeting, "you can analyze the key ideas and plans that are important to your various organizations, disciplines and operations, while I conduct a private executive meeting."

The executive was the ultimate Washington insiders club consisting of the Vice President, the Secretaries of State and Defense, the National Security Advisor and the Directors of the FBI and NSA. In attendance on this occasion were the second-in-command of the CIA, the Chairman of the Joint Chiefs of Staff, all the Joint Chiefs, the President's Chief of Staff, plus their top deputies. They went into private session with D'Amous.

"This is now a world of new realities and new threats," said D'Amous, once they were all settled. "Constraining U.S. freedom of action under a system of collective security is no longer in America's national interest," 'the Nostril' continued.

"I wanted to talk to you about – well, do you remember an operation called Project Bojinka?"

"Certainly," answered General Murray Meierhoff, Chief of the Joint Staffs, "it was picked up in 1995 by the CIA and FBI. In Phase I, Osama bin Laden was planning to hijack eleven

U.S.-bound airliners and blow them up over the Pacific Ocean and the South China Sea simultaneously. In Phase II, a suicide pilot would crash a small airplane like a Cessna, filled with explosives, into the CIA headquarters in Langley, Virginia. This came out during the trial in New York of Ramzi Yousef and Abdul Murad who were involved in the bombing of the World Trade Center in 1993 – an earlier FBI false-flag operation.

"Right. Bojinka, at the time, was used as the basis for intensive intelligence gathering," said the CIA Deputy, Herman Putzmeister. "We had every reason to take it seriously because, after all, it was our building that was one of the proposed targets. Evidence began to accumulate that flight schools were being used by international terrorists to learn to fly jumbo jets."

D'Amous interjected. "It doesn't matter whether the plans for Project Bojinka were actual creations of al-Qaeda or whether they were planted by us. What Bojinka now does is provide a plan around which we can shape our next strategy."

General Pierre Ness, a commander at NORAD, spoke up, "Could you be more precise? Are you suggesting some form of complicity?"

"I'm suggesting we could piggyback on an updated Project Bojinka. Osama bin Laden certainly isn't going to object, and it's my understanding that the Bojinka plan is still being worked on by his organization. They love the idea of using airplanes in attacks. Might it not be a good idea to give them some help?"

"To what end?" asked Meierhoff with interest, shifting forward in his chair.

"Demand for oil and natural gas from the growing world population is exploding at a time when we're reaching peak oil. We're heading for resource wars gentlemen. And who has those natural resources in abundance? The Middle East, Iraq, Iran, Saudi Arabia and all the 'Stans.' Our economy needs a big shot in the arm or our American standard of living is going down the dumper.

"I realize the planet hates American foreign policy and the American public are sick and tired of us meddling in other nations' affairs. But, someone has to do it, or all these little countries would go 'Cuban' and we can't have that. We're trying to bring freedom and democracy to the rest of the world and the only way that will happen is if there is an incident of the Pearl Harbor type to get the public behind our efforts."

"So true," Meierhoff chimed in, "nobody wants our help and some would just as soon shoot us on sight. Why? Because they don't understand our good intentions and they hate the things that we enjoy – our American way of life."

NORAD's General P. Ness chimed in, "We don't have to give a rat's ass about that, because we have an invincible army that can protect us from the consequences of any foreign policy errors which may inadvertently occur. I actually had some Canadian tell me just the other day, that as long as they're still talking to you, they're not shooting at you."

"One has to put up with that kind of crap from Canadians," said D'Amous. "Too bad they aren't all like that Mulroney fellow. We had him in our pocket. But our new President is doing a good job of bringing the Canucks back onside. Says he happens to think he's a pretty good diplomat. It's just that nobody else seems to think so. However, back to the point, gentlemen, our Project for a New American Century is in danger. Unless …," and 'the Nostril' stopped talking.

"Unless …," Putzmeister, taking up that train of thought, paused for several moments, his brow furrowed, "unless some Arab airline hijackers were to actually succeed in carrying out their old plan by attacking some prominent American icons."

"Precisely," said D'Amous. "*Aut viam inveniam aut faciam.* Where there's a will there's a way."

"Afghanistan is full of nasty Arabs like the Taliban. We backed them and they've now served their purpose," said Meierhoff. "And we could always use al-Qaeda as a potential enemy. Terrorism wouldn't be tolerated on American soil without retaliation against the perpetrators. We could then carry out the Pentagon's plan for an attack on Afghanistan, and on Iraq and that double-crossing bastard, Saddam Hussein – how dare he switch from petrodollars to euros. He would be a plausible culprit for any attacks on America. We need an incident, and the sooner the better. One that will provide a rallying point for the American public to back the attack. If we don't have something like that to justify our actions, the general masses aren't going to support going to war."

D'Amous secretly agreed with what Henry Rowan, onetime Assistant Secretary of Defense, had said about the Pentagon. "It's like a log going down the river with 25,000 ants on it, each thinking he's steering." Continuing to guide the assembled group toward the decision he wanted, D'Amous said, "The Vice President will be the titular head of – what shall we call it – maybe Project Piggyback, although that may be too suggestive. He'll be in charge of planning, and he'll be in complete control of FEMA, the DoD, the military, everything. The World Trade Center, the Pentagon and the White House are the obvious choices as targets, for many reasons."

"What reasons?" asked General P. Ness.

"The Trade Center complex has been attacked before," said the CIA Director, answering the question. "It houses vast archives of the criminal investigative records of a lot of agencies like the SEC, and also a paper trail of unknown size related to financial crimes, cooked books, inflated profits, government drug dealing and money laundering, and a lot of sundry other offences, and it wouldn't be a bad idea if it all went up in smoke."

"Anything else?"

"There are large amounts of gold and negotiable securities in a number of vaults in the trade center, many belonging to foreign banks," Herman Putzmeister said. "Could these be secretly removed and later claimed as destroyed or stolen? Just a thought ..."

"I'm not too keen on hitting the Pentagon," said Meierhoff. "Why do that?"

"An attack on the Pentagon," said the Vice President, "is vital for several reasons. First, in the event that sufficient popular support couldn't be garnered from the public over the loss of a financial center, then an attack on the Pentagon would certainly galvanize the military and even more of the population."

"If the White House were hit, FEMA could declare martial law and take over the government," said D'Amous. "But such things have to be arranged. They take a lot of time and careful planning. We have both but it may be too early to contemplate that scenario. Keep in mind that we can do a lot via Presidential Executive Order, whether it's constitutional or not. It becomes law by publication in the Federal Registry. Congress would simply be bypassed."

"What about the President?" asked Meierhoff.

"No problem," D'Amous replied. "I'll be talking to him, and I'll tell him all he needs to know."

"Who can we count on to both do a good job and keep their mouths shut?"

"There's an ultra-secret U.S. military and intelligence joint operation called Opposition Force," said Putzmeister, "or OPFOR, which has routinely played the bad guy in hijack exercises around the world and inside the U.S. It's a joint U.S.-Israeli operation. And we'd have the cooperation of the Israeli Mossad and certainly Inter-Service Intelligence in Pakistan."

"Let's think about using them as cutouts for the Vice and all U.S. agencies," said D'Amous. "Have them provide the plausible deniability and plan the cover story. And we always need protection from our own intelligence agencies and enforcement operatives who are out of the loop. Can't have them interfering with our plans."

"You can count on the Central Intelligence Agency," said the CIA Deputy. "The Agency knows every covert trick and black operation in the book, especially infiltration, intimidation and blackmail. Remember that Osama bin Laden was one of our assets, back in the days when we supported the mujahedeen rebels who were part of the Northern Alliance fighting the Soviets. We can also count on the five major corporate owners of the American media, who've always worked to protect the Agency and to keep the American public in the dark as to the nature of our activities."

No use dwelling on what these guys already know, thought the CIA's Putzmeister as the meeting came to an end. *The CIA is our own terrorist organization. We fund our activities by the profits of international drug smuggling, cooperating with both the drug lords and the Mafia, just as we did in the Vietnam War and in the Nicaragua War, and we'll do the same in the next war. The money has to come from somewhere, apart from the billions to be obtained from American taxpayers, courtesy of the government. Covert operations cost money. You can't finance them on milk and cookies, and you can't just pass up over one hundred and ten billion a year in drug trafficking profits. Besides, the 2.3 trillion dollars 'lost' by the Pentagon accounting gurus recently has been pretty helpful in keeping up the propaganda machine in the U.S. But control of all that black gold in the Middle East is essential for America, whatever the cost. The end really does justify the means. In any case, for the majority of Americans, whatever we tell them on TV and in the newspapers is what they will believe.*

"There is bound to be a certain amount of trouble running any country. If you are president the trouble happens to you. But if you are a tyrant you can arrange things so that most of the trouble happens to other people."

— *Donald Robert Perry Marquis (1878-1937)*, archy's newest deal

VI – Faulty Towers?

September 11, 2001, 9:00 a.m.

"We'll try to get to the 44th floor," said Lieutenant Hugh Mungo, talking to the firefighters assembled in the lobby of the South Tower. "The Battalion Chief and the Fire Marshal are on the 78th floor, and they report only isolated pockets of fire. They seem pretty sure we can put them out fairly easily. All it will take is a pair of engine companies and two hose lines to do the job. We'll work our way up there, while we help evacuate the building."

He led the way, looking for a working elevator. *There was no way they were going to be able to climb 78 stories with all that equipment,* he reasoned. There was only one elevator, in the first bank of six he came to, with its lights still on. It was a freight elevator that would take them up as far as the first sky-lobby on the 44th floor. "I'm going up to see if it's okay," Mungo said into his walkie talkie, and turning to Smoky Stover, a 20-year veteran New York firefighter, "Smoky, let's test drive this baby. Come on!"

When he and Smoky came back down safely, the first batch of firefighters and their equipment piled in and were taken up the tower. Smoky came back for a second load and then a third. The last fireman to get off was the irons guy. Smoky grabbed him by the back and said, "Hey! You gotta stay with me. We might need your tools."

The doors closed. Just as they started heading down, there was a huge explosion. The power went out. Everything went black. They couldn't see a damn thing.

"Holy sheepshit!" the irons guy yelled, "What the hell was that? Did another plane hit the building?"

The elevator doors wouldn't open. They were trapped!

* * *

Ian Stevens, a BBC reporter, was on the ground floor of the tower, trying to flag down evacuees to interview, when an explosion shook the base of the building. He ran outside just as a second explosion occurred, followed by a series of blasts.

* * *

After the first plane hit WTC 1 at 8:46 a.m., Tom Elliot, who worked on the 103rd floor of the South Tower, had decided to leave the building despite the fact that security was telling people they were safer to stay in their offices. He began running down the stairwell. When he'd reached the 67th floor he heard an explosion from below, which shook the building to its core. A tornado of hot air, smoke, ceiling tiles and bits of drywall came flying up the stairwell. The wall in front of him split from the bottom up, but he kept moving.

Then at 9:03, Flight 175 struck the tower above him between the 78th and 84th floor. He froze in horror for a moment, then continued his difficult descent through smoke and debris. He managed to get out before the tower collapsed at 9:59 a.m.

* * *

An *American Free Press* reporter buttonholed a man standing in a crowd about two and a half blocks from the South Tower. "Just before the tower came down, I saw about six flashes and heard a crackling sound," said the witness.

The German TV network SAT 1 captured video footage of a man talking about explosions. He was cut off in mid-sentence by two FBI agents who barged in, grabbed him as he was speaking, and hustled him away.

* * *

A minute after the plane struck the South Tower, a powerful explosion inside Building 6, the Customs House, hurled a cloud of gas and debris over five hundred feet high into the sky. A CNN broadcast image caught the rising smoke from street level near the base of the Customs House, originating at 9:04. Overhead views of the ruins later showed a large crater in the steel structure of WTC 6 that could not have been caused by fire, as there was none.

* * *

The elevator hadn't moved yet. The irons guy, thinking fast, pulled a spanner from his tool belt, the one he usually used to tighten the couplings joining lengths of fire-hose to a hydrant. He rammed the pointed end into the elevator door jamb. Using the spanner as a lever, he and Smoky began to pry apart the doors. Working feverishly, they managed to get them open a few inches, and then suddenly they popped wide open.

They charged out into the hallway, running to their left, looking for a stairwell. Finding one, they descended for six floors only to find it blocked by fallen debris. They ran across to the other side of the building, found another staircase, charged downstairs and made their way to the lobby.

As they ran toward the entrance, all of a sudden there was another explosion and the base of the building shook, banging them against the wall and jamming the lobby doors. Out came the iron guy's spanner again and they went to work with might and main. Just as they seemed to be having a little success with the door, another explosion picked them up and threw them right out onto the street.

Smoky looked up to the top of the tower, and saw perfectly synchronized explosions coming from each floor going all around like a belt, spewing glass and metal outward. One after another, from top to bottom, with a fraction of a second between, the floors blew to pieces. Smoky and the irons guy jumped up and ran as fast and as far as they could.

Just in time, for when they looked back, they saw the tower collapse into a massive pile of dust, smoking debris and twisted metal. They could hardly believe they'd been trapped like rats inside that big mother mere minutes before. From what they'd seen and heard, as experienced firemen, the only possible explanation for the collapse were the telltale signs of a controlled demolition job. *Somebody wired those buildings real good and that takes weeks of planning and a ton of talent*, thought Smoky.

* * *

While Smoky was coming down, Engineer Bill Delano, who had been working in the sixth sub-basement, was coming up. After a major explosion, he and a coworker went up to C level where there had been a small machine shop. There was nothing left but rubble and, on top of that, a fifty-ton hydraulic press was simply gone. They then went up to the parking garage, but found it was gone also. On B level they found a steel and concrete fire door which weighed about 300 pounds, wrinkled like a piece of aluminum foil. They got out just in time to follow Smoky down the street as fast as they could leg it.

* * *

FDNY lost 343 firefighters that day, exceeding the casualty count for the previous hundred years. The fires that seemed quite manageable were too high up for fire ladders, so they used the stairwells instead to get to the fires. They were able to fight the fires from within the skyscrapers with every degree of confidence. The reason for that was because no modern, steel-framed skyscrapers had ever collapsed as a result of a fire. On 9/11, the totally unexpected happened, the North and South Towers both collapsed, killing all but a few trapped in the basement.

> 'Experience ... a fine teacher, it's true,
> But here's what makes me burn:
> Experience is always teaching me
> Things I'd rather not learn!'
>
> — *Ethel M. Wegert*

VII – Guided Destruction Engineering

Jack Danielson lay sweating on his bed, fighting the urge for a drink for all he was worth. Images of corpses and rubble filled his mind and pursued him in fitful dreams. He knew having a drink wouldn't help, but try telling that to his body, which was still hooked after all these years.

The cops had once told Jack he'd blown the ass end out of the Breathalyzer, but Jack didn't think that was a fair comment. It was just that he reacted badly to an excess of alcohol. During Jack's marine stint in Desert Storm, the drinks had been strong enough to knock a buzzard off a gut wagon, and had created his addiction in the first place.

The only thing he'd really learned from his drinking experience was that shampoo and mouthwash looked the same but tasted different. After his discharge, he'd seen the writing on the floor, so he'd attended a couple of AA meetings. Though he'd been brought up in a Catholic family, religion had nothing to do with it, even though he'd decided to quit drinking at Christmas time. Jack believed the Yuletide holiday was Christ's retaliation for the crucifixion.

To distract himself from his struggle to stay sober, Jack had turned for help to his friend Sean Hennessey, who'd secured a short-term job for him a few weeks prior to the planes hitting the World Trade Center towers on September 11.

"Tell me why we're doing this again, Sean," Jack had said as he'd crouched next to Hennessey in the middle of the night, down in the seventh-level parking basement of the South Tower.

Hennessey, a handsome middle-aged Irish-American, could have been Jack's older brother with his black hair graying slightly at the temples. "The owners are afraid of what might happen if something else happened." Hennessey glanced sideways at Jack as he examined the steel pillar in front of them.

"What kind of bafflegab is that, you Irish jerk? I may be dumber than dog shit, but it sure looks like sabotage to me, and I don't want any part of blowing up this building, or anything else illegal."

"Calm down, Jack. You know there was a bombing attack here in '93. Blew out part of the ground floor and some of the basement, killed and wounded a bunch of people. Now, if something like that were to happen again, something which could impair structural integrity, then this tower might topple sideways, with God knows what horrific consequences to the surrounding area and the people in it."

"So?"

"So I'm told this is a precautionary measure. Controlled demolition will kick out the foundations and bring the building straight down, so no other buildings are damaged if this one goes. Aren't you glad now you got all that explosives training in the marines?"

"Yeah, it was useful experience for this kind of job. But Desert Storm was enough marine life for me."

"You're damn good at this demolition business, Jack, I wouldn't give it up if I were you," said Sean, as he rifled through the oversized kit bag he'd brought. "I'm so glad you've quit drinking too."

"Just don't bother telling Guided Destruction Engineering I'm working for you. I'm persona non grata with those guys. They still think I'm an alcoholic, which is why they turfed me."

"Don't worry about that. You're working strictly buckshee for me at the moment. They don't know about it, but I'll do what I can to get you on regular staff somewhere."

"I appreciate that, old buddy. But what about this building? It'll still go sideways unless the rest is wired to implode and come straight down. You'd have to set cutter charges on every other floor and set them off in sequence in order to pull the building safely."

"Not our job," Sean replied. "There's another crew looking after that. There's a bunch of engineers up there right now."

"But won't that take a lot of time and manpower?"

"No," said Sean, "the wiring was already done a couple of months ago when Harry Finkelman took control of the complex. "Now, there's only about ten guys needed to hook up the approximately 4,000 pounds of explosives in each building. They've been shutting down various parts of the towers over the last few days to get the job finished on time. But this basement contract's my responsibility, so let's get on with it. I think we can finish most of it tonight."

Jack stared at Sean. "It'd have to be some disaster to make them pull this puppy. We're right down to bedrock here. The central core of both towers is made of 47 huge steel box columns fourteen inches by thirty-six inches using solid steel four inches thick! Plus they were built to withstand winds of 160 miles an hour. No way they'll come down easy."

"Look, we've been placing charges every twenty feet or so all the way up each of the columns 'til we hit ground level. That should do it, plus it'll make hauling away the debris a cinch. If it's ever necessary, of course."

"You're right, Sean. Thanks for including me in on this gig. And for the big paycheck – now that's the best part."

"Yeah, the new owners aren't stingy by half."

"Especially when they know they're never going to have to use this so-called precautionary measure."

"Only fools are positive," Sean said, handing Jack some plastique.

"Are you sure?"

"I'm positive!" The two men chuckled and got back to work.

Several hours later and seven floors up, Jack helped Sean pack up the equipment. "Will you need me tomorrow night?" he asked.

"Ah, no. They've asked me to do another placement, but I can handle that by myself. I'll cut you a check on the weekend. You've been a big help, Jack. Thanks."

They packed their gear into a van and drove out of the basement of the South Tower, took Highway 78 through the Holland Tunnel and into Jersey City. They lived relatively close to each other, so Sean dropped Jack off at his digs.

"If we don't believe in freedom of expression for people we despise, we don't believe in it at all."

— *Noam Chomsky*

VIII – A Soul Ascending to Heaven

The Reverend Mosey Long had a Bible autographed by God, or so he said. He also owned his own television network and a multi-million-dollar personal fortune and enjoyed access to the ear of key U.S. Republicans. Mosey was running off at the mouth to his congregation, loud and clear, lest there be any mistake as to his meaning.

The Christian Intelligence Network (CIN-TV) was carrying the speech, and the sundry baloney-and-mustard-on-white-bread, truck drivin', Christian-bred, country music aficionados were lapping up his sermon. Mosey wet his larynx from time to time from the carafe on his pulpit that, judging from the content of his rants, some said contained a shot of vodka or two.

"Yes, brethren and sistern, I'm talkin' to you about sca-a-a-andalous, sex-yally suggestive nubile young pom-pom waving Salomés, pelvic thrusting and hip shimmying their way back to the sidelines of Hell itself, luring the attention of our community away from the wholesome Christian avocation of fine young men beating themselves senseless every Friday night on the football field. Can I get an Amen!?"

The congregation obliged, roaring their Amens.

"The nation that does not preserve its heritage is a nation not fit to survive. This is the challenge we face. God cries out to us as we slide deeper into moral and spiritual decline. 'Thus saith the Lord. Stand ye in the ways, and seek, and ask for the old paths, where is the good way, and walk therein, and ye shall find rest for your souls.' Jeremiah 6:16.

"But what is our nation's response? The ignorant pagan public say, 'We will not walk therein'. So what does God

46

do? He trumpets a final warning of what will befall them if they do not repent their individual and national sins. Also I set watchmen over you, saying, 'Hearken to the sound of the trumpet'. But again they say, 'We will not hearken.'

"Therefore hear, ye nations, and know, O congregation, what will happen if you just try to pull down the window shades on your lascivious and immoral behavior. 'Hear, O Earth: behold, I will bring evil upon these people, even upon the fruit of their thoughts, because they have not hearkened unto my words, nor to my law, but rejected it.' Verses 17 to 19.

"Dearly beloved, you are hearing this just in time to really do something about it!

"Other nations have left God out of the picture. But the United States will establish the wonder of God's direct and imminent intervention in human affairs. That very next event is prophesied to occur following the Tribulation and the Day of the Lord. Matthew 24:21, 29-30: 'The Son of God, the Prince of Peace, will soon return to inaugurate the perfect peace plan for mankind.'

"But first we have to deal with some very ungodly nations on this planet. China, Japan, the EU. They'll never pull the rug out from under our dollar economy. They have too much to lose! As for Taiwan, doesn't America have the most powerful navy in the world? Could we not literally steam roll China's navy to the bottom of the sea?

"Iran? Chief sponsor of global terror. It would not be smart to taunt America, the EU and the UN by developing nuclear weapons. Our American military could fuse them all into little glass pieces with one well-placed nuke!

"Russia? Putin's cuddling up to us. The President says we can trust him, he has too much to lose by resisting us. He's all talk.

"Europe? The Holy Roman Empire? Ridiculous! They have written God out of their constitution, so how can they possibly be termed holy? It is an enlightened free trade bloc. What's more, it is too disunited to be a real threat to America.

"Venezuela? We have a dangerous enemy to the south of us, brethren and sistern, and the name of this Satan is that commie-Castro-loving Hugo Chavez! Or is it Yugo Chovitz, because that's what he can do. He has destroyed the Venezuelan economy and made his country a launching pad for communist infiltrators and Muslim extremists, who will spread their evil across the entire continent of South America. If he thinks we're trying to assassinate him, I think that we really ought to go ahead and do it. It's a whole lot cheaper than starting a war. This man is a terrific menace controlling a huge pool of oil. This is in our sphere of influence, and we can't let him threaten to cut off our access to that oil. We have the ability to take him out, and I think the time has come for us to exercise that ability. We don't need another 200 billion-dollar war to take out one loud-mouth, strong-arm dictator. We just need to send in a few mercenaries to do the job. In the meantime I propose we stick a set of bagpipes up his ass and force him to fart Yankee Doodle Dandy until his eyeballs bulge out. Or send him a few special cigars like we sent Fidel. Maybe he'll be dumb enough to light one.

"The world can't afford to let the U.S. economy collapse. Too much depends on it. We're big enough to trade our way out of any amount of foreign debt. I've got a new mortgage on my home and a loan on my SUV, and my fridge is full. What more could anyone want?

"Another thing: The ignorant public's reasoning is that anything they do behind closed doors is none of our business, and there is no such thing as deviant behavior. They think that's just an old fashioned term to describe anything not permitted by the Bible. And they think they did away with those old repressive rules years ago. Well, they have another *think* coming. Right and wrong are absolute and unchanging, determined solely by the one true lawgiver – God – who is very interested in the sexual behavior that goes on behind closed doors.

"Satan is a powerful being that broadcasts, all over the Earth, a spirit of disobedience, which includes lying and deception. Ephesians 2:2. It is Satan who tempts all humans to lie. But in conclusion, let me remind you, 'This is where you will hear the truth!'"

A major player on the U.S. political scene, nobody argued with or interrupted the Reverend Mosey Long when he was operating in top fulmination mode; his intellect was rivaled only by garden tools, his mouth so offensive you'd be tempted to slap him with an harassment suit. Mosey was offensive in all categories including nose hairs.

"And now let's take a look at the domestic scene. What do we see? Janet Jackson's right mammary gland, that's what we see, right on TV! Her lascivious nipple completely exposed for anyone's vulgar gaze. Oh, it was enough to make a baby cry! Some have said to me, 'Reverend, it was only for 1.8 seconds and her action could have been accidental. No excuse, I say! Eighteen million people saw that boobie. Now if you multiply 1.8 seconds by 18 million people, it means that tit was exposed for 324,000,000 seconds. Divide those seconds by 60 and you get 540,000 minutes. Divide by 60 again and the result is 9000 hours those tits were viewed. Divide by two because only one of them was exposed, and the answer is 4500 hours in which a pair of boobs was on our tubes. Divide by 24 and the answer is that we were exposed to a sexually suggestive pair of tits for one hundred and eighty-seven and a half days, or 26.64 weeks, 6.66 months or over a half a year. UNACCEPTABLE! Just do the math people. We pay to bring television into our homes. We would be better off just to raise the salaries of those sinful, perdition-doomed TV performers and executives and let them be stupid in the privacy of their own homes; and stop bringing lipstick, perfume, high heels, underarm deodorant, breath mints, boobies and nipples into ours. Dare I say it and God forbid: tits and ass!

"These matters are a sinful stench in the nostrils, and an outrage in the souls of the righteous!"

* * *

Meanwhile, back at the ranch in Texas, the President was in a bind, because Mosey Long's multi-numbered Christian Fundamentalist Fanatics, largely congregated in the State of Missarkloutexana, had contributed heavily in money and votes to the President's election campaigns, contributed as much as the Miami Mafia and the Deadbolt voting machine company. Still, he had to distance himself from this ridiculous assassination statement by Long. The public was outraged.

There were more clowns in the President's administration than a three-ring circus, so why not call on them? Emulating the Lone Ranger, he immediately tasked Tonto, in the form of the Defense Secretary, to make a public statement. The Secretary, chagrined at this unwanted exposure of what was already standard practice of the CIA, stated, "Our Department doesn't do that kind of thing. And contrary to rumor, we don't stick red-hot pokers up anybody's ass, cold end first. It's against the law."

To further control the damage, el Presidente put in a call to his Eminence Grise, Nick 'the Nostril', and shortly thereafter a State Department spokesman added that the preacher, Mosey Long, was speaking solely as a private citizen, that his comments were inappropriate and in no way reflected U.S. government policy. Neither of them ventured to say that something should be done about the loudmouth, such as prosecution for a criminal statement that was much more threatening to hemisphere stability than the flash of Janet Jackson's breast during the Super Bowl half-time show.

"The case for government by the elite is irrefutable …
government by the people is possible but highly improbable."

— *J. William Fulbright, former Chairman of the Senate
Foreign Relations Committee, 1963 Symposium*

IX – My Head Hurts, My Feet Stink – But I Do Love Jesus

Texas, May 2001

Time was when the President had been plagued with an assortment of fears, a condition he could generally mitigate with a couple of drinks. That was before he'd read *The Wonderful World Tomorrow, What Will It Be Like*, after which he'd immediately begun to anticipate the greatest headline in history: JESUS CHRIST RETURNS! That time was coming, and the President knew it lay just ahead. He could feel the pulse of world events leading up to it. He was one of the chosen people, in fact, *the* chosen person, who had the real vision not only to see, but to control what was to come. He felt blessed by God, of whom he was not afraid. But as he walked toward the small office in one of his ranch outbuildings, he was forced to admit that the visitor awaiting him there scared the crap out of him.

Nick 'the Nostril' had his own nickname for his nominal boss – and that was *Truck* – because in his younger years the President had usually been loaded. It was D'Amous' idea to meet away from prying eyes in Washington, and he stood before a window looking onto an adjacent field, where a collection of thoroughbreds were grazing contentedly.

D'Amous scowled as he examined the bottom of one of his shoes. Damn! Was that encrusted horse manure? And this

51

damn state was too damned hot. He took off his jacket and hung it over the back of an old wooden chair, then flung the window wide open to take advantage of the slight breeze.

The President entered. The two shook hands and sat down on opposite sides of a well-worn oak table. *Sometimes D'Amous really looks like an Italian spik,* thought the President, *with that long nose and slightly pointed chin and the long, slicked back, black hair.*

D'Amous lost no time expressing his disdain for his surroundings. "Why does everything in Texas smell like horse shit?"

"Same reason everything sounds like it in Washington," the President replied, half snickering, "My granddaddy once told me that modern people who complain about the bad smell coming out of the exhausts of motor cars had never sat in a dray, four feet behind the two fat-assed horses pulling the wagon uphill. They could generate enough methane to fly Neil Armstrong halfway to the moon."

D'Amous, taking in Truck's checkered shirt and jeans tucked into his cowboy boots, asked sarcastically, "What's with the outfit, Boss? You have to do more than eat baked beans and fart around a campfire to be a cowboy."

"Good to see you too, Nick," the President replied, chuckling nervously. "I know why you're here, but I want you to run through the reasons why we should do this. A lot of Americans could get hurt."

"You've been in the armed forces, you know civilian casualties can't be helped," Nick added with a wry smile. "Now we just call them collateral damage. It won't be any worse than the last time in Iraq, and their people will be so happy to be rid of Saddam – so happy they'll welcome us with open arms and desert flowers. Given global overpopulation, it doesn't much matter how many get killed, now does it? Besides, *iacta alea est.* The die is cast."

"What about opposition here at home?" the President asked.

"Don't worry, we can handle that under FEMA and the journalists in Operation Mockingbird. If a full emergency is declared, only God would have more power."

Truck squirmed in his chair as he pondered the origins of FEMA. A body created without congressional approval during the Nixon administration by Executive Order 12148, the Federal Emergency Management Agency was capable of doing great good during and after a natural disaster. But its powers also included the ability to suspend the Constitution and the normal functions of civilian government, cancel or postpone federal and state elections, and throw the legislative and judicial branches of the government out of work, thus silencing the voice and legal redress of the people. Executive Order #11921 declared that when a state of emergency was imposed by the President, Congress couldn't review the action for six months. FEMA could allow the imposition of martial law in the event of nuclear war, widespread internal dissent or major opposition to an American military invasion overseas against a country that was threatening America, such as Nicaragua, El Salvador, Venezuela, Afghanistan, Iraq, Iran or Cuba – or even those socialistic bastards up in Canada. All that was required to unleash FEMA's sweeping powers was the President's official signature on an Executive Order.

The President's political masters had made him aware of one precedent – a staged national emergency simulation exercise in 1984, Rex-84 Bravo, authorized by President Reagan as National Security Decision Directive 52. The exercise was designed to test FEMA's readiness to deputize and assume authority over Department of Defense personnel and all fifty State National Guard forces, so as to avoid violating the Federal Posse Comitatus Act, which forbade using the military for domestic law enforcement.

Nick D'Amous interrupted Truck's musings. "The plan will work, believe me. We needed new ideas, new angles, and we've come up with them. *Aureo hamo piscara.* Money talks. To put it bluntly, you know you're the kind of guy who believes in government of the people by the elite for the corporations, with tax cuts for the rich. If that weren't so you wouldn't be where you are today. One dollar one vote, right?"

"We're talking eventually about open, aggressive, first-strike warfare. Some say it should be used sparingly," Truck replied, his busy hands betraying a degree of strain, giving the lie to his easy smile. "Such plans could eventually lead to what could be World War Three."

"If that's the case, then so be it and it must be fought rapidly and savagely, using all the tools and tricks we have at hand," D'Amous replied.

"I've never said I wasn't in favor of the plan, but I'm the one who has to deal with the people of this nation before and after it happens. And we both know that if this plan doesn't go right we could be cell-mates."

"Nonsense," Nick countered, "we merely apply our doctrine of self-exemption from international law and treaties. The U.S. is entitled to its own sovereign interpretation of all such matters. We have the Attorney General's legal opinion to support that."

"What about the Geneva Conventions?"

"The Geneva Conventions are just a set of rules allegedly governing the atrocities man commits in the name of some political ideology. We make our own rules in the good ol' U.S. of A."

"And the Charter that came out of the Nuremberg Tribunal?"

"Just like the World Court. Disqualified from judging United States actions, *ipso facto,* no legal restraints on our conduct beyond our borders." Nick paused, "or within, for that matter."

"And that damn Human Rights Watch, Amnesty International and the International Committee of the Red Cross? Those meddlesome bastards are always giving us a hard time."

"Mr. President, don't worry about them. We'll handle them; we've got people on their boards. As for the public, all you need to do is spin the end against the means. Give them the old flimflam, the feel good stuff, the old razzamatazz. Freedom is a priceless commodity, as is our American Way of Life, our family values, and our national security. Freedom demands constant vigilance to guarantee its longevity. We're going to hold their public noses to the roses we want plucked! And be sure and tell them *aut bibat aut abeat.*"

"For God's sake, Nick, speak American."

"You're either with us or against us."

The President nodded. *A great slogan. He'd have to give them the horns-on-a-steer speech – a point here and a point there, and a lot of bull in between – that sort of jingoistic nonsense,* he thought.

"But first we have to build up the terrorist threat to the United States," said D'Amous, mopping his brow and inwardly cursing the oppressive heat. "We badly need something to scare the living shit out of John Q. Public, because we no longer have the 'kill a commie for Mommie' syndrome to count on. We'll get plenty of help from the media. They're all controlled by a handful of mega-corporations that are owned by a few wealthy friends of mine. We can remain in the shade while they play the public like a cheap tin whistle."

"What about the knowledge and consent of Congress?"

"Screw them, they never stand up to us anyway. Not if they know what's good for them. Just remember that all

Congressmen have two things in common – they all have rectums and they all have opinions, and they should shove the latter up the former. We'll just use waivers of the CIA program MKULTRA."

"Remind me what that is. We passed a lot of stuff through Congress. Most of them never read the legislation anyway. And truthfully, neither do I. A waiver to what? Say again."

"Manufacturing Killers Utilizing Lethal Tradecraft Requiring Assassinations – MKULTRA. It means that you, as President, under certain circumstances, can authorize the CIA to brainwash a 'Manchurian Candidate' to carry out an assassination in order to protect the American way of life and our national security. Mr. President, you have to have the insight, precision and spine to allow us to carry out this operation. We must keep Americans safe from the terrorist threat that is knocking on our door."

"Well, I certainly want to do that. Which terrorist threat?"

"Fuck the details; you don't want to know. I'll tell you what to do in stages. And don't talk to the FBI. As far as you're concerned, there are no stinking details."

"The Secretary of State tells me we should try to get some other nations on our side, to form a coalition of the willing."

"Of course, and Rowland Fowler is just the man we need to convince everyone, including the UN, our actions are justified – even if we have to coach him on how to lie. Right?"

The President was pretty sure the New World Order didn't need his approval, so damn sure that he was going along with whatever game was afoot anyway. "You're right. Lying is a tool we must use when necessary. Hitler's Propaganda Minister Goebbels said it best: 'The bigger the lie, the more it will be believed.' Just keep telling it and eventually it becomes the truth in the minds of the public."

"You're a quick study. None dare call it fascism, for we'll only be doing the right thing for a noble cause."

"So be it then," said Truck. "God cries out to us to have the moral courage and collective will to use the sheer weight of our evident power to do the world a service and confront the denizens of the crazed, hateful anti-Christian nations in our midst. And anybody who is not with us is against us – that is, with the terrorists, right? I'll remember that. So fuck them all but six and save them for pallbearers."

"You're preaching to the converted. Save it," said D'Amous, running his hand back through his long black hair. Truck figured 'the Nostril' used Grecian Formula.

"Here's the first thing I want you to do," D'Amous continued. "Issue a homeland defense initiative in which you direct the Vice President to coordinate all U.S. government agencies in the event there's a terrorist attack on the United States. Military power must be subordinate to civil authority."

Nick picked up his coat jacket and plucked a piece of paper from the inside pocket. "Here's a copy of your official statement. Get familiar with it so you don't screw it up," he said, handing over the paper. He threw the jacket over one shoulder, saying, "Time for me to leave this horseshit heaven, but I'll be in touch when it's time for you to make that announcement."

"So long, D'Amous," said Truck as he watched 'the Nostril' step gingerly through the road apples in the empty corral on his way back to the farmhouse where he'd parked his car. Tapping the paper against his palm, Truck thought, *they didn't even consider that I might not go along with this, or did they?*

D'Amous' car headed down the road out of the ranch. When it disappeared from view, Truck unfolded the paper and read aloud:

'I have asked the Vice President to oversee the development of a coordinated national effort so that we may do the very best possible job of protecting our people from catastrophic harm. I have also asked the Director of the Federal Emergency Management Agency, FEMA, to create an Office of National Preparedness. This office will be responsible for implementing the results of those parts of the national effort overseen by the Vice President that deal with consequence management. Specifically, it will coordinate all federal programs dealing with weapons of mass destruction and consequence management within the Departments of Defense, Health and Human Services, Justice and Energy, the Environmental Protection Agency and other federal agencies.'

The President realized that this put the V.P. in charge of all planning involving a terror attack on America, with complete control over FEMA, the military, everything.

A strange, sly, sickly smirk crossed Truck's face. *Better him than me*, thought Truck.

"Since the plotters were flexible and resourceful, we cannot know whether any single step or series of steps would have defeated them. What we can say with confidence is that none of the measures adopted by the U.S. government from 1998 to 2001 disturbed, or even delayed, the progress of the al-Qaeda plot. Across the government, there were failures of imagination, policy, capabilities, and management.

The most important failure was one of imagination. We do not believe leaders understood the gravity of the threat."

— The 9/11 Commission Report,
Final Report of the National Commission
on Terrorist Attacks Upon the United States, *July 2004*

X – Military Intelligence
— An Oxymoron

September 11, 2001, 9:15 a.m.

Deep in the Presidential Emergency Operations Center (PEOC) beneath the White House, the Vice President was monitoring the unfolding drama in the skies over America's North East Air Defense Sector. A change in command policy had been put in place only three months before, and the Vice was in sole charge of both military orders to stand down and orders permitting fighters to shoot down rogue aircraft or hijacked commercial airliners.

After the second plane had crashed at 9:03 a.m. into the World Trade Center, requests had poured into his command post from fighter jet squadrons nationwide, offering to protect the skies over Washington. But the Vice President's stand-down orders prevented the military from intercepting any of the alleged hijacked aircraft.

At 9:20 a.m. the Secretary of Transportation arrived at the PEOC bunker where the V.P. was giving orders. The Secretary was in the bunker only 5 minutes when another hijacking was reported at 9:25 a.m. He rushed into the radar room, leaned over the shoulder of the Deputy Federal Aviation Chief and asked, "Do we have any clarification on this third hijacking?"

"We're tracking the target on radar, but the transponder's been turned off, so we have no identification," was the reply. The Secretary then returned to join the V.P. and other officials in the conference room.

A few minutes later at 9:32, a young military aide came in bearing news that the unidentified aircraft was heading directly toward Washington. "Mr. Vice President, there is a plane 50 miles out. Should we engage?"

The V.P. heard him but remained silent and motionless. The young man disappeared back into the radar room. A couple of minutes later, he reappeared again stating, "the plane is 30 miles out. Should we engage?" Again no answer from the Vice.

Two minutes later the same aide entered the room again, and stated for the final time, "it's only 10 miles out and – we've just lost the bogey! Do the orders still stand?"

The Vice President turned, whipped his neck around and said, "Of course the orders still stand. Have you heard anything to the contrary?!"

The aide chewed on his lip as he pondered the consequences. Did the officials and the Vice President know if this flight they were monitoring was real, or did they think it was just one of the war-games or terror drills that a multitude of air defense agencies were conducting this morning? What if someone had made a mistake and that was a real attack by some kind of plane or missile?

He didn't have long to wait. The bogey plowed into the Pentagon at 9:37 a.m.

"If you once forfeit the confidence of your fellow citizens,
you can never regain their respect and esteem.
It is true that you may fool all the people some of the time;
you can even fool some of the people all the time;
but you can't fool all of the people all of the time."

*— Abraham Lincoln to a caller at the White House
From Lincoln's Yarns and Stories, Alexander K. McClure*

XI – Chaim X. Zosted

September 11, 2001, 9:33 to 9:37 a.m.

Chaim X. Zosted opened his gas bar early. The X in his
name stood for Xavior, but he used it only as an initial. A
devout Israeli-American citizen, Chaim often pondered the
deeper spiritual meaning of things. That was the activity he
was engaged in, as he and his staff serviced the many vehicles
that pulled off the highway opposite the Pentagon, demanding
gas for their guzzlers.

Chaim wondered, *Is God the keeper of a database of
everything that's happened to every living creature on Earth
over all time? If so, he'd need one humungously big computer.
In all the time that Earth has existed, how many human beings
have inhabited this planet? And how long have we been using
petroleum to run our so-called civilization? A hundred years
or so? Just think, sixty years ago there was no Pentagon, and
no endless stream of traffic going by the largest office building
in the world and my little Citgo gas station here.*

It was at that point in Chaim's musings that an airborne
object executed an extremely difficult 270-degree spiral turn
over Washington D.C. and Langley Virginia, coupled with a
sharp, high-speed dive from several thousand feet.

Chaim, his staff and a number of motorists watched slack-
jawed as the object flew straight past the gas station, directly into

61

the Pentagon, streaking just a few feet above the ground. It ripped out five lamp poles and some trees before boring a small hole into the western side of the Pentagon – a wing assigned to the Navy but virtually unoccupied at the time, due to renovations.

The surveillance camera on the roof of the gas station recorded a four-minute segment of Earth time and that morning's most peculiar events, from 9:33 to 9:37 a.m.

Within minutes of the crash, as the occupants of the gas bar were reviving themselves from their shock and trying to grasp what had just happened, three men in dark suits and sunglasses entered the station. They confronted Chaim who was busy watching all sorts of fire and medical units appear at the Pentagon in a miraculously short space of time.

"What can I do for you guys?" Chaim asked, his eyes still fixed on the pandemonium across the road.

"We're here for your security camera tapes. We're confiscating them," the tallest of the three suits said.

Chaim's attention was fully on the agents now. "Why would you want to do that?"

"Mind your own business," the same agent snapped.

"I am. This *is* my business and these are my cameras, and my tapes. Got any I.D.?"

"For what?" another agent said, sneering.

"You can't just come in here and take my property without a warrant."

"We don't need no stinking warrant," the lead agent said.

"Why not?"

"FBI is why not," the man said, flashing his badge.

"But these are my tapes," Chaim repeated, "I haven't even seen them myself."

"And you're not going to."

"I don't like this one bit!" Chaim exclaimed.

"Okay," said one FBI agent, turning to the others with

him, "slap the cuffs on him. Take this man into custody for unauthorized possession of classified material."

"How can it be classified material?" Chaim protested. "Besides, the Pentagon's got plenty of surveillance equipment. They probably have tons of footage about that plane or whatever it was that crashed into the west wing. Why do you need my tapes? What difference will they make?"

"National security."

With that, the FBI agents took Chaim's video tapes and vanished as quickly as they'd appeared.

Later that day, Chaim heard CNN claim that the crash had been caused by Arab hijackers of Flight 77, who hated America and wanted to destroy the Pentagon, an icon of American military might. Apparently, the attack had taken the country's entire combined intelligence community by surprise.

Chaim wondered why the terrorists hadn't even been smart enough to just dive straight into the most heavily populated part of the Pentagon on the east side, the easiest target, and try to take out a few top military officials in the process. Instead, they'd chosen to hit a section of the building that was more difficult to hit, and the only area of the structure that was undergoing major renovations, which meant minimal damage and fewer casualties. *Something's fishy here*, he thought.

* * *

A man of many talents, Benny Fishal was trying to get out of Washington on the morning of September 11th, after hearing of the attacks on the World Trade Center. He made a wrong turn and found himself driving south on Washington Boulevard, the highway that passes the western side of the Pentagon. Fifty years old, Fishal was an electrical engineer, also a civilian pilot with a lifelong interest in both military and civilian aircraft – able to identify them quickly and accurately.

He was also trained as an emergency medical technician.

Shortly after 9:30 a.m. he noticed a strange object in the air. Along with other distracted drivers, Benny pulled over to the right shoulder, stopped his car and got out, the better to observe the fast approaching white aircraft that had no cockpit or fuselage windows.

That's bigger than a Gulfstream 300, he said to himself. One engine, located on the rear section between a V tail, reminded him of the Beechcraft Bonanza, with that funny looking front, shaped like a humpback whale. He watched the craft that he had not yet identified, approach from the north and make a 270-degree spiral turn to the right while descending, as it approached the Pentagon. It leveled off just above the ground and he heard a high-pitched whine coming from the single engine.

The plane dove downwards under perfect control over the highway cloverleaf southwest of the Pentagon, travelling about 200 miles per hour, then accelerated and leveled off as it aimed for the building, passing him at a distance of less than 500 feet. The engine configuration now reminded Benny of an older Boeing 727 that had a turbine jet engine located on the back of the plane above the fuselage. *Coming in so low, it's knocking down lamp poles, and it's very quiet, no roar like a commercial jet at full throttle would make,* he thought.

The craft flew with remarkable precision into the western façade and newly renovated section of the Pentagon, built on a low lying area formerly known as 'Hell's Bottom.' There was a bright orange fireball and a huge explosion.

Rushing back to his car, Benny reached into the glove compartment for binoculars and then swept the crash site scene. At first, a lot of smoke obstructed his view, but then, to one side, he saw a group of men wearing white shirts and ties. They all had binoculars. Benny saw some of them looking at him through theirs. He waved but they did not wave back.

Strange. Some were looking up into the sky and Benny did likewise. There was a four-engine jet at about 15,000 feet that looked like a Boeing 707 or a DC-8.

Back at his car again, Benny donned his emergency medical technician shirt and walked across the six-lane highway to assist in the initial rescue effort at the crash site, expecting to find wreckage, debris, dead and wounded. One of the first to arrive on the scene, Benny was baffled when he didn't find any bodies nor any substantial pieces of wreckage. All he saw was a 16 to 20-foot hole in the wall of the Pentagon, and some smashed up sheet metal lying around on the undamaged lawn. He found himself looking directly down at a bent and damaged 3-foot engine that was missing its turbine blades. It had not penetrated, and appeared to have bounced about 25 feet back from the two-foot thick limestone-clad wall. There was a strong smell of gunpowder or cordite. Planes do not simply evaporate; where was the wreckage? Maybe he could help with wounded inside the building.

"Hey, you," shouted a large and stern visaged man in a blue jacket and darker pants, exuding officialdom, "do you work for the Pentagon?"

"No, but I'm here to help," Benny Fishal replied, pointing to the EMT emblem on his T-shirt.

The official stared at the shirt for a moment, then said "Okay, you can help us over there."

"I'm willing, but who am I working for?" Benny wanted to know.

"Name is Erskine, FBI. Now get in line with those other people on the lawn and help pick up the debris. Here's a garbage bag."

"Aren't we supposed to leave it in place and flag it for the accident investigators?" asked Benny, who had been to other crash sites and knew the proper procedures.

"Look buddy," Erskine snapped, "just pick up the stuff. It's none of your damned business."

Benny did as he was ordered and joined a line of Pentagon employees walking slowly in a line across the undamaged lawn, picking up small pieces of shredded aluminum and carbon-fiber material which he noticed was rough with protruding fibers on one side and smooth and polished on the other. He was puzzled by the fact that rather than securing the perimeter and preserving the evidence, putting down orange flags for the forensic specialists and accident investigators, he and the others were treating critical evidence as trash. And how was it that the FBI in large numbers right after the crash – a crash that certainly didn't involve a large airliner? *I'm thankful for that, no bodies, no injuries to attend to. All I can see around here is that hole in the wall and this guy Erskine riding my ass behind me. Nothing like any crash site I ever saw or hope to see again. This is the same kind of carbon-fiber composite material they use for the wings and tail of those new jet powered, unmanned RQ-4 Global Hawks,* thought Benny. It was probably a 44-foot long surveillance UAV with a fuselage made of aluminum, a 115-foot wing span that can fly at 400 miles per hour, made by Northrop Grumman Systems Corporation and Raytheon under one of those multi-billion dollar defense project contracts. The plane could have been heavily armed with a missile of sufficient power to create a 75 to 96-foot wide entry hole in the first and second floors, and drill an exit hole through the third ring of the Pentagon about seven feet in diameter.

"Pick up every damn piece of debris," Erskine yelled as he supervised the collection.

I can't believe I'm doing this, Benny muttered to himself as he stuffed the evidence into his trash bag, *but I am dealing with the FBI and I'm not looking for any trouble.*

"A soldier told Pelopidus, 'We are fallen among enemies.'
Said he, 'How are we fallen among them
more than they among us?'"

— *Plutarch*

XII – Abu Ghraib

There is no visible difference between a Sunni and a Shi'ite Muslim in Iraq, just as it is impossible to tell a Protestant from a Catholic in the West. Mounir Malouf's mother had been a Sunni, his father a Shi'ite, so Mounir had become adept at walking the tightrope between the two opposing states of Muslim mind.

This ability was proving handy in the predicament in which Mounir now found himself – as handy as the mental trick his grandfather had taught him long before that wise man had been killed in an American bombing attack. The old man was not killed in the present conflict, but back in Desert Storm, in 1991. That war had been triggered by some fake incubator baby murders – a $10-million joint White House-Kuwaiti conspiracy of deception campaign which was used to create a public outrage against Saddam Hussein and support the invasion of Iraq. Then, as now, no Iraqi civilian, home, mosque, museum or medical facility, was spared from aerial or artillery destruction.

Mounir, a police dog handler and trainer who'd played no part whatsoever in the current insurgency against the occupiers, had nonetheless been picked up in an American military sweep through Kirkuk. He'd been handcuffed with plastic strips, put on a truck and incarcerated in the Allah-forsaken prison known as Abu Ghraib. There, he was considered an enemy insurgent terrorist until proven otherwise and was subjected to U.S.-style torture techniques.

The detainees were made to stand with their backs to the wall, knees bent and arms outstretched in front, so they were parallel to the ground. When they were unable to maintain this painful 'stress' position any longer, they were punched and kicked repeatedly. After 36 hours of this 'conditioning', combined with sleep deprivation, hooding and waterboarding, they were taken to a small windowless building for questioning. This was known amongst the troops as 'choir practice' – the shrieking and groaning of the Iraqis constituting the music.

A corporal had grabbed the head of one prisoner, a hotel worker friend of Mounir's, beat it against a wall three times and then repeatedly kicked the prisoner while on the ground. His friend died shortly afterwards from the multiple injuries he had received: broken nose and ribs, skull fracture, and renal failure.

Mounir was determined to find a way out of the prison – but not that way. Recalling his grandfather's trick, he leaned back against the cold cement block wall, closed his eyes and concentrated on relaxing his body. His mind's eye created a round black dot. He focused on the dot without thinking about its dimensions. It was simply a dot on a blank surface.

You can go in and out of that dot, he told himself, *but no one else can. Now you are going to pass through that dot to the far reaches of your brain, and there you will hide what you have just been thinking about. Lock up that thought and emerge from the black dot, leaving those thoughts inside until you get out of this hell-hole. No matter what is done to you, do not return to that place, nor reveal what is hidden away there. When it is safe, you will recall the password that will help you retrieve the thought you have just locked inside.*

Mounir's grandfather had said he could repeat the exercise with other dots in order to completely blank out his mind for long periods of time. The key was to avoid the conscious thoughts that could drive a person mad in a bad situation.

Oblivious to his surroundings, Mounir finally emerged from the black dot. Only then did he think of a password that would allow him back in. He chose the Arabic word for rosebud. He knew what else he had to do to survive in Abu Ghraib and give himself a chance to get out of there – ingratiate himself with his American jailers by using the Chalabi gambit, that is, volunteer as much false information as possible.

* * *

Bill Bailey stopped in his tracks. "Nobody move!" he yelled. He stooped to take a closer look at a metal object glinting in the dirt. "I got some wires here. Could be a bomb."

The rest of his team retraced their footsteps as they backed away from what turned out to be a large-caliber artillery shell, buried in the sand with some silver wires attached to it. The device was an improvised explosive, containing enough power to blow Bill and his mates to kingdom come.

The platoon sergeant examined the object and said, "I'm calling the combat engineering squad to disarm this baby and take it away for disposal. Lucky you spotted it, Bailey."

"I would've been okay, Sarge," Bailey quipped, "I had my safety goggles on."

"Always the joker, eh, Bailey? Let's just get on with the job."

The platoon blocked off the street and kept a close eye on the crowd of curious Iraqis who had gathered at a safe distance to observe the goings-on.

"They like seeing us get blown up," one jarhead groused.

"Don't worry about it. Just shitcan anyone who seems too interested," the sergeant replied.

Once the device was hauled away, the foot patrol unit of the military police continued its progress along the rubble-strewn, bomb-blasted Fallujah street. The foot soldiers and the tank accompanying them were tasked with mop-up operations following an attack by a heavily mechanized infantry division, whose path could be traced by the burnt-out scout cars and trucks which the general devastation had left behind.

Bill could see where they'd used white phosphorus on the Iraqis. The substance was generally used to light up combat areas, create a smokescreen or mark targets, but the bodies, burned down to the bone, testified as to its other main purpose.

The Iraqi insurgents had resisted the Americans by using civilian vehicles, but they'd been badly outgunned. Those who hadn't managed to escape had been slaughtered wholesale. Bill's military police job was to sweep up all the surviving men between the ages of 17 and 50 and throw them into Abu Ghraib.

The impressively high voter turnout for the recent Iraqi democratic referendum and election was marginally surpassed by the turnout for the ensuing riots, resulting in stepped up patrols by the occupying American military forces trying to quell the insurgency.

A group of Iraqi children crowded around the soldiers, begging for sodas, chocolate or army food rations. One of the grunts pulled a steel Humvee antenna from his belt and lashed the most persistent of the little beggars.

"What the hell are you doing?" Bill Bailey yelled.

The freaked-out marine blurted, "I hate these kids. I hate looking at 'em. I hate being surrounded by all these little Hajis."

"They don't look like insurgents to me," Bill said angrily.

"They could be, those little bastards," the grunt retorted.

No use appealing to the sergeant, Bill thought. Last month Bill had watched him lean out of a Humvee and smash a bottle over an Iraqi civilian's head as he went by. Bill was aware that most of the jarheads were in complete culture shock. Seeing all Iraqis as enemies, they lived in a state of perpetual fear.

The patrol moved on, making periodic forays down the side streets in search of Iraqi males. Suddenly an old car came slowly towards them on the main street, the passengers waving. The Sergeant yelled, "Stop, stop!" in English. The car's occupants either didn't understand or hadn't heard, and the car came closer.

Any approaching vehicle was treated with the utmost suspicion by the Americans. Without warning, the tank opened fire with its cannon at point blank range. Afterwards, the soldiers examined the remains of an Iraqi man, a woman and two small children, all blown to smithereens.

"Son of a bitch," Bill muttered. His platoon had just made enemies out of every member of these Iraqis' extended family. *Why do the people back home wonder why the so-called insurgents take up arms and hate us?* Bill thought. *What the fuck would they do if a Muslim army was wandering around in the States, breaking down doors and imprisoning our males, while they bombed the shit out of our cities?*

* * *

At Abu Ghraib, military police jobs rotated on a regular basis. Bill Bailey was transferred to prison duty. He finished the paperwork he'd been assigned and stepped out into the central yard. There were some five thousand prisoners in the complex – thieves, drunks and suspected insurgents – but over sixty percent were Iraqi civilians being held there for no specific offence. The red tape required to get them out would take at least six months.

Bill looked around. *What a dump*, he thought. Many of the prisoners were housed outside, up to eighty in a tent, hemmed in by razor wire, directly in the line of rocket fire from the insurgents. They had nowhere to run, and no protection from the mud and alternating heat and cold, no proper clothing. If one of the prisoners flouted the stringent rules, he was removed from the tent at night and left shivering outside. The military police used the cold weather to control the prisoners. If infractions continued, the prisoners' blankets were confiscated. Then their clothing would be taken away. Almost naked, in underwear, the prisoners of war would huddle together on an outside platform to keep warm. They were trapped and had to sit, wait and hope they would survive. The food was rotten and dysentery was rampant. Debris and muck were everywhere and the overcrowding was leading to an epidemic of disease, including tuberculosis.

The conditions were no better inside. Some prisoners were chained to walls, deprived of food and drinking water and kept in total darkness for long periods of time, or subjected to the blaring of loud rap and heavy metal music. Bill had heard one of them screaming his head off as he banged it against the wall of his cell.

Bill walked back to the low cement building where he had his own cell, a spartan room that gave him some shelter from the sporadic missile bombardment by insurgent forces. He flopped onto his bunk and took out the latest letter from his girlfriend Helen back in the States. Helen Weills, formerly of Tishamunga, Tennessee, but now of Washington, D.C., was hot and sexy, and Bill was anxious to get back to her. They had decided to marry as soon as his hitch was up.

Helen's letter informed him that she had just gotten herself a cat:

"I've decided to call it Asshole, because it won't do anything I want. Speaking of pussy, I sure hope you aren't getting any in Iraq. Oh yeah, my mother was horrified when I came back from college and told her I weighed 118 pounds stripped for gym. 'Who's Jim?' she asked.

"Love and XXX, Helen."

Thankful he had a girl with a sense of humor, Bill rolled over, pulled a blanket around his shoulders and, thinking about the lovely Helen Weills, took a nap.

An ungodly racket coming from the compound awakened him. He and several of his buddies rushed outside to discover the cause. Prisoners had torn up pieces of clothing and made banners protesting their living conditions. They were yelling for cigarettes. At least that's what Bill was told. He wasn't one of the few Farsi-speaking guards.

One prisoner, tense and unruly, perhaps more desperate than the others, approached the fence. He picked up some stones and pieces of wood and hurled them at his captors. One stone hit a young GI in the face, scratching his skin and bloodying his nose. The guard hauled out a machine gun and requested permission to shoot. Permission granted, he opened fire, killing three and wounding twelve others.

Bill was shocked to see such brutality coming from his own side. He knew the guard was a devoted family man, courteous and a devout Christian.

A few days later, Bill had occasion to talk to the soldier who'd done the killing. To Bill's further disillusionment, the man showed him photos of the execution. "I shot this rug-rider in the face. See here? His head's split wide open. This guy I shot in the groin, he bled to death."

"You shot unarmed men behind barbed wire for throwing stones! What do you want, a medal?"

"I said a prayer before I did it," the guard said defensively. "God knows these ragheads are inhuman shitheels, scum of the earth infidels. Anything we do to them is all right. They're terrorists and we gotta get revenge for 9/11." He posted the photographs on the guards' bulletin board.

A week later, Bill's CO called him into the office. "I see you've turned in your weapon and have applied to become a conscientious objector."

"That's right, sir."

"I understand your buddies are ostracizing you. You don't want to change your mind?"

"No sir," Bill answered, standing rigidly at attention.

"I also understand you've been writing to Congressmen and the media. That's unacceptable, soldier."

"All I said was that no one's taking responsibility for killing innocent Iraqis that have nothing to do with the insurgents."

"Your letters were never sent through, you little squealer." As Bill's lips tightened in anger, the CO said, " I want you to turn in your body armor. If you're not going to fight, you won't need protection."

"But I'll still be vulnerable, sir."

"I'm also canceling your leave. You're staying here."

"You're extending my tour of duty, sir?"

"For as long as I can. Tough titty. And I'm transferring you to an infantry unit of Bradley Fighting Vehicles. They're calling for more mechanics, and your record says you're a good one."

"I like to think so, sir."

"Maybe when you get your ass shot at some more, you'll want to burn some turbans, you unpatriotic yellow-bellied bastard."

Bill couldn't choke back his reply, "I love the fucking army, sir, and I guess the army loves fucking me."

"We're on our way to somewhere,
The three of us and you.
What'll we see there
What's gonna be there,
What'll be the big surprise?"

— Lyrics to Cuanto le Gusta,
by Gabriel Ruiz and Ray Gilbert
From the 1948 film A Date with Judy

XIII – Operation Sphincter

On a bright February morning in 2002, Luis Canon came home to his trailer in a park near Venice, Florida, to have a heart to heart with his significant other, Lorrie Van Halfton. The fruit of their common-law union, Minnie Van Halfton, was at a babysitter's two trailers away, as Lorrie was preparing to head off to work.

"What do you mean we have to move to Chicago?" Lorrie demanded after Luis had made his announcement. "I don't wanna leave Florida and go to no freakin' Chicago, and neither does Minnie. She'd have to get into a new school. And what would we do in Chicago, anyway? It gets colder there than the end of an Eskimo's tool."

"What do you know about the end of an Eskimo's tool? Anyway, we got no choice, we gotta go."

"Who the hell says so?"

"The FBI, that's who."

"Who in blue blazes are they to tell us where to go? I'll tell them where to go, all right."

"Look, they're putting me into their witness protection program. We gotta change our domicile and our names, that's what they said. It's for our protection."

75

Lorrie was livid, her jowly face turning purple. She stabbed a forefinger into Luis' chest. "Is this some new kinda bullshit you're feedin' me, Luis Canon?"

"No, honey. I've been workin' for the FBI on the side, to make a few extra bucks."

"Don't honey me, and what'd you do that you have to be protected? Is somebody tryin' to kill us? Who we supposed to be hidin' from, the Mafia?"

Luis thought it wise to put the kitchen table between them at that point. "No, no. You're not gonna believe this, but here's what happened. Just shut up and listen for once, okay? You heard about those Arabs taking flight training here in America, right?"

"Yeah, so what?"

"Well, the FBI knew about it way before 9/11 ever happened. The director said he had no idea, but if the wrong people find out he was lyin', things could get real embarrassin' for him. There's two flight schools out at the Venice airport, and they trained a whole bunch of those Arabs that crashed the planes into the towers and everything."

"What the hell's that got to do with you?" Lorrie interjected.

"The feebs asked me to rent a room for two of the Arab hijackers. Course, I didn't know who they were then. I was supposed to sorta look after them, babysit them, see that they knew their way around. It didn't take 'em long, that's for sure – knockin' back the rum and cokes and askin' for lap dances at the strip clubs." Luis grinned at the memory, but his smile evaporated as Lorrie advanced on him.

"Stupidity has never stood in your way before, has it, Luis? I bet you went right along with them, didn't ya, ya bastard! But why does that mean we gotta move to Chicago?"

"Because that Congressional inquiry found out that an FBI informant – me – had entertained and rented rooms for these hijackers. They wanna interview me."

"So what's the problem? You were just doin' what you were told to do by your government."

"The feebs don't wanna produce me as a witness. They wanna hide me. Us." Luis backed up a step as he added, "Also, I happen to know that a few hours after the planes hit in New York and at the Pentagon, a military C-130 Hercules flew into the Venice airport. It loaded up a rental truck with the records of those flight schools, ran it into the plane, and took off for parts unknown. I wish I'd never been there to see that, but that's the way it happened."

"So you're telling me that one bunch in the American government is gonna hide you out from another bunch of the same government? To cover up what both of them were doing illegally, and to keep the politicians from bein' embarrassed?"

"That's about the size of it."

Lorrie threw her hands in the air. "What kinda political cock-up is that? What if you just blow the whistle on them instead?"

"Listen to me, Lorrie. Three thousand got killed in the World Trade Center. Do you think a couple more is gonna bother whoever's runnin' this show?"

"If I thought they wouldn't nail me too, I'd blow the whistle myself. I swear to God, there's a curse on your family, Luis, and it fell on you. So what're they callin' this mind-bogglin' screw-up?"

"Whaddaya mean? It doesn't have a name."

"Darlin', you know they always have names for their dumb operations. All right, I'll give it a name: Operation Sphincter. You're all a bunch of assholes!"

Luis Canon could feel his own sphincter tightening as Lorrie Van Halfton started throwing dishes and cutlery at him as he tore out the door of the trailer.

"The land of the free and the home of the brave is becoming a police state in pursuit of its unwinnable War on Terrorism."

— *Doug Casey, International Speculator*

XIV – Sean Hennessey

July 2002

Way back in '96, Slippery Jack Danielson had ended a long quarrel and split everything fifty-fifty with his ex-wife. She took the house and he took the road. Now he lived in a rented bungalow on the wrong side of the tracks.

A great many people other than Jesus have found themselves crucified between two thieves – regret for yesterday and fear of tomorrow. In July of 2002, Slippery Jack suddenly became one of those people, and for very good reason.

Eating his bacon-and-egg breakfast at the kitchen table, he perused the morning paper. After dripping some ketchup on the sports page, he thought he'd take a quick look at the obituaries.

One obit jumped right off the page at him. *Sean Hennessey was dead!* His old pal who had hired him to help wire the Twin Towers with explosives. *Jesus, that's what it said, but how come?* Jack hadn't seen Sean for a bit, but there wasn't anything the matter with him as far as he knew, and Sean was certainly way too young to die of natural causes. The write-up wasn't specific but it left Jack with the distinct impression that Sean's death was not your everyday passing away. The last time the two had seen each other, and that wasn't too long ago, Sean had been in good health, mentally and physically, and was looking forward to spending a holiday in the sun with his wife.

Jack got on the blower to talk to someone who could give him more details. Sean's brother, Kevin, answered his call, explaining that Sean's wife, Colleen, was still too broken up to talk. The brother said he was just going out the door, and suggested that Jack meet him down at a neighborhood eatery called Sam 'n' Ella's Diner.

"Be there in half an hour," said Jack, who knew the spot.

They took a booth. "What's the story here?" he asked, coming right to the point.

Kevin was sad and serious. "I didn't want to discuss this on the phone."

"Why not?"

"Because there's something very fishy about Sean's death. The phone could be bugged."

"Why's that?"

"Because the cops are saying it was a suicide and won't listen to any other theory. Superficially it might look like suicide, all right, but I don't think it was, and they refuse to investigate further."

"I don't know the circumstances, but no way would I have thought he'd do that," said Jack. "What do you think happened?"

"Sean supposedly blew himself away while he was on the phone talking to his wife, who was at her mother's place. He never said anything that would indicate he was about to do it, and all she heard was a gun shot. Their young son was in the house at the time, watching TV upstairs. Maybe he heard the shot but thought it was just something on the box or a car backfiring in the street. When they found Sean, there was a shoulder holster on his desk, and a .45 Colt revolver in his hand with a spent cartridge in one chamber. Bullet hole straight through the head."

"Did the cops perform the usual forensics? Angle of shot, stuff like that?"

"They went through the motions, but to my knowledge Sean never owned a handgun. I'm his brother and he didn't ever tell me he had one, and I don't think he did. In fact, I know he didn't shoot himself."

"What about his wife? Did she know he had a gun?"

"Says she didn't know about it. Never saw the gun before."

"Any idea why anyone else would want to knock him off?" asked Jack.

"Not specifically," Kevin answered, "but I do know that something had been bothering Sean a lot lately. Once he even told me that someone might be out to stop him."

"Stop him from doing what?"

"Well, he wouldn't tell me."

"What exactly did he say?"

"He said, 'They'd make it look like suicide. I know how these bastards think. So I've got to do some heavy thinking myself.' He was worried, all right."

"About what?"

"Ever since the Twin Towers went down on 9/11. That had something to do with it."

That's when Jack's own knowledge of the wiring job he and Sean had done, in the bowels of the Twin Towers, kicked in and suddenly caused his stomach muscles to jerk with regret for the past and fear of the future.

Millions of people around the world had watched in near disbelief as the World Trade Center events unfolded live on TV on September 11, 2001. They'd seen huge clouds of smoke billow over Manhattan and watched the towers collapse in a very curious way. They hadn't toppled over; they'd exploded the way buildings would do if bombs planted inside had exploded outward. The explosions hurled debris over a wide area and the entire concrete part of both buildings was reduced to a fine dust, rather than breaking into chunks.

Some people knew what a controlled demolition looked like, after watching it happen on TV. Jack had been there, watched the collapse, and not only recognized it, but knew immediately what had caused it, which certainly wasn't the impact of aluminum airplanes. Nor was the collapse of any of those buildings the result of fire that melted the steel structure. He also knew Sean Hennessey didn't commit suicide.

Sean had been in possession of information, knowledge that was dangerous, that could conceivably rock somebody's boat. Something that made him a potential meddler, troublemaker, shit-disturber and whistleblower – therefore, politically unfit to live among patriots, as determined by the tyrannical shadow government of PNAC and their enforcement agencies.

I know pretty much the same stuff as Sean, thought Jack. *I helped Sean wire the towers; so where does that leave me?* *"No shit, Sherlock!"* his brain answered. *"Up Shit Creek, that's where, and you'd better start looking for a paddle."*

"Some day I'll pass by the Great Gates of Gold
And see a man pass through unquestioned and bold.
    'A Saint?' I'll ask, and old Peter'll reply:
    'No, he carries a pass – he's a newspaper guy'."

— *Edwin Meade Robinson,* The Newspaper Guy

XV – The Daily Grope and Flail

Walter Hunt had a problem. The corporate owners had ordered him to cut costs and increase profit. He had tried to do that, but the editor of *The Daily Grope and Flail* newspaper still had too large a staff in the newsroom and someone had to be let go.

The choice was between the beautiful, talented, and well-endowed Sue St. Marie, and the equally talented but comparatively ugly writer, Jack Gronnestad. Although he was attracted to the seductive Sue, whose revealing low-cut top indicated that she had absolutely no brassiere budget, Walter wanted to make the decision based strictly on ability. This was the cause of his dilemma, because it was a toss-up.

Walter picked up the latest article Jack Gronnestad had filed regarding the events of September 11, 2001:

On 9/11, I just happened to be standing in the lobby of the North Tower of the World Trade Center complex waiting for an elevator to take me to 'Windows of the World'. It was 8:46 a.m., and I was on my way up to interview John O'Dell.

Earlier in the summer, O'Dell, a counter-terrorism expert and Deputy Director of the FBI, had resigned in frustration over the continual stonewalling by the White House of his efforts to track down Osama bin Laden and al-Qaeda sleeper cells. Ironically, he ended up getting a job as head of security at the WTC the day before 9/11, on Monday, September 10th.

There were about 20 of us in the lobby at the time, waiting for different elevators. As we stood there looking up for our rides, we heard a tremendous explosion below us. The base of the building shook. People screamed, "Oh my God!" looking at each other, down at the floor and then at each other again.

Ceiling tiles began falling all around us. Without delay, we ran outside as fast as we could. A few seconds later, there was a second huge explosion far above us. As I turned back and looked up, I saw a huge fireball form, turning from bright orange to red and then to thick black smoke. It was pandemonium all around me. ...

Walter skipped further on down the article and read:

Curiously, no other newspapers or TV networks that I know of, have reported a bomb going off in the basement of the North Tower. Yet it was unmistakable, and heard by many of us in the lobby of the North Tower. ...

Walter read no further in the article, whose headline was *Bomb Explodes in WTC Basement*. Jack's story might well be true, and Walter figured it was, but he knew that if he printed it, the owners would not only turf Jack, but himself as well. Of course, that would take care of his problem as to which employee to terminate.

He was even more aware than Jack that a host of important questions about 9/11 had not been asked by the media. One question was why the American defenses had failed to halt the attacks. And why had the 47-storey Building 7, owned by Harry Finkelman, collapsed when there was no apparent connection between it and the attack on the Twin Towers? Walter's bosses, in the person of his uncompromising managing editor, had issued strict orders that he was to spike any story that threatened to cast doubt on the official version of the events of

September 11, or pointed to any conclusion that differed from the one the government was spinning.

"Damn it Jack, you know I can't publish that," Walter exclaimed aloud. He shot out of his chair and stared out the window of his office for several minutes, then sat back down at his computer. He called up Sue St. Marie's latest piece, which she'd slugged: *Ending Poverty Requires Understanding of its True Nature.* Walter scanned the article.

The poor are not those who have been 'left behind.' They are the ones who have been robbed. The wealth accumulated by Europe and North America is largely based on riches taken from Asia, Africa and Latin America.

However much we choose to forget or deny it, all people in all societies depend on Nature. Without clean water, fertile soils and genetic diversity, humanity will not survive. Today, economic development is destroying these onetime commons, resulting in the creation of a new contradiction: development deprives the very people it professes to help; it deprives them of their traditional land and means of sustenance, forcing them to survive in an increasingly eroded natural world.

Unable to survive under these new economic conditions, many peasants are now poverty-stricken and thousands commit suicide each year. In many parts of the world, drinking water is privatized so corporations can now profit to the tune of $1 trillion a year by selling an essential resource to the poor that was once free. And the 50 billion dollars of 'aid' trickling from north to south is but a tenth of the 500 billion dollars being sucked in the other direction due to interest payments and other unjust fiscal mechanisms imposed by the World Bank and the International Monetary Fund (IMF).

If we're serious about ending poverty, we have to be serious about ending the systems that create poverty by robbing the poor of their common wealth, livelihood, and income. Before we can make poverty history, we need to get the history of poverty right.

It is not about how much wealthy nations can give; it is about how much less they can take.

It was a very good essay, Walter thought. Could he print it as an op-ed? Maybe, even though the corporations wouldn't like it. Damn, both these writers demonstrated equal talent.

Walter went out to the water-cooler in the newspaper common room. As luck would have it, the pulchritudinous Sue was there also. Deciding to come right out and tell her of his dilemma, Walter blurted out, "Sue, I'll either have to lay you or Jack off!"

* * *

It was late in the afternoon and Walter, trying to recover from his gaffe at the water-cooler, repaired to the Flying Duck, a local watering hole not referred to in that exact manner by the reporters who frequented the bar. He joined a mixed group at the brass rail and knocked back a couple of stiff ones to calm his nerves, then headed for home.

As he was going out the door, a blonde on a barstool asked the other reporters, "Who's that guy? I've seen him here before."

"That's Walter Hunt, the editor of *The Daily Grope and Flail*," answered one heavily imbibing journalist.

Another joker farther down the bar chimed in, "He's got a brother named Mike. Maybe you know him."

"Mike Hunt? Mike Hunt? I don't know anybody by that … oh, you bastards!" She dropped her head onto the bar and laughed along with the rest of them.

"Blaze, with your serried columns!
I will not bend a knee!
The shackles ne'er again shall bind
The arm which now is free
I scorn your proffered treaty!
The paleface I defy,
Revenge is stamped upon my spear,
And blood my battle cry!
I'll taunt ye with my latest breath,
And fight ye 'til I die!"

— George Washington Patten (1808-1882)
The Seminole's Reply

XVI – Hidey Hole

Hilya missed her old home, but this new one wasn't bad, especially considering what had happened to the last one. When she was a puppy, her master Mustafa had played with her a lot, and she had reveled in his habit of scratching her belly and behind her ears. Mustafa's family thought she was a jewel, which was why they'd called her Hilya, and fed her scraps from their table.

One day when she was a little older, Hilya went on her neighborhood rounds with a couple of other dogs. She came back to find there was no home to return to; just bloodstained rubble. A small crowd had gathered. Some people were crying, while others shook their fists at the sky and cursed. Hilya hung around the ruins for a long time but never found any of her family.

She wandered the tear-stained streets of Baghdad trying to scrounge enough food and water to stay alive. That was how she met her new master, Mounir Malouf, who had just been released from Abu Ghraib, after months of playing the model prisoner.

86

Once he was out, Mounir recalled the password to the hidey hole in his head – rosebud – that enabled him to pass through the black dot once again and retrieve the hidden message: *Whenever you get the chance, kill every pig of an American you can find!*

Mounir immediately recognized the potential in a smart canine. He offered Hilya food and water in a bowl. The dog followed him through a bombed-out section of the city to an abandoned house. To Hilya's surprise, several other dogs inhabited the space. Mounir talked to the other dogs as he patted Hilya's head.

"Sit," Mounir ordered.

The other dogs obeyed, sitting straight up with their front legs tucked into their chests, hindquarters square to the front. Mounir attached a choke chain and leash around Hilya's neck and guided her to a corner of the room, placing her back against the two walls. Hilya began to lie down, but Mounir lifted her by the leash until she too was in the seated upright position. Mounir tucked her legs into her chest and patted her for doing a good job.

"Stay," Mounir said to the other dogs. They did so, remaining in position until Mounir gave the command to release them. Hilya, eager to please, followed the actions of the other dogs. In the days that followed, she learned the commands that went with the trick and was suitably rewarded. The longer the dogs sat without moving, the bigger the treat that followed.

Next came the down-stay command, which Hilya quickly mastered. This more comfortable position allowed her to rest her forepaws on the ground for long periods. Mounir hooked her up to a fifty-foot length of clothesline rope, stretching it flat along the ground away from the reclining dog. If Hilya moved, Mounir would step on the line, then snap it, yelling a command and forcefully placing her back into position. This routine was repeated until Hilya was able to sit or lie down and remain in either position for hours.

A dog handler and trainer in the Iraqi police force before and after Desert Storm, Mounir knew his business. He worked with a supply of dogs between ten months and a year-and-a-half old. Older than that, dogs were harder to train for any new purpose. He insisted on complete obedience, and immediately corrected any dog that broke discipline.

During the final stage of training, Mounir left the area altogether, staying out of the dog's sight but in a location where he could observe the animal. When he was satisfied that even introduced distractions would not move the dog out of position, he gradually extended his absences. Hilya proved to be the best at this exercise; she didn't even think about moving without a direct command.

In order to vary their training, Mounir taught the dogs to work as pack animals. They carried panniers of ammunition and went out with the Iraqi freedom fighters on missions involving machine gun action. The dogs ran through the ruined streets and alleys alongside the insurgents. They had a job and they enjoyed it.

When Hilya went out with the men, she could smell the mixture of fear and excitement in them, along with the odors of gunpowder, explosives and death.

* * *

Baghdad's Sadr City slum baked in the 115-degree heat. Children played in a garbage-strewn mud hole. A man scooped up putrid water in a tin bucket to take home to mix with powdered milk for his young family.

The overall neglect of Baghdad's water and sewer system during more than a decade of UN-sponsored economic sanctions had taken its toll. The pumping stations and underground pipelines were losing fifty percent of their water before it reached any household taps. The leaks were difficult and expensive to fix in a war zone, where insurgents kept blowing up infrastructure to undermine the U.S. client-government collaborators working with occupying coalition forces.

Fresh water and sewage mixed underground, water pressure was low or non-existent, and the resulting liquid was a stinking trickle that killed Iraqis as surely as bullets or bombs. Dehydration, diarrhea, vomiting, hepatitis A and typhoid plagued the city, and since there were no plans for the aftermath of the war, other than protecting the oil supply coveted by the invaders, there was little hope for a quick fix.

Iraqis of all persuasions were aware that the Yankees were drinking refrigerated bottled water and eating ten flavors of ice cream in their green zone ten miles down the road; goodies that were supplied by greedy American corporations with a lock on lucrative contracts in Iraq.

* * *

His school had been bombed into oblivion and no new quarters had yet been found, so 13-year-old Akim and his chum Omar decided to play freedom fighters. They'd been working, whenever it was safe to do so, on a bombed and rusted, burnt-out semi-trailer sprawled at the side of the airport road just outside Baghdad. They had assiduously dug beneath the trailer, then tunneled sideways, reinforcing the sides and top with whatever bits and pieces they could scrounge. When the vehicle had rolled off the highway, it had crashed into a small wayside shelter whose base had concrete walls.

Under his burnoose, which hid his brother's rifle, Akim was just a scrawny kid, so he didn't take up much room in the hidey hole he and Omar had dug, well under the carcass of the semi.

The boys placed a steel plate ripped from the vehicle across the tunnel entrance. They were aware of the risk of ending up sealed inside an underground tomb in the event of further shelling of the trailer. But as Omar pointed out, "If we can't dig our way out, then we die for Allah and go to Paradise."

"I haven't been with a woman yet," Akim confessed. "What would I do with seventy-two virgins?"

Omar, who was a bit older, smiled as he answered, "Buy them all ice-cream cones."

"That horned brute morose
that tossed the dog that worried the cat that kilt
the rat that ate the malt that lay in
the house that Jack built."

— George Shepherd Burleigh (1821-1903)

XVII – Harry Palm & Armand Legg

"This rat went into a shop with a stocking on his head and a gun in his mitt," said Harry Palm. "'Hand over the cheese,' he says to the shopkeeper, 'and keep your trap shut!'"

"Enough with the jokes," said Harry's henchman, Armand Legg, as they staked out the house across the street. "Jokes like that are one reason people take an instant dislike to you, Harry, which is good, come to think of it, because it saves them the time of getting to know you better."

"How would you like to kiss my royal American ass?"

"Let's not get romantic," Armand replied, lighting a cigarette.

"When I was in the Middle East we used to throw shit-disturbers down an old well. When they'd had time to think about the fact that justice for all didn't necessarily mean that it was equally distributed, we'd drop a hand grenade down the well. Nobody ever came out."

"So what did this guy do to piss somebody off at Homeland Security?" Armand asked, gesturing at the house with the hand that held the cigarette.

"He's a threat, all right. You remember that demolition expert, Sean somebody – Hennessey, I think – that we offed in his own home and made it look like suicide?"

Armand shrugged and said, "Sure."

"After we copied the contents of his computer, head office took a look and found out this Jack Danielson guy was mentioned as a buckshee worker on the project Hennessey contracted for. A boozer and explosives expert, whose name didn't show up on the payroll of the demolition company."

"I have to say it, these demo guys who know too much have been a big boost for the hit business. Sure pays to work for the government, doesn't it?" Armand slapped his leg and guffawed. "But why wouldn't they just make an anticipatory arrest?"

"What?"

Harry's clueless expression made Armand laugh all over again. "It's the natural evolution of the pre-emptive strike."

Harry grunted, then asked, "Hey, did you just throw that cigarette butt on the floor?"

"What?"

"Is that your cigarette butt on the floor?"

"No. Go ahead, you saw it first!"

"Aw, for Christ's sake," Harry moaned.

"So who's paying us for this job?" Armand asked.

Harry gingerly plucked the offending butt off the floor and dropped it out the window on his side of the car. "One of the other twelve alphabet intelligence agencies. They like to get the CIA to handle their dirty work."

"How and when?"

"We got a good retainer, but the main dough's going to be deposited to an account in the Midland International Bank and Trust in the Cook Islands – when we finish the job."

"Sounds good to me," Armand said. "Okay, his lights have been out for over an hour. Looks like he's turned off the TV and gone to bed."

"Time to hook up his car," said Harry. "This is as good a way to get him as any. Just make sure it looks like an accident."

The two men got out of the car and stuck to the shadows as they worked their way toward the house. Their target's vehicle sat in a carport next to the bungalow.

"Somebody's gonna have to crawl under the car," Harry whispered to his companion. "It looks like you."

"Who?" Armand whispered back.

"You."

"Why me?"

"Because my hernia's been acting up lately."

"Can you live with it?" Armand asked him.

"I've been married; I can live with anything."

"But does it hurt?"

"Only when I crawl under a car."

Working quickly and in silence, Harry and Armand attached a tiny black box to the base of the steering column inside the Ford Taurus. It was a remote control device that would allow a following vehicle to wrest control of the car from the driver.

Armand was under the car and Harry inside. Once the box's wiring was complete, Armand attached a small explosive device to the top of the gas tank. Something brushed up against his outstretched arm. "Holy shit!" he exclaimed, "What the fuck…?"

"Shut up!" Harry hissed, just as a woman stepped through the rear entrance of the house next door and began calling, "Kitty! Kitty! Here, kitty! Come on in now, Punkins."

"We don't want that dame coming over here looking for her cat," Harry whispered urgently from inside the car. "Get rid of it."

Armand muttered as he fended off the advances of the friendly feline. He stroked the cat's back with one hand and felt for its throat with the other, then got both hands around the animal's neck. He squeezed with all his strength, throttling the cat. But not before Punkins, in her death throes, scratched the bejeezus out of Armand's hands.

The cat's owner went back inside her house. The men completed their work and threw the cat's carcass into the shrubbery beside the adjacent house.

"You're bleeding on the upholstery," Harry said as he watched Armand tamping at his wounds with wads of tissue.

"Shut your cakehole, Harry! It's not funny."

"You're always complaining you don't get enough pussy. Then when you finally find some, you kill it and throw it away. That I find funny." Harry fired up the engine and drove them away from the scene.

* * *

Jack came through his front door, looking for his morning paper. As he stooped to pick it up, he saw his neighbor standing on her scraggly front lawn, looking worried and dejected. Jack had often thought about helping her clean up her property, maybe trimming back the shrubs a bit. Thus far, he'd successfully fought off the urge to do so, but he was proud of the thought.

"What's the problem, Mrs. Dover?" he asked solicitously.

"It's my cat, Punkins. She didn't come home last night and I can't find her." The woman seemed close to tears.

"Maybe she met up with a tom."

"I hope not. She's not that kind of a cat, really."

"Would you like me to help you look?" Jack offered.

"Would you? I've been around the whole neighborhood, calling her. She always comes when I call."

Jack went into Eileen Dover's yard and started searching the underbrush. He thought he spotted something in the midst of a dense bunch of sucker branches around the base of a French lilac. Parting the stems, he saw it was Punkins, all right, but she wasn't moving. Jack dragged the cat out by the tail. At the sight, Eileen Dover burst into sobs.

Jack examined the animal. Its eyes were bugged out and its neck was broken. Someone had obviously strangled the poor cat, but why? He lay the remains back on the ground, noting the blood on its paws. "I think we'd better find a place to bury your pussy Mrs. Dover," he said.

> "They wrote in the old days that it is sweet and fitting
> to die for one's country. But in modern war
> there is nothing sweet nor fitting in your dying.
> You will die like a dog for no good reason."
>
> — *Ernest Hemingway,* Notes on the Next War

XVIII – Depleted Uranium

April 2003

Marine Zack Zapata had arrived in Iraq a few months after the initial attack, but now it was a year after the alleged fall of Baghdad.

Meanwhile, the President, who liked to dress up in military uniforms and play the war hero he never was, had enjoyed his photo op on the aircraft carrier with a big 'Mission Accomplished' banner displayed behind him. The western mainstream media were adamant in their depiction of the United States as a force for good, a slayer of dragons, and not the military arm of the New World Order. His American detractors however, felt he depicted their beloved country in a new light – the Land of the Liar and Home of the Knave.

The War on Terror was far from over at Checkpoint Charlie on the highway that ran between the safety of the American Green Zone at the airport and the city of Baghdad. The politicians hid behind high walls and the embedded reporters were holed up in the Green Zone or in fortified hotels, leaving ordinary Iraqis to take pot luck driving their vehicles near military convoys or checkpoints manned by trigger-happy foreign soldiers.

Zack had already served his hitch, but here he was, still squatting with his buddies beside the troop carrier at the checkpoint, watching a fistful of sand drift through his fingers. He gazed up and down the highway, observing the sporadic traffic.

Strung along the edges of the road, abandoned houses crouched behind crumbling walls. Clumps of debris lay in the scrub-brush that somehow miraculously managed to survive in the murderous heat.

"Where are all the goddamn trees?" asked Terry Dunbar, another time-expired marine, as he removed his helmet and wiped the sweat from under the headband. "Last time I drew this duty, there were a least a few trees around those old houses."

Zack Zapata answered his buddy, "They were all cut down so snipers couldn't take pot shots at us."

Terry watched the trail of fine dust trickling through Zack's fingers and drifting away on the hot wind. "Stop that," he snapped. "You've got no idea how much depleted uranium's in that stuff."

Another grunt, Joe MacGillicuddy, glanced over his shoulder and asked, "Isn't that the stuff they haul away from nuclear power plants?"

"That's right; it's radioactive," Terry replied. "They've been using DU in the tips of some shells so they can slice through solid steel reinforced tanks and bunkers and such. Did so in Desert Storm too."

"What's so dangerous about it?" Joe asked.

"If you didn't know before you signed up, the army isn't likely to tell you now. DU projectiles are so powerful and get so hot when fired, they oxidize into aerosol-like particles less than ten microns in size."

"What the hell's a micron?"

"A hundred times smaller than a white blood cell and easily inhaled," said Terry, taking a slug from his water canteen. "It can pass through the pores of your skin, and when you breathe it in, it can go into your brain cells and mess up your mood-control mechanisms and your cognitive abilities."

"My what?" asked Joe.

"Your thought processes, dummy. Sounds like you've sucked in too much of the stuff already."

"Don't give me that smart-ass shit, Terry, you son of a bitch college boy. Anyway, it's depleted, isn't it? That means it isn't dangerous, so stop trying to scare the crap out of us."

Terry sighed in exasperation. "That's the cover story. Look, if you were in Bradley Fighting Vehicles in the first Gulf War and you sat on ammo boxes, you stood a good chance of coming home with rectal cancer. For a lot of women GIs, DU wrecked their uteruses – they just bled and bled."

"The army wouldn't expose their own troops to stuff *that* dangerous – to anybody, not just the damned ragheads," said Joe.

Zack, chagrined, brushed the sand from his hands. "I wasn't thinking. You're now getting the education the army recruiters promised you, Joe. Terry's right, it's just a matter of luck whether you breathe this shit in or not."

Terry, seeing Joe's expression, pressed his point. "The U.S. Army didn't tell its Vietnam troops about the effects of Agent Orange, did they?" asked Terry. "It's like the fallout from Chernobyl, or from atomic bomb tests. The wind carries millions of tons of dust and sand around the world, loaded with radioactive isotopes, soot, pesticides, chemicals, fungi, bacteria and viruses."

"That just sounds like lies bein' spread by people who support our enemies. Where do you get all this nonsense from, Terry?" the driver of the troop carrier asked.

Terry raked his eyes up and down the road, then settled back and continued, "The *Gulf War Review* or the Internet if you must know. There are basically two types of DU rounds. The kinetic energy penetrator is one. It's fired by our Abrams tanks, Bradley Fighting Vehicles, the HN Warthog aircraft, the

Navy Phalanx and some of our machine guns. They're gigantic darts of solid uranium, contaminated with all the other junk from the Department of Energy's facilities down in Paducah, Oakridge and Portsmouth, where they make the stuff. The Abrams round is a solid 10-pound rod of uranium about three-quarters of an inch in diameter, eighteen inches long. The A-10 fires one that's three-quarters solid uranium, at 4,000 rounds a minute. Then you have sub munitions land mines, or cluster bombs. The casing's DU, with high explosives inside. The absolutely perfect dirty bomb, bunker busters, have a uranium casing from the McAlester army ammunition plant. The guys who worked there got sick putting those things together, and I mean real sick. They had to shut the line down."

Joe was dumbfounded. "You guys are kiddin' me, right?"

"Wish we were," Terry replied. "It's what they call 'Gulf War Syndrome' but really it's DU poisoning that's causing all the cancer and severe birth defects which are becoming more and more common. Check out the Gulf War I veterans. They had DU in their equipment, in their clothes, in their semen. They were having normal babies before they came over here. Afterwards their babies had severe birth defects. They had brains missing, arms and legs missing, organs missing; they were born without eyes or had horrible blood diseases. Same thing's happening to the Iraqis here and the Afghans. And we're still using this stuff as we speak."

Joe slumped back against the troop carrier. "Holy fuck! How do I get outta here? And who's gonna clean this shit up?"

"Don't count on anybody doing it anytime soon. They can't," Terry said with a grimace. "The army won't even give you medical care. Anybody, here or back Stateside, who talks about this is called unpatriotic or worse, a traitor. They'll tell you you're psychosomatic and treat you like a nut case. If you don't want to get court-martialed, just do your job and shut up."

"But how can I tell if I'm breathin' the stuff in?"

"Some guys say there's a metallic taste – the actual taste of uranium. A day or two later, they feel sick, get muscle aches and lose their energy. Some become incontinent."

"In-*what*?"

"In adult diapers!"

"Jesus, I'm ready to shit my pants right now!" Joe exclaimed.

"Let's get back to watching the road, you guys," Zack urged.

The soldiers picked up their weapons and drifted back to their posts, leaving Zack and Terry crouched at the front of the truck.

"Damn, I'd love to be back breathing clean air in Alaska," said Terry.

"Never been there," Zack said. "Maybe I'll visit you when this is over."

"Great, I'll take you fishing. There's this place I keep thinking about." Terry broke off to stand up and lean over the hood of the vehicle. He braced his elbows and scanned the checkpoint area with his binoculars.

"What kind of place?" Zack asked as Terry sat back down.

"A stream comes down into the salt chuck from a trout lake higher up in the hills. I was walking the banks one day when I suddenly stepped into a little glade of young trees surrounding a small pool. Not a breath of wind, and the morning sun was filtering through the spring foliage. Must have been a trick of the light, but there was a kind of a – what's the word? – opalescence, because I swear I could see the air over the pool, which was reflecting like a mirror. Stopped me in my tracks for several minutes. Breathing was like drinking in moist air. Then, a young moose stepped out of the trees and wandered down the far side of the pool, not twenty feet away from me."

Terry shut his eyes briefly in remembrance, then said, "Yeah, I'd be glad to take you there. We'll go up to the lake and get us a nice mess of rainbow trout."

"Sounds great," said Zack. "Especially sitting here in the dirt with these jeezly fleas and mosquitoes. These bites are driving me nuts."

"Don't complain to me, tell the captain."

"That clown? Spends his days sending flowers to his wife and surfing the net. I swear, his receiver is off the hook. All he says is, 'Put some ointment on the bites and shut up about it'."

"The stores are out of ointment."

"We were supposed to have won this war by now and on our way home," Terry said. "But the administration's not here on the ground. These Iraqi insurgents are getting tougher. We need more troops."

"We may never get out of here, the way things are going. Not unless we get a lot more boots on the ground, and some spare parts. That last battle north of the city? Shit, the guys told me they had to ditch twelve vehicles afterward. No spare parts. I'm not asking them to bring in steak and lobster every week, just some parts and more armor plating for the personnel carriers."

"Not likely to happen," Zack remarked. "They make more money manufacturing new vehicles."

"Typical of this man's army," Terry said. After another pull on his water bottle, he stood up, leaned across the hood and scanned the surrounding terrain as before.

A bullet caught him right under the chin, above his flak jacket. He was flung backward onto the desert floor, clutching the place where his adam's apple used to be.

"SNIPER!" Zack screamed as he dropped to his knees beside his buddy, trying vainly to stop the spouting blood. The rest of his team ran over to take cover behind the truck.

"Where is he?" Joe barked.

"Gotta be from that burnt-out semi-trailer up the road."

"Let 'im have it," Joe shouted. They fired in unison, riddling the target with bullets.

"Cover me," Joe yelled. He ran toward the iron carcass while the others poured covering fire into it from either side. Joe lobbed two grenades into what was left of the old hulk, then ran back while the rest opened fire again. Nobody was getting out of that wreck alive.

Zack, tears streaming down his face, yelled out, "Help me get Terry into the truck. We've gotta get him back to base." But he knew already that Terry was going back to Alaska in a box, in the middle of the night, and that no images of the flag-draped coffin would appear on American television screens. *When is this madness going to end?* he wondered. *I feel like an alien in this damn country. We're doing our jobs, fulfilling our mission for Uncle Sam. But we're stuck in Iraq with no relief in sight, goddammit!*

Zack was convinced they'd hit a wall, because it was obvious the Iraqis weren't going to quit. Why? *Because we're not liberators, we're occupiers. We're stuck in the quicksand of another long-term guerilla war against a determined resistance movement. We don't understand the people or the culture. We're just here for the oil, to break the country up and kill people to get it. We didn't learn a damn thing from either Custer's Last Stand or Vietnam. Crap!*

* * *

Immediately after shooting the American, Akim dove back into the hole with his rifle, and amidst a hail of bullets pulled the steel plate over the tunnel entrance. After two grenades went off above him, followed by another fusillade, he thanked both Allah and the steel plate and lay semi-deafened in the darkness for a long time, his brother's rifle by his side. There was another muffled explosion from a distance, then silence.

Late in the afternoon, Akim finally felt it was safe enough to scramble out of the hole and scan for the enemy. They were gone. He scampered across the desert into Baghdad. He hid the rifle where his dead brother had always kept it, in the backyard outhouse. Tomorrow it would be Omar's turn in the hidey hole.

* * *

Zack Zapata's patrol lost no time heading for the security of the concrete walls enclosing the Green Zone, with its razor-wired and land-mined approach. As they proceeded down the highway, the driver noted that it was clear of traffic for the moment. A lone dog sat on the side of the road a few hundred yards ahead. Nice looking dog, he noted, recalling the one his children had back home.

* * *

Hilya was used to vehicles of all descriptions zooming up and down this long stretch of highway as she calmly waited for her master. She wasn't about to run away from the truck she saw nearing her position. Mounir, wearing the ubiquitous Iraqi outfit of black short-sleeved shirt over black trousers, watched from the shadows of an old wall, well back from the highway. He rested his back against a large rock, amongst the burned tires and barbed wire remnants of previous blockades.

As the vehicle drew closer, Mounir said a prayer for Hilya. When the troop carrier came level with her, Mounir sent a remote-controlled signal to the load of CX explosives in the dog's pannier.

The driver of the troop carrier was still looking at the dog when it disintegrated in a horrendous explosion. The precisely timed blast shattered the vehicle, blowing chunks of it skyward and across the highway of death, into the desert. The last thing the driver thought of before he bought the bloody farm was not of his wife and kids, but of his own dog, Barkley.

Hilya's last thought was of her supper – but this time she would be having it in Paradise with Allah.

* * *

Most of the GIs died or were fatally wounded in the attack. Zack was luckier, only suffering the loss of his right arm and left leg, plus a badly mangled right leg and a ruptured eardrum. His major injuries bought him a ticket back to the land of the free and the home of the brave.

Joe MacGillicuddy was the only one to survive unscathed. He reported what had happened. After the incident, American troops throughout Iraq agreed that this type of insurgent attack gave literal meaning to the expression *fucking the dog.*

I mused upon the Pilgrim flock
Whose luck it was to land
Upon almost the only rock
Among the Plymouth sand.

— *Alan C. Spooner* Old Times and New, *1846*

XIX – Serendipity

Mid-June 2003

There are many relationships that a person never forgets, whose termination leaves a loneliness that forever nags at the heart – the relationship between a mother and child, a happily married couple, old friends or lovers. This is especially so if the relationship is cut short by tragedy – even more so if the tragedy is man-made, evil in nature and strikes out of a clear blue sky.

Ella Vader's cherished husband, Darth, went to work at the World Trade Center on the morning of September 11, 2001, and never came home. In the midst of their grief, Ella and twenty other relatives of 9/11 victims refused to believe the story proffered by those in charge of the investigation into the WTC attacks that had deprived them of their loved ones – attacks that they believed could have been prevented. They refused to accept the sums of money proffered in full settlement of all claims, on the signed condition that they would not further discuss or investigate the matter.

After a year and a half of alleging that they were making progress in uncovering the truth about 9/11, the FBI finally agreed to meet Ella and the other relatives at the J. Edgar Hoover building in Washington, D.C.

Both parties knew that to call the investigation a pork-barrel project would be unfair to the pigs. Lester Square, the senior FBI agent, not looking forward to the interview, seated himself opposite the delegation of relatives, his pen poised to make notes as he hunched over his notepad like a dog screwing a football.

Ella had barely taken her seat when she launched into a barrage of questions. "With all the warnings about the possibility of al-Qaeda using airplanes as weapons, and the Phoenix memo from one of your own agents, warning that Osama bin Laden was sending operatives to this country for flight school training, why didn't you check out flight schools before September 11?"

"Do you know how many flight schools there are in the continental U.S.A.? Thousands. We couldn't possibly have covered them all and found these guys."

"Wait a minute," Ella said. "If there were so many flight schools, how come a few hours after the attacks, the FBI just happened to show up at the Double Decker Flying Circus Flight Schools of Venice, Florida – High Five Aviation, wasn't it? – where many of the terrorists supposedly trained?"

"We got lucky."

Ella's jaw dropped, but she recovered quickly and renewed her interrogation. "And how did you know exactly which ATM in Portland, Maine, would show you a videotaped picture of Mohamed Atta, supposedly the brains behind the attacks, when you claimed you didn't know *anything* about these people beforehand?"

"A degree of serendipity was involved there too, I'll admit," Lester answered.

"My definition of that term," said Ella, "is a lucky discovery made accidentally on purpose. Is that what you mean?"

Lester was used to asking the questions, not giving answers. He merely frowned and remained silent.

"There are more than 200,000 ATM machines in America! How'd you find the right one so soon after the attacks? Was it in order to implicate Atta, or did you just get lucky again?"

"What are you getting at?" Lester asked

"I think you were investigating some of these people long before 9/11, is what I'm getting at," said Ella passionately.

The other relatives started weighing in with their own questions, still hoping for answers in the face of what they had come to realize was a masterful display of cynical disinformation, stonewalling and ridiculous outright lying.

"How did you miraculously find one of the alleged hijacker's passports – supposedly belonging to Satam al-Sugami – in the smoldering rubble a block away from the WTC, in pristine condition, despite fires, explosions, mayhem in the streets and people fleeing for their lives? Was that luck, too?"

"If it was bin Laden who was behind the attacks, why all the secrecy around the investigation? You have pertinent information that you won't divulge, don't you? What kind of a puzzle palace is this, anyway?"

"And why did you let the entire bin Laden family leave the country by plane, right after 9/11, when there were restrictions on all other traffic in American airspace? No questions asked and the planes stopped in ten different American cities to pick them all up."

"If nobody knew ahead of time about the attacks, how could the government release 'bin Laden's' name within hours of the attacks and a list of the identities of the nineteen alleged hijackers just two days later? Not only that, but at least six of the hijackers who supposedly met their death that day, are, according to London's *Sunday Telegraph*, reportedly still alive. How do you explain that?"

Realizing the meeting was a big mistake and that he was losing ground fast, Square rose from his chair. "We've done our best to help you people," Lester said. "We're sorry for your loss, but there's nothing more we can say to these irrelevant questions. The investigation continues, and for national security reasons, we can't jeopardize it. I hope you understand."

"Understand?! What I understand," said Ella vehemently, "is that you use 'national security' as a stock reply to every question we ask and you won't answer."

Over the loud and angry protests of the relatives, who swore they would not give up, Square's agents efficiently herded the group out the door and down the hall. In the elevator, Ella asked the stone-faced escorts, "What's the difference between a porcupine and the FBI?" No one answered her.

"A porcupine has all the pricks on the outside," Ella said.

"Once more unto the breach, dear friends, once more;
Or close the wall up with our English dead!
In peace there's nothing more becomes a man
As modest stillness and humility;
But when the blast of war blows in our ears,
Then imitate the action of the tiger:
Stiffen the sinews, summon up the blood."

— *William Shakespeare,* King Henry V

XX – Helen Weills – She's Got It All & She's Reloading

"Okay, next patient, get in here and park your sphincter!"

Bill Bailey hobbled into the military infirmary. The clinic was run by a medic the GIs referred to as Numbnutz McCloskey. Bill hopped up on the examining table and gingerly removed his socks. The medic took one look at Bill's feet and raised his eyebrows. "How in Jesus name did this happen?" he asked.

"My army-issue boots just fell apart and burst into flames," Bill answered.

"Bailey, I know you have an open mind – and a mouth to match – so don't give me any camelshit."

"So help me God, it's the truth, Doc. I was on security patrol. Check out the heat on that tarmac if you don't believe me. Talk about a hot foot! How else would I get burns like this? I had one helluva time getting out of my boots."

Numbnutz had been in the Middle East for some time and really didn't have to be convinced. He knew what the desert heat could do to military equipment and uniforms. The variety of heat-related illnesses he'd seen included some serious cases of jock itch. In Oman, he'd seen a whole battalion of half-naked, barefoot soldiers hopping around scratching their willies. But this was his first experience with boots that had spontaneously combusted.

"Well, we've got the answer now, Bailey."

"What's that, Mac?"

"Rubber-soled boots designed to withstand temperatures of up to 572-degrees. Invented by the Brits."

"Are we planning to invade the Sun?" Bill asked.

"Only if we go at night," was Numbnutz's comeback. "You won't need 'em, though; your tour's nearly over. We'll get those feet fixed up just in time for you to go home."

"Fine by me," Bill replied, sighing. The officer who'd promised to keep him in Iraq indefinitely had been transferred back Stateside, and his replacement had turned out to be more sympathetic to Bill's situation. Barring further mishaps, Bill would be heading home for a month's leave in a few weeks.

"The new equipment's unbelievable," McCloskey was saying. "The best thing's the germ-fighting underwear." He dropped his pants to reveal the defense department's latest invention – unisex trunks made from anti-microbial germ-fighting fibers, designed to prevent sweating and chafing.

"What do you call those?" Bill asked in amazement.

"Mr. Magoos," McCloskey replied. "The Brits are also getting a new desert combat package complete with wraparound sunglasses, lighter Kevlar-nylon helmets and sandals for off duty wear."

"Are we going to get those items, too?" Bill asked.

"The top brass said no, because most of it would be useless in North Korea."

"Jesus Christ, I thought we were gonna attack Iran next. We could use the stuff in that hell-hole. The conditions could be worse there."

"One never knows, does one?" McCloskey commented.

Bill winced as the medic bandaged his feet. "When I get home, I'd like to spend some time where it's colder than a gravedigger's ass."

"Or the proverbial witch's tit," said Numbnutz. "Which ever's colder, right?"

* * *

Helen Weills was ecstatic. Bill Bailey was coming home and she felt like a born-again virgin. If she'd had an oak tree in her front yard, she really would have tied a yellow ribbon around it. She stocked up on champagne, along with a bottle of blue chartreuse. They'd listen to their favorite oldie, Glenn Miller's Blue Champagne, and get drunk.

She slipped into a tattoo parlor to create a special surprise for her lover. She intended to have nothing on but the radio when Bill arrived home.

* * *

From the airport, Bill took a bus to Washington, then grabbed a cab to Fairfax, Virginia, where Helen now lived with her brother, Heck, who was holidaying in the Caribbean. Bill paused, rehearsing what he'd say to his girl when she greeted him at the door. He didn't want to get all mushy, so he decided to fake a stutter and say, "Helen, you've been a cunt… cunt… cunt… cunt-in-ual in… in… inspiration to me!"

As Bill neared the door, Helen flung it open, turned her back and mooned him. The letter B was tattooed on each cheek of her shapely ass, in large print.

Bill stopped in his tracks, and spluttered, "Who in hell's B O B?"

* * *

Bill's leave was almost over. More than anything, he wanted to finish his hitch at home, particularly since he only had a few weeks left to go. He contacted marine headquarters and applied for an immediate discharge. They said they'd get back to him in due course. His leave ended without Bill hearing from them. Helen suggested he sit tight and wait until they deigned to reply.

Within a week, Bill was informed that his tour of duty was being extended yet again, under something called the stop loss program, and he was to report to the 9th Cavalry Unit in Texas, to be redeployed back to Iraq.

"Holy sheepshit, Miranda!" Bill exploded. "I'm not gonna go back to Iraq to kill civilians in downtown Baghdad."

The letter further stated that Bill had two options – go back and fight or go to military prison.

"I should never have told them I didn't want to go back," Bill moaned. "They're doing this because recruitment's down. Bastards! Nobody even wants to join the National Guard anymore. The recruiters are trolling for cannon fodder in the poorest communities. I never came across any grunts from what you'd call a rich or powerful family. And hardly any middle-class ones either. I've done my job for God and country, and look what I get. It's looking like they plan to be in the Middle East permanently, and I don't want any part of it."

"Oh, Bill, what are we going to do?" Helen reached across the breakfast table and took Bill's hand in her own. "I know this is a lousy time to tell you, darling, but I think I'm pregnant."

Bill leapt to his feet and grinned from ear to ear. "That's fantastic, honey, just fucking fantastic!" The news was a mixed blessing, given their current circumstances, but Bill was overjoyed. Between rapturous hugs and kisses, he asked Helen, "Are you sure?"

"I'll know for sure really soon."

Bill quickly sobered. "My dilemma now is I signed up hoping to learn engineering and get help with my education. Instead, I got sucked into a war I can't support anymore."

"So what about Canada? It's always been a haven for conscientious objectors. If you think the invasion of Iraq is illegal and criminal, maybe we could go there as refugees, saying you'll be persecuted in America if you go back."

Bill shook his head. "In the Vietnam War, the draft dodgers were civilians. I'd be a deserter as far as the military is concerned. I'd be subject to extradition, court-martial, and I could end up in jail for five years. They'd make an example out of me for sure."

"But Canada has already taken in some war resisters, and your hitch was up, Bill. Maybe they'll take you in too."

"I doubt it, but it's either that or go underground here."

"Whatever we do, we'd have to find some way to make a living."

"A tough proposition at the best of times, isn't it? I've worked for the military police, and I know how they operate. They'd be on our tails, and they are one mean bunch of bastards."

"How about making application as a conscientious objector?" asked Helen.

"I tried that in Iraq. It didn't work and I was lucky to stay out of the digger. Usually they just give you an order they know you won't obey and then charge you with insubordination."

"So we're tits up in bad karma, is that it?"

"Seems like it. Hey, did you ever play that game at the fair? I think they called it Whack-a-Mole."

"Never heard of it."

"They give you a big rubber hammer, and every time a little mole pops its head out of one of the holes in this big board, you have to whack it over the head. You got points for whacking as many of them as you could. I feel like one of the moles getting whacked everywhere I go."

* * *

A few nights later, the local police station received a 911 call about a domestic disturbance in Helen's neighborhood. Two gung-ho cops got the call. Unfortunately for Bill and Helen, the disturbance was in the house across the street from them, but the cops mixed up the street numbers and turned up at the wrong address.

Bill answered the pounding on the door wearing only his trousers, and found himself staring down the barrel of what looked like a .45.

The cop, Rick O'Shea, identified himself and his partner. "Get your hands up and turn around," he ordered.

"What for?" blurted Bill, remaining motionless except for putting his hands up over his head.

"I said turn around and do it now."

"Officer, I'm a U.S. marine. I just got back from Iraq. Why are you ..."

"Don't give me any shit. Shut up, keep 'em up and turn around."

Bill couldn't believe what was happening. He didn't move toward the cop but began to speak again.

O'Shea wasted no more time. He shot Bill with his Taser at point-blank range, sending 50,000 volts of electricity into Bailey's bare chest and abdomen. Helen, who'd witnessed the whole thing, began screaming as Bill lay writhing helplessly on the floor.

"What are you assholes doing?" she shrieked.

"He was resisting arrest," O'Shea said curtly. "This joker's not gonna beat you up anytime soon, lady."

Helen flew at the cop, pounding him with her fists. His partner grabbed her from behind and pinned her arms. Bill was rising unsteadily to his feet, so O'Shea blasted him with the Taser again, this time in the neck.

At that point, Helen's choo-choo left the tracks. She wrestled free, charged O'Shea and kicked him with all her strength in the nuts. "We'll sue your sorry asses," she yelled, as Rick slumped against the doorway clutching his family jewels. "You've got the wrong house, you dumb bastards!"

Rick's partner radioed for an ambulance, which arrived at the house in record time. The paramedics placed Bill's unconscious body on a gurney and checked O'Shea over before taking off for the hospital. The cops followed. O'Shea's partner drove his squad car while Rick alternately groaned, cursed and clutched his nuts, as he railed against the inherent danger in answering domestic trouble calls.

By the time they had him in a bed at emergency, Bill was coming to. O'Shea cuffed him to the bed and turned to the nurse. "This guy's on dope, I need a urine sample."

Bill was still in a daze, but he said, slurring his words, "And I'll give you one, you son of a bitch." He swung his feet off the bed, grabbed his penis in one hand and lurched forward, only to be brought up short by the handcuff restraining his other hand. "Piss on you!" he yelled.

Rick O'Shea, bathed in a stream of urine, shot Bailey for the third time with his Taser.

"Time after time in our history, in the face of great danger, Germans worked together to ensure that freedom would not falter. But not today. Motivated more by partisan politics than by national security, today's Social Democratic leaders see Germany as an occupier, not a liberator. And nothing makes me madder than someone calling German troops occupiers rather than liberators. Tell that to the Czechs, Poles, Frenchmen, and Belgians who have been freed because Adolf Hitler led an army of liberators, not occupiers. Tell that to the millions of men, women, and children who are free today from the Baltics to the Crimea, from Poland to the Balkans, because Adolph Hitler built a military of liberators, not occupiers. Never in the history of the world has any soldier sacrificed more for the freedom and liberty of total strangers than the German soldier. And our soldiers don't just give freedom abroad; they preserve it for us here at home. Right now, the world just cannot afford an indecisive Germany. Fainthearted self-indulgence will put at risk all we care about in this world. In this hour of danger, our Führer has had the courage to stand up with Him. God bless this great country and God bless Adolf Hitler."

— *Joseph Goebbels, German Propaganda Minister,*
in a speech entitled, The New Year 1939/40

XXI – Bob Loblaw

August 2006

Derrière Ltd. was a small French Canadian airline providing milk runs into the wilds of Northern Quebec and Labrador. Chartered by mining engineers, prospectors and fishing aficionados, Derrière planes landed at lonely spots on the region's innumerable lakes, which meant they needed floats in the summer and skis in the winter.

Nicolaus D'Amous waited for one of Derrière's Cessnas to cross Lac Lebleu and tie up at the dock on which he stood. The single passenger was Bob Loblaw, a well-connected Washington lawyer and former National Security Advisor. The two men were not great friends, merely acquaintances of long standing, but Nick knew Loblaw to be a like-minded individual and, in his day, a skilled manipulator of global events. At the least, someone with Loblaw's lengthy experience in the shadows of U.S. foreign and domestic policy could prove to be a viable confidante.

Loblaw, dressed in a fishing vest, green plaid shirt and rumpled pants, looked like a Henry Fonda stand-in from *On Golden Pond*. He clasped hands with D'Amous.

"Good to see you again, Bob," D'Amous said as the two walked up the wooden jetty toward the rustic lodge on the shore. "We don't get together often enough."

"That we don't, Nicolaus," Loblaw replied, taking in D'Amous' dark jacket and khakis. Typical D'Amous, he thought to himself. Even in the backwoods, with no one to impress with his sartorial splendor, D'Amous couldn't resist having the jacket tailored just so and the khakis pressed with knife-edged creases.

"We'll settle in for a bit, have some lunch, then take the boat out if you're amenable," D'Amous was saying. "Should be some great fishing here, courtesy of Quebec. There are some big rainbow and grayling in this lake. Whitefish too, but their mouths are so soft it's almost impossible to catch them on a fly. We can try, though."

"Sounds good to me," Loblaw said, smiling. "I've never caught grayling before." As they reached the porch, the pilot carrying Loblaw's gear dumped it and returned to the plane, where he cast off and taxied back out into the lake.

The two men stepped inside the lodge, and Loblaw breathed in the scent of the cedar planks that formed the walls, floors and raftered ceiling of the open-concept lodge.

"First things first," D'Amous said as he led the way to the bar along one wall. "Let me pour you something before we head out. Conditions are rather primitive, there's only one dogsbody here, but he's a damn good cook, as you'll soon find out."

Holding up the bottle, D'Amous asked, "Scotch? Or name your own poison."

"A Caesar, if you please, Nicolaus."

"No problem," D'Amous remarked. He prepared the drink using extra spicy Clamato juice, while Loblaw sank his bulk into an old lounge chair.

To know Bob was to sue him – he was such a crook – for he had been known as the Sultan of Sleaze, who drew his clientele from the government-by-bribe-and-threat crowd. Loblaw's many circumventions of the law had never been punished, and he'd ridden many political coat-tails and a string of buying and bullying tactics to a position of power within the Republican party.

They eyed each other as they raised their drinks. "You're looking as smart as ever," D'Amous offered. "Not like some."

Loblaw barked out a laugh. "Like our famous Under-Secretary of Defense, who was known as 'the fucking stupidest guy on Earth'. Inelegantly put, by our friend the General, but true enough, I'm afraid."

"Even the Oval Office has been, dare I say, graced with men of lesser intellectual stature."

"Right," Loblaw said, staring into his drink. "All the way from Reagan, who thought pollution was caused by trees, to our latest, who seems to be taking instructions from the Book of Revelations."

"Yes, President 'Truck'," D'Amous said. When he saw Loblaw's quizzical expression, he added, "Always loaded or at least he used to be."

"He may be all the things his detractors have said he is: affable exterior, hiding an insecure megalomaniac interior, stupid, ignorant, stubborn, mean spirited, even a bit unbalanced. But he's not half as tricky as the V.P.," said Loblaw.

"But he was perfect for the job. A tense, suspicious type with few real friends and a weak hold on external reality. In short, a person easily manipulated because he's falling apart inside from the fear of his own inadequacies, all of which he covers with braggadocio and an ability to deliver good fear-mongering speeches. Let's face it, Bob, these days, if your candidate isn't a born-again fundamentalist, right wing, holy roller Christian, you can't get him elected."

"I know what you mean," Loblaw said, nodding. "Ninety-two percent of that nutbar Mosey Long's followers – and they are legion – think God makes bets with the Devil, and that it is the Lord who decides who occupies the White House."

"I can personally state," Nick cut in, "that it wasn't God who came up with the Florida butterfly ballot with the hanging chads, or the Deadbolt voting machines. You know as well as I do that the last person we want in the President's chair is someone who's going to use reason instead of faith to make decisions. He might read things carefully before he signs them and start asking questions."

"I think you'd agree," Loblaw said, "that these fundamentalist beliefs are absurd, wretchedly superstitious and unworthy of the human brain, but I've heard that he's read books, and some of them in hard cover."

They repaired to the dining area and D'Amous waited until the cook had left the room after serving their meal, then said, "One of the reasons I suggested we get together, Bob, was that I feel I can speak frankly with you." He paused while he began to eat.

D'Amous had come to this conclusion knowing Loblaw's behind-the-scenes involvement in the Iran-Contra scandal, as unofficial counsel to Oliver North. It was Loblaw who had came up with the strategy for North to protect the President and provide him with deniability by testifying that he hadn't told him about arm sales to Iran to fund the Contra thugs in Nicaragua. Loblaw and North had deleted over five thousand e-mails related to Iran-Contra, but unfortunately, the e-mails had been automatically backed up by government servers. Loblaw had been found guilty on five counts of conspiracy, obstruction of Congress and false statements in 1990. Bob could not recall certain events in response to nearly two hundred questions during his testimony to Congress. The convictions had been overturned on appeal in 1991, on the laughably flimsy grounds that his testimony before Congress, which was given under immunity, may have influenced witnesses against him during his trial. Therefore he was a guy that could admire the sheer beauty of what was probably the world's greatest scam.

"You headed up the Total Information Awareness program, did you not?" D'Amous asked his guest.

"I did. It was a prototype database designed to detect patterns of communication that might be indicative of terrorist activity."

"And now that program has been signed into law under the Patriot Act."

"And a good thing, too," Loblaw said, dabbing at his mouth with his napkin. "In 1982, before TIA, we had the Defense Authorization Act. Sounds innocuous, but it was really revolutionary, in that it allowed the U.S. military to enforce civilian laws unrelated to military matters. As you know, Nicolaus, this used to be illegal under the Posse Comitatus Act. But drugs had been declared a threat to national security, so the War on Drugs was launched and the military was instructed to lend all appropriate aid in that war."

"The stated purpose of which was, as I recall," Nick put in, "to stop drugs from crossing into America, particularly from Mexico." At Loblaw's nod, D'Amous continued, "But it wasn't really designed to work, was it? Instead, everyone involved, including the banks that laundered the money, found the 'war' very lucrative indeed."

The two men sat in silence for a time, then Loblaw, his meal finished, leaned back in his chair and folded his meaty hands over his stomach. "Do you remember Operation Alliance in 1986? It brought together the FBI, CIA, DEA, Customs, the Bureau of Alcohol, Tobacco and Firearms, the U.S. Coast Guard, the Department of Defense and all manner of state and local law enforcement agencies. The border with Mexico was patrolled like never before."

Loblaw took a healthy pull on his third Caesar, then continued, "Which was ironic, because the CIA was flying the stuff into Mena, Arkansas and military bases elsewhere. Caribe Air, a proprietary CIA airline, used twenty different types of planes to transport illegal drugs into this country. We're fortunate that not many people care to inform themselves about this, but the CIA's direct and deep involvement in the international trafficking of heroin and cocaine created the enormous sums we needed to finance covert actions around the globe. And, via payments to Pentagon contractors, ensured the continued functioning of our military."

"Netted over a hundred billion in 1990, as I recall," Nick added. "The media knows this stuff but they always work to protect the Agency."

"To say nothing of the billions the Agency gets from the taxpayers, whether they like it or not."

D'Amous paused for a few moments as he studied Loblaw. The other man waited him out patiently. "You asked what I've been up to since last we met."

"Yes I did." said Loblaw, finishing off the last of his Caesar.

"You'll recall that after the planes hit the towers, Air Force One hopscotched across half the country, from the Booker Elementary School in Sarasota to the Offutt Air Force Base near Omaha, where the Strategic Command has its principle headquarters and a nuclear command bunker. Finally it flew to Andrews Air Force Base, where it didn't land until after 6:00 p.m. The public didn't hear from the President until he took a helicopter to the White House and made a speech at 8:30 that night. Have you ever wondered why that was?"

"Yes, I remember. What took him so long to respond?"

"The President was a player in the New World Order from way back," said Nick, "and knew the general outline of the scheme but not the total details. Everything had not gone exactly according to plan, particularly Flight 93, so we needed time to formulate a revised cover story. Furthermore, we had to keep the President out of the loop while doing so, because the Vice was the ventriloquist running the show and he didn't need or want help from the dummy.

"The President's only job was to make the televised speech later in the day, identifying al-Qaeda, Osama bin Laden and the governments of Afghanistan and Iraq as the evildoers responsible for the attacks."

"I knew plans of invasion of those countries had been in the works for quite a while," said Loblaw, "their sand has been covering up our oil for long enough."

"Correct," Nick answered. "You and I know the War on Terror is just a free market capitalistic enterprise, and the stock market prices of our patriotic corporations rise with the smoke from the bombs exploding all over the Middle East. For us, it's not a question of victory or defeat. It's a win-win-win situation for the New World Order allies like Carlyle, even if we lose the war."

"What about all our so-called intelligence agencies, the

CIA, the FBI, the NSA? How did you get around them?" Loblaw wanted to know.

"A certain small element of each was complicit in the plan. People tend to think it would involve thousands, but all it took was maybe fifty insiders and about the same number of highly trained commandos. Take the CIA for example. It is our own terrorist organization with its own banks, private companies and airlines, licensed to eliminate anyone perceived as a threat to American dollar imperialism and our interests here or abroad. So it is easy to bend them to our will. The same holds true for other agencies. We can always count on the Israeli Mossad, Britain's MI-6 or the Pakistani ISI to aid and abet as required, particularly in provocative false-flag operations."

"So you're saying that you, or the group you represent, engineered the whole thing."

"Precisely," D'Amous said, nodding his head. He leaned forward, "Our aim is to protect our worldwide corporate interests in perpetuity by establishing a U.S. dictatorship – plus a modern police state in America, with martial law, secret tribunals for dissenters, and strict controlled censorship of the media."

"Get rid of the Bill of Rights and the Posse Comitatus Act," Loblaw interjected. He thumped the tabletop. "Congratulations Nick, if I may call you by that name. I knew you were involved in 9/11 somehow. You want bragging rights, correct? Well, I can certainly understand. As you know, I've been the puppeteer for a few conspiracies in my time."

"Exactly why I feel you can be trusted with what I'm about to tell you – how we engineered the 9/11 attacks and then brought the American people around to our way of thinking. No one knows the full story. In case I should die unexpectedly or the evidence gets deep-sixed, I want someone else to know all of it. The whole 9/11 thing is just too grand a conspiracy to keep to myself. It makes the War on Drugs, the Pearl Harbor black-op,

Operation Northwoods and the Gulf of Tonkin false-flag op look like chickenshit. Let's face it, the War on Terror is not about just cause, it's nothing more than naked aggression for economic reasons. As you know, Bob, the U.S. government is owned and controlled by major corporations involved in munitions, banking, pharmaceuticals, oil exploitation and defense contracting – the so-called military-industrial-pharma-petro-media complex.

"Now, I trust I can count on you not to leak this to anyone whatsoever, after I tell you what went down."

"You bet," Loblaw replied. *But knowing it all, can be dangerous,* he thought, suddenly unsure whether he wanted to play Father Confessor to D'Amous, and remembering from past experience that by any other name, dogshit smells the same. "I'm eager to hear every bit of it. But if we're going to get any fishing in today, don't you suppose we should get going soon?"

"In ultrumque paratus." D'Amous said. Ready, come what may. He led the way to the dock, where the dogsbody had tied up a small motorboat with a 15 HP Evinrude motor and all the gear they'd need on this fine early afternoon in mid-August.

"What do we use for bait on these lunkers you were talking about?" Loblaw asked.

"Did I ever tell you about the time I caught a rattlesnake with a frog in his mouth?"

"No."

"I took the frog from the rattler, as they make good bait. Since this was such a dirty trick, I decided to pour a slug of scotch down the rattler's throat."

"You were always a generous fellow, Nicolaus."

"Later, when I was fishing, I felt something nibbling against my leg. I looked down – it was the rattler with another frog in his mouth."

Both men were laughing as they got into the boat and whipped out into the lake, looking to catch a mess of fish.

> "The whole aim of practical politics
> Is to keep the populace alarmed
> (and hence clamorous to be led to safety)
> by menacing it with an endless series
> of hobgoblins, all of them imaginary."
>
> *— H. L. Mencken, Editor (1880-1956)*

XXII – The Plan to Pull

$50,000,000 Reward to any current or former military or
public official of the United States government having
direct knowledge and verifiable proof that the events of
September 11, 2001 were not caused by Islamic terrorists.
Call 1-888-699-1234 toll free.

— Ad placed by the Wake Up America Project

"Is this Friday's coffee or today's?" asked Lance Boyle, the
young head watchdog interviewer for the Wake Up America
Project. He was thirty-two years old, weighed one hundred and
eighty-five pounds, and only six or seven of them were fat. His
hair was cut short, and he wore dark blue jeans and a lighter
blue pullover shirt. He swung his gray Bally loafers up onto the
desk. "It has a certain battery acid taste methinks."

Lance and the operator of the lie detector equipment,
Willie Maykut, were back at work on a Monday morning after
a weekend of rest and recreation. Willie was older, with a firm
pink face, looking closer to fifty than forty.

"Oh piss and bother," Willie replied getting up from his
chair, "I better brew a new pot. Doris usually does that. Where
is that girl?"

At that very moment, Doris Schutt, secretary and general
factotum, came through the office door. Nothing fancy, just an
average looking brunette in her thirties, slightly overweight,

wearing a simple black dress over tanned legs, taking in the scene with dark green eyes.

"How are you today?" asked Lance.

"I'd complain," Doris quickly replied, almost smiling, "only how long would you two listen? Anything new come in over the weekend for our big reward?"

"Nope. Who can blame them? But one of these days, someone will get cheesed off enough to squeal big time," said Lance.

"Trouble is," added Willie, "if identified, it's their ass that's in a sling."

"And maybe ours as well," said Doris. "This is a dangerous job. Especially if you're drinking that stale coffee." She grabbed their cups and poured the contents down the office sink, then started to prepare some fresh java. "I don't have to remind you guys that we're not too popular in many circles. I really don't know why I work here."

"Yes you do," said Lance, "It's because there is a war *of* terror going on against the American people right now – a psychological operation affecting all our minds and emotions – that began with 9/11, which is conditioning us into accepting the dictates of the full-fledged fascist, one-party government and police state world of perpetual war and terror."

"You've been writing a speech again, haven't you," said Doris. "If you want me to record that for you you'll have to start over again."

"Why not," said Lance, continuing his rant. "The United States has become the largest laboratory of Pavlovian dogs in the world, triggered by the methodical repetition of the fear and terror – the sights and sounds of the WTC attacks of 9/11. It's similar to the peasants in medieval times who were made to cower and shake in perpetual fear and insecurity at an enemy concocted, manufactured and marketed by the state and its corporate media propaganda mongers."

"You're in fine form to start the week, Lance," said Willie, "and, not to be outdone, may I add that the general public is still not willing to confront a very difficult mind game. They've been subjected for too long to propaganda-laced brainwashing that has left them in a hypnotized haze, preferring the warmth of ignorance over the upsetting fright of reality."

"Which is?" asked Doris, realizing her coworkers were warming up for the week's work on the 9/11 wake up front.

"The evisceration of democracy!"

"Which is about to change," said Lance confidently. "We are a real threat to the establishment if and when we uncover this, the greatest hoax in the history of modern man. Hopefully an informed public will rise up, the middle-class will refuse to be further decimated and the land of the meek and home of the slave will reject the status of peonage."

"Let's lighten up, you guys, it's too early in the week to get so serious," said Doris, sitting down with her own cup of fresh coffee and taking a long sip.

Willie was only too glad to comply. "Alright, I'll ask you two a new set of questions. Well, old actually, ones that were asked in my youth."

"To see if we're lying?" asked Doris.

"No, to see if you guys know the answers," said Willie.

"Okay, shoot," said Lance.

"What does every village need?"

"That's too easy," Doris answered. "An idiot!"

"Lance, who'd you like to go swimming with the most?"

"I know that one. It's from an old song, 'I love to go swimmin' with bow-legged wimmin and dive between their legs'."

"What does your mother wear?" asked Willie.

"What kind of a question is that?" said Doris.

"You and Lance are likely too young to remember that one," said Willie. "The answer is 'army boots'!"

"When Sir Galahad came to Camelot and asked for the Queen, the King said 'the Queen is in bed with laryngitis.' What did Sir Galahad say?"

Neither Lance nor Doris knew the answer.

"Galahad said 'Is that damn Greek here again!'"

Now do you remember the biblical story of Daniel and the Lion's Den?"

"Yes."

"What did Daniel do when the Lord called the lion forth?"

Just then, the phone jangled on the desk.

Lance's feet dropped to the floor, he swept some paperwork aside, picked up the receiver and listened to the caller. The male voice was raspy, perhaps disguised, but one that Lance felt was used to exercise authority.

"Yes, that's the type of information we are looking for," said Lance, his voice full of anticipatory hope. "Where are you calling from?"

"I'm in your city, calling from a pay phone. I'm sure you'll appreciate my caution, given the history of premature deaths among whistleblowers who got in the way of illegal government actions in this country. Where can we meet?"

"You know the Koffee Klatch at the corner of Main and Hastings?" replied Lance.

"No, but I can find it."

"Go there this afternoon and order a pound of fine ground Guatemalan coffee. While you're waiting for your order to be filled, you will be approached by someone to guide you to our location, so that we can meet personally."

Lance hung up the phone, then turned to Willie. "Well, what did Daniel do when the Lord called the lion forth?"

"Daniel slipped on some lionshit and came in fifth!" Willie answered. "Right?"

* * *

They sat in the Wake Up America safe house complete with polygraph equipment, assessing each other, gaining first impressions. "Do you wish to give us your name and position in the government or the military, sir?" asked Lance Boyle.

"That's going to have to wait 'til we've firmed up the deal and after you've heard what I have to say."

"Point taken," Lance replied. "You do understand, though, that we can only pay out the reward if we can verify that you're telling us the truth."

"Naturally."

"And you're willing to take a polygraph test as part of that process?"

"Yes, on two conditions. First, the fifty million must be in a safe place where I can access it undetected. The money will do me no good if I'm dead. Second, I need assurances that your organization will provide me with as much protection as is reasonably possible over the long term. The people I'd be blowing the whistle on aren't likely to forget about me in a year or two."

"I have a complete package for your perusal. You could become a national hero, there is that option. But I understand your concerns and I have the plans for your protection set out in a brief. We have blanked out some specifics in case you're a spook. Read the contents and see if our plan satisfies you." Boyle paused, then added, "Do you think the evidence you give us will convince the American people that the War on Terror is based on lies and deception?"

"We're *ad idem* on that score," said the man on the other side of the desk. "The American people's true enemies aren't *outside* their borders, but *inside* their own government, which at the moment is being held hostage by a criminal cabal."

After a few moments' silence the potential whistleblower continued, "I'm ready to sit on the stool and strain. But it's not because of the money. I've already done certain things I greatly regret, so I want to make amends, but I also want to live."

Willie Maykut studied the whistleblower as the polygraph expert hooked him up. The man was calm and determined, and both Willie and Lance were fairly certain they knew who he was, but said nothing on that score. As the lie detector went into operation, Lance launched into the Question and Answer session:

Lance: Let's start with Building 7, sir, the Achilles heel in the administration's conspiracy theory of the events of September 11. The Federal Emergency Management Agency says tremendous fires raged there for seven hours. But media images at 3 p.m. and just before the building collapsed at 5:20 p.m., showed only a few small fires on the 7th and 12th floors. No shattered windows, and only wisps of smoke. So what really happened to Building 7?

Whistleblower: Right. That's just an example of FEMA's usual bullshit. Those fires were so small you could've roasted marshmallows over them. No steel-framed high-rise building in the world has ever collapsed due to fire, not even raging infernos. FEMA tried to create a plausible explanation for the collapse of those towers, but have failed miserably. So, let's get it straight from the start. Fires had little to do with the collapse of any of these buildings. It is not a well-known fact that WTC 1 itself survived a serious fire in 1975. It started on the 11th floor and spread to six other floors, burning for three hours, yet the building didn't collapse.

Lance: Okay. How come they collapsed this time then?

Whistle: Here's the crux of why I'm here and I can supply the details, if we make a deal. The planes hitting the buildings were only an excuse for the official tale the administration had long planned to release immediately after the attacks.

Lance: The nineteen Arabs being run from a cave in Afghanistan by Osama?

Whistle: Yes, the 'official' cover story, which they knew would work on a gullible American public if the big lie were drilled in over and over again in the mainstream media. Their major problem in creating the collapse was overcoming the massive strength of the 47 steel columns in the Twin Tower cores, which were difficult to cut, even with powerful cutting charges. So quite a number of high-powered explosive devices were required throughout the basements. They used thermate for cutting these core columns along with traditional explosives, which generated powerful waves of upward pressure and extremely high degrees of heat – powerful enough to kill a lot of people and turn all the concrete infrastructure to dust.

Lance: So that's what you figure happened?

Whistle: No one mentions that do they? And it usually doesn't happen in a standard controlled demolition collapse. But with thermate, and high-powered explosives, the internal structure exploded extremely quickly and totally pulverized the concrete. People and computers were completely vaporized. Just take a look at the pictures and you'll see those terrific outward bursts of debris caused by the explosions.

Did you know that the towers were designed to withstand the collision of a Boeing 707? That's about the same size as a modern day 767. Not only that, but live loads on the peripheral columns could have been increased more than 2000 percent before failure occurred. Which means you could cut away all the first-storey columns on one side of the building and the rest of the building could still withstand further loads including a 100-mph wind force from any direction!

Manhattan was covered with about two billion pounds of pulverized, aerosolized building material, which is an extremely large amount of particulate debris from buildings whose total weight has been quoted at around three billion pounds. Debris removal has been quoted at 1.2 billion pounds. Therefore, based on those rough numbers, two-thirds of those buildings were turned into dust or vaporized. This is not possible in a gravitational collapse.

Lance: So how do you think they pulled this off?

Whistle: The buildings were wired ahead of time with explosives placed strategically on every other floor plus extra thermate charges were put in the basements. If you look at the video images and photos of the collapse, you'll see many features that can only be explained by controlled demolition: for example, the towers fell, straight down – and didn't fall over as you would expect; 'squibs' or streamers of smoke and dust can be seen shooting out of the towers well below the zones of total destruction; plus the towers collapsed at near free fall speed. All these were *prima facie* evidence of a controlled demolition. In short, gentlemen, the towers came down as a result of careful planning by someone on the inside.

Lance: Okay, can you be a little more specific?

Whistle: Well here's about all I can tell you. Security alerts were lifted and bomb-sniffing dogs were removed many days before 9/11. A few weeks before then there were an unusual number of evacuations from various sections of the towers, at various times, to allow for the placement of explosives.

Lance: I see. What happened, though, at WTC 7?

Whistle: That was the classic style of controlled demolition, an implosion. Contrary to what some say, it did not sustain any major impact damage from the èarlier collapse of the other two towers. If it had, it would have fallen *over*. In fact, Building 7 imploded into its own footprint, unlike the North and South Towers which *exploded,* 7's interior was brought down first, which meant the building's outer walls were sucked inward. When a building's internal structure is destroyed first, the falling mass encounters no resistance. You'll note that Building 7 collapsed in 6.5 seconds which is virtually at free fall speed

– only possible in a controlled demolition.

Lance: Okay, so we know how, but you haven't told us why.

Whistle: A little background history is in order here. You could start with why a New York property tycoon took a 99-year lease – in effect purchased the entire WTC complex – a few months prior to the 9/11 attacks. It was valued at 3.2 billion, and he got it for a down payment of 124 million dollars. From an economic standpoint the WTC was both a financial disaster and a four hundred thousand pound asbestos bombshell, which the buyers certainly knew about. The towers required, at least, 200 million in renovations and improvements to remove the asbestos health hazards. The New York Port Authority, the previous owners, had been legally prohibited from demolishing the buildings, even at the prohibitive disassembly cost of 15 billion dollars. The scaffolding alone would have cost 2.4 billion.

Lance: So why would anyone buy this lemon in the first place?

Whistle: Good question. Well, the complex was immediately insured for three and a half billion dollars and the coverage coincidentally included terrorist attacks. You may remember that following the attacks the owner filed two insurance claims based on two attacks, and eventually was paid 4.6 billion on an original investment of 124 million – not too shabby a profit.

Lance: Back to security for a minute. Who was in charge of the WTC complex?

Whistle: A new security company, Securiguard, was hired when the new landlord took over. One of the directors was the brother of President Truck, and the President's cousin was the CEO of the company. Coincidentally, Securiguard also provided security at Dulles International Airport and for United Airlines. So, there you have it, a small cabal not only owned the WTC complex, controlled its electronic security, but it also controlled the security of one of the airlines who had two aircraft hijacked on 9/11, as well as the Dulles airport from which Flight 77 originated.

One thing is sure – the destruction of the World Trade Center delighted many people, especially the destruction of Building 7. Thousands of sensitive files relating to the biggest financial scams in history, including Enron and WorldCom, were stored there, along with three to four thousand files of the most sensitive agencies in the country, including the New York offices of the Secret Service, the SEC, the Department of Defense, the IRS, NSA and the CIA. All these records were destroyed with the collapse of these three buildings, and, as a result, all cases involving criminal conduct of some pretty influential people can never be successfully prosecuted. Pretty convenient for so-called intelligence outfits like the CIA, don't you think?

Did you know Building 7 housed the mayor's command center, his Office of Emergency Management?

Lance: Yes.

Whistle: What you may not have realized is that the building was one of the attack operation centers for the gang who orchestrated 9/11. Building 7 was an important component for the planning and execution of the most audacious false-flag operation in the history of covert actions. A state-of-the-art bunker existed on the 23rd floor. The renovations alone cost taxpayers at least thirteen million dollars. The place had bullet and bombproof windows, an independent, secure air and water supply and the ability to withstand winds of 160-mph. It *also* contained directional homing devices for aircraft and high-tech equipment to control the explosive systems that had been planted in the World Trade Center buildings. This office was manned and monitoring the situation in lower Manhattan on the morning of 9/11. The people with their fingers on the buttons were in that building all day, until they got the order to evacuate.

Lance: Okay, so if they had all the bases covered, why did they leave the building standing so long after the towers fell?

Whistle: It was supposed to come down in the morning, after they guided the planes into their targets, and just after they set off the explosives in the two towers which brought them down. Right afterwards they were supposed to get the hell out of Building 7 and retreat a bit further to the north to a secure backup location at 75 Barclay Street and then implode 7 under the cover of all the dust clouds and smoke. But things started to go wrong when the fires in the South Tower didn't build because they were starved for oxygen.

Lance: You mean when the firefighters said they could probably put it out with two hoses?

Whistle: Yes, two fire officials had made it to the 78th floor and from that vantage point decided the fires could easily be put out with two hoses, so there was no need to panic. That's when the guys in Building 7 decided they had to pull the South Tower.

Lance: With all the firefighters still inside?

Whistle: Yeah.

Lance: And they pulled that before the North Tower.

Whistle: Right. Even though the South Tower was hit second and the fires there had only been burning for fifty-six minutes, it had to go down before the firemen could put the fires out.

Lance: You have to wonder why those fires were so feeble. Probably because most of the fuel exploded outside the building in that huge fire-ball we saw. Right?

Whistle: Yeah, you see it wasn't a direct hit. So even though the North Tower was supposed to go down first, having been hit seventeen minutes earlier than the South Tower, they had to pull the South Tower first or risk exposing the plot. The cover story was supposed to be that the collapse of the Twin Towers would cause so much debris to crash on top of Building 7 that it would look like it had suffered some major damage. Plus it could be said that the ensuing fires sparked fires in Building 7 which, in turn, set off a 40,000 gallon diesel tank on the ground floor, and that explosion kicked the feet out from under the building. All very logical.

Everything went according to the contingency plan, at first. They brought down the South Tower, then the North Tower, which sent up the huge cloud of dust and debris into the air, hiding all the surrounding buildings, including Building 7.

Lance: What happened next?

Whistle: Well they retreated to the safety of 75 Barclay Street, and pushed the button to demolish Building 7, but nothing happened. Malfunction! Now they had a big problem. They began to panic, because all the evidence of how they'd planned and executed 9/11 was in that building. The place was one massive crime scene waiting to be discovered. It had to go.

Lance: I can see that. The convenient cloud of debris that was to cover the collapse of 7 was gone by then, but they still had to get the explosives back on line, didn't they? And they hadn't prepared for that contingency, had they?

Whistle: Well, yes and no. They went back in and worked as fast as they could. It took them five or six hours to fix the problem. Of course, now they had to concoct another cover story to explain the building's collapse so late in the day. They set a number of fires, all the while staving off the firefighters. But the fires they lit didn't amount to much, so they gave up, cleared the area, told everyone it was about to collapse, then pulled the building.

Lance: We have a video of a broadcast which was shown on a PBS documentary in January 2004. It's an interview with the owner of Building 7, Harry Finkelman, in which he states: *I remember getting a call from the, er, fire department commander, telling me that they weren't sure they were going to be able to contain the fires in Building 7, and I said, 'We've had such terrible loss of life, maybe the smartest thing to do is pull it.' And they made that decision to pull and we watched the building collapse.* Tell me, doesn't everyone understand what is meant by the term 'pull'?

Whistle: Sure. It's industry jargon for a planned demolition. I saw that broadcast. Later the guy tried to say that he actually meant *pull the firefighters out,* but there were no firefighters in Building 7 before it came down. So that was B.S. The collapse of this building alone resulted in a nice little profit for the owner, five hundred million, I'd say.

Now, are you satisfied I know what I'm talking about? I was well placed in the administration and have even more information for you, when the time's right.

Lance: Would the President have known all this?

Whistle: It's hard to tell what the President knew and what he didn't. My guess is, information is fed to him on a need-to-know basis. But you have to ask yourself why he initially refused to testify before the supposedly independent 9/11 Commission, then agreed only if he could do so in the Oval Office with the Vice President, no tape recorders or transcripts were allowed and provided that those taking notes would have to submit them for redacting by the White House security personnel. Ludicrous.

Lance: All right, let's cut to the chase. Give us some names of those in charge of this hoax.

Whistle: I'm sure you can guess some of them. But first, turn off your machine and tell me whether you're satisfied I'm telling the truth. If you are, then I want proof that I can safely access the reward, and that I'll live to enjoy it. Then I'll name names and tell you the rest.

Willie Maykut shut down the polygraph machine. Once the connections were removed Lance said to the would-be whistleblower, "In the Aesop fable about sticking your head in a wolf's mouth, just being able to take it out intact was considered sufficient reward. But here at the Wake Up America Project we honor our contracts." Lance placed a folder on the table. "I think you'll find that adequate."

"Fine," said Whistle. "I'll get back to you shortly with my answer – likely in the affirmative." He rose and started to leave, then turned back. "I'll tell you one thing right now that might help convince you I'm on the level."

"Which would be what?" asked Lance.

"The administration has always contended they knew nothing about pending terrorist attacks prior to 9/11, which is a lie. All you have to do is ask for declassification of documents relating to a July 10th, 2001 meeting at the White House, between Truck's National Security Advisor and the Director of the CIA who briefed her about a so-called pending terrorist attack on U.S. soil by al-Qaeda. Apparently, she gave him the brush-off."

"Now that's quite incriminating," said Willie smiling.

"And the 9/11 Commission was briefed as to this meeting during their inquiry, but didn't include that in their report to Congress," said Whistle with a chuckle.

"I'm sure no one wanted that type of information to become public knowledge," Lance remarked. "Thank you."

"You're welcome. As I said, I'll get back to you shortly and don't worry, I'll corroborate everything whenever possible."

After he had gone, Lance and Willie looked at one another for a moment and then performed a high-five. "You know who that was?" said Willie.

"Yeah. Rowland Fowler!"

"I was wondering if you were going to bring up the subject of his infamous Iraqi weapons of mass destruction," said Willie.

"Naw. Would've been embarrassing and might've put him off. But that's the reason he'll decide to blow the whistle."

"The robb'd that smiles, steals something from the thief."

— *William Shakespeare*, Othello

XXIII – Hang Over Bar & Strip Club

Just because you're paranoid doesn't mean someone isn't following you, Slippery Jack reminded himself as he tooled down the highway, assiduously checking his rear-view mirror every few minutes. He'd seen that car before over the past couple of days, a run-of-the-mill beige Dodge Aries with two guys in it.

Jack slowed down and pulled onto the shoulder, watching as the Aries went past. He got part of the New York plate number, then cautiously eased back onto the highway. Five minutes later the Aries was on his tail again. He tried to convince himself it was nothing, and went about the rest of his day, doing his best to put the incident out of his mind.

The next day, Jack headed out to get groceries. Right after he hit the main street going into town, there was the Aries again. *Okay, no coincidence this time*, Jack thought.

He went to his bank, withdrew a wad of cash and transferred the rest of his money to his bank's affiliate in D.C. Back home he packed a suitcase with the bare essentials and dropped it off at a friend's place downtown.

Jack knew it was time to head for the hills like a bare-bummed Blackbird and disappear. The problem was how. He didn't take time to say goodbye to Eileen Dover, with whom he'd developed something of a bond since her cat had died, even though he'd never really been interested in her pussy. Jack waited 'til well after dark, piled into his Ford Taurus and took off.

He wheeled into the parking lot of the Hang Over Bar and Strip Club and stopped close to the entrance. *STAY ABREAST OF THE BARE TRUTH* was on the marquee over the front door, flanked by a list of the performers for the evening: Maria Wanna, Wild Cherry Knight and Mitzi Cupcake. Jack knew the establishment was a favorite hang-out for petty criminals and ne'er-do-wells, and he took note of the collection of rapscallions fouling the air with cigarette smoke by the club's entrance. Jack loitered, reading posters touting upcoming attractions as he watched for incoming cars. Sure enough, there was the Aries pulling in. It parked quite a distance away but the occupants stayed inside the vehicle.

* * *

Harry Palm and Armand Legg had pulled in less than a minute after Jack. Harry, who was driving, doused his headlights. Ignoring the available spots near the door, he parked well back from the entrance.

"I vote we go in," Armand said, licking his lips. "I could use a drink."

"No dice!" said Harry, tersely. "This is it; we've finally got him driving after dark and he's gotta go back down Ravine Drive to get to his place in Jersey. We can't afford to miss this chance." He snapped off his safety belt and heaved his bulk out of the car. "I'm gonna stretch my legs and have a smoke."

* * *

Jack went inside. The joint was wall-to-wall nookie, interspersed with males hoping to get some. There was a bar at one end with red leatherette stools, along with a huge color TV, a couple of small Boston pool tables, a shuffle-board and a little-used dartboard. At the center of the dance floor was the raised stage for the pole dancers or a band, but it was temporarily empty. The place reeked of a bad mix of beer, peanuts, B.O. and deodorant. The toilets were located down a back hallway on the way to the rear exit.

Taking a seat at the bar opposite the stage, Jack winced when the barkeep asked, "What'll youse have?"

"Soda water, ice and no disparaging remarks." The bartender's eyes widened, but he complied without comment.

Jack surveyed the crowd. It didn't take long for a likely candidate to turn up. The mark, in monochrome sunglasses, short-sleeved black T-shirt and black denim pants, plopped down on the adjacent barstool – one of the outside smokers, Jack figured. A tattoo of a pair of shapely female legs, in spiked heels of course, peeped out from just below the guy's left shirtsleeve.

Jack complimented the man on the Rembrandtian display, thinking that tattoos were everywhere these days, decorating bodies from arse to breakfast.

His companion flexed his sizable deltoids, and as the shirt rode up along his arm, the rest of the naked body was revealed.

"Impressive," Jack said, thrusting out his hand. "I'm Jack." He twirled his car keys around on his finger. "That work of art deserves a beer. Can I buy you one?"

"Yeah, sure, Corona. You can call me Duke."

Jack ordered the Mexican beer and kept up the chatter with Duke, sticking to women, cars, and sports, all of which Duke claimed to love. Jack made a show of sweeping his car keys off the bar and sliding them into the pocket of his brown suede jacket.

"Too damn hot in here," he complained, taking off the jacket and hanging it over the back of his stool.

"Ya got that right," Duke agreed. "But the strippers don't like too much air-conditioning."

Wild Cherry Knight took the stage, and Duke shouted over the rowdy applause, "Can I buy you a cold one, Jack?"

"Sure, right after I get back from the can," Jack said. "I've gotta take a crap. Watch my jacket for me, will ya, Duke?"

"Sure thing, Jack."

Wild Cherry Knight, looking bored, gyrated around the pole. Jack navigated his way through the drinkers at the bar, past the tables and gynecology row, then down the short passage leading to the men's can. Out of sight of Duke, he stopped, waited a few seconds, then slid back and peeked toward the bar. *The son of a bitch didn't waste any time*, Jack thought. *He's even taking my jacket!*

Jack whipped through the back door, crept along the back wall of the Hang Over and took a position behind a screen of shrubbery, where he could watch the front of the club. A heavily built man wearing a baseball cap leaned against the hood of the Aries, smoking a cigarette. Jack committed his face to memory. Seconds later, Duke emerged from the club wearing Jack's jacket, and climbed into Jack's Taurus. When he fired up the engine, the guy in the ball cap flung down his cigarette and jumped back into the Aries. Jack got the rest of the Aries's license number as it took off in pursuit of the escaping Duke.

* * *

Armand was about to take his turn outside the car when he spotted the brown-jacketed figure getting into the Taurus. "C'mon, Harry, he's moving!" Harry flipped his cigarette out into the parking lot and jumped back in and they set off after the Taurus, closing the gap between the cars as they sped down Ravine Drive.

* * *

Steering with one hand, his left arm hanging out the open window as the cool night air blew through his new wheels, Duke relished the joyride. He had several drinks under his belt, and he bellowed along to his favorite tunes on the radio as he did sixty down the only straightaway along Ravine Drive. When they played Watermelon Man, Duke sighed in appreciation of the best saxophone he'd heard in ages.

* * *

"This straight stretch comes just before the sharpest curve along the ravine," Harry pointed out to his partner.

"Certainly not the Grand Canyon," Armand said, peering over the edge, "but it'll do." He held the remote control gizmo in his lap. As soon as he spotted the sign for the upcoming curve, he pressed the button that froze the steering on the Taurus.

Their headlights illuminated the Taurus as the vehicle tore past the curve warning sign, crashed through the guardrail and sailed into space over the ravine. It hit once on its side, then rolled down the steep embankment, bouncing off rocks and fallen logs into the deep ravine below.

Harry and Armand heard a muffled scream as the car reached the bottom, then a great crash, followed by silence. Harry pulled up to the point where the Aries had left the road. He tried to aim his headlights into the ravine, to no avail. The two men got out and squinted into the blackness below.

"If that didn't whack him," Armand said, "this will." He pressed another button, which ignited the explosive charge strapped over the gas tank. A tremendous roar erupted from the depths of the ravine and fire began to rage. "Total destruction," Armand declared.

"That pig certainly won't squeal, and they'll even have a hard time identifying the burnt pork," said Harry. Spotting approaching headlights, he yelled, "Okay, the job's done, let's beat it." They ran for the Aries, and Harry spun the tires as they made their getaway.

> "The saddest aspect of life right now is that
> science gathers knowledge faster
> than society gathers wisdom."

> — *Isaac Asimov*

XXIV – Rick O'Shea & Pat Hand

"Let me ask you a question, O'Shea," the police chief said. "What's the difference between me and a proctologist?"

Rick O'Shea knew he was in deep doo-doo as he thought over this peculiar question. "I don't know, sir," he answered.

"No difference, dummy. We both have to look at one asshole at a time! And today I'm looking at you."

"It was a case of mistaken identity, Chief," Rick whined. "We got a 911 call about a wild drunk beating on his wife."

"And you went to the wrong address, did you?"

"Well, yes."

"And did you find a wild drunk there? No! The guy wasn't wild and he wasn't drunk, was he?"

"I don't know, sir." O'Shea shifted uncomfortably under the captain's glare.

"That's your standard answer, isn't it, O'Shea? You know damn well he wasn't drunk. The guy was a marine, just back from Iraq. Jesus Christ, they didn't shoot him there, so you figured to shoot him here? Do you remember the last time you were up before me for disciplinary action?"

"Yes sir."

"Some drunk tried to assault the naked female statue in the park and you charged him with statutory rape?"

O'Shea hung his head but remained silent.

"Well, this time I can't save your dumb ass. The Commissioner's office is insisting that you be charged with

143

aggravated assault, abuse of your authority as a police officer, and anything else the prosecutors can think of. You've created a public relations disaster for us, O'Shea!"

"Sir, he wouldn't do what I said. He wouldn't turn around."

"For God's sake, you Tasered him at close range, once when he had his hands over his head, once more when he was on the floor, and a third time when he was handcuffed to a hospital bed."

"But he was pissing on me," O'Shea protested.

"Rightly so, I'd say! And now it's my turn. Hand in your badge and gun. You're suspended without pay 'til your trial."

* * *

Helen Weills rinsed the mascara smudges from her cheeks, then pressed her flushed forehead against the cool glass of the bathroom mirror. Bill was still in a hospital room down the hall, languishing in a coma after being Tasered three times. It was time to stop crying and get busy. Whether Bill recovered, remained a vegetable or died, she was going to follow through on her threat to sue that s.o.b. cop and the idiot police force that had hired him.

She had little experience in finding a top-notch lawyer. She was aware of an old gypsy curse, "May you have a lawsuit in which you know you are in the right." But Helen knew what she needed – a fast, aggressive attack dog in the form of a cheap lawyer the cops didn't like, who wouldn't give her a lot of gobbledegook she couldn't understand – a lawyer with common sense solutions, arbitration skills and the belief that the most advantageous place to settle disputes is on the courthouse steps – a show-off guy who loved to win and hated to lose.

The courthouse was the place to start, she decided. She hung around for a day, observing, asking questions and handicapping the lawyers, just like she did at the racetrack before she placed her bets. Still, she knew she'd have to go on her gut feeling in the end. She came up with Pat Hand, a filly and a good mudder on the court circuit. Helen went to the lawyer's nearby office for her free half-hour consultation.

After Helen had laid out the situation, Hand said, "Tasers! Those numbskull cowboys sure love the latest toys. There are big problems with those electronic stun guns. I've just been reading about them, as a matter of fact."

Helen sighed and settled back in her chair, feeling she'd come to the right place. She studied the woman. Pat Hand looked to be in her early fifties, short and a tad overweight, with a pleasant face and graying hair pulled back so tightly it squeaked.

Hand continued, "The police did their own study on Tasers, called Review of Conducted Energy Devices. I figured that if they won't even call a gun a gun, they're unlikely to say the thing is dangerous, are they? And they didn't, in this study. They cited a number of other studies to prove that Tasers do not, by themselves, cause death. But we can counter that with expert testimony from doctors and forensic specialists. Bill's injuries speak for themselves."

"I'm not about to let those fools get away with this," Helen declared. "So I'm hiring you to do whatever it takes to make them pay."

"This case is clear-cut, I feel, like shooting the proverbial fish in a barrel. We'll leave the judge smiling, the defense lawyers humiliated, and the jury sobbing. I'll get these cops for you, guaranteed."

"How much will it cost me?" Helen wanted to know.

"We could negotiate a contingency agreement, whereby I assume the risk of success or failure along with yourself and Bill. If we lose I get nothing. If we arrive at a monetary settlement through negotiation or litigation, then I get a percentage of that settlement, plus out-of-pocket disbursements."

Helen thought it over. "What percentage, and who decides whether we accept a settlement?"

"The standard's thirty-three percent. I happen to think that's too high, so I generally ask for twenty-five, but you pay my out-of-pocket as we go along. How does that sound?"

"Better. As for my other question?"

"If during the progress of the case we get an offer, you and I discuss it and you'll make the final decision to take it or leave it. If we go to court, the judge or the jury determines the size of the settlement. Of course, my job is to try and get you the highest amount possible, either by negotiation or through a court decision, because what's good for you is good for me as well."

"Fair enough," Helen said.

"Okay, I'll marshal the facts, interview the medics, and talk to Bill as soon as he's able, then we'll hit O'Shea and the police department with a Complaint."

Helen decided to do her own research as well. That night she spent a couple of hours on the Internet at the library, hunting for anything she could find on Taser guns and their use by police forces.

She discovered that the electric charge emitted by a Taser was high voltage but low frequency. When it hits a human body, it confuses the nervous system, which also functions by sending electrical charges through its neural pathways. The brain receives mixed signals from the nervous system, resulting in great pain, temporary paralysis, spasms or convulsions. Tasers could disrupt the rhythm of the heart muscle and permanently damage the nerves.

The guns used varying amounts of current, but just 0.06 amps was a lethal charge. Anything over a three-second charge could disorient a person for up to fifteen minutes. The effect on the victim depended on their skin type and moisture content, body salinity, the clothing they were wearing and the stun gun's inner circuitry and battery strength. Since 1999, at least 126 people across North America had died after being Tasered.

* * *

The two doctors conferred outside Bill's room. "We can't tell how serious the damage is until he comes out of the coma."

"His nervous system seems severely affected, but I agree, we won't know the details until he tries to function normally."

"I've checked out his girlfriend's story and he's a marine, all right. She showed me his papers. So I suggest we ship him over to the Walter Reed Medical Center, where he'll be with the rest of his buddies."

"I concur," said the second doctor. "They've got some of the country's best neurological specialists there."

"As well as the latest equipment. Okay, I'll make the arrangements."

* * *

A few days later at Walter Reed, Bill came out of his coma. He had a splitting migraine and a vague memory of a dust-up with a cop. Helen was at his bedside, holding his hand and beaming as she wiped away tears of relief.

"What happe-pe-pened? Whe-where am I?"

"Thank God, Bill! You're in hospital, but you're going to be okay now. Just take it easy, don't get excited."

"My he-he-head hurts."

"I'll talk to the nurse. We'll get a doctor in here to explain everything to you. For now, just rest."

Rest was about all that Bill felt up to. He squeezed Helen's hand, then crashed back into sleep.

* * *

Over the ensuing days and weeks, the neurologist monitored Bill's progress. Bailey was suffering from involuntary eye movements and a stutter. He couldn't control the opening and closing of his eyelids, which made sleep difficult. The sleep deficit led to mood swings, with a preponderance of depression. He had trouble walking, and the tremors that would start in his upper limbs often spread to the rest of his body.

The neurologist was concerned that the toll on Bill's central nervous system could develop into Alzheimer's or Parkinson's disease, but he hoped that time, physical and drug therapy, along with counseling, would help his patient regain a normal life.

At least one of Bill's problems had been taken care of by the cops – he didn't have to go back to Iraq. Maybe two problems, because now he didn't have to become a deserter and go on the lam.

When Bill was somewhat more stable, the neurologist transferred him to a ward full of marines who'd been shipped home with a variety of injuries. They were some of the more than 15,000 soldiers wounded in action since the Iraqi operation began in March of 2003.

Bill was in a room with nine others, and he listened eagerly as the GIs swapped stories.

"Personally, I think there's a difference between living and being alive," one vet stated.

"True enough," said another. "Head injuries are about the worst, 'cause you could get brain damage, and then you'd still be alive, but you wouldn't be able to look after your wife or kids. Guess I'm lucky I only got my leg shot off." He grasped the stump of his right leg and aimed it at the first speaker as if it were a rifle, much to the other's amusement.

"How'd that happen?" the GI in the adjacent bed asked, indicating the stump with his chin.

"Combat outpost dump near Rawa near the border with Syria. It's on the Euphrates River in al-Anbar Province, a real hot spot for insurgents. One of our vehicles got bombed and we went in to help get our people out. The driver was stuck and screaming in pain – had a spinal injury. The rest of the crew was panicking. Total chaos. Then a rigged and buried artillery round exploded and tore off my leg. They flew in a medical team, who shot me full of morphine. Boy, was I glad to see that bird swoop in and take me and the other guys outta there. But I don't think they should have tried to save the guy with the spinal. His body armor was shredded and he had shrapnel in the head, chest and legs. Even with the morphine he was still screaming. If he's still alive, he's not livin'.""

"I was always afraid I'd get my nuts shot off. Now that would be a real bummer."

One soldier had had enough. "Knock it off, you guys. We should make it a rule not to talk about this stuff. Let's watch a video or somethin'."

The grunt in the bed next to Bill was a multiple amputee who hadn't said much of anything since he'd arrived. All Bill knew was that his name was Zack.

"Although we give lip service to the notion of freedom, we know that government is no longer the servant of the people, but, at last, has become the people's master. We have stood by like timid sheep while the wolf killed – first the weak, then the strays, then those on the outer edges of the flock, until at last the entire flock belonged to the wolf."

— *Gerry Spence,* From Freedom to Slavery, *1933*

XXV – Walter Reed

By the time Zack Zapata had arrived home from Iraq and undergone surgery to repair his damaged right leg, a minuscule piece of metal lodged in his spine had shifted, guaranteeing he'd never be able to use his remaining lower limb. How the doctors had missed it before then was a moot point. And now he had the same sane mind he always had in an entirely different body.

Medical experts believe the brain has a blueprint of body parts that persists even if they've been cut off. Hard-pressed by the phantom limb pain of the swollen and aggravated nerves that once served the limbs he had lost, Zack tried to alleviate his torment with the array of remedies on his nightstand – the medicated patches used for shingles, an electro-stimulation device, pills to combat depression. None of them worked too well. *What can I do, and with what? How can I face the world from a wheelchair?* he wondered.

Mangled, frustrated and scared, he entertained thoughts of suicide, but managed to shake those off temporarily by executing a strategic retreat into the recesses of his mind to keep from dwelling on his physical losses. He focused on his happiest memories – frolicking on the beaches of Mazatlan with his buddies and their girlfriends. Zack used to love water-skiing, unlike his girlfriend, whose sense of balance left much to be desired. She was afraid to stand up on the skis and steadfastly remained in a crouch as the boat gained speed and dragged her along. The majority of her body would remain under water, prompting Zack's friends to call it the 100-yard douche.

* * *

Nick D'Amous walked into the best facility of its kind, the Walter Reed Army Medical Center in Washington, on a mission not much to his liking, but one that he knew would be politically expedient. Of late, D'Amous had begun to be recognized as the power behind the throne. Though the President still caught most of the increasing flack over America's presence in Iraq, the alternative press in particular was painting D'Amous as the chief architect of an illegal and immoral war, and the opinionated prick who wouldn't listen to the U.S. Generals' insistence that they needed an exit plan.

Everybody thinks they're an expert, thought Nick. *Experts my ass! They imply I lack compassion for the jarheads fighting the war on the ground. I have two words for those ink-stained bastards and the last of those is OFF!*

"Some real bad casualties in this ward, sir," said the orderly who was conducting D'Amous' tour of the hospital. "We're doing our best to rehabilitate them all, but there are some who may have to stay with us permanently."

D'Amous, full of tension, had been rushing through the tour, impatient to complete the chore, barely listening as the orderly ran through the reason for each patient's presence in the hospital. But as he gazed into the large ward on the last floor of his tour, the orderly's words began to penetrate and despite himself, Nick was appalled at the catalogue of catastrophes these men had suffered. He moved slowly among the beds, thanking each veteran for his contribution to America's War on Terror and the depth of his sacrifice.

Although these soldiers had finally managed to touch his long-suppressed emotions, D'Amous stopped with relief at the foot of the last bed. The orderly introduced them, and Nick moved around the side to shake Zack Zapata's hand; except he didn't have one. D'Amous shuddered but struggled through the awkward moment, Zack offered him his left hand, plus a big sunny smile that D'Amous couldn't help but return.

"Tell me this isn't just about oil," were Zapata's first words.

"No, no," D'Amous replied, not entirely surprised by the question he had heard many times before. *Non semper ea sunt quae videntur*, he thought. "I mean, things are not always what they appear to be. It's about freedom, which is the Almighty's gift, and it's America's duty to make sure the entire Middle East has the same freedoms we enjoy."

Zapata, his smile still in place, said, "The Middle East is made up of some fifteen countries, and there are fifty-seven Islamic nations. Are we gonna take 'em all on?"

"No, son. We just wanted to get rid of Saddam Hussein, a terrible dictator, and bring democracy to the Iraqi people. We're there to win over the masses." Nick pulled a chair beside the bed and sat. "You've more than done your part in that effort, and I'm sorry you were injured. Tell me how it happened."

"I was a marine, sir. Bravo Company, 3rd Light Armored Recon Battalion. Went to Iraq shortly after the invasion of March 2003. I lasted about a year; then my patrol was ambushed by insurgents in a roadside bombing outside Baghdad."

D'Amous felt compelled to ask, "What is the extent of your injuries?"

"One ruptured eardrum, lost my right arm and left leg, and got severe wounds to my right leg. They may have to amputate that one, too. Doesn't matter, since I can't feel it, anyway." Zack's smile vanished as he told D'Amous about the metal in his spine.

"Maybe with artificial limbs –" D'Amous began ...

"Won't know for a while, but I hope it works. I'm really tired of having someone else wipe my ass."

The graphics of the situation came heavily home to D'Amous, Zack's stolen youth bringing on a sense of melancholy. He wondered whether Zack would ever be capable of the functions most people took for granted, including sex. He wisely kept his mouth shut on that topic.

The orderly standing behind Nick broke into the conversation. "Zack was declared clinically dead three times by military doctors in Iraq, sir. Infusions of 39 pints of blood helped save his life."

"Yeah, guess I'm lucky to be here at all. I've got buddies who aren't."

After a few more minutes, Nick rose and took his leave of the badly maimed soldier. He stopped in to talk to one of the hospital psychiatrists on his way out, surprising himself at how deeply Zack's plight had affected him. "Can these men really be rehabilitated?" he asked.

"Depends on the individual and his mental attitude. The psychological scars of amputation run deeper than those from more conventional wounds. They don't seem like the same people they were. Some will find a way to make a life for themselves. But the physical and psychological hurdles are horrendous. The patient's first job, apart from making it through all the operations, occupational and physiotherapy, is to get over the question of, *Why me?* That's usually a bigger problem for civilians, though. These soldiers knew the risks, even if they pushed the thought of those risks to the back of their minds in order to get the job done."

Nick drummed his fingers on the shrink's desk, then said, "I'm assuming this facility has procedures allowing well-wishers to offer special help to individual patients, over and above what the hospital itself and the Department of Veteran's Affairs provides."

"Of course," the psychiatrist replied, admiring the motivation. "That's not my department though. You'll have to talk to the admin office."

As he headed out to his car, D'Amous resolved to arrange financial assistance for Zack, who was going to need a great deal of specialized equipment. Nick even mused that, should Zack ever regain any sexual functioning, he could be supplied with hookers whenever the need arose.

* * *

Mood in the ward was volatile, depending on attempts at humor or explosions of anger. Zack was doing his best to tune out the hubbub around him as the orderlies wheeled in a gurney with another vet on board. They helped the patient onto a bed recently vacated by a grunt whose mangled body had finally mended enough to be shipped home, so his loved ones could experience the shock and awe the Republican administration loved to talk about.

Unusual for this ward, this guy had all his limbs, but seemed perpetually dazed. Zack waited a few hours until his neighbor appeared more *compos mentis,* then introduced himself to the grunt who said his name was Bill Bailey. A nurse showed up at Zack's bedside and began to tend his wounds. Zack wanted to keep his mind off the painful process, so he asked, "What happened to you, Bill?"

"I got sh-sh-sh-shot."

"Where?"

Bailey squinted and twitched with the effort to control his stutter. "Th-th-three times, in the ch-chest, and n-neck, I think."

"You don't know where you were shot?"

"It's hard to tell ex-ex-exactly."

"Well, was it in Baghdad, Tikrit, Mosul?"

"I was in Iraq, but I meant I c-c-can't be sh-sh-sure where on my body. Tasers don't sh-sh-shoot bull-bull-bullets."

"Who uses Tasers in Iraq?"

"Not there. Here. I got shot by a g-gung … gung ho … ho-ho … gaw-gaw-gaw damned eff-eff-effing cop!"

Zack's eyes widened. "No shit! How'd that happen?"

Bill, trying to control his stutter as best he could, explained his situation and his girlfriend's decision to launch a lawsuit. The nurse finished attending to Zack and moved off down the row.

The two men continued to talk "I was brought up as a dum-dum-dum-Dominionist," Bill said.

At Zack's baffled expression, Bill explained, "They're big in the S-S-S-South. Fun-fun-fundamentalist Christians, b-b-big time hell and brimstone Bi-bi-bible-punchers. You n-n-n-know, God is on the side of the U-U-United States, and everyone else is an ant-ant-anti-Christer infidel, trying to destroy our way of life. That's how I came to s-s-s-sign up in the first place."

"How's that?"

Bill described the rally where he'd met the mysterious and powerful Nicolaus D'Amous. "That hyp-hypocritical son of a bitch convinced me that I should help fight the Axis of Evil."

"He was just in our ward this morning!" Zack exclaimed. "I had a long talk with him. He seemed like a nice guy."

"He did when he was talking to me, too, but the result was b-b-b-bad."

"He might be coming back to see me," Zack said.

"That's good, 'cause I've got lots to say to him!"

"Back to these Dominionists, you don't sound like you're too happy with them, Bill."

"I'm not. Quit them cold. Now I'm a sec-sec-sec-sec-sec –"

"What, a sex maniac?" Zack prompted.

"Secular humanist. Polite word for an a-a-a-atheist. Don't

believe in G-G-G-God, Allah, or Yahweh."

"Is that possible?" asked Zack, pondering the possibility.

"Of course. It's intellectually s-s-stimulating. You f-f-find your own purpose and become responsible f-f-for your own life. That's exciting because you're free of all this b-b-bull-bullshit about being under the sur-sur-surveillance of God and second-guessing whether you're a-a-actions are going to send you to he-he-heaven or he-he-hell. You're free to speak your own mind and see-see-seek your own purpose, if you know what I mean. What about you?"

"Run-of-the-mill lapsed Catholic. That's a big lapse for a Latino, believe me. Happened about the time I got blown up and outta Iraq."

"And wh-wh-what are you now?"

"A disillusioned American patriot."

"Well, you can cow-cow-count me in on that."

"There sure are a lot of us," Zack said thoughtfully. "And not just vets, either. I'm talking millions of Americans who want to clean up this political mess, bring back some sanity to this country before it's too late."

"So wha-wha-what can we do?" Bill asked. But Zack had no immediate answer to that, and the two men fell silent.

* * *

The weeks passed, and over time, Bill's blepharospasms – the medical term for his damaged nerves – abated. He could now speak properly, but he decided to purposely maintain some of the stutter. His sense of balance had returned to nearly normal, but he pretended it still gave him trouble, too. However, he continued to have difficulty sleeping, which prolonged his bouts of depression and irritability.

The neurologist, with the aid of a sleep researcher, had diagnosed his condition as hypnagogic sleep disorder, a rare and curious phenomenon. He was getting stuck in a state halfway between wakefulness and sleep and having auditory and visual fantasies. The condition was believed to account for many out-of-body experiences. Bill also suffered from *hypnopompic* sleep disorder, which meant he experienced the same state on rare occasions when he *did* fall asleep. As he began to wake up, he would be overcome with visions that appeared to be very real.

"We've established that you see colors and geometric forms, flashing lights and colored rings," the neurologist said to Bill when they were in the sleep lab.

"That's right," he replied

"And images of people and places."

"I'm all over the map, doc. Back in Iraq, in base camp."

"Do you see entire scenes, including action sequences?"

"Yeah. Last night I was out on patrol with a four-vehicle convoy in Baghdad. We were driving slowly down a bumpy, half caved-in dirt road, looking for insurgents. We were supposed to find out if the route was passable and free from landmines, unexploded ordinance and other dangers. We s-s-stopped for a rest at what seemed like a safe spot. I was eating my MRE when I saw a coffee can. I don't know, I guess I was tired and not thinking straight. The coffee can was b-b-booby-trapped. The insurgents had attached a trip wire to some stuff they'd scavenged from dud U.S. bombs and shells and added a grenade. When I picked up the can, BOOM! Blood and guts everywhere. I didn't die, strangely enough, but I'd blown up several of my buddies. Not likely to help me sleep, huh?"

The neurologist nodded in understanding. "But of course it was an illusion."

"Yeah, I realize that once I'm awake, b-b-b-but these hallucinations are p-p-p-pretty damn scary. Sometimes I can see myself flo-flo-floating above my sleeping b-b-b-body, then

I fly thousands of m-miles away, and I'm looking down on other scenes."

"Yes, astral projection they call it, otherwise known as an out-of-body experience."

"Wha-wha-whatever, it's giving me the screaming me-me-meemies."

"Most of the time, people don't recall these events because they drift off into a deep sleep."

"Mine just jo-jo-jolt me back into be-be-being wide awake. You gotta do s-s-s-something, doc. My n-n-nerves are all sh-sh-sh-shot to sh-sh-sh-shit from this!"

* * *

A familiar voice came from down the hall. "Goddammit to hell, Zack! There oughta be a law against sending troops into a place they know is polluted with depleted uranium."

Zack hadn't seen Joe MacGillicuddy since the sniper shot Terry Dunbar, and he and Joe were then blown up on the highway of death between Baghdad and the Green Zone. But here Joe was, transferred to a room just down the hall from Zack, who'd been on his way back from the occupational therapy ward when Joe, sitting morosely in a chair by the window had hollered at him. Zack steered his wheelchair in next to his old buddy, who didn't waste any time before launching into his tale of woe.

"I'd never even heard about that DU stuff until that day Terry told us about it, remember? Just before that sniper got him. Now I've got that goddamned Gulf War Syndrome!"

"You're luckier than me," Zack replied with a wan smile. "Most of the platoon didn't make it out, Joe. I'm glad you did."

"Yeah, I guess I'm just grousing. But wait 'til you hear what else! I got a letter from the army saying they're gonna charge me seven hundred bucks for letting my body armor get destroyed."

"You're kidding me, right?"

"No sir," Joe said vehemently. "My body armor was wrecked in battle and incinerated as a biohazard, but nobody bothered to record that it happened. The last I saw of it, it was dragged off me while I was being evac'd from that highway ambush. I was grateful that the armor saved my life, but seven hundred bucks!"

"You gonna pay?" Zack asked.

"Not if I can help it! But it's not like I got a choice. The army's gonna deduct it from my pay."

"Get this," Zack said, glancing out into the corridor and lowering his voice. "There was this International Criminal Tribunal in Japan in December 2003. Our own federal government was convicted of crimes against humanity for using depleted uranium in Afghanistan. Can you believe it?"

"Where'd you hear this?"

"I got it off the Internet. You can bet CNN ain't gonna tell the public about that, or talk about how much damage this stuff causes. Well, you know, Joe."

"Damn right. I'm set to have major health problems for the rest of my short life."

"Our government's condemning its own troops, along with civilians all over the world, to thousands of years of toxic waste nightmares. Thanks to our weapons program and our nuclear plants, we've got tons of plutonium and U-236 uranium to get rid of and what better way than to sell it to munitions manufacturers. Plus it gives their explosives more bang for the buck."

"Like I said, there oughta be a law." Joe said, as he slumped in his chair, looking defeated.

"Hey, as long as 71 million eligible voters don't vote and people don't bother to find out what in the hell's going on, or don't care – as long as they're all snug and cozy in their gated communities, the government can keep on contaminating the environment and covering up the facts, here and overseas."

"A writer owned an Asterisk,
And kept it in his den,
Where he wrote tales (which had large sales)
Of frail and erring men;
And always, when he reached the point
Where carping censors lurk,
He called upon the Asterisk
To do his dirty work!"

— *Stoddard King*, The Writer and the Asterisk, *1923*

XXVI – The Customs House

September 15, 2001, 10:00 a.m.

"What do you mean, we can't inspect this building?" an irate Brian Pound demanded.

B.S. Pound's team of engineers was standing outside the tape surrounding the huge crater that used to be World Trade Center Building 6, commonly known as the Customs House. The building had housed such federal entities as the Department of Commerce and the Bureau of Alcohol, Tobacco and Firearms, and one private company, Eastco Building Services, Inc. Less than twelve minutes after the first plane hit the North Tower on September 11, Building 6's almost eight hundred employees were evacuated. The smoke around the stricken South Tower hadn't yet cleared when a mysterious and tremendous explosion shot hundreds of feet above the Customs House. Video footage of the blast aired at 9:04 a.m. and was confirmed by scores of witnesses, but it received no subsequent media coverage. None of the federal agencies whose offices had been obliterated would comment regarding the explosion, and they imposed a media blackout on all photographic evidence of this portion of the devastation.

"Blockage order from the New York City Department of Design and Construction. Acting on orders to keep you out," said the man blocking Pound.

"We're supposed to inspect what's left of Buildings 4, 5 and 6," Pound insisted. "We're with the American Society of Civil Engineers, and the inspections are authorized by FEMA."

"I don't care if you're King Tut from Turd Island, you can't inspect this site!"

Pound whipped out his cellphone and jabbed at the keypad. "I'm calling FEMA." He put the phone to his ear and announced to the listener, "We're down here at Building 6 and some joker's saying we can't do our jobs. What gives?"

"We agreed to a no data collection order," said the FEMA agent on the other end.

"Are you kidding? Listen, we need to take a close look at this crater. It goes way down into the basement. We were told the building came down because it was hit with debris from the North Tower, but I think there's something wrong about that explanation."

The FEMA agent replied, "Maybe there is, but it's a no-fishing hole."

Strange, Brian thought, completely frustrated. *At WTC Building 4 we were told that concerns about the gold bullion and cash that were stored there prevented our entry to that one too. This is a real tarfu – things are royally fucked up here! I wonder what's down there that they don't want us to inspect?*

XXVII – Hostel Destiny

Looking on the bright side, Slippery Jack figured he'd done well by avoiding either an untimely death or becoming a middle-management slave. He'd been forced to become a peon in the damned service industry, one of the few jobs available when you were on the run and trying to hide your identity.

But even menial work had proved hard to find. With all the overseas outsourcing, you practically needed a bachelor's degree to flip burgers at McDonalds or to clerk at Wal-Mart, and a Ph.D. to become a manager anywhere.

Jack eventually wanted to live in the South, where he could bunk outdoors if necessary. But first he was heading for Washington, D.C., on the theory that he could hide more effectively where his enemies wouldn't expect him to be – right under their noses.

If he were going to improve his lot, however, he'd need some fresh I.D. that would stand up to a modicum of scrutiny. So Jack went in search of the fake document specialists that existed in most major centers across America. He retained his first name and became Jack O'Reilly. He purchased a knapsack, figuring it would be less conspicuous and cumbersome than his

162

suitcase. Arriving in D.C., Jack found a cheap café where he ordered sausages and eggs.

"Coffee's over there. Help yourself, honey," said the scrawny waitress, indicating a side-table loaded with carafes, mugs and various condiments.

The restaurant was overcrowded, with only one vacant seat at a table occupied by an elderly man who looked down but not out. His disheveled appearance made Jack think that he might be wondering what had happened to him when he wasn't looking. He was the sort who just might know a good deal about the type of living quarters Jack was seeking.

"May I join you?" Jack asked politely.

The man looked up in surprise, then said, "Be my guest."

Jack sat down with his cup of coffee. "John Doe," he announced.

"That makes two of us," the man replied laconically. Jack detected a softened English accent.

"I sure needed this coffee as a pick-me-up," Jack said by way of conversation.

"You just passing through?"

"Maybe stay for awhile if I find some reasonable accommodation. Got any suggestions?"

The old man grunted, ran a hand over his splotchy skin and said, "Try the Hostel Destiny over by the Walter Reed Medical Center. Fine as long as you don't mind a few oddballs, like the vets discharged from the Disabled American Veterans' Hospital and the President Lincoln and the Soldiers' Home. Some of them don't have all their marbles. But the price is right."

The guy's definitely a limey, Jack thought. And the name, Hostel Destiny, is intriguing. "Thanks, John, I'll check it out. How about writing down the address for me on this napkin?"

"Down on your luck, are you, John?"

"Yes and no," Jack answered as the other man fished in his pocket for a pen. "Hoping to have better luck here than the last place I hung my hat."

"Ah! Success! The brief interval between a stroke of luck and a stroke of apoplexy." His laughter at his own remark turned into a coughing spell, then he carefully penned the names of the two crossroads which indicated the hostel's address.

Encouraged by Jack's chuckles, the Englishman continued, "I'll tell you something about success, young man. At age four success is not peeing in your pants, at age twelve success is having friends, at sixteen it is having a driver's license, at age twenty success is having sex, and at thirty-five it is having money. At fifty it's still having money, and at age sixty success is having sex. At age seventy success is having a driver's license, at age seventy-five success is having friends. And at age ninety success is not peeing in your pants."

Jack shook with laughter, spilling some of his coffee in the process. "What part of England did you come from?" he asked.

"Not exactly a Cockney, but I did come from a people kippered by the variable fogs and smogs of ten thousand bad days and nights. I was a Londoner."

"I always envied you guys, your command of language," said Jack. "But I could never understand the Cockney manner of speaking."

"Ah, yes. Difficult. You have to understand their version of the alphabet for one thing, and how they think for another. I could elucidate, if you were inclined to pass a moment or two."

"I'm not in any hurry," Jack said, as the waitress deposited his breakfast in front of him with a resounding thump.

"Well then, in Cockney, the alphabet goes like this:

A for orses
B for mutton
C forth Highlanders
D forential
E va brick
F for vesence
G for Police
H your neighbor
I for Norvello
J for oranges
K for teria
L for leather
M for Sis
N for a penny
O for a cold beer
P for a – damn, I've forgotten. Maybe 'for another penny'
Q for a bus
R for mo
S for Williams
T for two
U for me and me for U
V for la France
W your money
X for breakfast
Y for mistress
Z for his Zat"

"I'll be damned," Jack said. "I got most of it, but I didn't understand J for oranges."

"Jafor was a brand name of a long-gone English company that sold most of the oranges in England."

"I for Norvello?"

"Ivor Norvello, an old English singer and actor. Sort of like Bing Crosby."

Jack finished his breakfast, emptied his coffee, thanked his companion for an interesting conversation and went in search of the Hostel Destiny.

* * *

The establishment consisted of several adjoining rooming houses catering to all manner of itinerant workers, backpackers and resident eccentrics. A lack of planning, carefully executed, had rewarded Jack with a second-floor room in the last house in the row. As he settled into the eight-by-twelve, four-bit room, he didn't exactly feel like he was King of the Road, but decided the space would do just fine for the nonce.

In between his forays into the neighborhood in search of a job, Jack got to know the more singular inhabitants of the Hostel Destiny. There was the Egg Woman, whose nickname was Over Easy. She wasn't a prostitute, although she was known as an enthusiastic amateur. She ate a steady diet of eggs in order to absorb the vital life element in the embryo, and carefully destroyed the shells of the eggs she'd consumed so that they would not be harmed by any black magic that sorcerers might wreak upon them. She preached her cackleberry philosophy to anyone who would listen.

Jack liked eggs himself and wondered who the first guy was who said, *"I'm going to eat the next thing that comes out of this chicken's ass."*

Over Easy believed that eggs could be used for divination, to cure disease, in fertility rites and to explain dreams. A dream about an intact egg meant good luck, while dreaming about broken eggs was a warning of impending conflict.

"Would you like me to tell your fortune?" the Egg Woman asked Jack as he tried to slip past her on the way to his room.

"Why not?" he said, following Over Easy into the communal kitchen, where she put some water on to boil in a saucepan.

.   She asked Jack to select an egg from the carton. Taking it from his hand, she made the sign of the cross over the egg, then cracked it on the rim of the pot. She dropped the egg-white, but not the yolk, into the boiling water, then studied the swirls and shapes the egg-white assumed in the bubbling water.

"What do you see?" asked Jack with growing interest as he looked over her shoulder.

"The swirl around a center blob is a secret group joined by strands of intrigue." Over Easy's voice sounded dreamy. "Here is the Sword of Damocles hanging in the air from a grapevine."

"What do you make of that?"

She peered into his eyes. "You have a secret and you are in imminent danger, my good man. You had best be careful, lest the sword fall upon thy head."

How do you like those apples? Jack asked himself. *I thought this gal was a nutcase, but was that just a lucky guess or what?*

The hostel's warren of rooms was inhabited by a host of characters, caught up in the vortex of whatever destiny had dropped them there. What their real names were and what they were hiding was no one's business but their own. Jack figured he fit right in.

There was Duane Pyppes, an itinerant plumber, several nuts short of a full pouch. He reminded Jack of the famous forties band leader whose publicity used to say, "Eddie Duchin Himself at the Piano!" There was a tough streetwise gal named Connie Lingus, a garbage man named Horst Maneover, a German immigrant they called Herr Dresser and a has-been New Mexico politico named Don Kumbach.

Jack became intrigued with an African-American man with a deeply lined face, who went by the name of Urasmus B. Dragon. Also known as the Candle Man, Urasmus sported a gray, coffee-stained beard and chewed his fingernails.

When Jack asked him his age, he said, "I'm so old that the only thing I can get on is my clothes, and the only thing I can get in is my hearin' aid." Urasmus had a makeshift candle maker's shop in his room, and was adept enough at his craft that his candles were in demand at a few of the city's gift boutiques.

"Why'd you choose a moniker like Urasmus B. Dragon?" Jack asked him.

"People got reasons for not goin' by their right names. I got mine, likely you got yours. I got a story for you, help me make my point."

"Shoot," Jack said.

"This guy was drivin' through Atlanta, Georgia, when a cop stopped him for speedin'. 'Get out of the car,' the cop ordered and the guy did. 'What's your name?' the cop asks. 'Ralph,' the man says. 'I don't want your first name, you moron, what's your last name?' 'I'd rather not say,' the guy tells him. 'Don't gimme a hard time, dipstick, or I'll give you one,' says the cop. 'Now what's your last name?' 'Doodad,' said the man, 'my name's Ralph Doodad!' The cop starts to laugh. 'You see?' says the guy, real choked. 'That's why I didn't wanna tell you. Everyone laughs when I tell 'em my last name. Ever since I was a kid people laughed when I told them, so I tried to compensate by getting real good at everything. I became a doctor, and then I was Ralph Doodad, M.D. I got tired of that and got a dental degree. Then I was Ralph Doodad, M.D., D.D. I went to Mexico and got a social disease and became Ralph Doodad, M.D., D.D., V.D. Then the medical board heard about the venereal disease and jerked my license, and then I was

Ralph Doodad, D.D., V.D. The dental association found out and did the same thing, so then I was Ralph Doodad, V.D. Then the V.D. took over and I lost my Doodad. And then I was just Ralph, which is what I told you in the first place, officer.'"

"Okay," said Jack, when he finished laughing at this ridiculous joke. "Point taken, I get your drift."

Urasmus tried to recruit Jack as a salesman for his candle enterprise. "You could make a lotta money on this one candle alone," said the Candle Man, showing Jack one of the candles.

Jack saw nothing special about it, and said so.

"Why, this candle smells like Jesus! It'll go over real good with people of any religious persuasion. Could be a big seller."

"You figure?"

"Yeah, sure. You light one and everyone in the room says, "Jesus Christ! What's that smell?"

Jack howled with laughter. "How'd you discover a candle like that?" he asked.

"I was researchin' religious history," the Candle Man said, straight-faced. "The first clue I got that there might be somethin' called the odor of Jesus was when I calculated the number of times in the Bible that somebody wanted to wash Jesus's feet. Then I found the formula in a rare letter from Paul to the Judean sect of Aromatherapists. Praise the Lord who makes all candles shine. Please bow your head in prayer."

Jack complied.

"Our Father who art disgusted ..."

"People should not be afraid of their governments.
Governments should be afraid of their people."

— *From the film* V for Vendetta

XXVIII – Long Arm of the Law

Boy Scout Troop 3 maintained a summer camp near Lincoln Park and West Side Avenue near Jersey City, along a small stream that ran below Ravine Drive. It was the only wild spot left in the entire area, where no development was allowed and for which no building permits were issued. Each troop in the surrounding zone had been allotted a section of the wooded ravine, providing an outdoor experience for the city-bred youngsters. Each scout troop included a junior division of Wolf Cubs.

The stream didn't amount to much, but it flowed continuously and every so often provided a pool that served as a swimming hole. The Cubs had a great time learning to burn their food over an open fire, along with the usual knot tying, archery, first aid, camp-fire sing-a-longs and storytelling. They earned badges in various skills, performed community service, and when they got poison ivy the pain was 'in tents'.

Jimmy 'Jockstrap' Jorgensen and his best friend 'Rowdy' Reynolds were out on patrol, following a paper trail laid down the night before by their camp leader. The Cubs were timed to see which two-person team could finish the course in the shortest time, with the proviso that Scout's honor would prevail and no one would tamper with the clues. At each checkpoint the teams had to sign in to prove they'd been there.

"What're you gonna do with that Bible they hand out as a prize?" asked Rowdy as they trudged through the forest. "I know your old man's an atheist. You must be one too, and you lied to get in the Scouts, didn't ya?"

"It was the Christian thing to do. I swore on the Bible. So what? I'm not against readin' it."

"Whatever. But God is the hero of the Bible and we swear to him that we'll do our duty."

"Which is what? My Dad just tells me to use my noggin when I read the Bible. Don't take it too literally, he said, it's just a code of conduct. You can't believe that a corpse can rise from the dead and get beamed up to a place called Heaven, or that a pregnant woman can still be called a virgin."

"Hey, this could be a clue," Rowdy cried. He'd spotted something white on a pile of rocks high up on the embankment. He climbed partway up, then suddenly stopped and called back to Jockstrap, who joined his friend on the slope.

"What does that look like to you?" Rowdy asked.

"Like somebody giving us the finger. Waving maybe? Could be that pair of dorks that started out ahead of us. Let's take a closer look."

The boys scrambled up to the foot of the rock pile.

"That's no clue. Holy mackerel, Rowdy, it's a bloody hand!"

"Yeah, stuck in that crevice. Shit, what are we gonna do?" As his buddy continued to approach the hand, Rowdy yelled, "We gotta call the cops, Jockstrap! Hey, don't touch it!"

"I'm not, I'm just lookin' at it."

"What do you see?" asked Rowdy.

"It's a whole arm. Startin' to go bad. Birds or somethin's been peckin' at it. I think its got a tattoo!"

"Of what?"

"Wow, it's a naked lady!"

* * *

The incident, having passed the first two tests of newsworthiness – cleavage and car wrecks – got a big write-up in the local paper, with pictures of Jockstrap Jorgensen, Rowdy Reynolds, and the tattooed arm. The report made the connection between the discovery of the arm and a recent vehicular fatality on Ravine Drive, and it said the police were following up on this bizarre development. The next day a letter to the editor asked why the cops hadn't found the arm when they investigated the accident, as it likely belonged to the Jack Danielson identified as the deceased whose car had gone over the embankment and exploded.

At the station house the Chief of Police was asking his staff the same question.

"It's a long way from where that Ford Taurus ended up, Chief," said one of the investigating officers. "We did find the license plate part way down the hill; that's the way we I.D.'d Danielson so fast. His body was literally unrecognizable, and the car was in even worse shape."

"Okay, that's understandable. As I recall, we were up to our eyeballs in DUIs at the time," said the Chief, anxious to exonerate his staff. He cursed the coroner, who had to have noticed he had a one-armed body in his morgue.

"Yeah, we did figure the case was solved," the same cop went on. "Danielson was gone and there was nothing much in his estate except personal stuff in a rented house, which we donated to charity. His only next of kin was a sister in L.A., and she couldn't or wouldn't come to the funeral. Neither would his ex-wife, who described him as a jerk. Slippery Jack, she called him, and she said although he was a drunk, he was all foam and no beer."

The Chief suppressed a smile. "Talk about bad luck. He's the only guy I know who has ever been cremated twice."

* * *

Terror is a noun, terrorism just a concept, a tactic – like crimes such as kidnapping journalists, bombing mosques or shooting civilians. It's a tactic used by people who feel threatened and militarily powerless against a much superior force. There is no real defense against terror tactics other than to remove the reasons why people want to use them.

In the American police state there was the Federal Bureau of Investigation, the Central Intelligence Agency, the Drug Enforcement Administration, the Bureau of Alcohol, Tobacco and Firearms, the Department of Homeland Security, the Foreign Intelligence Advisory Board, the Naval Intelligence Branch, the Federal Emergency Management Agency, the National Security Agency, Foreign Intelligence Surveillance, Organized Crime Intelligence Division, the U.S. Secret Service and the Texas Rangers.

Every American state, city, town, municipality and hamlet harbored at least one member of these sundry alphabet agencies tasked with fighting terrorism. In addition, there were various police informants, squealers and stool-pigeons who monitored the news, on the lookout for any suspicious activity they could pass on to the same agencies, in hopes of advancing their careers.

One alert FBI agent glommed onto this news item and decided to visit Slippery Jack Danielson's neighbor, Eileen Dover. She told him that she'd often chatted with Jack while he was mowing the lawn. On hot days, he'd performed the task stripped to the waist and she was positive he had no tattoo of a naked lady on either arm. The agent investigated further and discovered that a local punk by the name of Alphonse 'Duke' Dukowski had sported such a tattoo, and none of his erstwhile companions in crime had seen diddly squat of Duke lately.

* * *

"Son of a bitch! Homeland Security paid two assholes, Harry Palm and Armand Legg, to put the hit on Danielson, and they've fucked it up! They killed the wrong guy and didn't even know it. I want their heads on a platter!"

The speaker was José Cardero, the new top American undercover spymaster, in charge of overseeing traditional human spying activities, or 'humint' in spy vernacular – the information gathered the old-fashioned way, by cold-blooded spies, as opposed to technology. Cardero coordinated all agency operations for the entire intelligence community. He occupied a key position created in the post-September 11 overhaul, devised to make the intelligence community more unified, coordinated and effective. Publicly he was referred to simply as 'José', the head of the National Clandestine Service. Privately, within his own organization, he was known variously as No Way José, or José Can You See.

Even in secret bureaucracies shit flows downhill and in due course, Harry Palm and Armand Legg were called on the carpet by the CIA cutout who'd hired them. They stood in front of his desk, trying to avoid the cold and beady black eyes that were staring at them like they were several fruit loops short of a full bowl.

"The guy's loose somewhere," their paymaster said ominously. "I'm not even sure you two deserve a chance to redeem yourselves by finding him. You took money from me under false pretenses. You were supposed to take Danielson out; you said you knew how to do the job, and you told me you'd done it."

"We could give the money back," Harry said apologetically.

"It's not the money, you morons. Danielson may only be a minor player, but he knows too much. Thanks to you, he knows his suspicions were legitimate, and now he's even more dangerous."

The man thought for a moment, then said, "Okay, you're going to give the money back, and you're going to finish the hit for free. If you fail, you'll be considered expendable, you dumb-ass experiments in artificial stupidity. Now get out of here and get busy."

The two bumblers trudged out of the office, got in their car and drove off, debating how they were going to find their target.

"Where would that son-of-a-slippery Jack go? He'll be just as elusive as *So-Damn-Insane's* weapons of mass destruction."

"And if we don't find him, it will be raining Shi'ites. Let's start checking bus stations, airlines and trains," said Armand. "He must've used one of those to get out of the city."

"That won't help," his partner groused. "He'll have paid cash and he wouldn't have given out a name; certainly not his own."

"Yeah, this is going to be one tough proposition."

"He probably took all his money with him," said Harry, "or stashed it somewhere. I say we check all the local banks for accounts in his name and see if we can track him down that way."

M.O. for the NWO

Restriction of politically incorrect speech in all forms of media
Implementation of martial law and FEMA concentration camps
Gun control laws, leading to elimination of private gun ownership
Introduction of one permitted official 'New Age' worldwide religion

Religious fanatics executed, imprisoned or sent to mental hospitals
Cash money eliminated; all payments made by implanted microchips
Surveillance, implants and mind-control used to keep critics in line
The United States Constitution to be replaced by a UN-style Charter

— Source: Wikipedia, *December 2006*

XXIX – New World Odor

"Truck has started drinking again," Nicolaus D'Amous said to Bob Loblaw. After yesterday's fine fishing, the two men had been too tired to talk about anything but fishing, and went to bed right after dinner. This fine morning, they'd set off at dawn in order to fish at the mouth of a river much farther down the lake. D'Amous had promised not to keep Loblaw in suspense about his 9/11 revelations any longer.

"You should have nicknamed him Label, because he sticks so close to the bottle. When did this Jim Beam and beer start?" asked Bob as the boat motored down the lake.

"When the levees broke in New Orleans, he reached for a Texas-sized shot of whiskey. Strange, because he knew the levees were going to break. I'm going to have to straighten him out, keep him sober until he finishes his term in office. After that, *liquor mortis* can set in, as far as I'm concerned. Still, he has been the perfect pain in the ass. We've rigged two elections for him, and that's all he's constitutionally good for. His approval ratings continue to slip because of faulty intelligence."

"His own, or regarding the WMDs in Iraq?"

"Both would be reasons, but no one talks about weapons of mass destruction anymore. They're starting to sniff around the last two rigged elections."

"What do you mean?" asked Bob.

"Well, the public seems to be onto the vote suppression and fraud, intimidation, ballot-box-stuffing and electronic hacking. However, the mainstream media are ignoring it, so the story's being smothered. Hopefully it's only a tempest in a teapot," said Nick. "Anyway, we've been working hard on a resolution allowing certain people who weren't born in America to run for President. A long shot, I'll admit."

He maneuvered the boat closer to shore and dropped anchor. Nick had decided to switch from spin to fly tackle, and cast a black gnat into an area where the small river ran into the lake. Loblaw prepared to follow suit.

"You're referring to our favorite governor?" Bob asked.

"Yes. If he could run we could elect him fair or foul, he's that popular. The guy's a natural and even stated in his youth that he dreamt of ruling the world. Fine by us, as long as he knows who's really the boss."

"Too bad about Truck," said Bob. "He had some bad old boozing days. If it weren't for the pretzels he'd have been entirely on a liquid diet."

"Well, he was enough of an artful dodger to sit out Vietnam in the National Guard, getting drunk and stupid Stateside, not even showing up for duty. That's really in the man's favor."

"And you have to hand it to the Vice for getting five deferments," Loblaw interjected. "Not an easy thing to do."

"But now Truck's approval ratings are plummeting. He's heading for the dumper, and I almost feel sorry for him." D'Amous reeled in his line and reached for the thermos of hot toddy behind him and passed it to Loblaw. "But we're not on the wagon, so let's have a drink."

"Why not?" Loblaw answered, imbibed freely, then handed the thermos back to D'Amous.

"I may even get primusinterplonkus," said Nick. "Out here I can let my guard down a bit."

Loblaw, whose own drinking habits continued to baffle modern urology, had heard that Nick had a vicious temper. However, he couldn't see how his host would ever let his self-control slip, but he kept that observation to himself.

"I'm babysitting an embarrassment, but the President's not doing any worse than we expected when we put the dipshit into office. He'll soon be used up, like a doped-up horse in his last race." D'Amous switched his fly to a strange concoction with a light orange color on top, dark on the bottom, with a trailing bit of mallard feather to change the silhouette. *Let's see if this will do the trick*, he thought, as he stood up again and made a long cast. The fly drifted slowly on the current until it hit the edge of deeper water. Nick felt a tug and, lifting his rod, set the hook. There was a swirl on the surface and something big began to tear the fly line from his automatic Shakespeare reel. Not giving the trout any sudden slack, Nick let the fish run. Suddenly, a three-pound rainbow arced out of the water and stood on its tail.

Loblaw whooped, "Zowie, that's a keeper!" He reeled in his own line and grabbed the net. "Don't let him throw the hook."

D'Amous played the trout through several runs and gradually worked the beauty to the side of the boat, where Loblaw scooped it up into the net.

Nick plunged his hunting knife through the trout's brain. "I'm taking this one back to Washington," he said. Both men admired the catch for a few moments before casting again.

"This is a terrific spot," Loblaw mused as their lines glinted in the morning sun. "All right, how about the other guy who really keeps this War on Terror going?"

"Who? Osama, the Vice President or Dick Tater at the Pentagon?" D'Amous asked with a sardonic smile. "I think I deserve brownie points for minding all of them. Quite a chore, I can tell you. The Vice is doing a good job of steering the President in the right direction. Bit of a brute, though, like Mussolini, Goering, Goebbels or Hitler. Shares the same kind of swinish hit man mentality and passion for war, without the burden of excess intellectual powers."

"And Osama?"

"Osama is more use to us free and on the loose."

"I've noticed that he's escaped quite a few times."

"You're right, and I'll tell you why. With patience, a terrorist organization can be infiltrated, influenced and ultimately controlled. Al-Qaeda was no different. Osama and his gang were very useful to us in the early years in Afghanistan against the Russians, then later in the Balkans. In 1995, the Sudanese offered us a gold mine of incriminating material on bin Laden and al-Qaeda, but we refused to accept it because we needed him at the time. In July 2001, while he was on the FBI's *Ten Most Wanted List*, he spent ten days secretly at the American Hospital in Dubai, courtesy of the U.S. taxpayer, receiving kidney dialysis. The CIA station chief kept a close eye on him while there. Also, we could've bombed him in Afghanistan, but we didn't. We had him surrounded on three sides when he was holed up in that cave complex in Tora Bora, but we let sympathetic Afghan mercenaries guard the fourth side. Naturally, he escaped into Pakistan as intended."

"What about when the Taliban wanted to put Osama under house arrest and hand him over to the U.S.?" Bob asked.

"They said they'd do so if we could present evidence of his involvement in 9/11. Well, we didn't have any evidence, as you know, and we certainly didn't want to see Osama spilling his guts in a courtroom. That's why we ignored them, let him escape, and started blaming Saddam for 9/11. Later, Osama was declared to be no longer of great importance. As for al-Qaeda, we encourage our media moles to make sure that every terrorist atrocity that occurs anywhere in the world, is somehow *believed to be linked to al-Qaeda*. You've noticed that, I'm sure. Got to keep the fear factor going. Now, if someone were to capture Osama, we'd have to eliminate him. He's old business, but if he's caught, I'm going to be madder than an alley cat in a dog catcher's wagon."

"Some people say Osama is already dead, that he died some time ago," Bob commented.

"I don't think so, but if it were true, and someone produced his body, that would create a big public relations problem for us – how would we explain all those phony Osama videotapes we've been broadcasting over the last four years?"

Staring at his line, Loblaw quietly asked, "Okay, Nick, so we know Osama didn't do it. I'm ready to hear what really happened and how you pulled off the 9/11 attacks."

D'Amous handed Loblaw the thermos again. "I'll tell you, but don't interrupt. I'm only going to tell you once. Now, *de minimus non curat praetor.* Don't bother me with petty matters."

Loblaw simply nodded as he sipped his drink.

Nick took a deep breath and began. "On the morning of September 11, we ran a series of airborne war-games, pre-planned and coordinated through the V.P., calculated to confuse our air defense forces and keep them away from New York and Washington. There was Vigilant Guardian, a hijacking drill; Northern Vigilance, which sent our East coast fighter jets to Alaska and Northern Canada; Northern Guardian, a war-game exercise using both real military and remotely piloted civilian aircraft; a NORAD exercise called Vigilant Warrior; a National Reconnaissance Office exercise simulating a plane crashing into CIA headquarters; and a FEMA exercise in New York involving a biochemical attack. These exercises occurred all at the same time as the real attacks on the WTC, and were used as a cover, part of which involved the injection of false blips onto radar screens."

"There was at least one live-fly hijack exercise, wasn't there?" Loblaw asked. "It involved a government-operated real aircraft posing as a hijacked airliner crashing into buildings including the Twin Towers. Right? That came out in congressional testimony from the fellow who was Joint Chief at the time. Correct?"

"I distinctly remember asking you to hold your questions until I've finished," Nick snapped. "Now, do you want to hear this or not?"

Loblaw's eyes narrowed, but he made no further comment.

"The Twin Towers and Building 7 were brought down by a combination of explosives and the use of pre-positioned cutter charges distributed throughout the towers. Thermate, a combination of finely ground aluminum and iron oxide mixed with two percent sulfur, was used to cut through the steel like a laser beam, producing a whitish smoke and temperatures of more than 4500-degrees Fahrenheit."

D'Amous hauled in his line and leaned the rod against the gunwale as he focused on his tale.

"As you will recall, American Airlines Flight 11 and United Airlines Flight 175 took off from Bostons' Logan Airport; AA Flight 77 took off from Dulles Airport in Virginia; and UA Flight 93 departed from Newark, New Jersey. Once they were in the air, they were all taken over by remote control. Next their transponders and radios were turned off. Then the passengers and crews were killed by depressurizing the planes, which is the easiest, cleanest, quickest way to eliminate the human factor, and is far less detectable than other methods such as nerve gas."

Loblaw's nose hairs literally curled, his throat convulsed and a spray of alcohol shot from his mouth as he spluttered and coughed, but he said nothing.

Nick smiled and continued. "It was accomplished using remote control technology originally designed to rescue hijacked planes. Ever wonder why none of the eight real pilots and co-pilots punched in the hijack code of 7700? All they had to do was press a few buttons, right in front of them on the panel. Thus all passengers and alleged hijackers were eliminated as witnesses.

"Well anyway, Flights 11 and 175 flew their predestined circuitous routes into the Twin Towers and we shot down Flight 93 over Pennsylvania. But Flight 77 was a little more challenging. You may be wondering why we decided to switch it for a 'missile' – as Dick Tater called it in *Parade* magazine. Well, we couldn't risk trying to hit the Pentagon in the least vulnerable spot with a real Boeing 757, because it would have been too difficult to pull off without the risk of something going wrong. What we needed was a plane that looked like a 757, but was as accurate as a cruise missile. The solution? A remote-controlled Global Hawk with a wing span of 115 feet, which is only 10 feet smaller than a 757. It fooled a lot of people, as you know.

"Less known is that the Pentagon had just completed a five-year renovation program, that very day, designed to reinforce the west wing which was nearly vacant of personnel. A Global Hawk crashing into that location would do the least amount of damage to the Pentagon, keep the military casualties to a minimum, and, would do no harm to the Department of Defense big shots stationed on the opposite side of the building who would be celebrating the 60th anniversary of the start of construction of the Pentagon that very morning.

"We wanted a reasonably plausible story that Flight 77, piloted by an Arab terrorist, had done the job – which would cause another 'helpful wave of indignation' – that we could ride into the Middle East. Also, we figured that the background debate as to what really hit the Pentagon would later wreak havoc in any 9/11 skeptics' movement.

"The plane switch took place at a closed-down air force base in West Virginia where we got rid of all the bodies. However, we kept some pre-distressed body fragments to ship off to the same morgue as the Pentagon rubble. Later, the body parts were identified by innocent military forensic doctors. Of course, all the standard post-disaster investigation policies and procedures were circumvented.

"So what, you ask, happened to the real Flight 77 plane? Under cover of darkness it was later flown by remote control out over the Atlantic and scuttled. Ended up in pieces on the bottom of the ocean."

Loblaw permitted himself an "Ah."

"And you'd want to know how we came up with the fake phone calls so quickly? Software exists for real time voice emulation using a sample of the person's voice. You plan ahead, that's how. Then Bingo! You've got your bogus evidence to confuse the skeptics. You know who some of the passengers will be, well ahead of time, by checking who purchased tickets on those flights. NSA phone surveillance is not new. Spooks gather voice samples to create fake phone calls all the time.

"Keep in mind that without special equipment, phone calls from that height and speed are impossible, but not many have figured that out. The alleged key-defining fake phone call of them all, was the one where the 'box-cutters' part of the official myth came from – which was later reinforced in bullshit propaganda movies like *United 93*. The guy who reported that call from his wife on Flight 77, Fred Molson, was a total insider. Actually he's one of the lawyers that persuaded the Supreme Court to get the President appointed in 2000, and who is on record saying it's okay for governments to lie to their people under certain circumstances – therefore a very dependable guy."

D'Amous held out the flat of his hand toward Loblaw. "I know, you're going to ask what happened to Flight 93. Shanksville,

Pennsylvania, may be in the middle of nowhere, but Indian Lake is highly visible from the air and was a good place over which to shoot down Flight 93. It disintegrated into very small pieces, scattering debris and other remains over the lake and nearby town of Indian Lake. A missile was then fired into the general area, to create a misleading crater near Shanksville, into which Flight 93 was said to have disappeared, leaving what looked, to some, like the debris of a crashed plane, in a small hole in the ground. We covertly had a truckload of scrap metal, from a nearby scrap yard, dumped into the hole for good measure. Strangely enough, very few picked up on the shoot down, despite the eight mile wide displacement of the plane's debris – one engine was found 2000 yards away!"

Bob's head was bobbing and his lips were moving. Nick nodded his permission to speak. "What about the hijackers?"

"There were no Arab hijackers on any of the planes and many weren't even in the United States on 9/11. In fact, no hijackers' names showed up on any passenger lists, and those faces you saw of Mohamed Atta and his buddy at the boarding gate were recorded much earlier. Our cover story has them all dead along with the passengers and crews. But glitches do occur and as many as seven are reported to still be alive in the Middle East, but not by major media in the States. Luckily only a small percentage of the public pays any attention to the British news. It just shows how easily the American public can be fooled.

"The alleged Arab hijackers who did take flight lessons prior to 9/11 were patsies, marching to the tune of our moles, and simply used to aid and abet the cover story. Before 9/11 these patsy Arabs were an essential part of the plan and could not be allowed to be rounded up and put out of action. Their presence as scapegoats was indispensable to the entire operation, because they were needed for propaganda purposes later. It wasn't an Arab sitting in an Afghanistan cave that defeated the air defense system of the world's sole military superpower. That was a patently ridiculous conspiracy theory at the get-go, with the least probability of any scenario, but the public ate it up because we pounded it into them courtesy of our friends in the mainstream media. On 9/11 we had full control over all defense, war-games and counter-terrorism departments.

"Okay Bob," said Nick, as he finished his explanation, "now you can open your trap."

As Loblaw shook his head in amazement, D'Amous picked up his rod again and attached a new dry fly. He cast sixty feet upstream and let it float down and across the current.

Loblaw remained seated. "That's incredible Nick! You're to be congratulated on pulling off perhaps the greatest scam of all time. But what about the lesser bureaucratic lights in our own government? Many of them must have known parts of the plan. Don't you think some of them might be tempted to talk?"

"The United States has been practicing false-flag operations for over a century, Bob, like 'Remember the Maine', the 'Gulf of Tonkin' incident and 'Operation Northwoods,' for example. A few people might have been appalled at the end result of what we'd planned, but not to the degree they'd jeopardize their careers. If we suspect that might change, the CIA will deal with them, as they've done in the past. Public scrutiny in matters like 9/11 has to be blocked, because the planning started years earlier and was developed slowly. High-level instructions were issued to the FBI and CIA to curtail investigations into 9/11 before it even happened – like Pentagon's Able Danger program which tracked al-Qaeda cells inside our borders. It was shut down just before the attacks.

"After 9/11, the Department of Justice wanted everyone to understand that this was now just a crime investigation – as opposed to an investigation into some covert operation – and that how and why it happened no longer mattered. This has, we hope, prevented further public scrutiny of any discrepancies. All FBI and CIA Directors were trained to do just that – block widely-known and discussed information from further investigation. They derailed attempts at taking preventative measures, using high-level directives, later claiming that any foreknowledge of 9/11 was newly discovered information that had not been previously known. Now they're deliberately withholding details about the alleged hijackers, where they trained in the U.S., why their names were missing on the official flight manifests, or any other specifics of what they knew, which was plenty – all part of the *modus operandi* of 9/11. The top strata of our intelligence agencies has unilaterally vetoed all routine appeals for action from their own counter-terrorist experts."

"I figured the investigation by the 9/11 Commission was a stroke of distortion genius," said Bob. "But I've noticed that some alternative press articles now refer to it as the '9/11 Omissions Commission'."

"Yeah, essentially it was the White House investigating itself, by ex-FBI, ex-CIA, and ex-Department of Justice ringers. Guylain Bardow, the Executive Director, ran the show and wrote the report. His job was to make sure that only the falsified White House version of events was ever considered, and that the government story about the 19 Muslim hijackers was taken as the gospel truth from the inception of the investigation. As Bardow himself has said, and rightly so, he wasn't going to dignify any other outrageous conspiracy theories by investigating or even reporting on the evidence. There hasn't been a bigger whitewash job since Tom Sawyer painted his sorry fence."

"I noticed the 9/11 Commission didn't even mention the policy of the New World Order, as stated in the *Project for the New American Century,*" said Loblaw.

"Yes, and derived from Zbigniew Brzezinski's 1997 book, *The Grand Chessboard,*" Nick replied, "where Zbig suggested that America's immediate task was to develop and simultaneously control a direct external threat which could be used to manufacture an attack like a new Pearl Harbor. Once the Cold War ended and we lost the *Evil Empire* as a foe, we required a new, credible and well-developed enemy. That's when PNAC, in its September 2000 report *Rebuilding America's Defenses,* stated the need for another Pearl Harbor-type attack. It would then provide a pretext for a massive military intervention in the Middle East to secure all that oil and gas that has been up for grabs since the Soviet Union buckled. But the mention of all this preplanning would not have looked too good in *The 9/11 Commission Report.* Right?"

"That's for sure," Bob remarked, "and there was certainly no censure of the people who were in charge of military defenses on 9/11, including the Chairman of the Joint Chiefs of Staff, the head of NORAD, and the Secretary of Defense."

"Certainly not," said Nick. "They were all commended for a job well done, especially Bardow. Since being put in charge of the commission, he has been made Counselor of the Department of State. Do you remember that in 1997, he coauthored a book with Truck's former National Security Advisor? Well he's now working with her again, as her senior policy advisor."

As if by unspoken agreement, both men hauled in their lines and D'Amous started up the motor. "This has been a damn good fishing trip, Bob, and it's been a pleasure to talk to you about things I couldn't possibly discuss with anyone else. Too bad I've got to go back to work soon. Gotta rachet up the fear factor again and raise the national threat level to orange, maybe even red."

"Is there evidence of a new terror threat?"

"Are you kidding?!" D'Amous said, as they headed for the lodge. "We're marketing terror 'til hell freezes over. We've got a crack team of strategist shit-shovellers in the Murdoch Manure Brigade, who are more than capable of keeping the

War on Terror front and center in the minds of John Q. Public. All this requires is constant reinforcement of fear and outrage in order to reap the benefits. So in the years following 9/11, all the administration will have to do is devise another and more ingeniously staged false-flag extravaganza to arouse fear and trembling in the global community of subservient citizens. Let's call it 9/11-2B."

"Meaning what?" Loblaw asked.

"Meaning it's not a matter of *if* it's going 2B, but a matter of *when* it's going 2B. Because we don't want any radical transition of power in the coming elections, such as an uncontrollable Democratic win in either the House or the Senate, which might result in independent investigations of the GWOT."

"The what?"

"The Global War on Terror," D'Amous replied. "Our goal is to lay the groundwork for a nuclear attack on Iran. It may involve exploding a low-yield tactical nuclear weapon at some distance from an American port."

Loblaw stepped out of the boat onto the dock and stared at D'Amous.

"You're looking a bit pale, Bob," D'Amous commented. "*Excitus acta probat.* The end justifies the means. Americans would be told that the ship bearing the weapon had been discovered and intercepted just in time, and towed to a safe distance away before the bomb went off, keeping death and destruction to a minimum. Then we'd say that Iran was to blame. We already have black-op teams in Iran trying to create an incident to destabilize the country. The ultimate form of control is fear, and that would be maximized. Fear and outrage would again blind the American people to the aims of our New World Order.

"Orwell's *1984*," said Bob. "All the alerts come to nothing. Occasionally an authentic terror attack occurs. No one can discover its real source, but it's blamed on the enemy *du jour.*"

"Yeah, we could say that the evil Canadians hate us, that they were going to storm across the border," Nick fantasized. "That hundreds of thousands of crazy Canucks had been unleashed and were about to come through our windows and doors with hockey sticks clenched in their hands, and nothing to protect us from being raped and murdered in our beds but the North Dakota National Guard. The American public would be sucked right in, and demand large numbers of police and troops on the streets, in the subways, on buses and ferries, a fence along the border. Random bag searches would be the norm, as everyone, even little kids, would have to be considered as possible terrorists, so as not to give the impression that the police were profiling according to age, race, gender or religion. They'd demand that we bomb Toronto in retaliation ..."

"And, at the same time, let the authorities trample all over the people's civil liberties, right?" Loblaw said vehemently. "Most of them are so stupid, they think the St. Louis Cardinals are appointed by the Pope."

"Or that the Kentucky Derby is a hat," said Nick.

Both men laughed as they stepped inside the lodge.

"Seriously Nick, if we're being frank with one another," Loblaw said as they flopped down into lounge chairs, "how are you going to achieve primacy? Nuclear weaponry may no longer be enough."

"The weaponization of space," D'Amous answered without hesitation. "What the U.S. Space Command calls *full spectrum dominance*. You've seen the patches on their uniforms, 'Masters of Space.' If we can aim space-based weapons against our enemies, we won't have to send troops to God-forsaken hell-holes like Iraq, Iran and North Korea. One salvo from space and all the other recalcitrants would get in line to do our bidding."

"An expensive proposition, I'm sure. How's the program coming along?"

"We need at least a trillion dollars. Problem is the American people won't keep giving more money to the military unless we continue to scare the living bejesus out of them. We've already raided Social Security, so there's nothing left there. Fortunately, there's still the civil service pension fund, and the middle class still have a big stash of cash we can target. Medicare and social services may have to go. We have to get our hands on all those funds, because as Lyndon Johnson said back in 1957, '*Space is the ultimate position from which total control of the Earth may be exercised.*' That's why we didn't ratify the Moon Treaty in 1979, which would have preserved space for peaceful purposes and secured all its resources as mankind's common heritage. Instead, we intend to fight in and from space with hit-to-kill mechanisms that engage terrestrial targets on land, sea or air. What we need is an arsenal with the ability to take out any satellites another nation might try to rely on, for anything from emergency communications to wireless bank transfers. In short, to deny others the use of space should we deem it advantageous."

"With what kind of an arsenal?" Bob asked.

"We're working on space-based lasers and kinetic energy weapons – munitions that work on radio frequency or high-power microwaves. There are directed-energy weapons that use millions of watts of power and large optical weapons that could deliver speed-of-light knockout punches to any nation of our choosing. We're aiming to have unilateral space control by the year 2020, at which time all other nations will have to kowtow to America."

"I'm duly impressed, Nick," Loblaw said. "From the time I first met you, I knew you were an evil genius."

D'Amous decided to take that as a compliment.

"Well, I look forward to spending the next two days with you," Loblaw continued. "The fresh air, the fishing and the bracing conversation are doing wonders for me."

"As Uncle Hugh used to say, 'If we remembered everything, 'stead of what we want to remember, we'd all be too ashamed to come out of the outhouse'."

— Lone Star Iconoclast, *Columnist Don M. Fisher*

XXX – Judith Priest, Shirley Knott & the Velvet Glove

"It's the educational system, or the lack of it, that keeps you dumb enough to enlist," Bill said quietly to Zack. "If I'd known I was just going to be an expendable cog in a military machine stuck in Iraq, I wouldn't have joined up."

"Yeah, screwed by the State," Zack said, as he dragged himself into a more upright position in his bed and fought with the pillows for a moment. "We were raised to be fools and tools. Grade school, you barely learn to read and write, and they turn you into a zombie who doesn't question the official version of history. But I'm beginning to smarten up now."

"Only about sixty percent of the population can read with any degree of effectiveness, despite the billions they spend on education," Bill groused drowsily. "Something's wrong when you have a class in drumming five days a week. I did that, for Christ's sake! My school was more like an entertainment center. Sports, music, art, but not much political science, world history or social studies. Just the usual bullshit about the great ol' U.S. of A …"

Zack saw that Bill was finally drifting off to sleep. He didn't feel like sleep himself, so he put his head back and thought over what he'd found out about Nicolaus D'Amous, the man who'd been so nice to him and who had promised to visit again. Given what he'd heard earlier from Bill, Zack had felt it prudent to dig up some background on D'Amous.

In years gone by, Congress had resolutely blocked passage of legislation that would allow the spreading of religious views in publicly funded government programs. Undeterred, the Religious Right had used their clout to establish beachheads in a host of federal agencies. Once inside, these people had diverted funding to programs supporting radical religious groups. Seeding key government offices with disciples of the Far Right had helped to cement a vast network of Christian fundamentalist organizations, whose political aims could finally be realized. The architect of this covert restructuring was none other than Nicolaus D'Amous, the most powerful White House advisor since the days of Herbert Hoover.

Zack had been appalled to discover how pervasive Christian fundamentalism had become in American public life. The Far Right wasn't far away from controlling most of the country's economy and its government at all levels, not to mention the prayer meetings in the Oval Office.

That morning Zack had watched a televised interview with a Bible brandisher named Mosey Long. Zack had been about to change channels when Bill exclaimed that he'd seen the preacher at the same convention where he'd met Nicolaus D'Amous. So they had listened to the program.

"The free market, free trade economic system is a perfectly designed instrument to reward Christian behavior and to punish the unrepentant," Long said in the interview. "And who are we to question a system blessed by the Creator himself? The trials and tribulations of hard labor, hunger and poverty are inflicted on working people as earthly tests of sinfulness and virtue, and are a necessary atonement for their original sin. Helping people out of poverty would endanger their immortal souls."

"Amen to that," said the saintly helmet-haired television host. "Any conduct – especially sexual – which deviates from biblical orthodoxy must be condemned. We must try to save the people from the evil twins, Sin and Satan, and be strong enough to smite our foes. That is God's will, is it not, Reverend Long?"

"That's right, sir. And if the infidels won't be saved, then to Hell with them! In the words of General Custer, 'We'll bring peace to this land, even if we have to shoot them all.' We must use the law to impose true belief and behavior on our fellow citizens, for their own good and ultimate salvation. We must prepare them for the Rapture!"

After a commercial break, the station had shown pictures of a string of fresh-faced young men and women being offered Bible sets, chances to win trips to religious retreats and tips on Christian home decorating. When the station cut back to the interview, Mosey Long launched into a fiery wrap up:

"Armageddon and the Apocalypse of the Second Coming are almost upon us. It will culminate in a world-destroying showdown between the forces of Good and Evil. Those who are pure, those who are virtuous true-believers, will be spared the gruesome fate of the evildoers, and will be transported directly to Heaven. There they will sit at God's side, to watch gleefully as our enemies below are annihilated. Christ will return to escort the deserving living directly into Heaven, where they will be joined by the deserving dead, who will be resurrected and restored to an incorruptible state. This will be preceded by years of tribulation and war, culminating in the final Armageddon in the Middle East. Nuclear holocaust is to be encouraged as a purifying agent, not prevented, and we now have that most powerful disciple of the Lord, the President of the United States, with his finger on the red button."

Zack, who was feeling drowsy himself, imagined telling a political fairy tale to the grandchildren he would never have: 'Twas the night before Armageddon and all through the White House of the faith-based presidency, the ultra-religious were stirring. This was the reign of the Mayberry Machiavellis ...'

He chuckled softly, starting to fall asleep, then shivered as he realized that *after Iraq, the next American target would be Iran. After that, what? World War Three?*

Those were his last thoughts until he awoke to the sounds of a lively exchange between Bill and the other jarheads in the room, on the topic of how to get laid in spite of their various physical handicaps.

"It's a prob-prob-problem all right," Bill stammered. "I don't know the answer."

"Least you got your arms and legs," one grunt complained. "And I've seen that hottie that comes to see you. She your girlfriend?"

"Yeah, she is. So just knock it off, she's not about to g-g-g-give you a ha-ha-ha-hand job, if that's what you're after."

Over the raucous laughter of the others, the same grunt said, "Hey, I'm serious. What are we supposed to do about sex?"

"Don't play with your rifle, Mac, it goes off too easily!" offered a stocky veteran who'd lost both hands.

A third GI chimed in with, "Didn't you read that sign in the men's can – *Be a man, not a fool. Pull the chain, not your tool!*"

"Whack it. Whack it. I'll hold your jacket," said another, laughing gleefully.

When the laughter had died down, Zack said, "I heard there are some women in the hospital somewhere – I don't know if they're employees, pros or whatever – but they'll help you out. I don't know what the deal would be, but I've heard it's available."

"How do you find them?" asked the handless vet. "I'm so horny I could screw the crack of dawn."

Zack grinned and said, "Ask an orderly if you can talk to Judith Priest, Shirley Knott or the Velvet Glove."

* * *

Jack Danielson caught the story about the Wolf Cubs finding the severed arm with the nude tattooed on it. *Damnation!* Jack thought. *Screwed by a tattooed tart.* He knew he'd have to keep his eyes peeled, because the people who'd been following him would soon be back on his tail again.

Jack needed to find work somewhere. He couldn't just sit around the Hostel Destiny contemplating his navel. Walking through some of the poorer areas of Washington, Jack had observed scores of needy families. Children, the disabled and senior citizens, in particular, depended heavily on food banks to get enough to eat. If Jack's grandfather were still alive, he would have said he hadn't seen so much homelessness and hunger since the Great Depression, and he would have been right.

If Jack didn't secure steady work soon, he'd run out of money and end up as poor as any of the wretches he'd seen in D.C. He concentrated his search on places where few questions would be asked about his background and his I.D. wouldn't be checked too closely. As before, that meant menial work at minimum wage.

The area's biggest employers were the hospitals, which always needed cheap labor to do the dirty work. On a community bulletin board close to the hostel, Jack saw ads for work in the maintenance section of the Walter Reed Medical Center. He turned up there the same day.

The only question he was asked was whether he'd had any experience in janitorial work.

About as much time as I've had in bed with virgins, thought Slippery Jack. "A little," he said aloud, and they hired him, just like that.

> "Give any one species too much rope
> and they'll fuck it up."
>
> — *Roger Waters*

> "Which would be funny if it wasn't
> so damn painful."
>
> — *Michael Nenonen*

XXXI – Ugly on a Gorilla

Jack Danielson had joined the marines in '87 upon graduating from high school and served in Iraq in Desert Storm, back in '91. While there, he'd been exposed to certain chemicals, drugs and vaccines. For a very short period he had been at the Khamiseyeh arsenal in southern Iraq where 15,000 soldiers might have been exposed to the highly toxic nerve agent sarin and possibly to mustard gas. The United States government knew that Saddam Hussein had this kind of material because, as the joke went, *they had the receipts to prove it.*

Years had passed by without any appreciable health problems, but now at the age of 36, Jack began to notice some worrisome and debilitating symptoms, a problem that was plaguing many veterans. He had spells of dizziness, lack of energy, occasional difficulty in swallowing, and his chest hurt. One problem he was having, which probably came from being exposed to the powdered glass on 9/11, were spells of blurred vision in his left eye. Seeking to correct the condition he went to see an optometrist, who asked him to look at eye charts through his optical equipment.

The eye doctor placed a single letter on the chart – an 'F'. "Close your right eye and tell me what letter you see with your left?"

"K," said Jack.

"Not correct," said the Doc, adjusting the optic machinery.

It's an 'F'. Try again at this new setting."

Jack took a long blurred look, then said, "Looks like a 'K' to me."

"No. That's still an 'F'," said the Doc. "Let's try again." Which they did with the same result.

"How come," said the Doc to Jack, "every time I see F you see K?"

* * *

In talking to other vets at the hospital, Jack learned that there were far worse symptoms to be suffered if he had indeed contracted Gulf War Syndrome. Loss of balance, memory loss, swollen lymph nodes, fever, personality changes, diarrhea, excruciating pain, severe sleep apnea, cardiac murmurs, upper respiratory problems, nausea, MS – you name it, they were getting it.

The media, in fact, had reported that there were very few U.S. casualties in Desert Storm, whereas, in fact, if you included those with Gulf War Syndrome there had been at least 100,000 – many more than that, if you included Iraqis. The Department of Veteran Affairs' was involved in a whitewash regarding veterans' illnesses. They refused to acknowledge the problem, and their medics stated that these ailments were being imagined. They claimed there wasn't enough evidence to link long-term health problems of Gulf War veterans with exposure to drugs, chemicals and vaccines while serving in Iraq and Afghanistan. Therefore, no conclusions could be drawn.

Jack didn't figure there was any genetic link to the symptoms he was experiencing, but thought maybe he should explore the possibility, as well as get a thorough check-up. But how could he do either without leaving a paper trail? He'd have to declare his real identity to the DVA.

Jack knew that by using tracking devices, security agencies and police could surreptitiously locate citizens via their cellphones, wireless internet connections, global positioning systems, wireless personal digital assistants, BlackBerrys and laptop computers, often even when the devices were turned off or their location features disabled. This was the case with any device that had both active and passive components; the active component could be controlled by the user, who could turn the machine on or off, but the passive device could be built in and accessible to the police at any time.

Jack believed the government had already built this plan into the electronic surveillance provisions of the Patriot Act. The President was already being criticized for authorizing secret surveillance of American citizens without obtaining proper judicial approval. But impeaching their leader for illegal wire-tapping would be like booking Jack the Ripper for littering. *How about indictment for complicity in 9/11, and the death of three thousand that day, and the tens of thousands in Afghanistan and Iraq later?* he thought. The President had surrounded himself with devious whisperers that filled his ear with comforting delusions; the most fatal being that he was invincible. As a backup plan, the President forced the Detainee Bill through Congress, although Jack preferred to call it the Death of the Constitution Act.

Jack felt that this invasion of the basic right to anonymity in free and democratic communities was becoming insidious in a society with such an incredible density of interconnectivity. Technology was rapidly making it increasingly difficult to remain anonymous anywhere in the world.

Slippery Jack was only too aware that the CIA operated on the assumption that everyone should be trackable, whether they wanted to be or not. So he no longer used a cellphone. If he wanted to use a computer he went to the public library. But how long would he have to wait before something either fortuitous or disastrous happened? What do you do when those who are supposed to protect you are the ones who are trying to kill you? He thought about blowing the whistle, but to whom could he blow it? They'd only call him a conspiracy wingnut – which really was nothing more than somebody who disagreed with the liars and whores of the press, the government and their intelligence agencies.

The more Jack thought about his situation, the more convinced he became that he had to do something. Everyone was afraid to stand up to the ruthless villains who were terrorizing the United States. There was really no one to complain to because everyone in charge had been hand-picked by, or was in cahoots with Big Nick the Sheriff and his Republican deputies, none of whom had been honestly elected but had instead bought their seats. There was no use going to the courts for help or to complain about abuse of power, because the courts didn't give a rodent's ass about anybody being free and equal. They were on the sheriff's payroll. And if you wanted to get gunned down on Main Street, in broad daylight, then just start disagreeing with the sheriff or any of his deputies. They could be downright mean and rotten when they ran you out of town.

The most revolting part of this whole scenario was that the sheriff was not the top man. He took his orders from an organization of slimy bushwhackers and rotten backshooters who crawled the desert sands of the wild west trying to steal everything you had, including your face. The Global Union, who employed Big Nick and his minions, never went out and did the dirty work themselves, because they could always hire plenty of willing varmints to do whatever rotten job they wanted done, while they hid safely under rocks like reptiles.

Like a rose, Jack had the feeling that someone was going to pluck him again. He didn't expect John Wayne to come riding into town on his snorting, sweating, spavined stallion, swagger into the stinking smoke of a shitty saloon and save his sorry ass. Like the Indians who doubted that the coming of the Iron Horse would bring them prosperity, Jack had reservations.

This was planet Earth in the 21st Century and not some western movie. And yet someone had to stop this band of hoodlums, these Asses of Evil, from taking control of the world before it was too late.

Too many Americans didn't want to investigate what had really happened on 9/11, mainly because they couldn't believe their government would attack its own people, then lie about it, despite the fact that their government had done just that so many times before. Something had to be done about it.

* * *

Harry was nothing but highly pleased as he broke the news to Armand. "They checked every fucking bank in Jersey and they got a trace on Danielson! The stupid motherfucker transferred thirty-three thousand dollars from his bank here to their branch in Washington, D.C."

"I'm surprised," said Armand. "He did such a damn good job of jacking us around the first time."

"Enough with the puns," said Harry.

"He just got unlucky, and all because of a lousy tattoo. I wish he'd gotten away with it. He'd be off the hook and so would we."

"But since we now find ourselves upon that hook, let's get our butts down to Washington and find the bum."

"It's a big mess down there – not going to be easy."

"Yeah, but he has to contact that bank sooner or later."

"And when he does?"

"His ass is in a sling. I've already made arrangements that we be immediately notified when he does. The bank will delay him, and –"

"And we'll be onto him like ugly on a gorilla." said Armand.

"Then drop him like a nun with a bad habit!" quipped Harry.

* * *

As an ex-soldier himself, Slippery Jack was happy that he had all his legs, arms and other body parts, along with his eyesight and hearing; so he felt a sense of guilt when he suddenly found himself in the midst of many who had not been so lucky in that regard. He didn't feel so hot himself these days, but he felt a surge of anger at all the stupid wars that produced these wounded souls, and the people who had caused them through faulty reasoning, avarice and self-aggrandizement. Now that he was working at Walter Reed every day, he hoped to be able to accomplish something other than mopping and sweeping the floors.

They had put him to work on the night shift at the hospital. He was shoving a push broom down the vacant pale-green hallways, to be followed later by a mop. The place was spooky in the middle of the night and Jack had the momentary sensation of having been abducted by aliens. It was the same feeling he used to have after drinking a bottle of vodka, when he'd invariably wake up in a strange place the following morning, having had his memory mysteriously erased. To cheer himself up, Jack sang softly to himself, *Two hours of pushing broom, buys an eight by twelve foot room. I'm a man of means, by no means, King of the Road!*

These were the wee hours of the morning when you heard an awful lot of Frank Sinatra, whenever you turned the radio on to a golden oldies station. Every time Jack heard Frank sing *'One more for my baby and one more for the road'*, one more time, Jack was sure he was going to get a 'sexual concussion' – that is, a fucking headache.

A strange sound interrupted his train of thought. He turned off his Walkman. Directly in front of him, the door to one of the wards was closed, but he could hear the low murmur of voices as he got closer to it. Maybe he should go in and check it out.

Silently he stepped into the room and listened to the conversation coming from behind the curtains of the first two beds. Jack coughed, the voices stopped and he whispered, "Hi, what's going on? Can I come in?"

The sudden silence was so great you could hear a horse turd drop, a mile off, in the snow. Then a whisper came back, "Sure. Who are you?"

Jack parted the curtains, stepped inside and found himself between the beds of two GIs who introduced themselves.

Jehovah:
"Did I ever mention publicly how Hell got started?
I don't think I ever did. It was this way: I thought I'd do
something nice for a lot of theologians who had, after all,
been doing the best they could, according to their lights;
so I gave them an enormous tract of Heaven to do what they
pleased with – set it apart for them to inhabit and administer.
I didn't pay any attention to it for a thousand years, and when
I looked at it again, they'd made it into Hell."

— Donald Robert Perry Marquis (1878-1937)
Chapters for the Orthodox

XXXII – Is There a Hope in Hell?

"I take it that sleep, the poor man's wealth, is not easily
come by?" Jack Danielson quietly asked the two veterans lying
in the beds at one end of the ward.

"Do we have a philosopher in our midst?" Bill asked.

"Nope, just your local janitor," Jack replied, giving his
broom a shove along the floor to prove his point. "Is this a
private conversation, or can anyone butt in?"

"We're just discussing our options," said Zack, "and
coming to the conclusion that we don't have many. I'm Zack
Zapata and this is Bill Bailey. So now you know our names,
what's yours?"

"I'm Jack O'Reilly," said Jack, nodding to both men in
turn.

"Oh really?" said Bill Bailey.

"No, O'Reilly."

"So tell us something Irish, O'Reilly."

Jack went with the first thing that came to mind. "The only
thing worth having in this earthly existence is a good sense of
humor."

That got big smiles and Zack said, "Good advice. Bill and I were just kicking around some thoughts on how we ended up stuck in this hospital, and you certainly need a sense of humor to consider that."

"Did you get it figured out?"

Jack, seeing Zack struggle to drag himself upright in the bed, went to help him adjust his pillows. Once he was comfortable, Zack spoke up. "It's the politicians running this country that head the list of who's responsible for all of us being in here." He waved his good arm to indicate the entire ward. "The official story about 9/11, and why we went to war in Afghanistan and Iraq, is full of holes. What bugs me is they keep changing the details. We were just trying to figure out what the truth is, that's all."

"Yeah, like how reinforced concrete can get pulverized into tiny particles and be exploded outward into what looked like a volcanic dust cloud. As if gravity can do that? I don't think so," said Bill. But, turning cautious, he added, "You can join in if you want, unless you're a die-hard Republican, or just not interested in any of this."

Jack said slowly, "Well, yes, I agree that the government's official story doesn't add up, but I've also seen evidence of what they do to people who try to point that out, or who just happen to know too much about what they're really up to."

Making up his mind to join them, Jack grabbed a chair and set it down between the two beds. "Their explanations are a total fabrication of lies, but you have to be careful how and to whom you express your views these days – especially after they passed Patriot Acts One and Two, which put the law on the side of anyone who wants to shut you up."

Bill and Zack began to warm up to their visitor, visibly relaxing when he told them about his Desert Storm experiences. The three continued their conversation, quietly into the night.

They agreed that all levels of government seemed to be filled with dangerous and incompetent narcissists, lunatic deviants and garden variety criminals who were out to loot the country for their own benefit. All the average Joe got out of the deal was a dose of clap and a second mortgage.

"My fiancée, Helen Weills, is coming by on the weekend," Bill told Jack with a shy grin. "Do you suppose you could buy a box of chocolates for me and drop it off on your next shift?"

Jack said he'd be happy to do it, then admitted he personally never wanted to get married again. "First there's sex in the kitchen, then sex in the bedroom, then sex in the halls, if you know what I mean. That's when you pass each other in the hall and you both say, 'Fuck you!' It's cheaper just to find someone you hate and buy them a house."

"Not gonna happen to me and Helen," Bill declared.

"Aw, I'm just kiddin'," Jack said. "I wish you wedded bliss." He got up and returned the chair to its place in the corner. "I've got a couple of floors left to clean, so I'd better get back to work. And you guys should try to get some sleep."

"Say, Jack, want to come by again tomorrow evening and talk? That's fine with us. Right, Bill?"

"By all means," Bill replied. "We could use some company. Maybe we could put our heads together and see if we come up with some answers to the mess this administration's gotten us into."

"Scraping the bottom of the barrel there," said Jack. "You couldn't get a bunch of bastards more dangerous to our freedom and democracy than this cabal."

Jack stepped back into the hallway and then strolled down to the supply room for a mop and bucket of hot soapy water. He was duly impressed with the two soldiers he'd just met. They were obviously hurting, especially Zack, but they didn't bitch, whine, sob or complain.

He couldn't tell them that he was one of the few people being hunted down because he knew too much about the 9/11 cover-up. Just to think, he and his good buddy Sean Hennessey had placed dozens of thermate charges in the basement of each of the World Trade Center Towers, which resulted in two large clouds of white smoke at street level ten seconds before the collapse of each tower. Scientific records had proven the ground shook prematurely on the seismic scale. A great many people had seen those pictures on the Internet. That, of course, coupled with the two tons of pre-planted explosives placed elsewhere throughout the entire structure of the buildings, was what had caused the collapse.

Jack had no doubt that a great deal of key 9/11 evidence had been seized, suppressed, or faked by the FBI and the CIA. In criminal trials, evasiveness, obstruction and destruction of evidence constituted strong circumstantial evidence that the accused was guilty, or at least not to be believed.

The administration was covering things up, so that the official Arab hijacker story would hold up. However, even by government standards, gross incompetence could not explain the systematic failure of the 9/11 Commission to follow the normal procedures of investigation into the crime of 9/11.

That's why the sons of bitches that liquidated Sean, as a basic security measure, are trying to deep six me as well, Jack thought. *Is there no arrest for the wicked?*

"Razors pain you,
Rivers are damp,
Acids stain you,
And drugs cause cramp.
Guns aren't lawful,
Nooses give,
Gas smells awful,
You might as well live."

— Résumé *by Dorothy Parker, 1999*

XXXIII – Jimmy the Slice

Money might be the root of all evil, thought Slippery Jack Danielson, *but the lack of it was almost as bad.* In his view, there were two kinds of people who never got rich: honest lawyers and good preachers. One worked for free and the other gave everything away.

Jack's job at the hospital was both menial and minimum wage, and as a consequence, he was running low on ready cash. He had to make contact with the bank that held the balance of his funds. It was not a magnificent sum, but significant nonetheless. It worried him that he might have already left too much of a paper trail, so he hoped to move his money out of the account to someplace safer. *Here today and drawn tomorrow,* as they say.

He sat in the common room of the Hostel Destiny, sipping coffee with a small group of the regular occupants. Don Kumbach got up, walked to the open door, yelled, "Bullshit," then returned to his seat.

Urasmus B. Dragon was expounding on the party he loved to hate. "Did ya hear what they did today? The National Committee announced that the Republican Party's changing its emblem from an elephant to a condom."

"I'm afraid to ask why," Jack said, prepared for the raunchy anecdote typical of this group.

"The committee chair said the condom more clearly reflects the party's stance today, because the condom accepts inflation, halts production, destroys the next generation, protects a bunch of pricks, and gives you a sense of security while you're actually getting screwed!" They all laughed.

Don got up again, went to the door, looked around and yelled "Bullshit."

Jack joined in the laughter, not really knowing why. He was preoccupied with how to get his dough out of the bank. He could show them his real driver's license and a plastic birth certificate card, but because he wanted to withdraw thirty-three thousand dollars, they'd likely give him their usual song and dance routine about a short delay while they authorized the release of that much cash.

He kept questioning himself about why he'd been so careless about the money transfer. Was it sheer laziness? Male reasoning usually ran along the lines of, "let's knock off early and go for a couple of beers." A second line of thought was the standard one for having done anything – "it seemed like a good idea at the time." That one had come back to bite him in the ass, and now he had to fix this banking error.

Those CIA bloodhounds had probably also read about the Wolf Cubs finding the tattooed arm and concluded he was still alive. They could have started checking banks in Jersey, found out where he'd transferred his funds to D.C. and be on his tail right now. So he could either try to get his money out now or just do without. *Fuck 'em,* Jack said to himself. *It's my money!*

As Jack took his mug to the sink for a rinse, Don Kumbach went to the door again, stepped outside and yelled "Bullshit!" several more times.

"What the hell's with Kumbach and this 'bullshit' business?" Jack asked the others. "Has he got Tourette's Syndrome or something?"

The Candle Man chuckled. "Oh, no, he's just calling his dog. You see, he crossed a bulldog with a shitsu, and…"

Jack groaned and put his face in his hands. "I know. He named it Bullshit!"

* * *

The next day, Jack cased the small branch bank to which he had transferred his funds. The neighborhood was a tough one. You could walk ten blocks without leaving the scene of the crime.

He had grown a short beard and bought a cheap pair of glasses in order to alter his appearance. He approached on foot and scanned the area. That's when he spotted an old beige Dodge Aries parked up the street from the bank. It looked familiar, but he wouldn't be able to see the license plate until he got closer, as the car was jammed in between two other vehicles. He decided to treat the car like an elephant with diarrhea – give it lots of room.

Jack ducked into a café sporting a sign saying *ALL DAY BREAKFAST,* and took a seat next to the window where he could watch the Aries. He ordered his usual: hash browns with toast and coffee.

Halfway through his second cup he spotted the guy he'd seen in the parking lot of the Hang Over Bar and Strip Club outside Jersey City. With him was an Hispanic-looking man. The two stood arguing on the street for several minutes, then got in the car and drove away. The license number checked out. *These were the guys who'd killed Duke the car thief, thinking it was me,* he surmised.

Perhaps his best defence was a good offense. The version of the Christian ethic he had grown up with was:

Do unto others what they have done unto you, before they did it to you again.

* * *

Obtaining a handgun in Washington was a piece of cake. Even Wal-Mart would be happy to sell him one, but Jack's situation required a less legitimate source, one that didn't ask any questions or keep records. He made some inquiries and the general consensus was that he should seek out a reliable source called the Rumgunner. A bouncer at a strip joint provided him with an address.

Jack went to the small gun sales and repair shop where the Rumgunner was supposed to hang out.

"I need a gun," he announced, after establishing that the scruffy, skinny man behind the counter was in fact the Rumgunner.

"Don't we all?" the Rumgunner said with a grin, exposing too many yellow teeth and inflamed gums. "What kind you want?"

"A snub-nosed .38 special for sure, but also something heavier that packs a bigger punch. With a silencer and a large ammo clip."

"You got it, my man. Anything else while you is here?"

Jack thought for a moment, drumming his fingers on the smudged counter. "Yeah, I could use a Kevlar vest, and maybe some plastic explosives."

"Not my usual line of merchandise, but leave it with me a while, and I'll see what I can do."

* * *

Back at the Hostel Destiny, Jack knocked on the door of an over-the-hill hippie known around the place as Jimmy the Slice. He was rumored to have once belonged to a biker gang that had since been wiped out by the Hell's Angels.

Slice ushered Jack into a shabby room furnished with a camp-cot, a table and chair, a faded rug and a broken washstand. The walls were covered with old Harley Davidson posters and Jimmy's clothes, hanging on nails. Slice believed that nothing is what most people did better than anything else. He only went to work when he felt like it, so he was usually so broke that he wore underpants fashioned from old newspapers. His motor bike, he said, still sported the logo of the now defunct Second Slice Pizzeria and he was an expert at navigating the streets of Washington, if you cared to know.

"I've got a job of work for you, Slice," said Jack without too much preamble, seating himself on the only chair. "I'd appreciate it if you'd do it as a personal favor for me."

"Depends on what it is, now don't it?" said Slice laconically, plopping down on his camp-cot and folding his fleshy forearms across his chest.

"All you'd have to do is ride the bike."

"I like the sound of that," said Slice, "but where and why?"

"I need to find something that I can't look for on my own. Not without wheels."

"Okay, so?" Slice asked, getting up from his cot.

"Here's a description of a car," said Jack, handing Slice a piece of paper. "The license number, along with a description of the guys driving it, and the place where this car might show up every so often. I want you to find out where the guys in the car are staying and where they park it while they're there."

"What're ya payin'?"

"Ten bucks an hour for as long as it takes."

"More than fair, man. You're on. But mightn't this take a long time? I don't like long jobs, cause I'm used to doin' nothing."

"The trouble with doing nothing, Jimmy, is that you never know when you're finished. Might take a few days, but I doubt it. Now I can do something that might make them show up regularly for several days. So be ready to start tomorrow morning. Breakfast is on me."

* * *

"We're getting close, Armand," Harry remarked as he lay back on the hotel bed, "so I want you to think twice before you act, unless the strain is too great …"

Armand, completing his shave in the bathroom, said, "I like you, Harry, but I can't stand your personality."

"Yeah, well maybe you should learn a trade so you'll know what kind of work you're out of."

Armand shot back. "It isn't the ups and downs in life that bother me. It's the jerks like you."

Harry and Armand were so used to insulting each other, they never really noticed they were doing it.

"What if we don't get him? He's slippery, all right."

"I agree, the guy's no dummy. So no mistakes this time. And stop complaining. I'll tell you a little story about that."

"Not another one of your stories, Armand."

"This one has a point."

"Which is?"

"There is always something to complain about. There were these three small kids. One was a bottle baby who complained to the others that the milk was either too hot or too cold. The second kid was a little older and he said his parents had switched him onto pablum and soft foods. "It's too runny, I miss my mouth with the spoon and the stuff dribbles down my chin. I sure don't like it." The third kid, the youngest, said that he was still being breast-fed. "Oh, that must be great," the other two said, "nothing to complain about there." "Oh yeah?" said the third baby. "Have you ever shared a pair of tits with a guy who smokes White Owl cigars?"

Harry actually thought this was funny, so although he laughed he also remarked, "Armand, you're an *ignoranus* – you're stupid and you're an asshole."

* * *

The next morning, Jack and Jimmy the Slice had breakfast at the greasy spoon near the bank, but they didn't spot the Dodge Aries. Jack was wearing a coat with a turned-up collar and a ball cap pulled low over his eyes. Just after the bank opened, he went in and asked to see the manager. Slice lounged outside, resting his bulk against a telephone pole beside his bike.

Waiting in the lobby, Jack noticed a crippled old man sitting in the corner with a push broom in his hands. Being a janitor himself, Jack wondered why the bank would have a crippled janitor on the daytime payroll who sat in a corner all day looking pitiful and doing nothing 'til closing time. Either the man was there so customers would have someone to feel sorry for while they were getting fleeced by the bank, or he was a security guard in disguise.

Finally the manager was ready to see Jack. "What can I do for you this morning, sir?" he asked once they were seated in his office.

Jack explained that he wanted to withdraw all the money in his previously untapped account, and produced the account number while offering his real birth certificate and driver's license.

The manager entered a few keystrokes, staring at the screen as the data came up. "Thirty-three thousand dollars in cash?"

"Is that a problem?" Jack asked.

"There are two problems, actually," said the manager with an oily smile. "Regulations require me to contact the branch from which this account was originally transferred and have them fax me a copy of the card with your signature on it, to validate your identity."

"I understand. How long would that take?"

"Anywhere from two hours to two days, depending on how busy they are."

"And the second problem?"

"Sums of that magnitude have to be sent from head office. We're a small branch, you understand. This is also a dangerous neighborhood, and we've been robbed before."

Jack smiled back at the manager. "A run on the bank would be short-lived these days, wouldn't it?"

"Yes indeed. It's the age of electronic cash."

"So how long will all this take?" Jack asked again.

"Perhaps we could have the money here by tomorrow."

"I was hoping to get it right away," said Jack, stroking his chin. "Okay, so when should I come back to pick it up?"

"Give me your phone number and I'll let you know."

"I'm afraid that's not possible." Jack said. "I'll come back tomorrow, how's that?"

"Can you give me a specific time?" ·

"Not unless you can," said Jack as he got up and headed for the door.

The bank manager had a third problem he hadn't mentioned. He needed time to get in touch with the pair of CIA bums that were hanging around the bank like two bad farts.

> "Government is a trust, and the officers
> of the government are trustees;
> and both the trust and the trustees
> are created for the benefit of the people."

> *— Henry Clay, from a March 1829*
> *Speech at Ashland, Kentucky*

XXXIV – A Bunch of Bull on Wall Street

October 19, 2003, Institute for Counter-Terrorism, Herzliya, Israel

Maverick analyst Daniel Weintrauber, an expert in stock options and derivatives and the criminal manipulation of same, was working on a briefing paper dealing with what he regarded as the world's largest insider trading scam. Hundreds of millions had been made on 9/11 and this suspicious deal had never been properly investigated. The great crime had received little attention from either the media, the SEC or the U.S. government, perhaps because their friends stood to gain billions of dollars.

Weintrauber's job was to provide information to his bosses, who in turn would inform the Knesset, about any suspicious movements in global stock markets that signaled the financing of radical Islamic terrorist plots against Israel. Daniel reviewed his thought processes:

According to a German expert, in the week before the 9/11 attacks, 15 billion dollars of put options – highly leveraged bets that a given stock's share price will fall – were placed on the Chicago Board of Options Exchange and the New York Stock Exchange. Huge profits had been made by savvy speculators as the stocks of United and American Airlines, of insurance companies and the brokerage houses of Morgan Stanley and

215

Merrill-Lynch that had offices in the WTC, plummeted in the aftermath of the September 11th disaster.

Try to purchase stock, futures, mutual funds or put options, without providing your identity. Try to do so anonymously and you won't get anywhere. Therefore the money trail was a smoking gun that could lead directly to those who had planned the events of 9/11.

Obviously, anyone who had detailed knowledge of the attacks before they happened, and thus traded on a stock exchange in order to profit from that knowledge, is at least an accessory to the planning of the attacks. The timing, specificity, size and unusual nature, indicates that the trades were carried out based on insider information. Overwhelming probability and common sense suggest that the trades were made by the same people who masterminded the attacks themselves.

Tracing the transactions to their real source would be difficult, because the trading is sure to have been done under false names, behind shell corporations, and in general to have been thoroughly obfuscated. This didn't mean that unraveling the threads of these transactions would be impossible, but it probably wouldn't be quick or easy.

Behind every great crime are great criminals who planned it well. Certainly if the perpetrators who placed the put options had been Islamic terrorists or fellow plotters, wouldn't Americans have heard all about it by now? But what if the conspirators were high officials in banking, finance or tied to the U.S. or his own government, then that would logically explain why no one investigated or prosecuted this scam. Was it possible the trail might lead to the CIA?

Wanting to verify some of his facts, Weintrauber placed a telephone call to a former chief of enforcement at the American Securities and Exchange Commission who had agreed to speak candidly about his own suspicions regarding the increase in trading volume just prior to 9/11.

The call went through, and after some preliminaries, Weintrauber began taping the conversation with his source: "There was a 9,000 percent jump in put options placed on United Airlines between September 6th and 10th, and a 6,000 percent jump above normal on American Airlines on the day before the attacks, plus more than 100 million dollars in illegal transactions were rushed through the WTC computers before and during the disaster. The regulators should certainly by now have been able to track down every trade, where the trade cleared, and from where the trade was directed."

"How do you know they were illegal transactions?"

"I still have some pull at the SEC," said the source. "There are people looking into this, but I don't know how far they're going to be allowed to go. It's too explosive."

"Okay thanks." He hung up.

According to his source, on the Thursday prior to the World Trade Center being destroyed, put options on United Airlines alone had surged to the phenomenal high of 285 times their average. There was also an unusually high volume in the purchase of five-year Treasury notes, which are amongst the best investments in the event of a world crisis, including a single five billion dollar transaction.

After a long period of silence following the attacks, Daniel knew that the Securities Exchange Commission had immediately undertaken the unprecedented action of deputizing thousands of key player private sector officials in its investigation. What happens when you deputize someone in a national security or criminal investigation is that you make it illegal for them to disclose publicly what they know. It is, in effect, a gag order – a smart move in a cover-up. Don't let anyone tell what they know was done-done, or you will go-go to jail, instead of those who were behind the criminal conspiracy.

In effect, the deputies become government agents and are controlled by the government regulations rather than by their conscience. In fact, they can be thrown in jail without a hearing if they talk publicly. This implied threat is used time and again with federal investigations, intelligence agents, and even members of the United States Congress who are bound so tightly by secrecy oaths and agreements that they are not even able to disclose criminal activities inside the government for fear of incarceration. This was how the SEC handled the insider trading by certain individuals who had obviously used foreknowledge of the attack to reap huge profits. *And this, right under the nose of the SEC, the supposed public watchdog, which didn't appear to be too interested in proceeding with any prosecution of these shysters*, thought Weintrauber.

Given the unusual increase in trades of put options prior to 9/11, Weintrauber wondered why anyone, with the notable exception of Representative Sydney McKinley, hadn't demanded a thorough and open investigation into the SEC cover-up? *Obviously*, he thought, *because powerful forces in America were blocking any such effort, aided and abetted by a compliant White House, a complacent Congress and Republican-stacked judiciary.*

The next day, Weintrauber phoned James Brannigan, managing editor of *Barrington's Weekly*, one of Washington's most respected business publications. Brannigan expressed his long-standing outrage concerning what had transpired on the stock exchanges. "It's true, all right," Brannigan said, audibly fuming, "and this could very well be insider trading at its worst, the most horrific, most evil use you've ever seen in your entire life. This would be one of the most extraordinary coincidences in the history of mankind, if it were a coincidence."

Weintrauber hung up the phone, chilled by the sheer immorality of the profiteers, and he worried that if the culprits were too highly placed in the U.S. administration, or involved with powerful corporate insiders who were intimately tied to the Republicans in office, there would be serious repercussions for his own country. If it ever came out that the Americans had engineered the entire disaster in order to make money and perhaps finesse a takeover of the Middle East, there would be an ensuing jihad the likes of which the world had never seen, one that would engulf Israel, since it was the handiest target of militant Muslim hatred.

Given the ties that bound Israel to the United States, or vice versa, the content of the article he was working on wouldn't have his own superiors, or national intelligence agencies, dancing with glee. He knew he should make his thesis compelling enough and sufficiently well-documented to try to force both governments into taking the proper action. But what that action might be, Weintrauber didn't know, and he wondered if he really wanted to find out.

What should he do? he wondered. *Submit the article or snuff it?* As he saw things, if he went ahead with it, he could end up as a canary in a coal mine, and he certainly didn't feel the need to be asphyxiated.

"These United States of America can never be destroyed from forces outside its borders. If America falls, it will fall from within. Brought down by apathy. When good people do nothing anarchy reigns."

— Abraham Lincoln in an 1854 letter to Congress

XXXV – Czar Nicolaus

D'Amous powered the small 15 HP outboard motorboat further down the lakeshore. A few minutes later, he eased the boat up onto a narrow sandy beach. The two fishermen clambered out of the boat with a lunch container in hand. Sitting in the shade of some shoreline trees, they each grabbed a ham and cheese sandwich.

"We've been talking a lot about politics, Nick. What would you say are the best rules to follow for success in that field?" asked Bob Loblaw, settling back against a tree trunk.

D'Amous took a big bite from his sandwich and chewed that one over. "Good question, Bob, and if you'll just crack open a couple more brew, I'll tell you.

"Well, first off, you always turn your own side's unconscionable lies and screw-ups into the fault of somebody else. Never apologize for mistakes. Ignore questions that require embarrassing responses. Blame the opposition and the media every chance you get. Don't hesitate to make the tough decisions that will likely kill innocent people in whatever number. Refuse to act on the wishes of the majority of Americans, even while ripping them off for taxes, and never consider the good of any other human being beyond yourself and your family."

"Political lore to live by. We were talking about al-Qaeda a while back. What's your opinion of that organization?"

"Al-Qaeda is actually a mythical name. It was given to bin Laden's rag tag operation in a Manhattan courtroom in

January 2001 so the US could legally go after him *in absentia*, for the embassy bombings in East Africa. It isn't some well organized 'Hate the U.S.A.' terrorist network orchestrated by Osama from some cave in Afghanistan."

D'Amous continued his explanation, the amount of booze he had consumed thus far making him more loquacious than usual. "Some of these terrorists were trained in Afghanistan by western intelligence and were being run as part of Opposition Force, or OPFOR, a joint American military and Intel operation. Fifteen or so of the so-called hijackers, who supposedly participated in the attacks on the WTC, came from or through Saudi Arabia, and got their visas through the CIA and the American Consulate General in Jeddah. Only a few were from Saudi families. They were from all over the Middle East and these guys were used to playing the villain in covert exercises around the world. Prior to 9/11, many were staying in a motel very close to the supersecret National Security Agency at Fort Meade, Maryland. Others were training at flight schools in Florida. They were under NSA and CIA surveillance and tasting all the joys that western culture had to offer, including strip clubs and liquor."

"Nothing the matter with that, is there?" Loblaw chuckled.

"Not unless you're Mosey Long or one of his bunch, but hardly the passions of a devout Muslim about to become a martyr. None of them even had an instrument rating, let alone the commercial jet ratings required to fly a Boeing 757 or 767. But the public was gullible enough to believe they could – all part of the conditioning process. Ever since the end of the Cold War, we were busy manufacturing a new external threat called 'terrorism' to replace 'communism'. The amount of work that went into this obviously paid off."

"I can only imagine the planning all this must have taken."

"It's taking a lot more work to keep the lid on the end result," D'Amous said, grimacing. "The FBI and other agencies are sitting on close to 7,000 photographs, videos and other evidence that would be invaluable to an independent investigation."

Nick laughed and added, "Just think of the money we've saved taxpayers – the government spent fifty million examining why the Columbia Space Shuttle exploded and another fifty investigating President Clinton in the Whitewater deal and probing into the Monica Lewinsky affair. Yet there's been less than a third of that spent on investigating 9/11."

They finished their lunch, got back in the boat and headed back onto the lake, deciding to switch from fly to spin tackle.

"This looks like a good spot," said Nick as he spun cast his lure toward a deep area under an overhanging cliff.

Bob took time out to see the results of Nick's efforts before taking a crack at it himself. His alcohol dampened coordination also played some part in that delay. "H-how many of the nineteen alleged ji-hackers. Uh ... hijackers are still alive?"

"I'm not sure of the exact number, but a lot of money is invested in good assets like Atta, Alomari and Alghamdi, and intelligence agencies need their covert operatives to trust them. Their greatest risk is being liquidated by their employers. So killing all of the alleged hijackers would have caused a mutiny among our assets, if they realized that they weren't going to be taken care of as promised. So some were expendable patsies and others were not."

"How and when did you decide to pull it ... ahh, off?" Loblaw got unsteadily to his feet and took a leak over the side of the boat. "I know America has targeted its own citizens before, but never anythin' on this shcale."

"In May, 2001, I instructed the President to place the Vice President in charge of all planning for a possible terrorist attack, effectively giving the V.P. control over FEMA, the military complex, everything. Then in June of 2001, the NORAD air scramble protocols that had been in place since 1976 were rewritten to take most decision-making powers out of the hands of the air force field commanders and given to the Secretary of Defense. This change provided deniability for the usual chain of command plus enough confusion for our plan to work."

"Some shay nine-eleven was quite similar to the Pearl Harbor attack," said Bob, "in that the President knew about it before it happened. But in that case, FDR didn't inform General Short, or Admiral Kimmel – who were in sharge – the classic Let It Happen On Purpose – LIHOP scenario. Right?"

"Not really," replied Nick, noting Bob's sliding verbal precision. "That would have been too difficult – too much could have gone wrong. No, we planned and coordinated the whole thing, using inside moles and outside operatives from other countries. Some call it MIHOP – Make It Happen On Purpose. Others would call it *an inside job*. You see, we engineered the World Trade Center catastrophe, programmed the public reaction, and offered them the solution – problem, reaction, solution – one of the oldest tricks in the book. It was dreamt up by the German philosopher Hegel at the beginning of the 19th century. It's something he referred to as the 'thesis, antithesis, synthesis paradigm' and is used in an underhanded way to sway public opinion."

"Brilliant," said Bob, clumsily zipping up his fly. "Tell me sh'more."

"In a minute," Nick continued. "You know, I prefer fishing to hunting. You usually catch something – big or small, whereas hunting is eternal expectation and perpetual disappointment."

"I'm more of a fisherman myself," Loblaw said, nodding agreeably. "Lasht time I shot a buck was in a crap game."

Nick smiled at the remark. "To further answer your question, Bob, back when we planned this thing, it was bad times, and alarms were going off everywhere you looked concerning peak oil. The economy had already been milked close to collapse by 1998. It was time for the major transnational corporations and the big players to cash out and that's what they were doing – pumping and dumping their stocks, sucking the wealth out of pension plans and mutual funds. Trillions of dollars of shareholder equity were wiped out, while the people on top cashed out and moved their money elsewhere."

Loblaw, being one of those who had cashed out, said, "Yeah, I know how our system works." He reached for another cold one and cranked the top off. "We were faced with a choice of masshive panic and collapse of the financial markets, plus a loss of public faith in the political system."

"Which would have meant the loss of most of our power and wealth, if the public ever caught on. As you know, this is a very lucrative crap game, being played by an all-party government system that functions like organized crime – full of corruption, cooked books, lack of transparency and accountability, destructive of life for the sake of net profits and supremacy."

Bob cut in; "A prime example of that would be the resource grab in the Middle East. Correct?"

"Exactly," Nick agreed. "These war protestors regard the Iraqi war as the illegal sucker trap of all time, a quagmire from which we should pull our troops. What they don't comprehend is that from our point of view Iraq is a success, exactly what we wanted – mission accomplished – a deeply destabilized country with a puppet government that owes its existence to America, a completely broken infrastructure, civil war that inevitably leads to splitting up the country into three separate States, made up of Sunnis, Shi'ites and Kurds. A place where we have established military bases in areas we seek to control, immediately adjacent to strategic oil fields and next to countries where we intend to do the very same thing as we did in Iraq."

"Which never could have happened if you hadn't come up with a plan like 9/11. Right?"

"Yes. There were ample reasons for using a terror attack," said Nick. "We got together with a few major players to plan how to make such an attack happen, that already had some legs."

His curiosity rising, Bob asked, "How many guys did it take?"

"Only about fifty – consisting of a handful of top government officials, a half-dozen foreign political operatives, a few top honchos in the intelligence field, and maybe a dozen specialists with expert demolition skills. Also a small company head with the technical electronic skills to control planes by remote control, some rich money-men connected to the New York real estate market to acquire control and access to the WTC complex, and finally a dozen skilled technicians to operate the collapse. Oh yes, and a top official at the FAA who made sure such things as the air traffic control tapes were destroyed after the New York attack. Plus if you add me," said Nick, "then fifty-one people engineered 9/11. Others were peripheral players, befuddled generals at the Pentagon or NORAD, bewildered FAA air traffic controllers or USAF pilots – these guys were simply pawns."

Faintly incredulous, Bob asked "What if >*hic!*<, one of them came forward and plew the plot wide open?"

"They all agreed the end justified the means. Not only that, but each of them stood to gain from the operation," Nick replied. "So why would they blow the whistle? That would mean suffering ridicule and recrimination, threats of harm to themselves and family, or pay the ultimate price – death!"

"Yeah, that's enough to keep their mouths shut forever," Bob firmly agreed.

"September the 11th was not a new idea, Bob. The Clinton administration kept the idea alive as a contingency. We began dragging old plans off the shelves, like Bojinka – plans to manufacture, develop and control a direct external threat by staging an attack on the U.S. It was as obvious as a hernia at a weight lifter's convention that we needed a *new Pearl Harbor*, as some people call it now. This provided the pretext for the later massive military interventions to secure America's energy supplies in the Middle East, Africa, and Colombia – although it's not working well in Venezuela at the moment. We're committed to this path; all we have to do is make certain that terrorists conveniently turn up on schedule in each situation. There have been mistakes in the execution and subsequent cover-up of 9/11; I'll be the first to admit it. However, we're plugging all the holes."

The two men were both feeling good, particularly Bob. "These things never go as smoothly as one would like. But I'm curious, Nick, as to just *who* was responsible for coordinating the multiple war-games running on 9/11. That was a brilliant idea."

Nick had learned, even when drinking, to make every attempt to maintain an awareness of any situation. "Same question that the 9/11 Commission asked General Eversharp, who was in charge of NORAD that day."

"What'd he shay?" Bob slurred.

"All he said was, 'No comment'," replied Nick. 'National security'."

"And the commission never insisted on a proper answer, did they? That figures – why would they? They were all hand-picked cronies who had good reason to see that the truth never came out. Right? So who was it then?"

"No comment," said Nick smiling. "But just remember that you can now take off, fly, and land commercial airliners from here to Australia by remote control, with no pilots involved."

"Whoa ..." said Bob, surprised. "Just how does that work?"

"A lot of technical details, but it's all wrapped up in planar antenna technology. High gain microwave antennas on the tail sections make very fine control possible through downlink telemetry and guidance. The planes were controlled by an expert pilot from a military AWAC plane flying high above the scene, as each plane flew toward their targets; all coordinated with the command post in Building 7. Meanwhile, on the ground, we basically paralyzed the few remaining air force interceptors – which weren't deployed to Alaska – with false radar blips and live-fly hijacks that morning. We sent the Otis fighters out to sea 'so they wouldn't collide with all the other domestic traffic over New York' and the Langley jets were delayed until it was too late. These tactics staved off any interference that might have developed from the air force. This stuff is confidential and if you asked General Meierhoff of NORAD, or the Vice President, they'd deny it. The administration has been under strict instructions to make damn sure that no significant investigations into 9/11 would ever be carried out," Nick continued, "and none were."

"Do you remember those French guys filming a fire-fighting documentary on the streets of New York that day? They got some great pictures of the plane hitting the North Tower."

"*Vitam regit fortuna non sapientia.* That was mostly a matter of luck" said Nick.

"Hey," said Bob, picking up his rod, "maybe we, ahhh, we should get back to a little fishing."

"Good idea. This lodge owner told me that sometimes you can catch panfish right out in the middle of the lake. There's a spot there that's relatively shallow, only about ten or twelve feet deep. A lot of bottom weed around that spot attracts fish, because of a big spring that feeds the lake at that point. So let's head out there."

"Shounds like a plan, Stan," said Bob, reaching into the cooler for another beer.

They headed out to the middle of the lake, found the spot and cut the engine, the sudden silence ringing in their ears now that the motor's drone had quit.

"Cheers to the coup on 9/11!" said Bob, lifting his bottle. "But damn it, these hard seats are making my ass sore."

"Damnation! You're right. We forgot to bring the cushions." Nick took off his life jacket and placed it under his butt. Bob did likewise.

"There, that's better, now pass another bottle, will you, Bob?"

Due to the drink, the two men now were more interested in talking than fishing, as they knocked back more beer. Neither of them was in a hurry to begin further decimation of the fish population.

"One brilliant scenario," Loblaw mused, "was the supposedly heroic actions of the passengers aboard Flight 93 over Pennsylvania."

"Never happened. Couldn't. We faked it! There's a gag order on National Security Operations Center personnel. It was an unfortunate slip of the tongue when the Secretary of Defense addressed the U.S. troops in Baghdad at Christmas a couple of years back, when he referred to a plane being shot down over Pennsylvania.

"Well, he knew perfectly well who the people were who attacked the United States, and who shot down Flight 93, and it certainly wasn't Osama bin Laden and his scary band of nineteen Arab hijackers. We later concocted the passengers' revolt story for propaganda reasons. Comes in handy whenever we need to inject a little patriotism into the official story.

"One of the beautiful things about the operation is that no passengers were left alive to reveal what really happened. The gullible American public, who would for the most part be unwilling to believe what did happen, is later propagandized with Hollywood-made movies that give them an action-adventure version of the event. We've relied heavily on the fact that even intelligent people just won't bother to investigate the facts because they can't bring themselves to believe their leaders are capable of carrying out a false-flag operation of this magnitude – no matter how many times we've done it in the past."

"How shtupid can they get?" Bob mused.

"The average American has twelve million brain cells, and 11,900,000 of those are unemployed. Sixty-two percent of Americans are functionally illiterate and one in five believes the Sun revolves around the Earth. If the public thought about these things seriously, then we'd be in deep shit. They'd soon see that the talking heads of mainstream media, religion, government and business are all subservient to a greater global power."

Loblaw simply stared at D'Amous, waiting for more.

"This is a large enterprise carried out by an invisible international network of power interests, with the U.S. government at their disposal. They literally own the U.S. military, NATO, the Secret Service, the CIA, the FBI, the NSA, the Federal Reserve System, the Supreme Court and many of the lower courts, including state, county and local law enforcement agencies. We call the shots, and for decades we've indoctrinated the masses through the media, which we also own. Television, radio, newspapers and magazines have been flooding living rooms with New World messages, and the public has bought in completely," boasted Nick.

"You don't shay?" Loblaw interjected, his speech slurred, suddenly feeling drunk. "Surely shum mishtakes were made."

"We've taken control of fiscal and monetary policy, natural resources and politicians in all countries in which we operate. We're fishing in Canada right now. We spent years grooming the new Prime Minister. He proved himself in a speech he made to the Council on Foreign Relations a few years back. If Canadians were aware of the content of that speech, they'd know he was going to go right along with the U.S. administration, who goes right along with us."

"So whash the name of this shadow empire again, Nick?"

D'Amous winced, his nose wrinkling just a fraction. "Don't you remember? The Global Union."

"And I shuppose you're the chzar?"

D'Amous detected a note of derision in Loblaw's voice, and realized that the older man might be dismissing what he had just said. Self-controlled or half swacked, D'Amous did not suffer fools gladly.

"More like the Executive Director," Nick said, bristling. "The people I work for know I'd never hesitate to sacrifice those who get in our way."

Drunk is the future of drink, so Bob replied, "Whish is why you're not very well liked or admired, right Nick? You don't even bovver to hide your ruthleshness. Judging by wha people call ya behind your back, you're not sho firmly in control as you'd like to think."

"Is that right? What do they call me?" said Nick testily.

"'Nick 'the Nostril'', for one thing."

"Bastards!" D'Amous snapped back. His opinion of Bob's reliability had plummeted. He now knew that secrecy and alcohol would never be a successful combination with the man; *LIABILITY* was echoing over and over in his mind. "So what?" He barked,

"Sho, if they ever found out wha really happened on nine ... nine eleven, they'd take Nick 'the Nostril'," Bob paused and smirked "to the nearesh tall tree with a low limb ..." He broke into laughter at his own remark, too far gone to remember or care about D'Amous' occasional fits of rage.

Nick's face flushed with the rush of blood to his head, thinking, *Maybe I've told this guy too much ... He's getting downright disrespectful.* "Any other jokes you'd care to relate, Bob?" Nick queried.

Loblaw swayed on the boat's seat as he tried to attach a new spinning lure to his line. "In Biblical times it wash a miracle if you could get a jackass to speak; now issh a miracle if you can get 'Nostril' D'Amous to shut up! Get it? Nostradamus!" Bob roared with laughter.

"Who said that?" D'Amous said, snarling.

"I jush made it up," said Loblaw, bursting into laughter again. "What's the difference between Nick D'Amous and a Huggie?"

Looking daggers, D'Amous asked, "Well, what then?"

"They're both full of sh ... shit, but the Huggie doesn't leak it!" Laughing uproariously again, Loblaw awkwardly stood up in the boat and drew the fishing rod back over his shoulder, about to make a bad cast. His back was to D'Amous.

"You know, Bob, some people never learn when to shut up. You can befriend them, you can bribe them, and you can threaten them all you like, but sometimes it's easier if you just make sure they never open their big traps again."

"Words to live by," Bob Loblaw carelessly responded, making a very sloppy cast into the lake. He staggered as the line went out, but held his footing. He hiccupped loudly.

"*Mordui non mordent*! Dead men carry no tales!" D'Amous shouted as he shoved Bob overboard with his foot, then revved up the boat's engine. He drove the craft a few yards away from Loblaw, who was spluttering and gasping, getting weaker by the second, as, fully clothed and unable to swim, he tried to stay afloat. The cold water momentarily restored a semblance of sobriety to him, and though his gasping prevented him from crying out to D'Amous, his eyes were pleading for assistance, promising solemn secrecy and radiating icy fear.

D'Amous watched coldly as Loblaw's struggles ceased, his eyes fluttered shut and he abruptly sank below the surface. Turning the boat back to camp to report the fishing accident, Nick said to himself, *The V.P. shot a lawyer in the face; I should at least be entitled to drown one. Too bad Bob was such a blabbermouth.*

"And in that town two dogs were found,
    As many dogs there be,
Both mongrel, puppy, whelp, and hound,
    And curs of low degree!"

— *Oliver Goldsmith,* An Elegy on the Death of a Mad Dog, *1766*

XXXVI – Retroactive Birth Control

Jack jumped behind Slice on the old bike and they got to the greasy spoon early in the morning. By now the café staff was treating Jack as a regular.

"Hey Jack," the waitress, Tarara Boumdier yelled. "Whaddaya think? I told these guys, just because you spend a hundred bucks on a woman doesn't mean you're entitled to a piece of ass."

Tarara was a woman of many parts but a lousy assembly job. She was wearing a sheepdog brassiere – one which rounds them up and points them in the right direction. Jack figured that if her blouse had been cut any lower it would have been a belt. She was out to catch a man, but was more likely to catch a cold.

"I found that out when I got married," Jack said affably, as he and Slice took seats at the counter. "She kept telling me she loved me, but if she loved me so much, why didn't she marry somebody else?"

"You know why they call it a piece of ass, don't you?" asked Tarara.

Slice bit. "Why's that?"

"Because nobody gets all of it!"

"When I got divorced," said Slice, "the judge asked me the reason I wanted one. I told him it was because I lived in a two-storey house. The judge said, 'What on Earth would that have to do with getting a divorce?' I told him, 'Well, the first story was, 'I've got a headache,' and the second story was, 'It's the wrong time of month!'"

Whatever her physical faults, Tarara was a good waitress. She moved faster than a bubble dancer working with a ping-pong ball. Between customers, Tarara sank her torso into the seat beside Jack and Slice.

"You ask me, a woman's love is like the morning dew." she remarked.

"That's rather poetic," Slice observed.

Tarara completed the analogy, looking directly at Slice. "In my experience, it's as likely to settle on a horse turd as on a rose."

Jack smiled, then looked around the café. It was the best place for a stake-out, but it was a refuge for all kinds of kooks, has-beens and wannabees. One skinny guy at the end of the counter, pretending to be a political pundit, was expounding on the War on Terror.

"You people are fools," he declared loudly, directing his gaze at the man on his right. "Your opinion proves that liberals can't be trusted to make their own decisions. War's good for the economy, and if a few soldiers die in the process, then kiss my ass and call me Charlie! It's their job. The world doesn't hate America, it fears it, and that's a good thing. Better than being just one of the sheep. And there's a reason it's called the Patriot Act – if you're against it, you're a goddamn traitorous terrorist, plain and simple."

"Now just a minute, Mac, are you questioning my loyalty to the flag?" said another man, getting off his stool beside him. His fists were clenched.

"Up yours! We hold all the cards and we'll make sure that no dumbocrat ever holds power again. You'll just have to shut your yap and do what you're told. The President is a great man. He won't hesitate to wipe all you bleeding heart liberal scumbags off the face of this great nation. God bless America and no one else!"

In the silence that followed, Jack thought, *Ah, the cry of the beer-swilling nutjob redneck!*

"Maybe we should kick the living shit out of that Republican bootlicker," Slice muttered to Jack.

"Nah, he's just an idiot spouting shit that's so stupid, it's funny. Besides we've got other business to attend to."

Just before the bank opened, they struck paydirt. The Dodge Aries rolled slowly down the street and parked half a block away.

Jack handed Slice a couple of twenties for meals. "You might have to wait all day, but you know what to do. I'll walk back up the street and catch a bus back to the hostel."

* * *

Jack had booked a week off from his night shift job at the medical center, but he couldn't quite get used to the change in regimen. He was trying to get some sleep, but kept tossing on the bed, his mind churning with indecision about how to handle the two government killers on his tail. He had the explosives, so he might be able to wire their car and blow them to smithereens, which would be tit for tat. But that move might also kill a lot of innocent people, and in their profession these guys would likely check out their vehicle as a matter of course.

He thought about all the western movies he had seen as a kid, but he wasn't Hopalong Cassidy, Lash LaRue or John Wayne and he hadn't fired a gun in years. *What the hell*, he said to himself, *death is the only thing that doesn't get worse every time Congress meets.*

* * *

Later that night Slice reported back. "I trailed them to a motor inn about fifteen minutes from the café. They're on the second floor of the main building, in room 214. Their car's in the parking lot below the room."

"Excellent work."

"Whaddaya want me to do now?"

"I have a score to settle with those bastards," Jack explained. "Are you game to take me out there tomorrow morning, real early?"

"Yeah, sure."

"Could be dangerous," Jack warned.

"Listen, Jack, I was slidin' into the pit, feelin' sorry for myself. You're gettin' me off my ass, and besides, it's time I had some excitement."

"Okay, here's the situation." Jack explained.

* * *

Very early the next morning, Jack loaded his guns and strapped on the Rumgunner's allegedly bulletproof vest. He sat behind Slice and the two roared off to the motor inn. A few overnight guests were just starting to pull out of the parking lot, which was still filled with cars.

Jack got off the bike and laid a hand on Slice's shoulder. "I'm not sure what's going to happen here," said Jack. "There could be some gunplay."

Slice took this in stride. "I'm just gonna sit here and tinker with my hog. I'll be ready to roll as soon as you come out."

"Thanks for the vote of confidence. But if I don't come out, don't hang around. Dammit! I forgot one thing!"

"What?"

"I could sure use a drink to pull this off."

"Good thing I came prepared," said Jimmy, pulling a flask of whiskey from his pocket. He took a slug and handed it to Jack.

"Jesus weeping on a cross," Jack moaned. "I'm only one drink from going back on the bottle. If I take this drink, then whichever way this comes out, those bastards will have killed me." Jack pulled back his outstretched, trembling hand. "Forget it Slice, I gotta go in sober."

Jack climbed the stairwell to the second-floor balcony that ran the length of the building, and stopped in front of room 214. He touched the waistband at the back of his pants to ensure the .38 was still there, and grasped the .45 in his right hand. He pressed the buzzer and waited. No response. He pressed again and announced in a falsetto voice, "maid service!"

He heard voices and muffled cursing. Suddenly, the door was flung open and a bare-chested Harry Palm, a shirt dangling from one hand, stared straight into the muzzle of Jack's gun. Harry dropped the shirt and backed slowly into the room with his hands up.

Armand was sitting on the edge of his bed reaching for his pants, which hung from a chair next to his shoulder holster.

"I understand you two butt ugly bastards want to kill me," said Jack, stepping into the room and kicking the door shut behind him, his terse, cold tone belying his churning guts. "Now's your chance. You murdered my friend Sean and made it look like suicide. If you've got guns, this'd be a good time to go for them, because this is the only chance in hell I'm going to give you."

Armand didn't need to be asked twice. He lunged for his spring-loaded shoulder holster as he rolled off the bed onto the floor. Jack's first shot missed the moving target, but his second hit Armand in the thigh. The silencer muted Jack's shot, but Armand's gun roared as Jack fired a third time. The simultaneous shots hit both men in the chest. Jack staggered back, his vest absorbing the impact. *Thank you, Rumgunner!* Armand was done breathing and started to bleed all over the carpet. Maid service wasn't going to be happy, because Armand had also crapped himself, and he wasn't wearing any shorts.

Harry backhanded the .45 out of Jack's grasp before he could shoot again. The gun flew across the room, bounced off the wall and fell to the floor. *Shit, should've shot him when I first came through the door*, thought Jack.

Harry's right cross connected with Jack's jaw and knocked him sprawling into the table and chair by the window. Harry dove for the gun on the floor. Jack was dazed, but he fumbled for the .38 in his waistband. He pulled it out but kept it behind him as he stared up at a shit-eating grin.

"You're slippery, all right, Danielson," said Harry, in no hurry as he had the drop on Jack. "But this time we won't have to fake a suicide. You got shot after you killed my partner. Now I've got no one left to insult. That pisses me off so much I'm going to have to shoot you in the nuts, then the head, and finally in self-defense."

"Could I just say something before you do that?" asked Jack as he tightened his grip on the snub-nosed .38, hoping he hadn't lost his ability to shoot from the hip.

"Go ahead. Be my guest," Harry said with a sneer.

"Fuck you, fuck everybody that looks like you, and fuck the fucking CIA!" Jack yelled as he rolled sideways. Harry's bullet slammed into the wall above his head. Jack swung the .38 from behind his back, aimed it at Harry's heart and pulled the trigger.

His aim was off. The bullet missed Harry's hairy chest, but it sure wiped the grin from his face, which exploded into an unsightly mess of blood and brains.

Choking back bile, Jack leaped from the floor, picked up the .45, stuck it in his pocket and walked out of the room just in time to join the motel guests pouring out of their rooms, wondering what in the hell was going on.

Jack faked the rubbernecking act with the crowd for several seconds, then calmly descended the staircase and walked over to the motor bike, whose engine was running, with Slice in the saddle. Jack hopped on and they took off in the proverbial cloud of date pits and camel dung.

Slice couldn't contain himself. A few blocks from the motel, he shouted over his shoulder, "How'd it go?"

"There's good news and there's bad news," Jack replied, starting to shake as he clung to Slice's back.

"What's the good news?"

"Those two are as dead as the Pope's pecker. Dumb fucking luck, but if there's any justice, those two are now roasting in Hell."

"And the bad news?"

"Their bosses are likely to send more twisted dickheads after me. Anyway, let's get to the bank. It's safe to get my money now, and then I can show my appreciation for your services. And Slice? First thing you do back at the hostel is paint out that Second Slice Pizzeria sign on this Harley. Someone at the motel might've picked up on it."

"Right. You don't look so hot, Jack. Sure you don't want that drink?"

"No thanks."

"Hey, you're welcome. I'm glad we were able to deliver a little justice today."

"Right," Jack replied. "But as my Uncle Hugh used to say, 'if you like sausages and respect justice, you should never see either being made.'"

> "As nightfall does not come at once, neither does oppression. In both instances, there's a twilight where everything remains seemingly unchanged, and it is in this twilight that we all must be aware of the change in the air, however slight, lest we become victims of the darkness."
>
> — *Justice William O. Douglas*

XXXVII – Don Shivagitz

February 28, 2005

Fate flings odd casts of characters together at coffee break klatches, where many jokes are told and deep discussions of grave problems run rampant. It happens every business day in diverse eateries and coffee-houses across North America. This meeting of the minds was taking place at the Algonquin Hotel in New York at the morning session of the Golden Circle Quiver and Shake Club.

An irregular attendee, the famed law professor and TV talking head, Don Shivagitz, was there, twisted, demented and ghoulish as usual. How did that distinguish him from other lawyers? *Good point,* thought the rest of the members.

There was Bertha de Blooz, an aging and itinerant cabaret singer, whose high-C at one time could spay a dog at twenty paces. She was accompanied by her sidekick, Glorious Sternum, who had been robbed four times but couldn't get raped, and who had once sung in a female quartet called the Four Skinner Sisters.

Successfully fighting a weak urge to return to his office at the local newspaper, was Lloyd Mongull, whose name continually haunted him every time he looked at the staff listings or in a telephone directory. Leif Tabaca, a psychiatrist who'd had a Norwegian mother and a Japanese father, had just arrived with his born-again, ex-patient, Athol Ludencrude, who ran the Gateway to Paradise Rest Home.

Already on his second cuppa was Justice Haughton Bauthird, who was so sick of being kidded about his name that he was having the surname shortened to Bauth, but could not guess that the same fate would befall his grandson, Haughton Bauth III.

Hans Downe, a former ballistic engineer, had brought a binder of information relating to 9/11. He opened it to a page featuring a pair of images he thought would interest the female architect in the group, Ingrid Locke, a pleasant, intelligent woman in her late forties. On the left was a photo of Madrid's 'Windsor' high-rise building fully ablaze on February 12th, 2005. It had burned out of control for about seventeen hours but never collapsed. The other photo was of the South Tower of the World Trade Center collapsing less than an hour after much smaller fires had burned on only a few floors.

He showed the pictures to Ingrid. "Why would the South Tower collapse so quickly when the Madrid tower remained standing?" he asked her.

One quick look and Ingrid replied, "Because the Madrid tower was fireproofed."

"You just made that up, didn't you?" said Hans involuntarily, playing the part of the jester.

"Yes," Ingrid admitted, and everyone at the round table laughed.

"So why was that your answer?" asked Downe when the laughter stopped.

"Well, I guess I had to resolve the discrepancy, so I figured the Twin Towers couldn't have been fireproofed."

"What if I told you they were?"

"Well then it must have been blown off due to the impact of the planes."

"So you buy into the administration's official story?"

Ingrid thought about that for a moment while the others waited for her response. "Yes, of course! I believe the official explanation like everyone else does, besides, the government wouldn't lie to us about that type of thing. Those two pictures don't prove anything," she said. "What you're implying doesn't make any rational sense, in my way of thinking."

Hans asked Leif Tabaca for his opinion about the architect's knee-jerk reaction.

The psychiatrist scratched his chin and looked at her, saying, "In my opinion, your mind functioned to short circuit your rational thought. Most people, when they hold forth on 9/11, make up a set of facts for themselves on the spot, without really knowing what they are talking about."

"So the point is," said Judge Bauthird, "that there is a great deal of difference between the official 9/11 *story* and the 9/11 *evidence* which our friend here seems to be ignoring."

"Yes," said Hans. "Her initial reaction to the photos doesn't make any sense whatsoever – that some sprayed-on asbestos keeps a burning Madrid office tower standing for seventeen hours through a raging inferno. She infers, incorrectly, that somehow the alleged lack of fireproofing – something she merely assumed in order to back up her hastily concocted theory – causes the Twin Towers to entirely disintegrate despite the small fires of short duration."

"I was getting a massage last week," said Glorious Sternum, never one to be left out of a conversation for long, "and I asked the masseur why he thought the towers had collapsed. He replied 'It was the fires. They explained all that shortly after it happened.' 'Did they?' I said, 'and who are they?'"

"It's the manipulation of mental machinery," said Lloyd Mongull, "to get us, the audience, against our will, to entertain a proposition that resolves the incongruity the situation presents. They provide us with a cover story which subconsciously reinforces our belief system in a government which serves and protects us, even though the same story ignores the facts and disregards certain evidence. Ultimately this creates a belief system which is a cover-up for the inside job. And *this* is what we are up against in trying to expose it all – the universal cover-up."

"Easy for you to say," said Bertha de Blooz to the newspaperman, "but I don't want to talk about it. If 9/11 was an inside job then monsters rule me. I don't want to live in that kind of world. So let's talk about something else."

"Like what?" asked Ingrid Locke.

"Well, like what do you think about me, for instance," said Bertha.

"I think your wheels are spinning but the hamster's dead. Now what was the masseur's answer to your question, Glorious?"

"He said, '*They* are the authorities people listen to: CNN, FOX, ABC, you know, *The New York Times*, *Washington Post*, the so-called experts. Even if there are a few discrepancies and there's a better explanation to explain them, I won't believe it.'"

"Well, there you have it," said Hans, "the average U.S. citizen's attitude in a nutshell. Even when the laws of physics and structural engineering prove that jet fuel based fires do not attain temperatures above 1800-degrees Fahrenheit under optimal conditions, and that the melting point of steel is 1000- degrees higher – which means that the steel could not melt – they choose to believe it did. Even though we all saw black clouds of smoke emanating from the buildings, which means oxygen starvation and that the heat was far below 1800-degrees, some people will still stick to their guns. They have to rely on an erroneous belief system, ingrained by the perpetrators, who tell them how it all happened. But one always has to look for 'the dog that doesn't bark' as Sherlock Holmes would say."

Don Shivagitz had kept his mouth in his coffee cup while he listened to what he considered to be about enough of this load of codswallop, and he now bespoke himself in no uncertain terms. Don didn't have ulcers – he gave them. "You paranoid, unpatriotic loonies make me want to puke, with your asinine deluded conspiracy theories. It's preposterous to believe that the government of the United States would attack its own people. Criminal gangs may have ruled in other countries like Italy, yes, but it's never happened here and cannot happen here. Any evidence to the contrary is entirely bogus, I don't know anybody who believes this crap."

"Whoa down there, Don," jumped in Lloyd. "As Mark Twain once said, 'It ain't what you don't know that gets you into trouble. It's what you know for sure that just ain't so!'"

"Don't get sarcastic with me, Lloyd, you pinko," said Shivagitz. "We are the world's greatest democracy. We all have a chance to vote. I voted for the President and his party and I'm not a criminal or a traitor, so they can't be either, because we, the people, are the government."

"Did I say you looked like a criminal?" asked Haughton. "If I did, I'd be as guilty as the businessman who was chosen for jury duty. He was so busy at work that he badly wanted to be dismissed from performing his civic duty. He tried every excuse he could think of, but the judge believed that everyone, no matter what their social status, should serve on a jury at some point, and refused to excuse the businessman. On the day of the trial, the businessman decided to give it one more shot. As the trial was about to begin, he asked if he could approach the bench. 'Your Honor,' he said, 'I must be excused from this trial because I am prejudiced against the defendant. I took one look at the man in the blue suit, with the dishonest face and those small, beady-black eyes. I said, 'He's a crook! He's guilty! Guilty! Guilty!' So Your Honor, I can't possibly stay on this jury!' With tired annoyance, the judge replied, 'Get back in the jury box. That man is his lawyer.'"

They all loved that one, except Don, who took it personally, chagrined at this slur on his profession, especially coming from a judge.

"What do criminals and traitors look like, anyway?" asked Athol.

"They look like Arabs, Germans, Japanese and Chinese," said Don. "They look like some of you. That's what they look like. And history is about accidents, bungling, lone nut cases and coincidence – not conspiracy. And like no other nation in history we are an unparalleled success, we are heroes, we are the good guys, we are exceptional and we trust our government to be the same."

"Self-admission being the criterion of veracity," muttered Hans.

"I didn't know you had an office in Disneyland, Don," said Leif the psychiatrist.

Don slammed his cup onto the table, splashing coffee across the cloth. He glared around the table, pushed back his chair and rose to make his exit. "I'm leaving," he said, "and you can all kiss my royal American ass goodbye."

"How romantic!" said Bertha.

"We don't know what we'll do without you," said Glorious with a smile, "but we're willing to try."

"Some say you look much better at a distance," said Ingrid Locke. "You should go far – and none too soon. Goodbye."

"A word of advice," said Don, coldly. "You folks keep up this kind of talk and you could find yourselves in a PDF."

"What did he mean by that?" asked Athol Ludencrude, as he watched Shivagitz pass through the door and into the street.

"Abbreviation for Political Detention Facility," Lloyd explained, "they are being built all across the U.S., as we speak. They changed the name, which was originally CILF, or Civilian Inmate Labor Facility, same thing though."

"Suppose you were an idiot;
and suppose you were a Member of Congress –
but I repeat myself."

— *Mark Twain*

XXXVIII – Crap-Can Con Artists

Meanwhile, down in the Southern States, some things would have been better left unsaid. An over-refreshed Reverend Mosey Long was about to spout another of his amazing revelation sermons to the brethren and sistern of the faithful, in which he examined some of the tenets of the Fundamentalist Church of God. This speech was both live and being broadcast to a national television and radio audience. Mosey was determined to pull out all the stops, leave no sinner unsaved, put the feet of the flock to the fire. They were about to get answers to questions they never asked. He gripped the lectern with both hands, steadied his breathing and stared red-faced at his congregation and the array of microphones and cameras.

"Am I right or am I right?" Mosey shouted. "You're damned right I'm right, you know I'm right. So, don't waste your time arguing the obvious.

"Genesis, the very first book of the Bible, clearly states that there is no way, no how, and never was there the slightest possibility that there ever was such a process as Evolution! That theory, promoted by God-forsaken eco-maniacs, is pure dung of the dog and you and I know it. Merely a clever trick performed by that dimwit Darwin, who made a monkey out of Adam. So, listen people, fill your mind with the truths that I am about to reveal unto you and then nail it shut, so that none of these gems can escape.

"Now tonight, let us examine some of God's words in the Bible. What does He have to say about the question of the separation of Church and State? He saieth, 'What God has joined together, let no man put asunder.' Now, what could be clearer than that? God's hand is needed to guide the State, which is why you should always vote Republican in any election.

"Listeners in radio and TV land, do not touch that dial. It is right and proper that politics should be preached from the pulpit, and what I am about to say is important to this great United States of America, and to the entire God-fearing, Bible-loving free world.

"Revelations tells us that the end is nigh and only the righteous Christian faithful shall be saved and allowed to enter the Paradise of Kingdom Come. On the eve of Armageddon, yea, those that hearken not unto the words that God has exclusively inspired me to speak, shall be put to death. God is going to punish those of you who think that Sodom was a fun city and that Gomorrah was merrier; and he's going to do it real soon." Mosey paused for a moment to lubricate his tonsils from the carafe on the podium, then continued.

"Why? I'll tell you why – because God is sick and tired of crap-can con artists and shit disturbers, Popes and papists, foreigners with beards who don't speak English, murdering abortionists, dope-addicted punks, rock and rollers who smoke weeds and partake of white powders, liberal and social democrats, chickenshit secular humanists, cellphone users in public places, gun-control nuts and treehuggers, telemarketers, rapists, bullshippers, prairie oyster eaters and crotch-watchers. Third World United Nation representatives, Kofi lovers, citizens of those countries who owe money to the World Bank and won't obey WTO rulings, welfare mothers and unemployment recipients, desperate housewives, the White Queen of the Gama Huchi Islands, joggers, nigra-loving judges and defense lawyers, onanists and women who use twelve-inch vibrating dildos, whoremongers and harlots, anyone with B.O. or halitosis, nudists, crotchless pantyhosers, inner Mongolian idiots and cripples, people who break wind in elevators and then get off on the third floor when you're going to the twenty-third, used car and Viagra salesmen, insurance con men, cock-teasing 25-year-old blue-eyed divorcées, *filles de joies*, bicycle-seat sniffers, make-out artists, bung-starters, gangbangers and belly dancers, haberdashers and toastmasters, pooper scoopers and storm troopers. Chickenshitters and cat housers, labor organizers and union members, peckerheads and schmucks, bagpipers and accordion players, and anyone who doesn't give a rat's ass about our President or Jesus. In the last days, these sinners will all be killed and cast down into Hell to burn forever, unless they change their, and I mean it, goddamned ways!"

Mosey paused, wild-eyed, flecks of spittle dotting his lips. Nor was he concerned by the expression of shock on some of the faces of pissed-off parishioners in front of him, as he plunged full speed ahead into his diatribe.

"Now, you may ask why I have left out queers, queens, faggots and fudgepackers, bungholers, corksackers and dicklickers, chocolate speedway artists, knob gobblers and premature ejaculators, ass kissers, and circle jerk weirdos? I know that formerly I have told you that ever since the date in history when man was created by the Trinity, namely the 26th of October, 4004 B.C. at 9 o'clock in the morning, God has frowned on these homo-degenerate practices. But does the Bible approve of homosexuality? Theologians of the Bible Institute of America have searched the Good Book for a definitive answer to this question, and they have found some disturbing new evidence. The answer may not be as clear as we once thought. Three times in the Bible it says, 'Get thee behind me, Satan!' This has created some doubt, and I understand that these passages are being used in the defense of some ass-bandit priests who sodomized their choirboys. Should they be let off the hook? There are a great many votes in the gay community, and we want to be fair-minded in all things. So you figure it out in your own hearts."

Mosey wiped his mouth, dismayed that several people at the back of the church were filing out, and that one camera jockey was actually filming their escape! *Jesus Christ! Am I blowing this sermon? Better lighten up!*

"Now, it is true that we took the Ten Commandments from the Zionists. I'm here to tell you that we may have taken them, but a great many of you have not kept them. That has got to stop. Go on home now, and study your Bible, for there is much that you can learn by doing so. For example, a lot of people say that if it weren't for venetian blinds it would be curtains for all of us. If you turn back to Genesis you'll realize that Eve was the first woman to persuade her husband to turn over a new leaf. Well, we all need to follow suit."

"If you'll recall, when the Ark landed on Mount Ararat, Noah told the animals, 'go forth and multiply.' That's why the two snakes stayed behind because they were only adders." Mosey's nervous chuckle was one of the few to be heard in the auditorium. "Just a little religious levity there, folks, to overcome the gravity of the situation. But to be serious for a moment, just remember that when we pass the collection plate, we want a little more than praise for the church. Dollars are what are required, because in this world you get what you pay for. Verily, I say unto you, it is no harder for a rich man to enter the Kingdom of Heaven than for a needle to go through the eye of a camel!" The gears in his brain were starting to slip and Mosey was really starting to lose it. "And remember, folks, if you can't tune a piano, you can always tuna fish."

What the hell am I talking about? I'd better wind this up! he thought. *I'm trying to keep in mind that every blade of grass is a sermon and therefore is best kept short and neat. A sermon should be like a woman's skirt – short enough to retain the interest but long enough to cover the essentials.*

"So I thank you, Father, Son and Holy Ghost, for choosing me as your messenger. Teach us nothing but Creation, but deliver us from Evolution, for thine is the Republic, and the power of Old Glory, for ever and ever. Amen."

* * *

Jack was waiting in an empty cubicle, curtains drawn, for the return of the medical intern who'd agreed to check out his increasingly debilitating symptoms. The intern almost always got the graveyard shift, and had a soft spot for the down-and-outers on the night-time maintenance crew.

Slippery Jack's health seemed to have gone into free fall. His whole body ached and he'd developed a painful, itchy rash. He was beginning to wonder if, instead of getting Gulf War Syndrome back in Iraq during Desert Storm, he'd become ill from the airborne toxins that had enveloped him on 9/11, and later, when he'd been on-site during the clean-up. *Wouldn't that be ironic retribution for helping Sean Hennessey and Guided Destruction in the controlled demolition?*

In the first 24 hours after the attacks, the EPA and New York City Health Department had issued warnings about the air in downtown Manhattan being highly poisonous. A few days later, the EPA spokesperson Chris T. Witless declared the same air 'safe to breathe' at the World Trade Center site. Jack figured she had been pressured to do this by the White House, in order to re-open Wall Street the next week.

The intern came back with the test results, which he'd gotten a buddy in the lab to run for him right away. Regardless of the source of Jack's illness, the truth was that his chimney was clogged and his slinky kinked. There was too much yardage between the goalposts, and all the while he had been trying to water-ski in Nebraska. These goofy metaphors allowed Jack to face the fact that he wasn't going to live to any ripe old age, and that his final years were likely to be sixty-four cents short of a dollar.

* * *

Jack Danielson was not the only one who was suffering from the toxic fallout of the 9/11 attacks. Benny Fishal's cleanup experience at the Pentagon on 9/11 had continually bugged him too. He was upset in a patriotic sense, especially after he was diagnosed with a form of lymphoma. He wondered if he was somehow a victim of his own proximity to the events of 9/11 at the Pentagon site. If the missile that had likely been fired into the building by remote control had been armed with a blockbuster type of weapon, then was this a possible cause of his condition? These were the thoughts that went through his mind as he took chemotherapy.

Wishing he had done so earlier, Benny came forward with his ground-breaking testimony on radio talk shows and the web site RBNive.com. His description of the aircraft that struck the Pentagon fit precisely with that of a Global Hawk, a relatively unknown UAV, which was still being tested in 2001.

"The government version that a Boeing 757 hijacked by Arabs hit the Pentagon is bogus," Fishal said. "All the hype about the video frames released by the Pentagon showing a 757 is a lie if I ever saw one. The American people need to know it was not a Boeing 757 that hit the Pentagon. No way."

* * *

Nick didn't really want to, but he forced himself to make a return visit to the Walter Reed Medical Center. The place gave him the creeps, a feeling he abhorred as a sign of weakness. However, he had promised the young amputee, Zack Zapata, and on this occasion, he felt compelled to keep his word. Perhaps he just wanted to assuage the sense that he was in some way responsible for the young man's predicament. Obviously the war had been necessary to reach America's goals and was therefore, as he had written into a speech for the President, a noble cause. That some others might not think so was immaterial. So, *nulla dies sine linea*, he said to himself, you've got to keep at it.

As he strode down the hallway to Ward F, he recalled reading somewhere that the old building was about to be replaced. He'd been pleased at that, then surprised that he would care. He stepped through the doors of Zack's ward and approached the young veteran's bed.

"How are you today, Zack?" he asked. "You remember me, I hope. Nicolaus D'Amous."

Zack looked up, obviously startled, and quickly shut down the program he'd been running. "Of course, Mr. D'Amous," Zack said. He closed his laptop.

"This must help pass the time," D'Amous said, indicating the computer. "What were you doing? Games or research?"

"Just catching up on the news," Zack replied.

D'Amous glanced at the vet in the adjacent bed.

"This is my friend Bill Bailey," Zack said by way of introduction. "Bill, this is Mr. Nicolaus D'Amous."

"A p-pleasure, Mr. D'Amous," Bill said. "B-but we have met before."

Taken by surprise, D'Amous exclaimed, "You have the advantage there, son."

"You like-likely don't remember. C-couple of years ba-back at the Do-Dominionists' Reclaiming Am-America Convention. You and I talked for a bit over cof-coffee. Mostly about my j-joining up to f-f-f-fight for America."

D'Amous wondered whether he was responsible for this soldier's wounds. He said cautiously, "Yes, I recall now. Good to see you again, although I wish it could be under better circumstances. I take it you were in Iraq."

"D-did a tour there, yes, sir."

"And you were injured?"

"Yes, bu-but not there. He-here. By the cops. They Ta-Ta-Tasered me."

D'Amous paused for several seconds. "Now that is ironic," he said.

Bill nodded. "I th-thought so too, sir."

"How did that affect you?" D'Amous asked.

"Nerv-nervous system disorder."

D'Amous perfunctorily expressed sorrow. "Well, I hope you get well soon." He turned back to Zack. "I'm having a prosthetics expert call around shortly to assess your needs, Zack. I've also arranged to have you kitted out with a top-of-the-line wheelchair."

Zack was flabbergasted, but managed to thank D'Amous, who extended the awkward conversation as long as he could, then said his goodbyes and walked out of the hospital. By the time he reached his car, he'd shrugged off the uncomfortable emotions the visit had aroused in him and was back to his usual stone-hearted, ruthless self.

"To grasp this sorry Scheme of Things entire,
Would not we shatter it to bits – and then
Re-mould it nearer to the Heart's Desire!"

— *Omar Khayyam, Stanza 99,* Rubayat, *1859*

XXXIX – Miz Sarah Bellum

Jack had been given a slow death sentence and that took a little time getting used to. He fought his way past three saloons on his way back to the Hostel Destiny, but refused to take a drink. He fell exhausted onto his bed and tried to calm his racing thoughts and get a few hours of fitful sleep before going back to Walter Reed to put in his shift. He'd tell the news to Bill and Zack at their nightly bull session.

"Where's Bill?" he asked that night when he entered the ward and saw the empty bed.

"He got a three-day pass to go home with Helen. He's feeling a lot better these days."

Jack told Zack the results of his tests and that his condition was going to greatly reduce the length and quality of his life. "Them's the breaks, I guess, but nothing compared to *your* problems."

"Sorry to hear we have similar situations," said Zack, "Join the club. But I've got news of my own. Maybe you've heard, there's a big Republican gathering next month at the Washington Convention Center. The President's going to announce his new foreign policy direction in a speech to the nation, live."

"Hadn't heard that," said Jack, "and I doubt that *we're* invited."

"And that would be where you're wrong," said Zack, with a wide grin on his face. "Nicolaus D'Amous has told me that the President is going to explain the administration's policy for Iraq and hopefully halt his slide in the public opinion polls. It's down to a measly 31 percent right now, you know. And D'Amous wants me to be the poster boy for the veterans of the War on Terror."

"Are you going to do it?!" Jack exclaimed.

"Yeah, told him I would, but I said I'd want someone who's familiar with my condition and needs to come along with me. He agreed, and that's where you come in. I want you to go with me."

"I'm not exactly an orderly."

"Doesn't matter, you know what to do, how to help me when I need it. You've been doing that all along. And thanks, in case I never told you before, I appreciate it. D'Amous is going to give me some notes for a short speech he wants me to make on behalf of the veterans."

"That's really something, Zack."

"Something bigger than you might think. I have an idea. It may not be feasible, but I want to discuss it with you."

"Fine by me."

"It's pretty wild."

"So what?"

"Plus, it would take a little money to pull it off."

"I've got some dough. Go ahead, shoot."

* * *

Back at the hostel the next afternoon, Jack spent an hour carefully trimming his beard, then hunted through his closet for a presentable shirt and pants. He took the subway downtown, emerged at street level and saw the convention center. Located in the heart of the nation's capital, the long glass and steel building covered two city blocks, and was flanked by N Street to the north and Massachusetts and New York Avenues to the south – over two million square feet of space in total. He walked the perimeter. The place was so big, he could hardly tell one back entrance from another.

He was halfway around when he came upon a couple of janitors sharing a smoke break outside a set of double doors.

After a few minutes of swapping jokes, Jack asked whether there was any work to be had at the center.

"Part-time or full-time?" the larger of the two men asked.

"Either one would be good. I'm looking for a job that's handier to my digs."

"What kind of work?"

"Janitorial, maintenance," Jack replied.

"Well, full-time's tough, but you might get one covering for guys who are sick or want to book off for some reason or other." The man appraised Jack for a moment, then said, "Wait 'til I finish this smoke and I'll show you which door takes you to the human resources office. Come by tomorrow morning and ask for a Ms. Sarah Bellum. She's the one to see about hirin' and firin' guys like us."

The next day Jack turned up in his good duds, his curly hair neatly combed, and waited while his presence was announced to the support staff manager. After a fifteen-minute wait, Jack was ushered in to see Sarah Bellum, a gray-haired, middle-aged, overly made-up woman clinging to the wreckage of a once-fine figure.

Bellum fiddled with her eyeglasses and the pencil in her hand, not looking up from the papers on her desk, as Jack sat down in front of her.

"Got any references?" was her first question after Jack made his pitch, turning on the charm.

"I could get some from Walter Reed. Been doing some work for them. But I'd rather work for you," he said, grinning.

Sarah, who'd probably heard her fair share of blarney,

smiled despite herself and said, "Okay, give me your particulars, Mr. O'Reilly. Where can I get in touch with you?"

"I'm in the process of moving. Could I just check in with you in a day or so?"

"Fine by me," said Bellum, still smiling. "This place is huge and we need a lot of maintenance people to cover it all. People come and go in this town and never tell me why. I'd be happier if they'd tell me they were leaving, although some of them don't seem to think that'd be the polite thing to do. So I'll check out the situation and you can call me tomorrow. We'll see what we can do for you, Mr. O'Reilly."

"Thanks, Miz Bellum, and just call me Jack, okay?" He stood and extended his hand. "It's been a real pleasure meeting you, ma'am," he added, holding onto Sarah's hand just a little longer than necessary.

* * *

Instead of calling, Jack turned up again the next day. He didn't have to wait as long this time. "You're timing is good, Mr. O'Reilly, I've got a guy off on holidays as of today, and we can't afford to be short-staffed with this Republican love-in coming up. If you like, you can start right away."

Jack thanked her profusely, shaking her hand again. Bellum, looking a tad flustered, said, "It'll give me a chance to find out if you're as good at working as you are at talking, you Irish smoothie."

* * *

Jack quit his job at Walter Reed with some regret, but continued his visits with Bill and Zack.

At his first opportunity, prepared to use his janitorial cover or pretend he'd lost his way, Jack cased the 52,000-square-foot ballroom where the Republican event and the speech by the President were to take place. One problem apparent to Jack was the excessive number of security officers in the building. He realized that the success of the plan depended on the location and sophistication of any detection devices they might set up. The wheelchair switch he and Zack had in mind would have to happen past that point.

So where was the most likely spot? What was the most usual excuse for having to leave a room? Easy as pie. Going back to grade school, you put up your hand when you wanted to leave the classroom and the teacher gave you permission to go to the can.

Jack found a set of washrooms in a corridor leading into the lounge, which served as a holding area for people waiting to go onto the ballroom stage. And as Irish luck would have it, the door beside the men's washroom was an entrance to a supply room. Perfect – that was Jack's department and he of all people was allowed in. Such places were usually no more than cubby-holes, but like everything else in the convention center, this one was humungous. Shelves lined the sidewalls, and there were a couple of racks down the middle of the room. Large cardboard cartons of supplies were arranged along the back wall. Move those around a bit and they could provide a good place to stash the dummy wheelchair, hopefully long enough – a day or two before the event – to go undetected before the switch took place.

Jack spent a considerable chunk of his newly obtained cash on buying an identical wheelchair to the one D'Amous had supplied to Zack, and took it back to his room at the Hostel Destiny, telling his motley neighbors there that he was fixing it for a disabled veteran he'd befriended at the hospital.

After another trip to the Rumgunner, Jack went to work on the wheelchair, filling the hollow tubing of the frame with deadly plastic explosives, hooking a detonating system into the guts of the complicated operational panel of the chair. He did it carefully, because he didn't want to blow the hostel to smithereens along with the Candle Man, the Egg Lady and Jimmy the Slice. He also installed a second remote-controlled firing device to the explosive charge as a backup.

It wasn't long before Jack was ready.

* * *

Slippery Jack hired a truck to transport the chair to the convention center parking lot, steering the truck toward the incoming freight shed belonging to the complex.

"Where you goin' with that?" The question brought Jack to a halt. He turned to face the beefy, bald security guard and got ready to do some fast-talking.

"Medical meeting scheduled for the fourth floor. They want this contraption for a demo," Jack flashed his maintenance worker's badge.

"I haven't heard about a medical meeting," the guard said.

"Well, the wheelchair company rep dropped it off and the office told me to deliver it pronto," Jack explained. "Hey, would you like to take it for a spin? Quite the machine." As the guard shook his head, Jack performed a wheelie with the chair, and said coaxingly, "Come on, try it."

"Nah, I haven't got time to horse around. Besides, I might screw up the mechanics or something."

"Okay." Jack took off toward the elevators, and spotted one that was empty. Taking that to his floor, he then tooled down the hall and into the supply room. Once inside, he concealed the chair behind the cardboard cartons of toilet paper and towels stacked along the back wall. The chair would have to stay hidden for a couple of days, so Jack made sure there were plenty of open cartons of supplies near the front of the room. Only through dumb luck would anyone discover it before they went on-stage.

> "The thing is with democracy, the people who are elected
> are never dumber than the people who elected them,
> or else they wouldn't have been elected."
>
> — *Bertrand Russell*

XL – The Omissions Commission

Fall 2002

While enjoying a leisurely breakfast, Dr. Guylain Bardow was listening to a country and western radio station. They were playing 'hurtin music,' your basic sobbin'-in-my-Budweiser, woman-done-left-me, sheriff-shot-my-hound-dog music. The tune was 'If I Said You Had a Beautiful Body, Would You Hold It Against Me?'

His housekeeper entered and announced that his car was waiting out front. He finished his coffee as the song ended, gathered up his briefcase and walked out to the curb, where an idling black limousine awaited.

Opening the rear passenger door, Bardow was startled to find the back seat occupied by a jovial looking individual he recognized as the second-in-charge at the National Security Office.

Bardow had just been appointed Executive Director of the 9/11 Commission because of his Republican connections, including having been on the President's Foreign Intelligence Advisory Board since 2001. His lengthy service with the GOP was not widely known outside Washington power circles. Bardow had navigated the ethical and legal slough of two other commissions of inquiry into potential political disasters in a manner that hadn't threatened the administration's agenda. This had established his reputation with the neoconservatives as a fair and thorough man, whose primary interest was getting at the truth of their preference.

259

"Get in, Doctor, we have things to discuss," said the man.

When Bardow had taken his seat and the car was in motion, with the privacy window in place, the official congratulated him on his new post, then said, "You do enjoy the perks of a life well lived, don't you, Guy?"

Guylain could see where this was going, as he had been down this street before. Not wanting to change his life in ways he wouldn't like, he didn't answer in the vulgar vocative, but opted for the affirmative. "Yes," he replied.

"You realize, of course, that the White House is essentially investigating itself, which is why we've chosen you to do this job."

"Which is what exactly?" asked Guylain.

"As you probably know, the Family Steering Committee for an Independent 9/11 Commission forced us into doing this and by God, we're going to see that it's done – our way."

"And you want someone to run the show so that it doesn't look like the fix is in. Right? What about the Chairman? Isn't that his job?"

"Look, the Chairman is just the titular head. The Executive Director runs the show. It'll be up to you to determine the focus and direction of the Commission's investigation. Decide what they look into and what they don't. See to it that you and maybe only one other member is allowed to review all the intelligence records, and make your own notes before reporting back to the Commission. And when they finally finish the job – and we don't care how long it takes – you write the final report."

"Who else will be on the commission's board?"

"Don't worry about that," the official said. "We'll have the board packed tighter than the borrowed flight suit that Truck wore for his photo op on the U.S.S. Lincoln."

> "The individual is handicapped by coming face
> to face with a conspiracy so monstrous he
> cannot believe it exists."
>
> — *J. Edgar Hoover*

XLI – Guy Fawkes Redux

"Man, this is some wheelchair," Zack exclaimed as he sat working the controls with his left hand, popping a couple of wheelies in the patient's lounge. The room was empty except for Bill and Zack.

"The standard army issue models are good, all right, but that's a Cadillac," Bill agreed, watching his friend maneuver the wheelchair around the chairs and coffee tables.

"Damn nice of D'Amous to get this for me."

Bill was glad to see his buddy smiling for a change, but he was a realist. "With him being such a *big shot* in the government do you think this is his way of working off guilt for the mess he helped cause in Iraq?"

"More like a *big shit*, I'd say," Zack observed. "Everybody seems to kiss his ass, and I think we're just starting to see how big a role he plays. I'll bet when he says jump, even the President says, 'How high?' But I am grateful for what he's done for me."

"Do you think we're getting too wound up in all this political stuff?" asked Bill. "I can only take so much before the whole thing depresses me. I see all these guys coming in here, basket cases most of them. Over six hundred sent back for psych treatment since we first went into Iraq. Almost two dozen suicides – that we know of – and they figure one in five of us is gonna end up with post-traumatic stress disorder. Like those zoned-out homeless guys, half of them Vietnam vets who just couldn't get it together when they got back home."

Zack swung his wheelchair around to face Bill. "What else can I say? Let me think. So D'Amous is helping me for whatever reason, it doesn't matter. That doesn't change the fact that we've got a fascist dictatorship for a government and he's in it up to his neck. I can't ignore that."

"Fascist dictatorship? In the good ol' U.S. of A.?" Bill said, feigning the cowboy drawl again. "I know the sheriff's nothing but a steaming pile of manure with a badge on, and that they're up to no good in the White House, but –"

Zack spun the chair in a 360-degree circle as he warmed to his topic. "Look, who's in charge in this country these days? A President who stole two elections and set up a shadow government quite literally run by criminals. *That's who!*

"Why have a secret government operating out of the basement, like Reagan did, when you can have one operating upstairs in broad daylight in the White House, supported by a lame duck Congress? A government that spies on its citizens while utilizing old Nazi tactics. One that spends its money on foreign wars while its own people suffer, and that subsidizes the military and the corporations who, in turn, fund both parties to the hilt. You marry politics to corporations and fold in the church and what do you think you get? Fascism! *That's what!*"

"The world situation has never been so dangerous," Helen Weills said as she walked into the lounge. "You've got our President, who thinks he's being guided by the hand of God and is just waiting for the Second Coming of Jesus. You've got Muslim leaders who think they're guided by the hand of Allah, like the president of Iran, who's waiting for the Twelfth Imam to come back to Earth in time for Judgment Day. We've got nukes; maybe even Iran's got 'em. Hell, the wacky President of North Korea's got nukes. All God's chillen got nukes! And who's going to get their asses blown off when these nutbars clash? None of these so-called leaders are capable of running a brothel, let alone a country. Something's gotta be done about these idiots. Starting here at home! We can't just do sweet essence of bugger-all."

Jack Danielson chose that moment to enter the lounge, bearing a tray of coffees for everyone. "I heard some of that," he said, setting the tray on the table and sinking slowly into a chair. His muscles, which had become increasingly sore of late, protested. "Does religious ideology have anything whatsoever to do with fascism? Don't think so. Bobby Kennedy Jr. said it best: *While communism is the control of business by government, fascism is the control of government by business.*"

Zack spoke up. "In that case, Jack, you're describing the schmucks who are holed up in the White House. I hope you're here to tell us we're going ahead with our plan. I've read about all I can stomach about 9/11. In fact, I'm so steamed I can hardly stand it. It's either do something drastic or roll over and die in my bed. Except I'd need help rolling over."

"Why don't you catch Helen up on what you've found out, Zack?" Bill suggested. "When she and I are together, politics ain't exactly uppermost in our minds, if ya know what I mean." He slipped an arm around Helen's waist as the others chuckled.

"Okay," said Zack. "We all know the official story, right? Nineteen Arab hijackers crashed three out of four airliners into symbolically important American targets allegedly as part of an ongoing terrorist war against this country. So if that's true, how come there were no Arab names on the passenger lists of any of the four planes? Of that list of nineteen hijackers who supposedly went down with the planes, half a dozen or more now say they're very much alive and well and living in the Middle East. The alleged Arab hijackers were either double agents or patsies.

"The planes were flying popular routes, so they were usually packed, or even overbooked. But on 9/11, American Airlines Flight 11 was only at 30 percent capacity, Flight 77 at 27 percent, United Airlines Flight 175 was at 26 percent and Flight 93 at just 16 percent capacity."

While the others listened raptly, sipping their coffees without taking their eyes off Zack, he continued his exposition.

"Why did it take an hour and a half for the air force to scramble any fighter jets? On 9/11, the Vice President, we know, was in full control of America's air defense system; in fact, he was overseeing at least five war-games going on that day. So when the attacks happened, most of our jets were off on a training exercise way up in Alaska, instead of patrolling the skies over Washington and New York. Even the ones that were available were sent out over the Atlantic for some goddamned reason. Or ordered to chase down phantom Flight 11 which they thought had miraculously survived the crash into the South Tower and kept on flying! Does this sound like something Osama bin Laden and his terrorist groupies, huddled together in an Afghani cave, could cook up? No, the war-games were staged to facilitate the attacks and then used as an excuse for failing to prevent them."

Zack paused for breath. He smiled his thanks at Helen, who pressed a coffee into his hand. "No modern high-rise steel-framed building has ever collapsed because of fire of any kind, before 9/11 or since. And yet, that day three skyscrapers collapsed into a cloud of dust. Count 'em: WTC 1, 2 and 7. Well, now we know from Jack here, that it was controlled demolition that brought the World Trade Center buildings down – because *he helped wire 'em*! There's no shortage of witnesses, including firefighters, who heard and saw the explosions popping and flashing all over the place before the towers collapsed."

As Helen stared mutely at him, Jack rubbed a hand over his face. "Look, I'm not proud of my role in 9/11," he said. "I had no idea what was planned by those bastards. And I guess I'm paying the ultimate price now. One of my best friends was just murdered. I'm a wanted man. And, whether it's from the first Gulf War or the crap I breathed in on 9/11, I haven't likely got all that long to live anyway." Helen's look softened to one of sympathy as Jack added, "Payback's a bitch, huh?"

"Don't sweat it, buddy. No way you knew what was going down that day, so cut the guilt, okay?" Zack resumed his narrative. "Let's look at what happened right after the attacks. The day after 9/11, the federal government declares war on all so-called rogue States, and targets Iraq as part of an 'axis of evil.' Truth is, the plans to attack Iraq and Afghanistan were already in place, had been since Truck took office. It's our government, or the CIA if you want to be specific, that helped set up the Taliban in Afghanistan, and we know what holy terror those guys unleashed on the Soviets. Then when the Taliban took over and wouldn't cooperate on the building of the oil pipeline we wanted, we used the 'Osama did it' story as an excuse to bomb the shit out of them.

"We now know there never were any 'weapons of mass destruction' in Iraq. But the Iraqis had those huge oil reserves we wanted plus, thanks to Saddam, the petrodollar was under attack. After ten years of economic embargoes, we gave up. So when 9/11 came along, it gave us the very convenient excuse to go in and secure America's oil supply, and be able to deny it to our competitors. Or so we thought. And why are we focusing on Iran as the next villain? Because of the oil *they're* sitting on. What else? Bring them U.S.-style democracy?!

"Within a week of 9/11 the American media were speaking with one voice. All dissent against what the officials said were facts, was labeled a conspiracy theory, and anyone with a difference of opinion was called unpatriotic and a nutcase. The official story was agreed on – that the fanatics from al-Qaeda did it, probably with help from Iraq. That was a slam dunk and no doubt an investigation would clear up the details."

"I'm appalled at the scale of this," Helen said, shaking her head in disbelief. "How have they been able to get away with such a massive conspiracy?"

"By discrediting anybody who tried to poke holes in the government's story, and calling them a *conspiracy wingnut* or worse, *traitor*. By making sure that the media, nearly all of whom are controlled by mega-rich corporations, dance to the official tune. By passing the Patriot Act, which went through a complacent do-nothing Congress like crap through a goose – no one in Congress even had a chance to read the draconian legislation before it was passed – we now have secret prisons, torture chambers and people being killed for trying to blow the whistle on the cover-up. No wonder the Senate and Congress are afraid to rein in the administration.

"So there you have it. The War on Terror is bullshit and the perpetrators are now real nervous that what *they* call conspiracy theories are quickly gaining credence among a growing number of Americans, that the wars they started were outright frauds, and that their dirty tricks and perjury will all be found out.

"We're being ruled by a government headed by a fundamentalist frat boy who barely understands the speeches that are written for him, and who's under the thumb of Ubermeister Nicolaus D'Amous. For kissing the President's ass while Truck farts in their faces, government departments are packed with the Christian faithful, eager for their shot at screwing the country. Ironically, the intelligence agencies like the CIA and FBI, who failed us on 9/11 and helped create the disaster, got huge budget hikes. Meanwhile, by exercising their right to be uninformed, apathetic Americans are asleep at the wheel and headed for disaster. We're talking the end of personal freedom in this country. And, just to think, the Republican regime's shoveling money at their corporate cronies in the form of tax breaks and pork-barrel politics – which is one reason our national debt is so bad that this entire country might be bankrupt by 2009. The question is, do we let them get away with it?"

"Okay, I'm good and pissed off now," Helen declared. "So what do we do? It's no use preaching to each other here. Who else can we talk to about this?"

"Nobody that I know of," said Jack, "but we either act to end it or know that we are accomplices to traitors, tyranny, murder, maiming and torture. Now is the time for action, and regime change of these neofascist pigs in this administration – both parties for that matter – starts here!"

"Well, I can hardly say any of this in the speech D'Amous wants me to give at the convention center," said Zack "But Jack's got a plan. Tell 'em, Jack,"

Looking each of them in the eye, Jack said, "You all know I'm a veteran, one of over a million of us who've been used and abused in the two Iraqi wars. So I've definitely got an axe to grind. Add to that the fact that I'm probably going to be hunted for the rest of my life – which probably won't be too long anyway – and I'm highly motivated to take a big risk."

"As for me," Zack interrupted, "you guys know I don't much care if I live or die, and that actually I'd prefer the latter. Jack and I have talked about assisted suicide and cases like Terry Schiavo. The docs tell me I've got other problems besides being an amputee. My life is shit. I'm going to buy the farm, and I know it."

"What?!" Helen said, looking at the others in dismay. "Get to the point, already!"

Jack leaned toward her, pitching his voice low. "I bought a wheelchair just like Zack's here. I've added some features, like packing the hollow tubing of the chair with plastic explosives."

Helen let out a gasp and covered her mouth with her hand.

"D'Amous wants Zack to give a 'wounded vet' speech at the Washington Convention Center. The President and most of his administration will be there, along with about three thousand Republicans – foreign policy types. All we have to do is switch Zack's wheelchair for the one I bought."

"How do we do that?" Bill interjected.

"As a matter of fact, I've already cased the ballroom area and the security set-up. The operation's all set to go."

"What do you want me to do?" Bill asked.

"Nothing," Jack said emphatically. "You're not helping, and neither is Helen. You two have family about to happen and a full life ahead of you. Zack and I don't want you taking any part in this gunpowder plot. In fact, it doesn't require your help at all. Just your moral support. Another thing, we never had this conversation."

The two protested, but Zack and Jack were adamant, going on to explain the final details. "Zack will be with D'Amous before he goes on stage."

"But, don't forget, we need time to make the wheelchair switch." Zack put in.

"Right," Jack said. "And given Zack's condition, we're counting on the security people to give us enough slack for this to happen."

Just because we've done it
wrong for all these years,
is no reason to change things now.
So let's avoid thuzzy finking
and ...

XLII – Do It Rihgt

November 10, 2006 – The Oval Office

The past was perfect, the present is tense, and the future comes soon enough, thought Nick 'the Nostril', *and the only sure thing is that people always act in their own self-interest. Which is why plans should be implemented right away before future events can create roadblocks to an overall goal.*

He was in the Oval Office of the White House talking to the joint incumbents.

The President leaned across the desk on his elbows, a smirk on his face, "Didn't the UN Committee on Torture say that some of us here were in violation of international treaties by condoning torture?"

The Vice President scowled and said, "The UN doesn't know chickenshit from chicken salad."

"Yeah, right," Nick 'the Nostril' agreed, "They're a pain in the neck, unless you have a lower opinion of them. You guys are in the clear, so don't sweat it. It's now U.S. law that we don't have to obey international law. The Military Commissions Act you signed on October 17th sanctions human rights violations or bad executive decisions by the United States throughout the War on Terror, and also includes the use of torture – above the waist, that is – and the denial of *habeas corpus*."

"What's that again?" asked Truck, scratching his head.

"We can arrest anyone we don't like, even U.S. citizens, label them as 'enemy combatants' and put them away forever. That'll come in handy for some of those damn peace protestors and 9/11 skeptics who are getting in our way. No right to a lawyer – of their own choosing, at least – no right to see the evidence held against them and, best of all, no right to a fair trial by judge or jury within a reasonable period of time. Basically, we can black-hole them for an eternity," 'the Nostril' explained with a grin.

The V.P. nodded his approval. "The mainstream media guys have done a pretty good job of keeping *that news* off the front page. I was expecting an uproar about the famous writ of *habeas corpus* being shredded, but all we got was a few squawks from the ACLU. The New World Order is dancing on the grave of *habeas corpus* and the First Amendment, to boot! As for 'peaceful' political protestors they can either stay home or end up getting a free, one-way ticket to Gitmo Bay."

But D'Amous had other things on his mind. His immediate problem was the unexpected outcome of the November 7th midterm elections for the House of Representatives and one-third of the Senate seats, and that was why he was here and the subject was up for discussion.

"*Experto credite,*" said Nick as he paced back and forth. "Believe me when I tell you that this is not defeat. A small road-block, a setback if you will, but just one from which we can take immediate advantage. A lull in which we can consolidate our gains to date."

"How so?" asked the President, anxious to keep in the loop from which he often felt excluded.

"The midterm elections meant nothing," Nick replied, "and that's exactly what the American public can expect. The fix is always in with eighty percent of Congress, who are bought and paid for, whether they are Republicans or blue dog Democrats.

Nothing dire will happen. The main concern of most members of both parties is how to stay elected, and they can't do that without the massive financial assistance supplied by our wealthy backers. How else will they be able to afford all the television advertising necessary to win in 2008? As we all know, America doesn't have a two-party political system. It's one party, with two different colors. The same special interests control both."

"True enough," said the Vice from his position by a window. "At least we have accomplished one of our goals: the destabilization of Iraq. We've incapacitated their conventional forces and it has become a basket case about to split into three pieces. Now, if we and our allies can do the same thing to Iran ... and Syria ... we'd be all set. Besides there are only a few House Democrats who want significant change in U.S. foreign policy, or an immediate withdrawal from the Middle East, like Dennis what's-his-name, and he doesn't count."

"That's right," the President chimed in, "the Democrats unanimously voted for both Patriot Acts, and passed every funding bill for the Iraqi and Afghanistan wars, even agreed to the donation of munitions and jet fuel for the southern Lebanon attack."

"Keep in mind it is only a one seat congressional majority and we made sure that the key independent was elected, and he knows it." Nick continued, in a self-congratulatory mood, "furthermore, you should be glad that I got the President to sign the *John Warner National Defense Authorization Act for Fiscal Year 2007.*"

The President flipped through his desk calendar. "Hey, that was back on October 17th too. What was that all about again?"

Nick gave a sigh of resignation. "It handed you the power to subvert the authority of each individual state, to call in the military, including the state National Guard, to serve under your command and federalize state law enforcement."

"Ah right!" said Truck, as he leaned back.

"Also," said the Vice, a broad smile on his ego-mad face, "it gives the military the authority to ask Congress for 462.8 billion dollars in funding, plus another 70 billion dollars to get new army and marine corps equipment, which is wearing out faster than hindsight replaces foresight."

"Not only that but you can send in the military," said 'the Nostril', "to police any trouble spot in this country regardless of the wishes of any state Governor, including that actor in California."

"What kind of trouble?" asked the President.

"Any kind. And you can dragoon all National Guards into the federal service, in any State or possession of the U.S., 'to restore public order and enforce the laws of the United States, as a result of natural disaster, epidemic, other serious public incidents, *or any other condition'*."

"It's like ketchup," said the Vice, "it covers a multitude of sins, such as insurrection, domestic violence, unlawful conspiracies."

"The key phrase was *or any other condition,*" said Nick proudly. "That was my idea. Slipped it in as a rider because I knew nobody would study the Bill. They never do. And now it's already passed."

"Sounds good," said the President. "I didn't read it all back then. I got put off by that term 'Posse Communitis' or whatever it's called."

"You mean, 'Posse Comitatus' – that's an 1878 Act which basically states that the military cannot be used to execute the laws of the land within the United States and whoever authorizes such an action could be fined or imprisoned."

"Good thing we got rid of that. So you mean, I'm now the dictator of a police state and I can send in a military police force to any city in the nation, whenever I like?"

"That's it," said Nick, "on a whim."

"Hmmm ... then isn't it about time we shut the big mouth on that Iranian camel driver ... you know, the one with the name no one can pronounce, Mahmud somebody? Drop a few big boys on his *nuculer* facilities. I've been wantin' to do that for a long time."

There are not many ideas that get past Truck's hair, thought Nick. "You could," he answered tersely, "but don't forget the deal. Those kinds of decisions have to be vetted by me on behalf of the Global Union. So don't go off half-cocked. We'll tell you when we want to start another war. Now let's get back to this new Democratic Congress bit. Best you show a little contrition, Mr. President, a little less of the cowboys and Iranians persona, if you please."

The President grimaced but stopped talking. *Damn this bureaucratic heifer dust anyway,* he thought.

"So, for public consumption," Nick continued, "we need to throw somebody to the wolves. They are howling for a scapegoat now that this election is over."

"Like a designated fall-guy?" said the Vice. "I sincerely hope you aren't suggesting me or the President?"

"Au contraire," said Nick, switching to French. "Someone who was in charge of the planning of the Iraqi war and whom the public perceives as having royally fucked it up."

A short silence ensued, dominating the room as they looked back and forth from one to the other.

"Are you thinking what I'm thinking?" asked Nick. "There's only one logical choice for that role. The public, even the military, hates his guts."

"You're thinking of ..." said the President.

"You don't mean ..." said the Vice.

"Who else," said Nick. "... Dick Tater!"

"Good choice, although too bad we don't have Bob Loblaw around any longer," said the Vice, smiling at D'Amous. "But that brings up something else that we have to think about."

"What?" asked Nick, turning suddenly and dropping into a chair.

"Who do we bring in as his replacement for Secretary of Defense?"

"No problem. I have a guy already warmed up in the bull pen," said Nick, running his hand back through his hair, "who can pitch big curve balls. We picked him on waivers from the Iran-Contra team, one of their top-notch pitchers."

"Has he got a name?"

"Yeah, you know him," said Nick. "Denny Grayshen. The guy most responsible for institutionalizing political corruption of intelligence analysis, and who always shaped it to suit our needs – *contra bono mores* – against society's best interests."

"So we're still in business," added the Vice. "It's mind control as usual, instilling fear above and beyond the level of the real threat. Americans are so monumentally gullible it defies description. So shall we tell the public we're going to pull the plug on our troops in Iraq and Afghanistan? – Not!"

"Today Americans would be outraged if UN troops entered Los Angeles to restore order; tomorrow they will be grateful! This is especially true if they were told there was an outside threat from beyond, whether real or promulgated, that threatened our very existence. It is then that people of the world will plead with world leaders to deliver them from this evil. The one thing every man fears is the unknown. When presented with this scenario, individual rights will be willingly relinquished for the guarantee of their well being granted to them by their world government."

— *Henry Kissinger, in an address to the Bilderbergers at Evian, France, May 21, 1992*
(Transcribed from a tape made by one of the Swiss delegates.)

XLIII – Show Time

A wheelchair-friendly hospital transport vehicle took Zack and Jack to the Washington Convention Center, where they were met by a pair of White House staffers who escorted them through the checkpoints. Both the visitors and the wheelchair were subjected to electronic and physical searches at several stations, but the process became more perfunctory as soon as Nicolaus D'Amous turned up. He welcomed both men and hailed Zack as a war hero, at which point the security people lined up to shake his only hand.

D'Amous escorted the two men to the lounge adjacent to the ballroom. He pointed out a few of the high-powered politicos streaming into the room, engaged in intense conversations and bringing with them an air of mild excitement. With thirty minutes to go, the President arrived with an entourage of his closest aides and hangers-on. D'Amous offered to introduce Zack to the President, at which point Jack beckoned D'Amous aside and whispered in his ear, "Zack's upset because he's

275

occasionally incontinent, and he's worried that all the stress of being here and giving a talk might bring on an unfortunate incident. I'd like to take him to the men's room before the speeches get started."

"Good idea," D'Amous replied. "We don't want him pissing himself on national television. Go ahead, as long as he's ready to go on stage with us at eight o'clock."

* * *

The President was also upset as he walked around pressing the flesh, but he was well schooled in the art of hiding his emotions behind a fake mask. He was under pressure from all sides, now that the American GI body count had reached the same level as those killed on 9/11. The soldiers' families were screaming for his blood. Congress was challenging his God-given right to spy on his fellow citizens and even the media, the double-crossers, were starting to question American interrogation and 'prisoner handling' tactics at Guantánamo Bay and other holding facilities for suspected terrorists. Truck was furious at the rising tide of leaks detailing things that were supposed to have been kept secret from the American people. *As for the whistleblowers, when I get my hands on them, they'll get a personal tour of some prisons that would make the torture at Abu Ghraib seem like a Sunday school picnic. Accusing me of illegal actions! I'm not just their democratically elected leader, damn it all, I'm their King and the United States Constitution is just a goddamned piece of paper.*

He had his new foreign policy speech in the inside pocket of his jacket, and by God, he was going to seize the chance to blast his enemies as well.

* * *

Zack executed a practiced 180 and he and Jack headed out of the lounge and down the hall toward the washrooms. Once the lounge doors closed behind them and the hallway was clear, they slipped into the supply room, where Jack flung aside the cardboard boxes concealing the second wheelchair. He pushed it out beside the one in which Zack was sitting and completed the hook-ups that armed the substitute chair. He helped Zack get into the rigged chair, then wheeled the other one toward the back of the room.

Suddenly the door opened and in stepped an officer from Homeland Security, who raked his eyes over the scene. "What's going on here?" he demanded, walking past Zack toward Jack at the rear.

"Just helping my veteran friend here get ready for his speech," Jack said, straightening up quickly.

"How come you need two wheelchairs for one amputee?"

Zack already had his left hand wrapped around a toilet plunger with a metal handle. He rear-ended the guard with his wheelchair; then as the guard fell backward, Zack brought the toilet plunger handle down on the man's head with all his might.

At the same time Jack delivered a right cross to the guard's jaw. The man let out a grunt and toppled sideways onto the floor, out cold. Jack was on him like a fat kid on a french fry, rolling him over onto his back. "Nice work, pal," he said to Zack. "Still a good soldier, aren't you, who knows what to do in the clutch."

Zack beamed, then said, "We don't have much time, Jack."

"I know," Jack replied as he hoisted the guard into the wheelchair, then grabbed a roll of handyman's helper – duct tape – and sealed the man's mouth and secured him to the chair. "No calls for help from this bird," Jack said as he wheeled the chair with the unconscious guard behind the cardboard boxes, and taped it to a standpipe.

Back in the lounge, a relieved D'Amous greeted them. "I was beginning to be concerned about you two," he said. "Now, don't be nervous, Zack. You'll be fine. Remember, *fortuna favet fortibus*. Fortune favors the brave. This evening will make a national hero out of you. Something that, in my opinion, you richly deserve."

Zack hung his head. A sad expression came over his face and he surreptitiously brushed a tear from his eye. "I kinda wish you hadn't said that, Mr. D'Amous. But if it happens, it'll be because of you. I want you to know that, and no matter what happens, I'd like to thank you for everything you've done for me."

"Not at all, my boy. Okay, let's get this show on the road."

"If you will not fight for the right when you can easily win without bloodshed, if you will not fight when your victory will be sure and not too costly, you may come to the moment when you will have to fight with all the odds against you, and only a precarious chance for survival. There may be a worse case. You may have to fight when there is no chance of victory, because it is better to perish than to live as slaves."

— *Winston Churchill (1874-1965)*

XLIV – The Deadly Digits of Destiny

Three thousand of the usual suspects applauded vociferously as the influential, administrative big hitters of the Republican Party strode onto the stage and took their allotted seats surrounding the podium. Luminaries of the obscenely rich American dynasties formed a neoconservative pantheon in the audience. Sitting front and center were members of Christ Inc., the Religious Right, taking time out from bilking gullible followers out of their social security checks. If a roll call could be taken, several key figures from the Skull and Bones Society, the Bilderbergers, the Council on Foreign Relations, the Trilateral Commission, PNAC and their associated think-tanks, would have declared themselves present.

Mosey Long opened the proceedings with a short blessing that embraced the audience, the current administration and America as a whole. He was followed by introductions of a few of the luminaries, each of whom responded briefly. Then it was Nicolaus D'Amous' turn to take the podium. He cut to the chase.

"Many people in America with big fat mouths – and not all of them Democrats – are demanding an immediate withdrawal of our military from Iraq. To those people I say, 'Shut up and

279

let our troops do their job!' We're going to stay the course and win this battle despite what some wimps would have us do!" His words were met with thunderous applause.

"There's a young man I want to introduce you to this evening, a man who has proudly served Uncle Sam and who, I have no doubt, would cheerfully do so again. He risked his life and lost his limbs in Iraq, but he has no regrets about having fought for liberty and the protection of our God-given, American way of life. This man has a tale to tell of surviving hell and how it feels when his buddies were wounded or killed. When he sees the American flag, this man is not afraid to cry. I know this man, and so will you when you hear what this true patriot has to say. Like all veterans, this man has earned a place in history. This veteran is with us on stage tonight. His name is Zack Zapata. Let's give Zack a big hand." D'Amous led the crowd in a standing ovation.

Zack wheeled up to the podium with Jack right behind him. The techs had adjusted the microphones so Zack could speak from his wheelchair. Zack reached up and exchanged a high five with Jack. "Ladies and gentlemen," Zack said, leaning into the mikes, "I thank Mr. D'Amous for his kind words, and I thank you all for giving me this opportunity to tell my story and express my views to you and to the American people.

"I hope that tonight we'll find out if patriotism really is the final refuge of scoundrels. Contrary to what the administration might say, if servicemen and women in Iraq are reaching out to help the people in that country, then they're pretty well doing it on their own. Why do I say that?"

The audience had begun to stir, and the media, who had resigned themselves to covering another boring Republican love-in, suddenly perked up.

"It is now a proven fact that some people in this administration planned the second war in Iraq years before

9/11 because, they claimed, *our* oil was under *their* sand and our self-interest required that we control that oil and protect the petrodollar. The reason we got 9/11 was because our government needed another Pearl Harbor to drum up support for an illegal war on yet another resource-rich sovereign nation. On the false pretext that Iraq had weapons of mass destruction, we invaded that country and are doing our best to destroy it."

The audience sat in stunned disbelief, as Nicolaus D'Amous sprang to his feet, shouting in protest. "That isn't the speech I gave you! He's double-crossing me!" He lunged for the podium.

"Shut up and stand back!" Zack yelled. "I've got a bomb!"

D'Amous froze in his tracks, while a communal gasp rose from the audience.

"This wheelchair's loaded with explosives, enough to blow this whole stage and a good part of this room off the map. Under the thumb of the only hand I have left to give for my country, there's a button that'll blow all of us to Kingdom Come, or Hell, or wherever. If anyone tries to leave this stage I'll set off the bomb, so don't move. Mr. D'Amous. Just back off and listen to what I have to say."

Every political mother's son and daughter in the banquet hall sat as if in a horror movie, eyes riveted on Zack. D'Amous slowly backed away. He looked around and spotted the security people circling the podium. He hoped they had a sniper in position.

Zack and Jack had thought of that possibility as well. "Just so you know," Zack said into the microphones, "this trigger won't set off the explosive charge until I release the pressure of my thumb. If I'm shot, I'll let go and the bomb will go off. But if my demands are met, the release mechanism can be disarmed.

"Another thing. If the networks, like Fox, or the Christian Intelligence Network or CNN try to cut off the live feed into this hall, I'll know about it, and I'll set off the bomb. So keep those cameras rolling, folks.

"I'm not afraid to die; what about you? You wouldn't be afraid either, if you'd suffered what I have. So here's your chance to get your ass blown off for your country.

"Why am I doing this? The answer is, I want our President here to explain to Americans what his role was in 9/11. I want him to confess everything he knows about the false-flag attacks on the Twin Towers and the Pentagon, and I want him to talk about Building 7 and the shoot down of Flight 93 over Pennsylvania."

The assembled Republicans on stage muttered furiously among themselves. "How much does he know?" "How much does who know?" "The President?" "I don't know. Who knows what he knows? But he likely knows plenty." "I think this guy Zapata means business." Their eyes turned to the President, who was now standing on shaky legs and looking pale. "I think he's about to crap himself." "I doubt he can do that standing up." "Oh no, I've heard about soldiers running scared with shit coming down one leg."

No one checked the President's drawers, but he was whining to Zack, "It's the Vice President who fields these kinds of questions; you'll have to ask him to respond to these scurrilous allegations."

"Not this time," Zack insisted. "He's slicker than snot. I can see his mind working right now on how to weasel his way out of this situation. No sir, Mr. President, you have to make your own speech."

"What about Nick 'the Nostril', I mean Nicolaus D'Amous?"

"I don't want to see him or any spin doctors up here at the mikes," Zack said. "The world deserves to know what the Commander-in-Chief knows about the 9/11 attacks being planned in order to convince Americans we needed a War on Terror and that the suspension of their rights as free citizens was necessary. We want to know why your administration perpetrated the 9/11 scam. We want the names of all those in the government, the military and the intelligence agencies who were involved in carrying out this mammoth false-flag operation. We want you to admit that criminal elements within the military-industrial complex, the Project for a New American Century and the Council on Foreign Relations are the real puppet-masters behind the government of this country."

"You know who did it soldier! Al-Qaeda and Osama bin Laden!" the President bleated.

"As we say in the military, Mr. President, don't give me that bullshit! This is your chance to come clean with the American people."

"Anything I did was part of God's plan. How can I blow the whistle on *Him*?"

"Because *He* hates liars, Mr. President. Jesus may love you, but everyone else thinks you're an asshole. So just tell the people the truth. You can start by telling us all about the next stage of America's so-called War on Terror."

The President stood mute, racking his brain for a way out.

"Maybe I'm not getting through to you, Mr. President," Zack said. "If you don't start talking, you're going to die, and you're going to take a lot of your co-conspirators with you. That may be for the best, but it's not for me to say. Maybe it's better for the American people to hear what you have to say and to decide what to do about you. This is your own personal Armageddon, Mr. President. You claim to have a direct line to God – what's He telling you to do?"

"Look, what's done is done, and I do have opinions of my own – strong ones – but I don't always agree with them. Jesus Christ, goddammit ..."

"No swearing, you could be about to meet your maker. Do you want to face Him after taking his name in vain?" Zack was clearly enjoying himself by this point.

D'Amous stepped forward, his hands up in a conciliatory gesture. "Zack! Please, for Christ's sake! Let me have a word with the President. Just let me talk to him for a moment before you kill all these people. Two wrongs don't make a right. I think I can help."

Jack whispered in Zack's ear, "I don't think we should trust him, but it's your call."

"Okay, Mr. D'Amous, but make it quick," Zack said.

D'Amous seized the President by the sleeve, pulled him to one side and put his mouth close to his ear. "The fat lady just sang! Your big show is canceled, just like we told you it would be someday. Just say, 'Yes, I admit it.' Later we'll say it was an admission made under duress, which indeed it is. You'll fake a nervous breakdown and go into seclusion for a while in an asylum for the mentally incapacitated."

At Truck's alarmed expression, D'Amous said quickly, "Oh, don't worry; we'll take care of you, just like we did the rest of your family over the years." *Truck's got to take the fall for us,* thought Nick. *We may not save the man, but we've got to save the plan.* He continued, "the New World Order will bring in a hand-picked new cast, fresh faces. The V.P. will take over from you and we'll be back in business sooner than tomorrow. Zack and this other guy will get life in Gitmo.

"Now get out there and give the performance of your life. Take the blame for everything. Say you had foreknowledge of the 9/11 attacks but failed to act, and apologize for your error in judgment. Tell them the buck stops with you. Declare your intent to resign and state that your successor should do whatever it takes to indict the perpetrators. Go on, Americans love a good TV show, and it doesn't get any better than this. You're a cunning little runt, now do your stuff."

This last message was delivered with a push to the small of the President's back, projecting him back out onto center stage.

The President took one lurching step toward Zack, thinking, *I'm being played like a two-dollar ukulele. I sure hope this Zapata guy buys this, or else it's game over ... for all of us. Where the hell do I start?!*

Just then, Jack tapped Zack on the shoulder and whispered in his ear again. "I want to say something before the President gets to spill his guts."

"Sure thing, Jack."

Jack leaned toward the mikes, "Fellow Americans, I want to tell you that ..." he paused. "I know for a fact ... 9/11 was an inside job ... because I myself helped install the controlled demolition charges in the basement of the World Trade Center Towers. My friend Sean Hennessey had a contract to wire the basements with explosives. The CIA or the NSA then murdered him and made it look like suicide. They are presently on my trail trying to do the same to me. This administration does not want you to know the truth about 9/11."

Jack turned toward the President, "But I'm hoping, sir, that you will enlighten us as to the true nature of your administration's bold plans to rule the world – by undermining the domestic economy, turning the Bill of Rights into toilet paper, and restarting the Crusades in the Middle East to steal all that oil – or are those things just some vain, insane exercise in self-aggrandizement, Mr. President?"

Zack swung his wheelchair to look squarely at the President, the man who had been sold to the American public as an uncomplicated man of action, a Christian cowboy redeemer, a man who could scare evildoers back into their Afghan caves in abject terror. He no longer looked like the self-authorized captain of the universe, but more like a draft dodging Connecticut frat boy. "I'm waiting," Zack said, "and I have to tell you, whatever choice you make, has to be a plus for America."

Truck stood in stunned silence, starting to hear organ-grinder music inside his head. He forced a smile onto his face, the one he always used when in the presence of cameras. Once again he began acting out the part of the dancing monkey of corporate capitalism, but he didn't feel much like dancing.

With ashen face, and failing to affect his usual John Wayne swagger, the President stepped up to the microphones, trying to quell the voices screaming inside his head. *You bastards! I'm the President! Now I'm the one who has to pay the price because you've left me twisting in the wind. I was afraid the American people would eventually find out I'd screwed them. Damn!*

"I didn't know what I should've known," Truck began haltingly. "I came into office, like many others before me, with few ideas beyond a basic desire to rule the roost and to appoint my good friends to key offices." His brain churning, his glands pumping adrenaline, his lungs gasping for air, the President fought off his flop sweat and hit his stride. "I soon became the front man for an invisible government that considers me a moron, who'll meekly go along with whatever it wants, without considering the welfare of you, the American people, or bothering to uphold the Constitution." He pulled a handkerchief from his breast pocket and wiped his brow. "I was deceived into committing war crimes under the Geneva Conventions and the War Crimes Act!

"If I was provided with bad advice, and didn't know any better than to follow it then ... then I unwittingly assisted in committing the crime of 9/11. By the time I'd realized it, it was too late to turn back from a course of action that I now sincerely regret. You've got to understand, I'm only a figurehead taking orders from people who are the front men for others behind the scenes, of whom I am unaware. This should not be the case, and the American people deserve better. So I'll tell you what

I know about 9/11 and the subsequent attacks on Afghanistan and Iraq. I deeply apologize for my part in 9/11. Going after all that oil to protect our economy and America's standard of living ... well, it just seemed like a good idea at the time."

The President struggled to suppress the fear gnawing like a rabid rat at his entrails and offered up a silent prayer to save his sorry ass. *Jesus Christ, you were supposed to have died for my sins, so don't desert me now, 'cause if they catch me lyin', I'm dyin'. God's gotta be able to get me out of this fiasco. I've always had trouble with telling the truth. How much of it is enough to get me off the hook this time?* He looked out at the audience, glared back at his 'supporters', then glanced sideways at Zack and his thumb which held down the deadly red button. "Please!" he whined pathetically, "I'm not just a dumb-ass President who wants to screw up other people's lives. I'm better than that. I'll tell you all I know. I'm willing to confess everything."

Standing back from the wheelchair, a grim visaged Slippery Jack Danielson fingered his backup remote control detonator in his pocket and listened as the President started to open up. *This had better not be another thin veneer of lies,* he thought.

From the gallery, the TV cameras took in the scene unfolding before them. Several shots of Truck's nervous, pallid face were intercut with panoramic shots that swept across Jack and Zack's determined gazes, and over to D'Amous' edgy but calculating eyes flitting from the audience to Truck and then to Zack. Zack's finger was growing weary of holding down the button that was holding back the viciously explosive forces packed and wired into his wheelchair. The muscles in his thumb were beginning to quiver slightly, small spasms of exhaustion creating gentle tremors that betrayed the lactic acid build-up in his hand.

D'Amous' eyes had zoomed in on this detail too, even as his mind tried to calculate the odds of getting out of this situation alive. As the President began to reveal his part in what really went down on 9/11, Nick, feeling nauseous, started to wonder, *is dumb Truck going to double cross me, like Zack?* He thought about running for it, but that wouldn't work. Zack could release pressure in an instant and tear everything in this room to shreds in milliseconds. Even getting a bodyguard or two between himself and the blast source would probably do no good at all. Definitely, it was going to take some deft finessing, verbal and psychological, to escape this nightmare.

Slippery Jack, looked on, wondering how the evening would end, based on all that he knew and all he was learning now, as the President spilled the beans to a shocked, awed and stupefied audience. He refocused on the President, with some degree of pity, as the former puppet began to cut his strings.

A quick look down to match Zack's momentary glance up, confirmed to each of them what the other knew – this was the ultimate sacrifice and no matter what the outcome, they were doing the right thing. If things didn't work out as they hoped and they were taken away, under promises of immunity, those promises would be tossed on the trash heap faster than a losing lottery ticket – in which case they would both spend their remaining time alive in some very uncomfortable surroundings, answering a million questions they knew would satisfy no one, and having to make admissions that would only serve the interests of the Global Union's attempts to reassert its dominance and position regarding 9/11.

On the other hand, if Truck came through, Jack and Zack could end up being applauded, rewarded and treated as heroes in the media, thanks to public pressure. The real perpetrators would be forced to admit their part in the greatest crime of all time, which would give the American public an opportunity to put the bastards behind bars and clean up Washington. Then new lawmakers could transform the American Republic back to what it was meant to be in the first place – government *of* the people, *for* the people, and *by* the people – not some clique of lizardly plutocrats. That then, would be the end of the *New World Order*, hopefully.

Truck didn't fail to deliver the goods. His speech was punctuated with admissions that undoubtedly would *have* to be analyzed, reviewed and covered in every paper and on every news channel. All the unanswered questions that had been suppressed by the mainstream media and covered up by the 9/11 'Omission' Commission were now out in the open and would have to be examined with the intensity and care they should have had from the beginning. In his *mea culpa*, President Truck didn't forget to implicate everyone he knew was involved, including Nick 'the Nostril' D'Amous. While some in the audience were horrified with Truck's *last stand*, many were mightily impressed.

Finally, with a sense of relief, Zack Zapata thanked the President and said ominously to everyone, "Now, we have to decide what action of ours is the right thing to do for the people of America, who must now be awakening to a reality they have been avoiding, for whatever reasons, for so long."

He glanced up again to Jack, who had just turned to look at him. Each knew their respective fingers controlled a certain outcome. They could use deadly force to instantly obliterate many members of the cabal who had deliberately murdered so many innocent people on 9/11, or they could abort their plan, leaving it up to the American people to cry out and demand justice.

Either way, for the New World Order conspirators, all their plans were about to change – fucked by the five fickle fingers of Fate, dashed by the deadly digits of Destiny, screwed, blued and tattooed, all in one go – by two lowly war vets.

∞

Dedication

This novel is dedicated to three propositions:

First, to the Iraqi people, in the cradle of civilization, who may soon no longer exist. Along with its infrastructure, 84% of Iraq's institutions of higher education and museums have been burnt, looted and destroyed, many of its academics assassinated. Their civilization lasted for approximately 7000 years, until terminated in the early 21st century by the illegal occupation of the neocon, fascist world power, the United States Incorporated; a once-upon-a-time great and well-liked democracy that fell from grace and became a world military bully dictatorship.

The major incredible international crime perpetrated by the world's bully was the use of radioactively contaminated depleted uranium 238, that is spreading through Iraq, Afghanistan, other neighboring countries and the world, via dust storms and global air currents, and becomes deposited in human bone, causing cancer and congenital anomalies. If the U.S. administration is allowed to use nuclear weapons on Iran, then mutually assured destruction and annihilation becomes only a matter of time.

Secondly, to Secular Humanists, open-minded atheists, if you will, whose philosophy sets people free to think, investigate and judge for themselves; frees them from ghosts, gods and myths, from ignorant and cruel creeds, from priests, popes and preachers, from sanctified mistakes and holy lies, with no need to cringe, crawl, bow or lie.

Thirdly, untutored emotions of ignorant people are the material that enables evil deeds; and when I have shuffled off this mortal coil I want to leave concrete proof that I was not one of the willfully blind or deliberately ignorant persons unwilling to question the ridiculous government story of what happened on 9/11; unable to entertain the irrefutable evidence of the administration's complicity and participation in the attack on the World Trade Center and the Pentagon.

This novel is my attempt to get people to take an intelligent look at the overwhelming evidence that once again the United States government and its New World Order masters indulged in a state-sponsored false-flag covert operation that killed their own countrymen, with a view to blaming it on a new enemy they wished to create in the public mind, and to drive fear into the hearts of Americans by hyping imaginary terror threats. What the administration now truly fears is not terrorism, but, instead, the movement which is demanding the truth about 9/11. May this novel help true American patriots re-establish a lawful government of the people and for the American people, by ridding themselves of the present foreign and domestic policies that are causing the U.S. to be despised and resented on a worldwide scale.

* * *

Due to advancing years this may be my last novel. All that seemed necessary to write it was to utilize all available news stories and political information of the last sixty years, in order to discover what led up to what really happened on 9/11, and as a consequence subsequently caused the present world situation in Afghanistan, Iraq, Israel, the Middle East and also in America.

The major content regarding that defining event has been taken from the research of others; taken from the internet, alternative newspapers, videocassettes, DVDs, documentary movies, television, radio, websites, books, magazines, periodicals, whatever and wherever I found the researched material.

I went into the Internet like Stanley into deepest Africa, hacking my way through walls of dense verbiage, dragging my canoe behind me, to bring out the most pertinent information I found there; then created a story-line to frame the factual news and political research of the times. The genre could be termed historical-political-action-adventure, applying fiction to facts, or vice versa; ending up with *a work of faction* – the welding of factual information, scientifically researched explanations and informed political opinion, into novel form, using the information gleaned from researchers, journalists, writers, investigators, whistleblowers, soldiers, scientists, ex-intelligence agents and military experts, politicians and lawyers, who presented their investigations and analysis thereof so well.

I believe in Newton's theory of gravity and have never found any need to keep dropping apples out of trees to prove the basic laws of physics. Those researching this subject have been trying mightily to expose some truths behind the many government lies the public is exposed to these days, particularly regarding 9/11 and Iraq; and I think they want that information to reach as many people and readers as possible. By doing the same in novel form I am trying to help in the dissemination of that information, hopefully in an entertaining manner, to a whole new readership.

Why did I read reams of material and sift it through my brain? Because unless you believe in reincarnation, you are only going to pass this way once. I do not want to depart this planet leaving the impression that I was a few beers short of a six-pack, and so stupid I couldn't understand some aspects of how this world unfortunately operates.

Most of us take the raw events of our lives and try to turn that material into meaningful experience. We do this joyously in our youth and desperately in old age, and to that I plead guilty.

So, what can any one individual do, besides cry with tears as big as road apples, to help in the abominable situation in which the world finds itself? I'm writing this novel about the *Modus Operandi* of *9/11* – what happened before and after the so-called defining moment in modern world history.

I'm not Fathom J. Dooley, a very deep guy. I'm Hal Sisson, a member of the rabble in good standing. You know who you are. We ignore the increasing assaults on civil liberties and *habeas corpus* at our own peril. Perhaps, if everyone does a little bit, together we can contribute to whatever rectification is still possible to make this world a better place. By all means, have a good time while you're in your prime, cause it won't mean a thing when you're dead. But if we don't do something to stop the Fourth Reich now, then our descendants will be living in a fascist police state, compounded by poverty, violence, genocide, tyranny and disease.

∞

Bibliography

Listed below are works that were consulted as reference sources, and from whence I derived or deduced the facts and ideas regarding what really happened on 9/11, and how this humungous false-flag scam was pulled off, as unearthed by these great and tireless researchers and writers:

Andreas, Joel. *Addicted to War – Why the US Can't Kick Militarism,* AK Press, 2004.

Adams, Patricia. *Odious Debts,* Probe International, June 2002.

Ahmed, Nafeez Mosaddeq. *The War on Freedom,* Olive Branch Press, 2002; *The War on Truth,* Olive Branch Press, 2005.

Begich, Nick & Manning, Jeanne. *Angels Don't Play This Haarp,* Earthpulse Press, 1995.

Biddell, Jack L. *Reclaiming Canada's Sovereignty,* 1996.

Butler, Brigadier General Smedley D. *War is a Racket,* Feral House, 2003.

Caldicott, Dr. Helen. *The New Nuclear Danger: George W. Bush's Military Industrial Complex,* New Press, 2004.

Chang, Matthias. *Future Fast Forward: The Zionist Anglo-American Empire Meltdown,* American Free Press, 2006.

Chomsky, Noam. *The Chomsky Trilogy: Secrets, Lies and Democracy*; *The Prosperous Few and the Restless Many*; *What Uncle Sam Really Wants,* Odonian Press, 1995; *Failed States, Metropolitan Books, 2006.*

Chossudovsky, Michel. *The Globalization of Poverty and the New World Order,* 2003; *America's "War on Terrorism",* Centre for Research on Globalisation, 2005.

Clarke, Tony. (with Dobbin, Murray and Finn, Ed) National Insecurity – CCPA, *Bowing to U.S. 'Security' Demands Will Make Canadians Less Secure.*

Corn, David. *The Lies of George W. Bush,* Three Rivers Press, 2004.

Diamond, Jared. *Guns, Germs, and Steel: The Fates of Human Societies,* W.W. Norton & Co., 1999.

DiEugenio, James and Pease, Lisa. "The Assassinations", *Probe Magazine*, (On JFK, MLK, RFK and Malcolm X), Feral House, 2003.

Dowbenko, Uri. *Bushwacked: Inside Stories of True Conspiracy,* National Liberty Press, 2003; *Hoodwinked: Watching Movies with Eyes Wide Open,* Conspiracy Digest, 2004.

Dobbin, Murray. *The Myth of the Good Corporate Citizen: Democracy Under the Rule of Big Business*, Stoddard Publishing, 1999.

Dyer, Gwynne. *Future Tense: The Coming World Order*, McClelland & Stewart Ltd, 2004.

Eggleton, Andre Michael. *Thieves in the Temple – America Under the Federal Reserve System*, Milligan Books, 2004.

Erlich, Paul R. & Anne H. *The Population Explosion*, Touchstone Books, 1991.

Fing, Wing F. Reverend M.D., PhD., L.L.D., D.V.D. *Fuck, YES!: A Guide to the Happy Acceptance of Everything,* Shepherd Books, 1988.

Franken, Al. *The Truth with Jokes*, Plume, 2005.

Franklin, Benjamin. *Fart Proudly: Writings of Benjamin Franklin You Never Read in School*, Frog, 2003.

Gagnon, Bruce K. *Come Together RIGHT NOW*, Just Write Books, 2005.

Griffin, David Ray. *The New Pearl Harbor: Disturbing Questions about the Bush Administration & 9/11*, Olive Branch Press, 2004.

Griffin, Des. *Fourth Reich of the Rich*, Emissary Publications, 1998.

Helms, Harry. *Inside the Shadow Government, National Emergencies and the Cult of Secrecy*, Feral House, 2003.

Heinberg, Richard. *The Party's Over, Oil, War and Fate of Industrial Societies*, New Society Publishers, 2005.

Hellyer, Paul. *Funny Money,* 1994; *Surviving the Global Financial Crisis: the Economics of Hope For Generation X,* 1996; *The Evil Empire: Globalization's Dark Side,* 1997; *Goodbye Canada*, 2001, Chimo Media Ltd.

Hixson, William F. *It's Your Money*, Comer Publications, 1997.

Hoffman, Don Paul and Jim. *Waking Up from Our Nightmare, the 9/11 Crimes In New York City*, I/R 2004.

Hurtig, Mel. *Pay the Rent or Feed the Kids: The Tragedy and Disgrace of Poverty in Canada*, McClelland & Stewart, 2000.

Iggulden, John. *Silent Lies: Things You Need to Know that You Weren't Ever Taught, A Survival Handbook into the 21st Century*, 1996.

Jalkaran, Jacques S. M.D. *Debt Virus, a Compelling Solution to the World's Debt Problems*, Glenbridge Publ. Ltd., 1995.

Klare, Michael T. *Resource Wars, The New Landscape of Global Conflict*, Metropolitan/Owl Book, 2002.

Korten, David C. *When Corporations Rule the World*, Kumarian Press Inc., and Berrett-Koehler Publishers Inc., 2001.

Krehm, William. *A Power Unto Itself, the Bank of Canada, the Threat to our Nation's Economy*, Stoddart Publ. Co. Ltd., 1993.

Marrs, Jim. *Rule by Secrecy*, Harper Collins, 2001; *Inside Job, Unmasking the 9/11 Conspiracies*, Origin Press, 2004.

Martin, Al. *The Conspirators, Secrets of an Iran-Contra Insider*, National Liberty Press, 2001.

Millegan, Kris. *Fleshing Out Skull & Bones: Investigations into America's Most Powerful Secret Society*, Trine Day, 2004.

O'Rourke, P.J. *Parliament of Whores*, The Atlantic Monthly Press, 2003.

Palast, Greg. *The Best Democracy Money Can Buy*, Pluto Press, 2004.

Perkins, John. *Confessions of an Economic Hit Man*, Plume, 2005.

Perloff, James. *The Shadows of Power: the Council on Foreign Relations and the American Decline*, Western Island Publishers, 1988.

Piper, Michael Collins. *The High Priests of War*, 2004; *The Judas Goats*, 2006, American Free Press.

Ruppert, Michael C. *Crossing the Rubicon, the Decline of the American Empire at the End of the Age of Oil*, New Society Publishers, 2004.

Saul, John Ralston. *The Collapse of Globalism and the Reinvention of the World*, Penguin Canada, 2006.

Soros, George. *The Bubble of American Supremacy, the Costs of Bush's War In Iraq*, Harper Collins, 2004.

Swanson, Gail. *Behind the Scenes – Ground Zero: A Collection of Personal Accounts*, TRAC Team, 2003.

Tarpley, Webster Griffin. *9/11 Synthetic Terror Made in USA*, Progressive Press, 2006.

Thauberger, J.A. *Inflation: Bankruptcies Unemployment Can Be Beaten*, The New World Publishing Company, 1994.

Thorn, Victor. *The New World Order Exposed*, Sisyphus Press, 2003; *The New World Order Illusion*; *Guilty: 9/11 on Trial, The World Trade Center Collapse*, Tree of Life Publications, 2006.

Tucker, Jim. *Bilderberg Diary*, American Free Press, 2005.

Woods, Ian ed. *9/11: The Greatest Crime of All Time – The Best of Global Outlook – Vol. 2*, Global Outlook, 2006.

Zarembka, Paul ed. *The Hidden History of 9-11-2001*, Research in Political Economy (Vol. 23), Amsterdam: Elsevier, 2006.

Zwicker, Barrie. *Towers of Deception, the Media Cover-Up of 9/11*, New Society Publishers, 2006.

Other writers from the Internet, newspapers or magazines:

Abdul-Khaaleq, Nashid	Asner, Ed	Baez, Joan
Baker, Jeremy	Barrett, Kevin	Berg, Phil
Bollyn, Christopher	Bowman, Robert	Brechin, Gray
Brouillet, Carol	Broeckers, Mathias	Carlson, John
Casbalt, James	Chin, Larry	Cohen, Marjorie
Corcelli, John	Davey, Monica	Davis, Walter
Denver, James	Deitrich, Michael	Dewdney, A.K.
Diebenow, Nathan	Dobbs, Lou	Douglas, Bill
Edmonds, Sibel	Elmasy, Mohamed	Fernandez, Ken
Finn, Ed	Fisher, Don	Foreman, Liz
Floyd, Chris	Franklin, Jonathan	Gagnon, Bruce
Garver, Lloyd	Galenby, Gavin	Galati, Rocco
Goff, Stan	Golust, David	Gorman, Beth
Guinnane, Marilyn A.	Guliana, Lisa	Heard, Linda S.
Hecht, Jamey	Herman, Douglas	Hence, Kyle
Hightower, Jim	Hoffman, Jim	Icke, David
Jackson-Sczbecki, Sybil	Jamail, Dahr	Jenkins, Ken
Johnson, Rosita	Jones, Steven T.	Kane, Michael
Kay, Joe	Kimmel, Thomas	Klein, Naomi
Larouche,Lyndon H.	Levis, Nick	Lindorff, David
Livergood, Norman	Lynn, Joyce	MacKay, Neil
Martin, Al	Martin, Harry V.	Mariani, Ellen
Matsui, Jennifer	Mazza, Jerry	McMurty, John
McKinney, Cynthia	McGovern, Ray	Meyer, Michael
Moore, Oliver	Moore, Steve	Moser, Bob
Nichols, Bob	Nimmo, Kurt	Nenonen, Michael
Olbermann, Keith	Olmstead, Thomas R.	Palast, Greg
Paul, Don	Pentz, Lynn	Perkel, Colin
Pitt, Wm. Rivers	Pickering, Russell	Potvin, Kevin
Potvin, Sue	Quinn, Joe	Reese, Charlie
Reynolds, Morgan	Roberts, David	Roberts, Paul Craig
Rockwell, Paul	Rowley, Coleen	Ryan, Kevin
Sanders, Richard	Schoenman, Ralph	Schwartz, Karl W. B.
Sheehan, Cindy	Skolnich, Sherman H.	Smith, Leon
Steele, Edgar J.	Steinberg, Jeffrey	Szymanski, Greg
Tenuto, Jerry	Thompson, Doug	Thompson, Paul
Victorian, Armen	Von Buelow, Andreas	Waters, Sharon
Watson, Joseph	Watson, Paul	Whitney, Mike
Wickstrom James P.	Wilson, Jamie	Woods, Ian
Valenzuela, Manuel	Vandana, Shiva	Zwicker, Barrie

and … Wayne Halyn & Glen Acorn 'humorous name aficionados'

Films:

9/11 – The Greatest Lie Ever Sold – 2005, Anthony J. Hilder.

9/11 Open Your Eyes: the War on Terror is a Lie – 2005, Snowshoe Films.

9/11 Emergency: Conspiracy Theories or Conspiracy in Practice – Black Cat.

Aftermath: Unanswered Questions from 9/11 – 2002, Guerilla News Network.

Blast Force – 1998, Controlled Demolition Inc.

Celsius 9/11 – 2005, Jeremy Wright, with highlights from two International Citizens' Inquiries into 9/11 – March 2004 in San Francisco and May 2004 in Toronto, Canada.

Insights Into 9/11 – 2007, *Part I, Design of a Deception* with Ken Jenkins and host Ian Woods.

Liberty Bound: Is the US Bound for Liberty – or does it just have Liberty Bound? – 2005, Filmmaker Christine Rose.

Loose Change 2nd Edition – 2006, Directors Dylan Avery & Korey Rowe.

Martial Law – 9/11: Rise of the Police State – 2005, Alex Jones.

Money Masters: How International Bankers Gained Control of America – 1998, Bill Still and Pat Carmack.

Painful Deceptions, An analysis of the September 11th Attack – 2002, Eric Hufschmid.

Spiral Into It, Episode 28 & 29 with Carol Brouillet – 2004, Director Fiske Smith.

The Oil Factor: Behind the War on Terror – 2004, Free-Will Productions.

The Great Conspiracy – The 9/11 News Special You Never Saw – 2005, Barrie Zwicker, with highlights from the Toronto International Citizens' Inquiry into 9/11, May 25-30, 2004.

The Power of Nightmares, November 3, 2004, BBC 2.

The Truth and Lies of 9/11 – November 8, 2001, Michael Ruppert at Portland State University.

Truth and Politics: Unanswered Questions about 9/11 – 2005, David Ray Griffin.

What I've Learned About US Foreign Policy: The War Against the Third World – 2002, compiled by Frank Dorrel.

World According to George Bush – 2006, CBC's Passionate Eye.

Newspapers and Magazines:

American Free Press, Address: 645 Pennsylvania Ave. SE, Suite 100, Washington, D.C. 20003. Tel: 1-888-699-NEWS.

Global Outlook, Ian Woods, Publisher and Editor. Address: P.O. Box 222, Oro, Ontario, Canada LOL 2X0. Tel: 1-888-713-8500 or 1-705-720-6500. Fax: 1-705-728-6500. Website: www.GlobalOutlook.ca.

Idaho Observer, Address: P.O. Box 457, Spirit Lake, ID, 83869. Tel: (208) 255-2307.

Press for Conversion, published by the Coalition to Oppose the Arms Trade; Richard Sanders, Editor. Address: 541 McLeod St., Ottawa, Ontario K1R 5R2. Tel: (613) 231-3076, Fax: (613) 213-2614, Website: www.ncf.ca/coat/.

Secular Humanist News, Victoria.

The CCPA MONITOR, published by the Canadian Centre for Policy Alternatives; Address: #410, 75 Albert St., Ottawa, Ontario, Canada K1P 5E7. Tel: (613) 563-1341, Fax: (613) 233-1458, e-mail: ccpa@policyalternatives.ca.

The Lone Star Iconoclast, Editor-in-Chief, W. Leon Smith. Address: P.O. Box 420, Crawford, TX 76638. Tel: (254) 675-3634 Fax: (254) 675-4090.

'The Republic' of East Vancouver, Kevin Potvin, Editor. Address: P.O. Box 50672, Vancouver, B.C. V5L 5E2. Tel: (604) 218-4952.

Victoria Street Newz, Jeanine Bandcroft, Editor. Address: 1027 Pandora Ave., Victoria, B.C. V8V 3P6.

Weekly Telegraph, Britain's Global Newspaper.

Why not subscribe to these independent alternate news sources yourself – and get the stories and the truth that the mainstream media covers up and is afraid to print.

Internet Websites: (www.)

911Dossier.co.uk

911Visibility

911Busters.com

911Research.WTC7.net

911Truth.org

ArcticBeacon.com

Buzzflash.com

CommunityCurrency.org

ConspiracyDigest.com

CooperativeResearch.org

CounterBias.com

Emperors-Clothes.com

FromtheWilderness.com

GlobalResearch.ca

Independent.co.uk

InsiderIntelligence.com

KarlSchwarz.com

LibertyBound.com

NY911Truth.org

PolicyAlternatives.ca

Radio4All.net

Resisters.ca

SkolnickReport.com

Serendipity.li/

Space4Peace.org

TakeBacktheMedia.com

TVNewslies.org

WhatReallyHappened.com

WsWs.org

911Proof.com

911Blogger.com

911Inquiry.org

911SharetheTruth.com

911Review.com

AlMartinRaw.com

CommonDreams.org

ConspiracyBias.com

ConspiracyPlanet.com

CounterBias.cocurioustimes.com

CloakandDagger.ca

Flight93Crash.com

GreatConspiracy.ca

GlobalOutlook.ca

InfoWars.com

Justicefor911.org

LegitGov.org

NewMediaExplorer.org

OnlineJournal.com

PrisonPlanet.com

Rense.com

ScholarsFor911Truth.org

SeptemberEleventh.org

SnowshoeFilms.com

SummerofTruth.org

TruthOut.org

UnansweredQuestions.org

WTC7.net

ww1.SundayHerald.com

WhatDoesitMean.com/$50MillionReward.htm

"It's not about Right or Left.

It's about Right and Wrong!"

— LooseChange911.com

Other Books by Hal Sisson ...

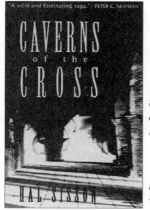

Fiction, Paperback, 164 pages
ISBN: 1-55152-049-4
1997, Arsenal Pulp Press
$16.00 cdn / $ 15.00 us

"Hal Sisson's amazing tale covers much new territory – for him and for us. But it's a solid and fascinating saga with some inspiring and astonishing insights."
Peter C. Newman

"Sisson's lively plot has more twists and turns than the Roman catacombs. He writes about: murder, blackmail, a miracle contraceptive, industrial espionage and sinister forces within the Roman Catholic church,' all set against a backdrop of the world population explosion." **Robert Collins**

Caverns of the Cross is an intriguing roller coaster of a novel that moves from the naked jungles of Brazil to the sacred halls of the Vatican. In the midst of the Brazilian rainforest, a Canadian scientist has been working on the development of a natural contraceptive, distilled from South American flora.

The formula is finally complete, and *Naturcept* is poised to revolutionize the way society perceives contraception and pregnancy. But the individual, company or group that controls *Naturcept* will be in a position to determine the course of society. Pharmaceutical companies recognize that there is money to be made. Sects within the Catholic church, realizing that societal attitudes have changed, are fighting amongst themselves to determine whether *Naturcept* should even be released into the hands of the faithful.

Whose hands the formula falls into depends on a complex web of murder and conspiracy – those involved will stop at nothing to get what they want. Pitting altruism against avarice under the powerful gaze of the Vatican, *Caverns of the Cross* is a gripping and raucously entertaining novel.

Available from *Global Outlook. See order form p. 311.*

Or call 1-888-713-8500 within North America or 1-705-720-6500.

The Big Bamboozle by Hal Sisson

Fiction

Paperback, 354 pages

ISBN: 1-894012-03-8

April 1999, Salal Press

$11.00 cdn / $10.00 us

Dear Children:

Sit down quietly and I will tell you about a gorilla named Bamboo, who lived in a lovely jungle somewhere in Africa. Now nasty things were happening in Africa. The jungle was quickly disappearing because people were cutting down trees – yes Johnny, just like MacMillan Bloedel – and destroying the place where the gorillas live. Can you say 'habitat'?

Poor Bamboo was quickly running out of quiet places where he and his lady friend could grab a quick, um, snack. So one day, Bamboo and his lady gorilla friend were, um, snacking, and this big meanie snuck up behind them and used a tranquilizer gun – right, Brittany, just like Mummy's Valium – because he wanted to take Bamboo far, far away to Canada and put him in a zoo so he could, um, snack with other lady gorillas.

Meanie Man really hurt Bamboo and doctors had to fix him up and much to everyone's surprise, Bamboo learned to talk. Isn't that wonderful, children?

Okay, yes I know gorillas can't talk, but when they fixed Bamboo they did something to his throat – no Johnny, not like when they fixed Rover so he couldn't make puppies. Anyway, the Big Meanie man was really a bad person because he wanted to snack with Bamboo's girlfriends, too, as well as with anything else he could … Uh, children, how would you like to hear about Lassie, who rescues little Timmy when he falls into an open mine shaft – yes, Tyler, I KNOW Lassie is really a he. And no, he is NOT a dog in drag …

The Big Bamboozle is great fun, guys, although I can see where the odd zoo might get a titch nervous about selling the book! Personally, I don't think a little bestiality ever hurt anyone, but some zoos have no sense of humor. A welcome relief from the usual do-gooder's factual, oh-so-worthy, save-the-animals-or-they-will-disappear and IT'S-ALL-YOUR-FAULT book, which I realize does have its place. — *Dina Sudlow,* book reviewer.

Available from *Global Outlook. See order form p. 311.*

Or call 1-888-713-8500 within North America or 1-705-720-6500.

Coots, Codgers and Curmudgeons

by Hal Sisson and Dwayne W. Rowe

This hilarious collection of tales from rural Western Canada, originally published by Orca Book Publishers, evokes a time when the funeral parlor's hearse doubled as an ambulance and baseball games pitted Red Deer against Butte, Montana.

With singular wit, Sisson and Rowe depict an unforgettable house call, a pair of ministers in an impromptu stand-up comedy routine, back country entrepreneurs and the perils of home brew and accident-prone youth. Sheer entertainment for those who remember how 'things were back then' and anyone visiting these slices of Canada's past for the first time.

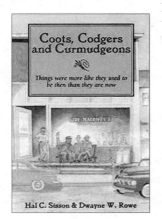

Non-Fiction
Paperback, 176 pages

ISBN: 1-894012-04-6
June 1999, Salal Press

$16.00 cdn / $ 15.00 us

"Sisson and Rowe write with confidence and humor."

BC Bookworld

"An appealing and detailed sketch of an era almost lost. Thoroughly enjoyable."

The Independent Senior

Available from *Global Outlook*. See order form p. 311.
Or call 1-888-713-8500 within North America or 1-705-720-6500.

A
FAT LOT
OF
GOOD

Hal Sisson

Poor Phil Figgwiggin! Someone with a taste for rump steak fresh from the victim has bumped off his doctor; he can't sleep and he's in danger of losing his driver's license. His partner Mike Fowler could drop dead any minute from angina or S&M party games.

With nitro spray firmly in hand and tongue firmly in cheek, Phil and Mike brave bombs, bombshells and coronary crises as they close in on the murderer.

Fiction
Paperback, 304 pages
ISBN: 1-894012-06-2
June 2002, Salal Press
$11.00 cdn / $10.00 us

Two unusual heros raging against the foibles of old age show – there is life after seventy.

"A Great read! [Sisson's] plot was as twisted as a box full of Slinkys, dialogue sharper than a scalpel and his many life observations made me laugh out loud."

Laurence Gough

Who killed Dr. Dex? You'll get some belly laughs from the wise-ass characters you'll meet on your way to finding out."

Bob Collins, author

Available from *Global Outlook. See order form p. 311.*
Or call 1-888-713-8500 within North America or 1-705-720-6500.

Garage Sale of the Mind

Hal Sisson & Dwayne Rowe

Non-Fiction
Paperback, 220 pages

ISBN: 1-894012-07-0
October 2002, Salal Press

$16.00 cdn / $15.00 us

The salty humor and quirky take on life that authors Hal Sisson and Dwayne Rowe brought to their first short-story collection, *Coots, Codgers and Curmudgeons*, is back with a vengeance. Now the wryly witted pair presents more tales of colorful characters they've known, including a vengeful dog catcher, a turncoat bootlegger and assorted oddball relatives.

In *Garage Sale of the Mind*, politicians are skewered, authorities parodied and nostalgia affectionately indulged. The stories are as bawdy as Greek comedy and as sweet as a stroll down memory lane.

This fresh collection of short stories is perfect to take to the living-room rocker, the porch swing or onto public transit, where passengers heard laughing aloud are generally given lots of room.

"Fans of W.O. Mitchell ... will find this book irresistible."

Stitches, the Journal of Medical Humor

"Puts the boots to the widely held belief that lawyers lack a sense of humor."

Vancouver Courier

Available from *Global Outlook*. See order form p. 311.

Or call 1-888-713-8500 within North America or 1-705-720-6500.

MAQUILADORA MAYHEM

Hal Sisson

A dead CEO, found naked and bloodless in the desert and the organized injustice of corporate globalization take senior sleuths Phil Figgwiggin and Mike Fowler into Mexico's maquiladora zone. Their efforts to solve the murder become entangled with the machinations of an American corporate executive and manic-depressive terrorist. Armed with a stash of cash and their trademark cheeky wit, Figgwiggin and Fowler team up with a beautiful investment expert to fight the ravages of time and the arcane forces of the New World Disorder.

"I couldn't put the book down and I chuckled throughout."

Sue Potvin,
Discourse & Disclosure

"You're going to love the 'old farts' gang. Thank God for a hero over 50!"

**Jackson Davies, actor,
producer, *The Beachcombers***

**Fiction
Paperback, 380 pages
ISBN: 1-894012-08-9
Sept. 2003, Salal Press
$11.00 cdn / $10.00 us**

**Available from *Global Outlook. See order form p. 311.*
Or call 1-888-713-8500 within North America or 1-705-720-6500.**

*"You should live so long to see a book that covers religions, government plots, secret societies and the New World Order, in a manner both illuminating and humorous. But you're in luck. Canadian author **Hal Sisson** has accomplished this very thing in this rollicking mystery novel – with those down-but-never-out superannuated sleuths, Phil Figgwiggin and Mike Fowler. Who's the victim of Sisson's most recent murder plot? No less than Mother Earth herself. Don't miss this fun foray into mysteries, myths, mayhem and plain old skullduggery."*

Fiction
Paperback, 521 pages

Jim Marrs, best selling author,
Crossfire and Rule by Secrecy

ISBN: 1-894012-09-7
Sept. 2004, Salal Press
$11.00 cdn / $10.00 us

Peace River, Alberta, *Record-Gazette* editor Sydney Selvon compared Sisson to Michael Moore, saying he prefers Sisson because he is more successful than the American writer in subduing the leftist harangue in favor of the supreme mission of fiction writers to truly entertain their readers. "You will not put the novel down until you have reached the epilogue and at times will howl with laughter. Sisson shows an immense knowledge of the world's oldest historical accounts, providing credibility to the speculation that stories about ancient gods fighting epic battles on this planet have extra-terrestrial origins in some unknown planets. Did mankind coexist in very ancient times with beings from a superior civilization who had flying engines from which they viewed the planet and gave detailed descriptions of the landscape that could not have been possible from the ground? Passages in the Bible and the Ramayana of ancient India would seem to bear that out. Find out how this relates to American and CIA blunders, as they engage in a war against terror, i.e. fighting the same forces they financed and armed to the tune of billions of tax dollars. Those who are hostile to left-leaning writers should not shut themselves off from subversive, irreverent literature unless they have become intolerant of the freedom of writers."

Available from *Global Outlook*. See order form p. 311.

Or call 1-888-713-8500 within North America or 1-705-720-6500.

SORRY 'BOUT THAT
a tribute to burlesque

Hal Sisson

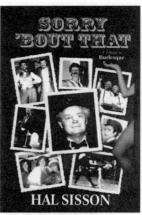

Ft Lauderdale, September 2005: The art of burlesque is in the midst of an awesome comeback, according to featured articles in many popular magazines and by the number of new clubs being launched in New York and Los Angeles. Additionally, auditions are being held for a new burlesque troupe this week in LA, while an eye-popping, pastied and tasseled group of striptease artists are heading to a convention in San Francisco at the month's end. Burlesque's heyday may still be in its future.

Non-Fiction
Paperback, 258 pages
ISBN: 1-59526-493-0
Sept. 2005, Llumina Press
$22.00 cdn / $20.00 us

Yes, burlesque theater is enjoying a popular revival across North America, and Hal Sisson rides the crest of that growing wave with *Sorry 'Bout That*, an affectionate tribute to his twenty years producing and performing in Western Canada's longest-running burlesque review. With his encyclopedic memory for jokes and his love of the craft of comedy, Sisson steals the show with this hilarious compilation of songs, gags, naughty poetry and fast-paced skits.

No arena of human activity is spared and no apology actually intended as Sisson pokes fun at the quirks and pretensions of magicians, lawyers, preachers, medics, psychics and salesmen. The humor in *Sorry 'Bout That* is enriched with Sisson's genuine appreciation for the lengthy tradition of comedy theater in England and North America.

Sisson's book includes a salute to the greats of burlesque, British music hall and vaudeville and reminiscences of performers who have trod the stage with him, furnished him with lively material, or shared the privilege of a life spent leading an audience to laughter.

Available from *Global Outlook*. See order form p. 311.

Or call 1-888-713-8500 within North America or 1-705-720-6500.

About the Author

Hal Sisson

Proud Canadian, Hal Sisson was born in Moose Jaw, Saskatchewan. He served in the Royal Canadian Air Force for four years during World War II as an armourer – in Alaska with #135 Hurricane Fighter Squadron, and in Ireland and Wales with #422 Sunderland Flying Boat Squadron of Coastal Command.

Majoring in English at the University of Saskatchewan – with a stint as a reporter – he graduated from Law in 1951. In 1984, Hal retired from practising law in Peace River, Alberta, where he was involved in provincial politics. Happily married to Doreen they have two children.

Hal is the Ranking Canadian and U.S. player of six-wicket USCA and International Croquet and an avid old hand and machine-made marbles collector and is also a championship player of 'Ringer', the old schoolyard style of playing marbles. His talents also include a stand-up comedy routine of the burlesque and music hall variety, a founder of 'Peace Players' theatre troupe and writer and producer of *'Sorry 'bout That'*, the longest running – 20 years in all – annual burlesque revue in Western Canada based on his novel of the same name.

Sisson's major interest since retiring as a Queen's Counsel (Q.C.) is his writing. He has authored 9 books so far. His novels feature daring and imaginative plot lines and subject matter from murder mysteries (three novels in a series featuring old fart octogenarians Phil Figgwiggin and Mike Fowler); to collections of humorous reminiscences on the vagaries of life in rural Western Canada during simpler times (with Dwayne W. Rowe); to the dignity and humane treatment of animals and great apes fighting off extinction; to exposing the ways in which we are truly being controlled by those in power, and the lengths to which they will go in order to feed their insatiable greed; and to sinister forces of blackmail and unscrupulous legal drug dealers and Catholic church cults, contraceptive industrial espionage within the Vatican, set against a backdrop of the world population explosion.

In all of these great stories Hal uses many comedic devices to address very serious concerns, providing fascinating skitters of wit and wisdom through the sub rosa of the mind; a wake-up call which provides offence to all those who want to believe things are exactly as they would have them. These days, Sisson's goal is to keep writing as much as possible before it's his turn at kicking the winning ball through the goalposts of life.

A Note from
the Publisher, Author & Editors

If you enjoyed reading this book and would like others to read it, here are a few things you can do:

1. **Tell your friends about this book and where to get it.** You can order any or all of Hal Sisson's books mentioned in the previous pages by filling out the order form on the next page and mailing it to Global Outlook, P.O. Box 222, Oro, Ontario, Canada L0L 2X0 or phoning us (toll-free) in North America 1-888-713-8500 or 1-705-720-6500 from overseas.

2. **Ask your local bookstore or library to carry it.** Have them contact us for our distributor or how to get a library copy.

3. **Get extra copies, at special bulk discounted rates, to give to your friends or to sell at rallies. Please visit our website at www.GlobalOutlook.ca for rates or phone us for details.**

If you would like to learn more about 9/11 please visit our website: **www.GlobalOutlook.ca** or call us and ask for our free catalog of books, magazines and DVDs on 9/11.

* * *

The author wishes to thank Ian Woods and Clare Forbes for their invaluable assistance in the editing of this novel. Special thanks also goes to Vandana Shiva for her inspiring passage on pages 84 and 85.

* * *

The author and editors would like to thank the following proofreaders and fact-checkers for all their efforts: Wayne Halyn, Elizabeth Woodworth, Sequoia (Jen), D. McCorkell, Ken Jenkins, Joyce Nelson, Lea Gilboe and Jennifer (Kueneman) Hopp.

Order Form

4 ways to order! **PHONE** with credit card: Toll-free in North America: 1-888-713-8500 or from overseas 1-705-720-6500. **FAX** order form with credit card info to: 1-888-713-8883 or from overseas 1-705-728-6500. **SURF** to our secure web-store www.GlobalOutlook.ca and use PayPal, MasterCard or VISA or **MAIL** your credit card information, cheque or money order in U.S. funds with this completed order form to:

Global Outlook
P.O. Box # 222, Oro, Ontario CANADA L0L 2X0

1. **Modus Operandi 9/11***	($11 cdn/$10 us)	$_____
2. **Caverns of the Cross**	($16 cdn/$15 us)	$_____
3. **The Big Bamboozle**	($11 cdn/$10 us)	$_____
4. **Coots, Codgers and Curmudgeons**	($16 cdn/$15 us)	$_____
5. **A Fat Lot of Good**	($11 cdn/$10 us)	$_____
6. **Garage Sale of the Mind**	($16 cdn/$15 us)	$_____
7. **Maquiladora Mayhem**	($11 cdn/$10 us)	$_____
8. **You Should Live So Long**	($11 cdn/$10 us)	$_____
9. **Sorry 'Bout That**	($22 cdn/$20 us)	$_____

(*Please add $6.00 Canadian or $6.00 US for postage and handling for the first book, $2.00 more for each additional book.)

Sub Total $_____ + S&H* $_____ = $_____ Total enclosed

Name: _____

Address: _____

_____

_____

Phone #: _____

E-Mail: _____

VISA / MC #: _____

Expiry (MM/YY) _____

Conspiracy Theory?

It's not a theory, if you can prove it.

— *Loose Change 2nd Edition*